D1028195

Reecah's Flight

Legends of the Lurker

Book 1

Richard H. Stephens

Acknowledgements

Reecah's Flight began as a magical idea that came to me one day quite by accident. While writing *Into the Madness*, I realized I wanted to explore the world that had shaped Melody and Silurian's lives. To tell the story of Mase's legacy. The next day, I randomly came across an image of a woman and a dragon. As soon as I saw it, I had to have it. It was as if fate had intervened. So excited, I wanted to put *Into the Madness* on the shelf and jump right into *Reecah's Flight*. That wouldn't have been fair to the amazing fans of the Soul Forge Saga, so I finished the trilogy—working in the back story as I went.

I am forever grateful to the people behind the scenes, without whose involvement, Reecah's Flight would never have gotten off the ground.

First off, I wish to thank my beta readers for reading Reecah's Flight on such short notice. Your input, as always, is valued more than I can ever express. My sincere appreciation goes to: Joshua Stephens, Matthew Lane, Paul Stephens, and of course, Caroline Davidson who is always the first one to read it, and the last.

Thank you to my editor, Michelle Dunbar. Through her patient instruction, my writing style has evolved. If you are an aspiring writer, check her out: http://michelledunbar.co.uk/

Thank you to my cover and interior picture designer, Katie Jenkins. The cover helped fuel my inspiration for Reecah's Flight. You can find Katie at, KJ Magical Designs: https://kjmagicaldesigns.com

The image for Grimelda's Clutch was created by my amazing partner in life: Caroline Davidson, to see more of what Caroline offers, please visit her website: www.thefunctioningexecutive.com

Credits:

During the writing of *Reecah's Flight*, I decided I wanted to give back to you, my readers—a way of thanking you for sticking with me as I grow as an author. Subsequently, I ran a dragon naming contest in which I asked people to think up a name and anything else they thought would be important to their dragon such as colour, gender, alignment, etc. so I could use it in my dragon series. Thank you to the following individuals for naming a few characters in the Legends of the Lurker Series. Their creativity and insight have made the series that much more fantastical.

Sandy Fosdick for naming the purple, female dragon: Silence

Georgiana L. Gheorghe for naming the red, female dragon: Scarletclaws

Angela Carter for naming the high king: J'kaar.

I am always searching for dragon names and invite you to connect with me on my Facebook Author Page: @RichardHughStephens

In addition, for book 2 of the Legends of the Lurker Series, I decided to run a, 'name the female warrior contest.' I look forward to sharing her name in *Reecah's Gift*.

Reecah's Flight is dedicated to anyone with a dream. Don't let life slip by without attempting to realize your dream. You're the only one in control of your destiny. Work hard. You're worth it. Your dream isn't as far away as you think.

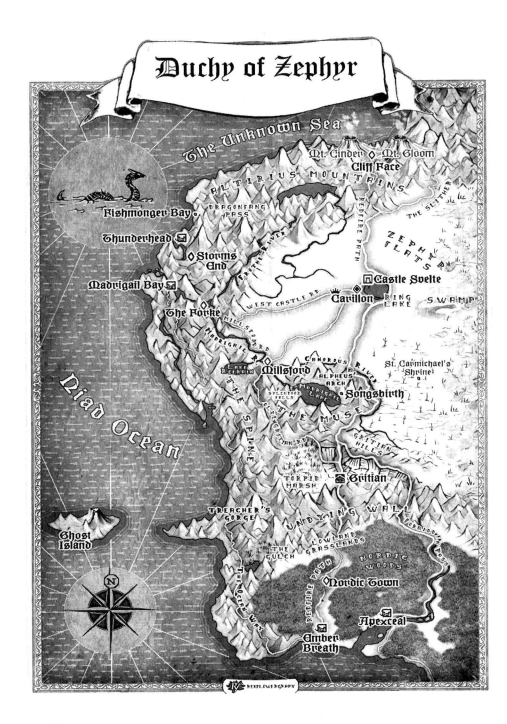

Duchy of Zephyr

Table of Contents

To view the full colour maps in the Soul Forge realm, please visit:
www.richardhstephens.com

Reecah's Flight

Legends of the Lurker

Book 1

Reecah's Flight

A Rare Day

"**Poppa,** do you think I'll ever be able to fly?"

"Of course, little poppet. You can do anything you set your mind to."

Reecah's dimples creased her pudgy cheeks, the sunshine twinkling in her eyes. Lying on the side of a steep, grassy hill, she put her hands behind her head and stared skyward. "Do you think I could fly as high as a butterfly?"

Viliyam Draakvriend smiled at his six-year-old granddaughter daydreaming like he was wont to do. She reminded him of her mother—a girl daring to envision a better life. She reminded him of himself.

Viliyam spotted the monarch butterfly Reecah tracked with a pointed finger. "Higher."

Reecah giggled. She scanned the sky and thrust her arm out. "High as that bird?"

Viliyam spotted the seagull squawking above the steely waves of the Niad Ocean. As long as Lizzy didn't get wind of their conversation, what was the harm? "Higher."

"Higher?" Reecah's high-pitched voice squeaked. "Wow."

He loved her innocence. Oh, to be a child again, oblivious to the cares of the world—her hazel eyes full of wonder, searching the sky. He felt warm inside. Lying here with Reecah allowed the pressures of everyday life to ease away. It wasn't often he got to know peace.

1

Reecah's Flight

It was a rare day in Fishmonger Bay. Viliyam had made sure his chores were completed before the sun crested the lofty heights of the Spine. Days like these only happened a few times a year. There was no way he was going to miss out on his favourite activity—stomping across the mountainside in search of life's simple treasures with Reecah. She was growing up much too fast.

A warm breeze wafted over the hill, ruffling Reecah's dark brown hair. She pointed excitedly up the coast to an unusual jut of flat rock. "How about as high as a dragon?"

Viliyam sat up and squinted. "You see a dragon? Where?"

"There Poppa, by the cliffs."

The joys of getting old, Viliyam mused, his imperfect vision unable to see what Reecah was going on about. He followed her crooked finger. If there was a dragon up there, he couldn't see it.

"You see it, Poppa?"

"Yes, poppet, a big one."

Reecah frowned, too smart for her britches. She knew he hadn't.

Viliyam searched the area with concern. It wouldn't do to be caught unaware on the hillside if a dragon *was* about. "We should go now. Grammy will be worried."

"Aw! It's not even late. Can we go down to the shore? You promised." Reecah crossed her arms, pouting.

Viliyam couldn't help but laugh. The little devil knew how to play him. Her cute scowl did it every time. Lizzy was right to call him a sucker. Reecah pulled his strings and everyone knew it.

He searched the cliffs, hoping he wouldn't regret his weakness. "Last one to the bottom is a slimy serpent!"

Reecah squealed, on her feet in an instant.

Gingerly climbing to his feet, Viliyam winced at the stiffness in his back. His trekking days would soon be over.

Reecah's Flight

Reecah bounded ahead, her little legs barely keeping up with her body as she charged down the hill without a care in the world.

"Grammy! Grammy!"

Reecah's boots clicked across the porch Viliyam had built earlier in the spring; a job Lizzy had been after him to complete for the last several years. There was always something needing fixing around the blasted place.

Reecah burst into the hut, the thin door banging off the interior wall and slamming shut again. "Guess what Poppa said?"

Viliyam groaned, holding the door halfway open, unsure whether he wished to enter or not.

"Gracious, child, what did Poppa tell you?" Viliyam's grey-haired wife turned her chair away from the old loom she worked at and caught Reecah in her embrace, depositing her on an apron-covered lap.

Reecah beamed at Lizzy, her smile cleaving her face from ear to ear. "Poppa said I'll be able to fly one day!"

The happiness slid from Lizzy's wrinkles. She locked eyes with Viliyam; her look promising him they would be having words.

Lizzy gave Reecah a weak smile. "He did, did he?"

"Yes, Grammy. High as a dragon!"

Viliyam stepped into the one-roomed hut, unwilling to meet his wife's brooding glare.

"We've been over this before, my little flower bud. People aren't able to fly."

"That's not what Poppa says. He says I can, long as I really wanna."

"Sometimes Poppa doesn't know what he's talking about."

Reecah's Flight

Reecah gazed into her grandmother's eyes, her pout not nearly as effective.

"People aren't built for flying. We don't have wings."

Reecah's face twisted in thought. Not liking what her grandmother said, she crossed her arms. "Well, Poppa says I can."

Viliyam dared to look across the room. Reecah's pout never worked on Lizzy but it had him melting again.

"Poppa was just being silly." Lizzy glared at Viliyam. "Weren't you, Poppa?"

Viliyam felt like a dog with its tail between its legs. He nodded and said softly, "Yes, poppet. Poppa was joking."

The hurt look he received broke his heart.

Reecah jumped from Lizzy's lap, a loud, "harrumph," escaping her as she stormed over to her blanket in the back corner. She sat facing the wall, clutching a crude wooden dragon he had carved for her mother when she was around the same age.

Lizzy indicated with hard eyes for him to step outside. He swallowed and followed his skinny wife onto the porch.

When the door banged shut, she didn't waste time. "How could you?"

Viliyam didn't bother replying. There was no point when Lizzy got herself worked up. He found it best to let her vent until she worked the frustration out of her system, and then apologize. Even if he didn't think he'd done anything wrong.

"We agreed not to fill her head with this dragon nonsense."

"I know, but—

"But nothing! You want Reecah to end up like her mother, father, and uncle?"

"No, but—"

"Dammit, Viliyam! She's all we have left of Marinah."

Reecah's Flight

"She's only six, Liz. It's a phase she's going through. She'll have forgotten about it by tomorrow. By then she'll be dreaming of sailing the high seas aboard Jonas' brig."

As soon as he mentioned the grizzled sea captain's name, he regretted it. The anger in Lizzy's eyes was evident in her squint. "I told you never to mention that name around here."

He held his palms up. "Sorry, a poor example." He stepped off the porch and spun to face her. "Come on. You know I didn't mean any harm. If I get home before dark tomorrow, I'll take her back to the hill and explain why she can't fly."

"And then what? Fill her head with more of that fantastical shit? Like you did with Rina and Davi? Look what it did for them!" Her wild green eyes appeared on the verge of tears.

The sting of her words slapped Viliyam hard. There wasn't a day went by that his heart didn't die a little bit more since their children's horrific death. If Lizzy could only feel the hurt her blame instilled in him.

"I'm not about to lose her to your fanciful dreams and promises of adventure." Lizzy glared, heaving heavy breaths. "I'll be damned if Reecah ends up like her mother."

Viliyam flinched as the hut's door slammed open and banged shut, marking Lizzy's passage into their darkening home.

He walked down the path to where it joined the main trail and gazed at the ocean—the waves awash with a gorgeous tinge of orangey-red refracting the setting sun.

It was a rare day in Fishmonger Bay indeed. It'd be good to get back in the boats.

5

Reecah's Flight

Oh, to Fly

Reecah stared at the ocean swells hundreds of feet below her dangling feet. She pitched a pebble into the wind and watched it fall away, willing it to soar through the air and avoid a watery resting place, but it was soon lost to sight.

She pulled her worn cloak tighter, fending off the cutting chill. She wished Poppa were here. *"There were fish to catch and chores to be done in Fishmonger Bay if they wanted to eat and keep the clothes on their backs"*—Grammy's words echoed in her head. The same thing every day. Work and toil, clean and boil. Poppa never played with her anymore. Ever since that day Grammy yelled at him.

Grammy's angry words replayed themselves, *"I'll be damned if Reecah ends up like her mother."*

Being the only child on the hill was a lonely business but Reecah preferred it that way. Every time they visited Grammy and Poppa's friends in the village, the kids made fun of her. Not in front of the adults—they'd be whipped for that. No, they waited until the adults sent them out from underfoot. No one understood her dream of flying. Whenever she brought it up, the other kids laughed. The nastier kids pulled her hair and teased her about her patched clothing and grimy skin. They called her reeky Reecah and hopped around holding their noses.

Some of the boys would go as far as trying to pull her breeches down. No matter how the visits started out, they always ended the same. Reecah receiving the cane from an irate parent after one of their kids ran home with a black eye or bloody nose. Reecah didn't mean to fight, but when the kids pushed her hard enough, she reacted like a cornered badger. Grammy said she had her mother's pluck, whatever that meant.

Lonely and cold on the black jut of rock, she chewed at her lower lip. She hadn't known her parents. Grammy told her dragons took them—her father one autumn day while off hunting, and her mother and uncle Davit the following year while climbing the mountains in search of dragons.

Blinking rapidly, a gust of wind blew her hair around. Way out over the ocean she caught sight of a tiny speck flying high above the waves.

She marvelled at the ease it stayed aloft without exerting any effort. Oh, to fly.

She smiled. Someday. Despite what Grammy said.

The speck grew in size—much bigger than a bird. Born on the wind, it became apparent the flying creature was unmistakably a dragon.

Even at six, she knew that sitting exposed on the outcropping wasn't a great idea. She laid flat on the edge like Poppa had shown her, unafraid of the fatal drop a hand's width away. There was nowhere else to hide.

The dragon flapped its wings occasionally, preferring to glide on the air currents, turning gently one way and then the other. As it neared the shore, Reecah noticed it was actually dirty-white in colour. According to Poppa, that meant it was an older female losing her colour.

The dragon's flight took it north of Reecah's position. Just when she thought she was safe, it craned its horned head in her direction. She squeezed herself against the rock, her cheek mashed on the brink, and held her breath.

The relentless surf thundered into the base of the cliff, unseen far below. Reecah swallowed, trying to quell her fear.

Reecah's Flight

If the beast spotted her, she decided she would throw herself over the edge.

The dragon kept its head pointed her way as it glided toward a towering cliff face. At the last moment, it flapped its leathery wings and rose into the heights and out of sight.

Reecah wasted no time scrambling across the great promontory and down the rock-strewn embankment to a thin strip of sand at its bottom.

Barely keeping her feet beneath her in her headlong descent, she darted across what remained of the beach. The tide was coming in. If she wasn't quick, she'd be stranded until well after dark.

She knew all too well what that would mean. A tongue-wagging from Grammy at the very least. More like a couple of licks with the cook spoon and a lecture, *and*, if Poppa were home, he'd likely receive the same—without the swat from the cook spoon. Grammy always blamed him whenever she got into trouble.

By the time Reecah ambled up the far side of the beach onto the steep hill leading home, soaking wet and exhausted—the tide had reached the cliff wall. Swimming the last bit, she had made it in time.

She stopped and disrobed, wringing out her clothing. More to prevent Grammy from asking why they were wet than to keep the cold wind from nipping at her. Explaining to Grammy what had happened wouldn't end well. Grammy had forbidden her from climbing the Summoning Stone.

"Reecah, my little flower bud, you clean up the table and sweep the floor while Poppa and I go for a walk."

Reecah cast Poppa a furtive glance. Where were they going? It was dark outside.

Poppa feigned fear and rolled his eyes.

Reecah's Flight

Reecah's snort turned Grammy's attention on her.

She lowered her eyes, fighting the laughter threatening to land her in trouble—the tenseness of the moment making it that much more difficult to hold it in.

Grammy looked from her to Poppa. "Honestly, you two. You're enough to give me grey hair."

Poppa let a guffaw slip through his lips, and Reecah burst out laughing.

Grammy stared at them, shaking her head. "There isn't a lick of sense between the two of you." Her chair scraped the wooden floor. "Come on, Vili, walk with me."

Reecah watched them leave. What were they going to talk about this time? Her probably, but she hadn't done anything wrong. At least not that they knew of…or did they?

Reecah tiptoed to the door and listened. Nothing.

She pushed it open a crack, cringing at the squealing hinges, but Grammy and Poppa weren't on the porch.

Gravel crunched down the path toward the main trail. Searching the shadows to be sure neither one had remained behind, she slipped through the door, careful to shut it quietly behind her.

Slinking down the path, she couldn't help wondering if Grammy knew where she'd been earlier. She didn't think so. Grammy wasn't one to hold back. If she knew, she would've yelled at her already. She swallowed. With Grammy, no one could ever be too sure.

Lost in thought, she almost yelped. Out of nowhere, Grammy stepped into the open in front of her. Luckily, Grammy faced the other way.

"I don't like it, Vili. You're getting too old."

Poppa stepped into the open beside Grammy, his hands on his hips as they glanced at the sparkling night sky. The ocean lay unseen over the crest of the hill, but even from this distance, the rhythmic slap of the surf carried on the breeze.

9

Reecah's Flight

"I don't like it either. You know my feelings."

"It's a wonder they asked you at all."

Poppa ran his hands through his thick, grey hair. "Because I know how to find them."

"Tell them you can't handle the journey anymore."

"You know I can't do that. If Jonas suspects me of lying... Well, you know. Besides, if he thinks I've become weak, he'll let me go, and then where will we be?"

Grammy sighed. "Where will we be if something happens to you? What about Reecah? Who'll look after her?"

Reecah swallowed. *Who'll look after her?* Why? Where were they going? She wanted to let them know she was listening and ask but thought better of it. She'd be in trouble for disobeying, and Poppa would take the brunt of Grammy's wrath.

Poppa shook his head and threw his arms in the air. "I don't know. That's what scares me the most." He turned his head, seemingly looking straight at Reecah.

Reecah held her breath.

Poppa stared a moment longer before turning away. "We should get back. The season has started. We shouldn't leave her alone after dark."

Reecah's eyes grew wide. *The season has started?* She backstepped several paces and fled up the trail.

By the time Poppa and Grammy came back, the interior of the hut smelled of dust as Reecah furiously plied the corn broom. She smiled up at them.

Grammy studied the interior, espying the dirty dishes. She glared at Reecah, poised to say something, but thankfully changed her mind and went to sit before her loom.

Poppa latched the door behind him and sat down on the edge of the rickety pallet he shared with Grammy.

Reecah watched him until she caught his eye. When he smiled at her, she knew it wasn't genuine.

Reecah's Flight

Reecah kept an eye on him as she bustled about the hut, churning the dust to fall in other places. Something was wrong. Poppa wasn't his usual, happy self.

Grammy must've noticed she'd stopped sweeping.

"Keep your mind on what you're about, child. The hut won't clean itself."

Reecah's broom jumped into action, but she kept her eyes on Poppa until he glanced up at her again. She gave him one of her heart melting grins and skipped away.

Poppa's melancholy noticeably lifted.

Reecah's Flight

The Day the World Stood Still

Several days passed since Poppa had departed dressed much differently than normal, a rope over his shoulders, his old sword buckled to his belt, and a black quarterstaff in hand.

Reecah studied Grammy sitting before her loom in the flickering candlelight, never once pushing down on the foot pedal to operate the cumbersome machine. Grammy's faraway gaze told Reecah her mind was elsewhere.

"Where's Poppa?"

Grammy looked up and blinked a couple of times. A grim smile fluttered amongst her wrinkles. "He's off hunting with the villagers."

Reecah frowned. Poppa often hunted for food, but he usually took his bow. "He's been gone a long time."

"Come here, flower bud."

Grammy held her arms out for Reecah to climb into her lap.

"Remember when we told you about the seasons?"

Reecah put a finger to her lips in thought, her hazel eyes searching Grammy's face. "I think so."

Grammy kissed Reecah's forehead and gave her a patient smile. "Let me remind you. Every three years around this time, we must be extra careful with the dragons. Fishmonger Bay has the biggest population of the beasts anywhere."

"Why Grammy? What happens?"

"Hmm. I'm not sure how to explain it so that you'll understand. You see, every creature, be they mice or people or dragons, find someone to love. When a couple loves each other, they become close and, um, well, they mate. And then they have babies."

Reecah frowned deeper. "What does mate mean?"

Grammy's face reddened. "Well, heh, let's just say they snuggle close."

Reecah had no idea what mating meant. She wrapped her arms around Grammy's thin body and hugged her tight. "You mean like this?"

"Yes, something like that." Grammy cleared her throat. "But that's not what's important here. The point I'm trying to make is that during the dragon mating season, the beasts become overly protective of their territory. Fishmonger Bay lies within a major dragon territory and that means other animals, including people, must be extra careful."

"Is Poppa hunting dragons?"

Grammy didn't respond right away. "Poppa is with a bunch of men trying to keep the dragons from encroaching on our village."

Reecah nodded, not really knowing what that meant either. She did, however, understand Grammy's serious tone. "Is Poppa going to die?"

Grammy pushed Reecah to arms length. "Gosh, child, no. Don't ever think that."

Reecah smiled and snuggled into Grammy's bosom. "I like it when we mate, Grammy."

Grammy stiffened and began to stutter, but the sound of boots clomping on the porch had them gaping at the door in anticipation.

Reecah flew off Grammy's lap as the door banged open and Poppa stomped inside. "Poppa's back!"

Poppa's glum face brightened. He caught Reecah in a huge embrace and lifted her off the floor.

Reecah kissed his face all over before she leaned back with a wrinkled nose. "You're stinky, Poppa."

Reecah's Flight

"Hah!" Poppa put her on the floor and hugged Grammy who had walked up behind them.

Lying awake in the dark cabin, Reecah hugged her wooden dragon, stroking its scaly spine and listening to snatches of her grandparents' conversation from their pallet on the far side of the hut.

Grammy's voice sounded sad. "Why must you go back out again? I thought you showed them where to go?"

"Aye, but Jonas is afraid there'll be trouble. He wants as many swords as possible."

"He can't be serious. If he provokes them, he'll risk bringing the entire dragon community down on us."

"I agree. Told him that, too, but you know Jonas. You can't tell him anything."

Silence settled over the hut. Reecah's thoughts drifted. She wasn't sure she dreamed her grandparents next words or not.

"I don't like it, Vili. What would we ever do without you?"

"Shh. It'll be okay Lizzy. I won't let that happen. I promise."

Early the next morning, Grammy hugged Poppa by the door, tighter and longer than usual; her face damp.

Reecah pulled on Grammy's apron. "What's the matter?"

Grammy let Poppa go and forced a smile, sniffing. "Nothing, child. Just saying good-bye to Poppa."

Reecah looked from Grammy to Poppa, confused. When her eyes met Poppa's, his face broke into a wide grin.

"Come here, poppet. Give Poppa a big hug."

Reecah held out her arms and was whisked off her feet in Poppa's loving embrace. He opened the door and walked outside into the cool morning air with Reecah proudly sitting in his arms. Without looking back, he strolled down the path

Reecah's Flight

"Viliyam!" Grammy called after them.

Poppa said loudly, "It's okay. I'll send her back when we reach the trail."

Reecah watched Grammy over Poppa's shoulder—her grandmother didn't look pleased.

At the end of the trail, Poppa put her down. Reaching inside his tunic, he pulled out a walnut sized, crimson gemstone and crouched down to her level.

"Wow." Reecah accepted it in her small palm. "For me?"

Poppa smiled. "That was your mother's. I need you to take care of it for me until I come back. Can you do that?"

Reecah nodded.

"Promise me you won't tell anyone else about it."

"Not even Grammy?"

Poppa's response surprised her. "Especially not Grammy."

Reecah turned the multi-faceted stone over in her hands, running a finger along its one flat side. "What's it do?"

Poppa swallowed, his eyes on the verge of tears. "There's no time to explain it to you. When the time comes, it'll all become clear, okay?"

She nodded.

"Promise me. No one."

"I promise, Poppa."

Viliyam knelt on one knee. "Good, now give me a hug. It's time I was going."

Reecah hugged him around the neck so hard she heard him gasp. "When are you coming back, Poppa?"

She felt him tense, but his soft voice calmed her.

"I will always be in your heart, little poppet. Don't ever forget that." He held a hand over her chest. "As long as I'm here, it'll be like I never left."

15

Reecah's Flight

Six days passed until the sound of heavy boots clumped upon the porch. The sun had lost its grip on the land while Reecah and Grammy were having supper. As one they turned expectant eyes on the door but it never opened. Grammy held out a hand to keep Reecah in her chair.

A heavy knock rattled the door.

Grammy's brows knitted. "Now who could that be?"

Reecah didn't miss the fact that Grammy clutched her meat knife as she stopped behind the door. "Yes? Who is it?"

"It's Jonas Waverunner, ma'am," a deep voice answered. "I need to speak with you."

Grammy's shoulders slumped. For a moment, Reecah didn't think she was going to open the door.

A hulk of a grizzled man stood on the porch, his great, blonde-bearded head hung low—Poppa's sword belt and quarterstaff clutched in filthy hands.

Where was Poppa? And why was Grammy suddenly leaning against the door, crying?

"I'm sorry, Lizzy."

Grammy glanced at Reecah sitting in the chair watching. At once she pushed by Jonas and closed the door behind her.

Reecah stared at the door, not knowing what to do. The big man had upset Grammy.

The sound of Grammy's raised voice brought Reecah to the doorway.

"There was nothing we could do."

"Damn you, Jonas. There was plenty you could've done. Why did you have to involve Vili in the first place? He's too old to be prancing around the heights chasing monsters."

Reecah's eyes went wide. Poppa was chasing monsters?

"No one tracks like Viliyam. Without him, we'd have spent weeks trying to find the colony."

"Weeks!" Grammy was never a mild-mannered woman, but Reecah had never heard her speak harshly to a head villager.

16

Reecah's Flight

"To find creatures bigger than my hut? You must be as blind as you are stupid! Who's going to look after me and Reecah now?"

Reecah frowned. A sudden feeling seeped into the pit of her stomach and twisted. Her throat tightened and her round eyes teared up. They couldn't mean that. They just couldn't.

"I will send one of the boys up to stay with you. At least until the season passes."

"You'll do nothing of the sort. I don't want your charity. You can bloody well shove it up your ass. Look what it has done for us so far. You're a bigger fool than everyone says. Shame on you."

Reecah put her hands over her face and backed away from the door, trying hard to hold onto the tears dripping down her cheeks.

Suddenly, nothing seemed real. She couldn't focus on the conversation outside—the words meant nothing to her anymore. It was as if the world stood still.

She stumbled to her blanket in the back corner, unable to breathe. Though they never said it, Reecah pieced together the meaning of their conversation along with Jonas' presence carrying Poppa's weapons.

She stuck her fingers into a hole in her ratty, feather pillow and fished out the crimson gemstone Poppa had given her. A tear splashed on its surface as she cupped it in her shaking hands.

Poppa wasn't coming home. Not tonight, or any other night. Her best friend was gone forever.

Reecah's Flight

The Package

During the ensuing years, Reecah withdrew into herself, shunning everyone who tried to speak with her—except Grammy. But Grammy had her own concerns to deal with and Reecah made a point of not making life any harder for her.

Six years passed slowly in the deteriorating hut on the hill. Grammy tried her best to keep their home in good repair but her advancing age and years of tending the family gardens had taken their toll.

Reecah did her share, but nothing she did lifted the bitterness from Grammy's heart. Many nights she heard her grandmother sobbing—mumbling in the dark about how someone needed to take action against the tyrant, Jonas.

Through it all, Reecah kept her deepest desire closely guarded. Only once, in a moment of weakness while thinking of Poppa, did she let it slip to Grammy how wonderful it would be to fly. The dark look Grammy gave her convinced her never to bring it up again.

The spring of her twelfth year found Reecah yearning to spread her wings. She loved Grammy but she was suffocating being isolated on the hill. Her secret treks to the Summoning Stone no longer filled her with the joy they once had.

"Grammy, do you need anything from the market?"

Grammy, at her usual place in front of the old loom, squinted—her failing eyesight painful for Reecah to see. "What's that, my flower bud?"

18

Reecah's Flight

"I was thinking of going down to the village to stretch my legs."

Grammy's scrutiny made Reecah uncomfortable. The old woman had the knack of seeing through her. Knowing how Grammy felt about the villagers, Reecah feared she would forbid it, but Grammy surprised her.

"Actually, there is something I would like you to deliver for me."

Reecah's face lit up. "Really?"

Grammy struggled to her feet. Using the loom for support, she pushed off and hobbled, stoop-shouldered, to her pallet. With a great deal of effort, she pulled open a sticky drawer of an old cabinet by the footboard and rummaged through its contents. "Now where did I put that blasted thing?"

"What's that?" Reecah asked but Grammy didn't respond.

Grammy pulled open another drawer. "Ah, yes." She tucked something under her arm and straightened up the best she could.

"Come here, child."

Grammy stared at Reecah standing eye-to-eye before her, seemingly considering her next words. Finally, she held out a small package wrapped in an old cloth. "I've been meaning to take this to Grimelda ever since Poppa died. I'd forgotten about it until now."

If there was one name that instilled more fear into Reecah than Jonas Waverunner, it was the village witch.

Grammy patted Reecah's hand. "It's okay, child. Grimelda and I go way back. She won't harm you."

"But. She's a...a—"

"Witch?"

Reecah nodded.

"She's been called worse, but I guess that's what people call her now. Regardless, Grimelda will not harm you. Take this, and be careful. Whatever you do, I need you to promise me you won't look inside."

Reecah went to grab the package but Grammy pulled it back, lifting her eyebrows.

"I promise." Reecah laughed, accepting the bundle. It was heavier than it looked.

"Good. Now, turn around. Let me braid your hair. Can't have you going to town looking like a ragamuffin."

Reecah winced and grimaced as Grammy used a bone-toothed comb to tug at her tangles.

"My, how long your hair has gotten. It'll be at your waist before long," Grammy said as she separated three equal amounts of hair and intertwined it.

"That's better." Grammy smiled at her and shuffled to the door. The hinges squealed. "Be quick about it. I don't want you out after dark. With the snows freshly gone, dragon season will soon be upon us."

Reecah paused to kiss her wrinkled forehead, the skin cool on her lips. "I'll be as quick as a hungry troll."

Grammy gave her a playful shove. "See to it that you don't fill the hungry troll. Now be gone. I'll have supper ready when you return."

Reecah bounded down the faint path, a renewed spring in her brown suede boots, but when she hit the main trail she stopped, hesitant to visit the witch on her own.

The south end of Fishmonger Bay lay visible far below through newly budding trees. In another week or so, the derelict buildings would be hidden from view.

She gazed longingly at the Summoning Stone in the opposite direction. It reminded her of Poppa. How she wished he were here to accompany her. Poppa wouldn't be afraid.

Poppa's memory provided her with the courage she needed. The sooner she got it done, the sooner she would be back on the hill.

Reecah's Flight

Stepping off the trailhead onto the gravelly main street of Fishmonger Bay, she was greeted by the mournful clanging of Father Cloth's service bells.

Living on the mountainside and having little contact with the villagers, Reecah never knew what day it was. Every now and then Grammy would tell her about an important date coming up, but other than the passing seasons, Reecah never bothered to worry about it. If Grammy hadn't prepared a special supper a fortnight ago, she'd never have known it was her birthday. Poppa had said her birthday fell on the spring equinox—whatever that meant.

A few stragglers scurried across the commons, past the mercantile toward Father Cloth's ramshackle temple, paying no attention to her; except one man loping along on his own. Reecah stopped and stared at the size of the man, wondering if he was one of those giants the kids had gone on about when Grammy and Poppa used to frequent their friends in the village.

The man stopped and motioned for her to go ahead of him, likely thinking she was attending the service. He doffed his worn leather sailor's cap and bowed his head—his great black beard bunching on his massive chest.

Reecah smiled at the man and shook her head, motioning for him to go first. As he should. She was taught to respect her elders.

"Why thank you, li'l miss," was all the man said, a great smile lifting his bushy mustache, and off he went.

She had seen the man many times while in Poppa's company. Apart from his size, his disposition separated him from the rest of the villagers. He was always happy.

She waited until everyone disappeared up a steep flight of steps and through the temple's double doors before she

Reecah's Flight

strolled across the commons. On her right, the Niad Ocean broke along a rickety pier jutting into the water—lapping gently against the shore.

She paused in front of the mercantile, the largest building in Fishmonger Bay besides the temple. Carved dragon corner posts held aloft a great porch sheltering the shop's grimy windows. Broadcloth and fanciful wares were displayed amidst an odd assortment of armour and weaponry. Trappings for the well-to-do.

"Reeky Reecah!"

She froze. A group of boys burst out from behind the sagging warehouse near the pier. Jonas Waverunner's establishment. She recognized the youths as the ones who had caused her grief when she was younger.

She glared at them, too afraid to say anything. They were much bigger than her now. Clutching her package tighter, she scrambled past the temple, a place she absently thought the boys should have been, and spotted the most colourful building in Fishmonger Bay.

Glancing back, she cringed. The boys were following.

Picking up her pace, she bounded up three, broad, flagstone steps onto the porch of a lavender washed cabin; the building surrounded by an odd assortment of dragon statues and carvings.

A large shingle in the shape of a dragon—its wings spread wide—appeared to float in the air of its own accord. Written across the dragon's belly were the words: *Grimelda's Clutch*.

The top half of a stained-glassed door was held open by a thong. Reecah glanced back the way she had come. The boys had stopped by the temple. Seeing her look their way, they pinched their noses and doubled over laughing.

Reecah's ears reddened. She had broken more than one of the boys' noses once upon a time—especially the three, blonde-haired, Waverunner boys.

The cobwebbed interior of the shop smelled of incense, herbs and something stronger Reecah couldn't identify. Clear jars lined ill-designed shelves bearing insects and animal parts, salves and powders of varying colours.

She jumped as a raven cawed noisily from the back corner. The scruffy bird, perched on a gnarled branch embedded into the log wall, provided the proprietor with a warning that someone had entered the shop whenever the witch was elsewhere.

Mustering her nerve, Reecah strolled through the bizarre array of goods toward the counter at the back of the room— the beady-eyed bird watching her every move. She couldn't remember, but she was certain the raven hadn't been here several years ago—the only other time she had visited the shop, with Poppa and Grammy.

"Can I help you, dearie?" a gruff voice sounded behind her.

Panic leapt through Reecah's body.

A wizened old woman scrutinized her with wide, bloodshot eyes on either side of a hooked nose. An old smock draped the witch's bony frame; her thin waist cinched tight by a grubby apron.

Reecah's Flight

Reecah tried to step backward but the counter held her firm. The raven cawed in short bursts, as if laughing at her.

Even though she spoke the words, Reecah recognized the grizzled woman confronting her. "Uh, I'm looking for Grimelda. M-my grandmother sent me."

The old crone tilted her head. "Reecah Draakvriend. What brings *you* here? You were a wee lass when I saw you last, no?"

"Um, yes. I was, uh, four or five."

Grimelda cackled and poked Reecah's thigh with the knobby stick she used to support her hunched frame. "A fine specimen you have become. Marinah's daughter for certain, eh?" She ran a long, yellowed fingernail down Reecah's exposed forearm.

Reecah shuddered, instinctively pulling her arm back.

"Hmm. I wonder…" Grimelda let her hand trail away and limped around the end of the counter, almost disappearing behind its height. She stopped before a dusty shelf and removed an octagonal brass bowl, the unwieldy object seemingly too heavy for the old lady to lift. Blowing the worst of the dust from its tarnished surface, Grimelda lifted the bowl to the countertop.

Reecah's curiosity got the better of her. She placed her package on the counter and observed the witch polish the dust and grime from the peculiar object. Large runes etched into each of the bowl's eight sides materialized from beneath the tarnish. Reecah had no idea what most of these particular runes meant, but she remembered Poppa reading to her from books inked with similar pictographs.

Grimelda worked quickly, her tongue between her lips. Smaller runes appeared around the circumference of the bowl's flattened rim. Apparently satisfied, the old crone disappeared beyond a ratty, plaid blanket covering the doorway to a backroom.

Reecah's Flight

Just when Reecah thought the witch had forgotten about her, Grimelda pushed past the blanket, a large flask in hand, and poured its contents into the bowl.

Reecah couldn't contain herself. "What's that?"

"A curious creature you are, hmm? Good. Good. Much like Marinah," Grimelda said as she adjusted the position of the bowl on the counter and dispensed several pinches of a powder she obtained from an apron pocket.

Watching the powder dissolve, Grimelda broke the surface of the opaque liquid with a fingernail. Small ripples, more than should have occurred as a result of her simple touch, made their way to the centre of the bowl, curiously narrowing into a triangular formation before disappearing. "Are you ready for an augury?"

"A what?"

"A vision, child."

Grimelda reminded her of Grammy in a strange sort of way. "I don't know what you mean, ma'am."

Grimelda cackled. The raven emulated her.

"Oh, child, you are too naïve to be a Windwalker."

Reecah frowned. "I don't know what you mean." She looked over her shoulder, hoping for a distraction of any sort. The old woman gave her the creeps. She fleetingly hoped the boys would take it upon themselves to enter the shop. "Um, I should get going."

Reecah stepped away and was about to bolt, but Grammy's package caught her attention. She swallowed her rising tension and pointed at the cloth-wrapped bundle. "Th-that's for you. It's from Lizzy Draakvriend. My grandmother."

Grimelda's disturbing eyes flicked to the package before boring into Reecah. "I know who it's from, child. It's about time the foolish old woman sent it. Perhaps with you here, I can put it to use, eh?"

Reecah's Flight

Reecah had no idea what was inside the cloth bundle, nor did she wish to stick around to find out.

"Sure, I guess. Um, I have to go. Grammy will flay me if I'm not home before sunset." Reecah didn't wait for an answer. Knocking into a dusty, life-sized, stuffed mountain lion in her haste to escape the mystic shop, she stumbled down the centre aisle.

Grimelda's raspy voice followed her from the store, "Don't you want to know what happened to Viliyam?"

As much as that statement startled her senses, Reecah was too frightened to stop. She burst through the door and leaped the three flagstone steps, crunched into the gravel, and ran north through the village.

The boys were sitting on the stairs in front of the temple but by the time they noticed her, she had run wide of the building and was past them.

The boys gave chase, calling after her—the older ones slinging sexually crude innuendoes. Most of what they said didn't mean a lot but her cheeks flamed hot. She wasn't totally naïve.

By the time she hit the trailhead, the boys had fallen far behind. Living in the mountains, evading the potential dangers, and clambering the grueling surfaces, Reecah had become a proficient runner. She was a quarter of the way up the long hill before the boys stopped at the trailhead, giving up their sport. Their voices followed her up the hill long afterward.

Reecah's Flight

Confronting a Bully

Reecah's insatiable need to understand what had led to Poppa's death consumed her after her visit with the witch. She had always wondered what had happened, but when she asked Grammy, the old woman refused to say any more on the subject.

Something about the crone's words resonated deep within her. Perhaps it was Reecah's age. At six, she hadn't the maturity to question Poppa's tragedy, but now, reflecting on that fateful day, Reecah's curiosity demanded an answer.

Sitting in the darkening hut, studying Grammy before her loom—the old lady staring vacantly out of the grimy front window—Reecah saw the pain etched on her features. She wished she knew what went on inside Grammy's head. Was there ever a time she didn't think of Poppa?

Grammy became blurry as Reecah fought to contain her welling tears. It had been over six years, and yet her grief was no less. It still felt as if Jonas had just arrived on their doorstep.

Jonas! He knew what had happened that day. The brute had *led* the hunting party.

She swallowed her misgivings. From everything Grammy told her of the ruffian, she wasn't sure she was brave enough to confront the man. If Grammy found out what she planned to do, she'd tan Reecah's hide like there was no tomorrow.

Lying back on her blanket, the gemstone in her pillow jabbed the back of her head. She adjusted the annoyance until she couldn't feel it anymore and gazed at the deepening shadows.

Reecah's Flight

The sight of her wooden dragon sitting in an imperfection in the log wall filled her with bittersweet memories.

Her dream of flying had been quashed with Poppa's death. Seeing the carving sent a twinge of regret through her. Why should she give up on her dream? What else did she have? Grammy wouldn't be around forever, and then what?

Early the next morning, Grammy braided her hair, as she usually did after breakfast, and asked her to chop wood up on the slopes. Enduring the seclusion from their regular activities during the dragon mating season had seen their meagre stockpile dwindle. Up until a few days ago, Grammy hadn't allowed her to so much as stray from the yard. Now that summer was just around the corner, Grammy allowed Reecah the freedom to wander the nearby hills, provided she stay away from the higher heights and the Summoning Stone—both places Reecah frequented immediately. Her fondest memories of Poppa were there.

Throwing the old axe into the hand wagon, Reecah slipped into the woods. As soon as she was out of sight of the hut, she abandoned the wagon and made her way down the hill into Fishmonger Bay.

She'd no sooner stepped into town and sighted Jonas' warehouse when she regretted her decision to leave the axe behind. Two of Jonas' boys sat out front, pitching stones at a tree, their shoulder length, blonde-haired heads perking up at her approach.

The older boy, Jonas Junior, scanned her from head to toe. "Well look who we got here. Reeky Reecah." He spat on the ground.

Jonah's third son, Jaxon, laughed and imitated his brother, but his spittle drooled down his chin.

Junior laughed. "Ain't you a fine sight. Perhaps you're sweet on little Miss Reeky, huh?"

"Stuff it, JJ."

Reecah's Flight

Reecah stopped well out of spitting distance and rolled her eyes. Jaxon was around her age, while Junior was probably four or five years older. She fondly remembered drawing blood from both of them.

"What do you want, whelp?" Junior said.

Reecah glared. Oh, to split his smug lip! She didn't dare. Junior was fast becoming a man. His broad shoulders and the beginnings of facial hair had transformed the gangly youth into a powerful young adult. His heavy brow and long nose bespoke of his beefy father.

"I want to talk with your father, please."

"You're too young for him," Junior said and belted his brother in the shoulder. Jaxon had started laughing but shot his brother a dirty look after being hit.

Reecah frowned until his words set in. She struggled to keep her words steady as she spoke through nervous breaths, feeling her cheeks redden. "Please guys, it's important."

Jaxon leaned toward her, his brows raised. "And whatcha gonna give us for it? You ain't looking like you got much to offer, Reeky."

Reecah restrained the angry retort threatening to leap from her tongue, unsure what Jaxon meant.

Junior spoke up, "What's so important you can't speak with us?"

"It's about my Poppa."

"Your Poppa?" Jaxon blurted out.

Junior scowled and spat. "He's dead, ain't he?"

Reecah tried to keep the emotion from her voice. "Yes."

"Then who cares about Reeky Poppa—" Jaxon spouted off, his words catching in his throat.

Reecah leapt at the boy, fists swinging. Jaxon tried to turn and run but Reecah was quicker. She battered him twice, once in the stomach and once in the mouth—his teeth cutting her knuckles.

Reecah's Flight

They went down in a heap—Jaxon howling in pain and Reecah screaming at him, delivering a flurry of round house punches, "Don't you dare say anything about my Poppa again or I'll kill you. You hear me?"

Junior pulled her off his brother and slammed her into the wall but restrained himself from pummeling her. Their commotion had attracted the attention of several villagers.

The front door of the warehouse banged open and one of the biggest men in the community stormed out.

Jonas Waverunner took in the scene and the villagers milling about. "What's going on?"

Junior released Reecah and backed away from his father. Neither boy answered.

Jonas loomed over Jaxon, the whimpering boy nursing a busted lip and missing tooth. Blood covered his hands.

"Who did this to you, boy?" Jonas demanded and glanced around. The only people close enough were Junior and Reecah. His eyes fell on Junior, who shook his head.

Jonas turned an angry scowl on Reecah. "You did this?" His tone unbelieving.

Reecah glared. "He insulted my Poppa."

Jonas' scowl fell on Jaxon. "Get yourself cleaned up. There'll be more of that when I'm through with you."

Jaxon scrambled to his feet and disappeared into the warehouse.

Jonas focused on Reecah clutching her bleeding hand. "You're hurt."

"Poppa used to call that a 'welcome smarting'," Reecah mumbled, not meeting the big man's glare.

Jonas' face softened. "Aye, your Poppa always had a clever tongue. He's missed around here, let me tell you. He was a good man."

Reecah's ire heightened. "Grammy says you killed him."

Reecah's Flight

"Whoa girl, now hold on." Jonas's eyes took in the gathering crowd. "I don't know what Lizzy told you, but I assure you, I never did anything of the sort."

"Grammy says you forced him to hunt dragons."

Jonas nodded. "Aye, Viliyam accompanied us on the hunt, as was his duty. I'll not deny that."

"Grammy says you're reckless and shouldn't be trusted to lead men."

Jonas' face darkened. "Oh, she does, does she?" He jutted his prominent chin to the hill north of the village. "What does she know cooped up on yonder hill when the rest of the good people of Fishmonger Bay work themselves weary to keep the village thriving?"

Reecah fumed. First Jaxon attacked Poppa and now his father called out Grammy. She had half a mind to kick the man between the legs. Instead, her gaze took in the dozen buildings visible to them. "You call this thriving? One good wind and half these shoddy places are kindling."

A few of the villagers grumbled at her assessment. She didn't care. Every time she came to town, trouble had a way of finding her.

Jonas puffed out his considerable chest. "I think these good people take issue with the way you speak of their fine establishments. Perhaps we should band together and leave you and your grandma to your own devices up there."

"Ya? Well, by killing my Poppa, you've already done that now, haven't you?" Reecah couldn't believe she actually spoke to Jonas Waverunner this way. She glanced at the onlookers, hoping to find sympathy, but to a person, they glowered back at her.

Jonas' purple face belied his barely controlled voice. "I suggest you take your haughty self and disappear before I lose my temper."

The villagers nodded.

Reecah's Flight

Reecah bit her lips. She wanted to scream at the arrogant man, but Grammy had taught her to respect her elders. She inhaled deeply through her nose, looked at the blank faces gathered around, and walked away.

She stomped across the gravel commons, sobbing. Jumping into a run, she fled between the buildings leading to the trailhead and made her way up the slope. By the time she reached the top of the hill, she couldn't see through her tears.

She was tired of being bullied.

Reecah's Flight

Age of Discovery and Darkness

Ever since her run-in with Jonas and his boys, Reecah dedicated herself to learning about the dragon hunt. The reason for it, the weapons and tactics the hunters employed, and the conditioning required to deal with the giant beasts.

In her fifteenth year, she had lain in wait for Jonas and his men to commence their hunt, and followed them into the precarious mountain heights, careful not to be seen. The larger men carried great shields and axes, while others had two swords strapped to their hips. During her observation, she learned that these were the *fire breakers* and the *slayers*.

The most curious of the group were the ones bearing quarterstaffs—the *trackers*; the first contact with the dragons. Responsible for finding the nests and ensuring the adult dragons were not at home before they proceeded to prod and poke the large holes in the cliff face the beasts called home.

Of the three groups, the trackers had the shortest lifespan. If their information proved incorrect and an adult dragon remained in the nest as they attempted to lure the babies into the open, they suffered a horrific, fiery fate.

That knowledge struck Reecah hard. Poppa had been a tracker.

She knew only too well how dangerous the beasts were. According to Grammy, her mother, father, uncle, *and* Poppa were victims of the dragons. That knowledge did little to soften the brutality of how the men stabbed and cut apart the dragonlings. The horrific sight made Reecah sick.

Many were the nights afterward that sleep evaded her, haunted by the baby dragons' pathetic squealing as they were put to the sword. There had to be a better way to deal with them.

After the hunting season was over, when not tending to Grammy, whose advanced age left her in failing health, Reecah spent her spare time training her body. The upside to Grammy's condition was the fact that she could no longer keep track of Reecah's movements.

Reecah snuck Poppa's weapons from the old steamer trunk he kept them in and stashed them in a small cave not far behind the hut. Having no experience with weapons, she satisfied herself by running the trails and ridgelines with the same type of weapons she'd seen the hunters carry, strapped to her body or in her hands.

As the long summer days passed, her endurance increased to the point where she could run the treacherous route to the Summoning Stone and back four times without stopping—a route that used to take her and Poppa most of the morning to traverse one way. Many were the times when the tide precluded her ability to run that route. On those occasions, she found a way across what most people considered unnavigable terrain. If poor Grammy had found out about the extreme places Reecah found herself in, she would have had a stroke.

At eighteen, most of the boys no longer called her Reeky Reecah. In fact, they seemed uncomfortable speaking with her at all. Long lashes, full lips, captivating hazel eyes, long, brown hair kept in a tight braid, and a shapely physique separated her from the other girls in Fishmonger Bay. The boys who used to tease her mercilessly, suddenly became tongue-tied in her presence.

Reecah had filled out in so many ways due to her insatiable desire to become stronger, faster, and more agile than any of Jonas' hunters. She took comfort in the fact she could sprint the entire way up the hill from Fishmonger Bay to the path leading to her and Grammy's hut with Poppa's quarterstaff in hand and his old sword and bow strapped across her back.

During those torturous training sessions, she often caught sight of curious villagers standing at the trailhead watching her. If they were there when she arrived at the bottom, she would smile at them, turn, and sprint back up—their presence motivating her to run even harder.

Along with her eighteenth birthday came the dawning of the new dragon mating season. Instead of following Jonas' men into the mountain heights, she went on ahead and hid within crevices at various junctures she knew they had to pass to access the outlying dragon warrens. Once they made it to her position, she would slip away and take a more dangerous route, again beating the hunt to its destination. Reecah knew every nook and cranny on the mountainside for several leagues in any direction. Had Jonas asked, she could have saved his men days of needless hardship, but Jonas had it coming.

She secretly hoped to see the day the brute slipped up, promising herself to personally shake the claw of the dragon responsible for ending him. Though many men died during this year's hunt, Jonas wasn't one of them.

On one of the last expeditions, Reecah watched in horror as Jonas' second eldest son was carried away by an irate mother dragon that had returned while Janor clung to the cliff face he was working.

Reecah's Flight

With the mating season drawing to a close, Reecah skulked into her hut shortly after dark. At eighteen, she still feared Grammy's wrath if she disobeyed the rules.

The hut lay in darkness. "Grammy?"

Grammy didn't answer. Nor was there the usual aroma of food cooking.

Reecah pulled a thin stick from the kindling pile and stuck it into the ashes of the hearth. The residual heat of the embers sparked a flame to the end of the stick and she lit a nearby candle, looking toward Grammy's loom. She wasn't in her usual spot.

A faint wheeze came from the direction of Grammy's pallet.

Reecah set the candleholder on the cabinet beside the bedside and knelt on one knee, feeling Grammy's forehead with a dirty hand.

Grammy's yellowed eyes flicked open, blinking several times. Her pale lips turned up at the corners. "My child. You made it back to me."

Reecah's face tingled, her inner senses warning her of something she refused to believe. Her eyes welled up. "Of course, Grammy. I always come back. You know that, silly." She tried to smile past a trembling lower lip.

"Don't be sad, child." Grammy lifted a wrinkled hand, shaking more than usual, and ran her fingers along Reecah's cheek. "You have such a pretty smile. You are as beautiful as your mother." A tear dropped down Grammy's aged face.

Reecah wiped it away, her voice cracking, "What's wrong, Grammy?"

Grammy's faint smile widened. "Please, my sweet child, do not cry for me. I have lived a good life and have known a love like no other."

Reecah shook her head. "No Grammy, don't talk like that. You're going to be okay. You have to."

Reecah's Flight

"It's time I joined Poppa. He's been too long without me. There's no telling what mischief he's gotten himself into."

Reecah could barely breathe, let alone talk. "You can't leave me, Grammy. I can't live without you."

"Bless you, my child. Your cheerful presence all these years since Poppa left us has been a blessing. Your beautiful smile has given me the strength to last this long." Her watery eyes studied Reecah's face. "My flower bud. You're stronger than you know. Prove to Jonas you're a better hunter than the rest of his men put together."

Reecah swallowed. All she could do was stare.

"Aye, sweet Reecah. Don't you think for a moment that I didn't know what you were up to. Running to the Summoning Stone and parading about with Poppa's weapons."

"You knew?"

"Grammy knows everything."

Reecah spit out a wet laugh, even as her heart continued to break.

Grammy's cold hands wrapped weakly around Reecah's right hand. "You're your mother's child as much as she was Poppa's. You've become everything I feared. I warned that rascal, but Poppa hadn't the heart to set you right."

Reecah's face scrunched up in confusion.

"It's okay, sweet child. It was me who was wrong. I should never have stopped Poppa from encouraging you to become the woman you are destined to become…despite my best efforts to deter you."

"It's okay. You did it to keep me from following in Momma's footsteps. To protect me."

"No, child. I did it to protect *me*."

Reecah frowned.

"You're all I have left of your mother. I couldn't bear to lose you to those damned dragons. I'm sorry, Reecah. I was selfish." A weak cough interrupted her train of thought. "I hope someday you'll find it in your heart to forgive me."

Reecah placed her other hand on top of Grammy's and squeezed. "Don't say things like that. There's nothing to forgive. I love you."

Grammy's smile seemed forced. She closed her eyes.

For the briefest of moments, Reecah feared she had passed, but when her eyes opened again, her voice came out stronger than before.

"Poppa gave you a special family heirloom the last time we saw him alive."

Reecah's eyes widened.

"Aye, child. Remember? Grammy knows."

Reecah didn't know what to say so she just nodded.

"That stone is special. Been in the family longer than legends are old." She paused as if deciding whether she should say what was on her mind. "Your great-grandmother possessed the gift…You know what I'm speaking of?"

Reecah thought hard. "Magic?"

Grammy nodded. "It skipped me, but your great-aunt was touched by it. I've been watching for it in you, afraid to see it foster. By keeping you secluded, I have done you a disservice." She broke into a fit of raspy gurgles, pain evident on her face.

Reecah used the corner of the blanket to dab at the spittle on Grammy's lips.

"Fetch the gemstone for me."

Reecah didn't want to leave her, fearing the worst would happen before she returned from across the room, but she did as Grammy asked. Gathering the gemstone, she tried to hand it to Grammy, but the old woman shook her head.

"If you reach into the second drawer, you'll find something I want you to have."

Reecah frowned, placed the stone on top of the cabinet, and opened the drawer. Buried beneath a pile of old shifts, she

Reecah's Flight

located the same cloth wrapped package Grammy had her deliver to the witch years ago. She had no idea how it had come back. Turning it over in her hands, she marvelled anew at the weight of the small bundle.

"Open it."

Reecah fumbled with the cloth folds until she managed to unweave the intricate bands and withdrew a pristine, leather-covered book, embossed in fancy gold script: *Reecah's Diary.*

Reecah's eyes bulged. She opened the book and flipped through hundreds of blank pages. Turning the book over, she noted a walnut-sized impression in the back cover.

Grammy's smile was bigger than Reecah had seen in years.

"Take the gemstone and place it in the hole."

Reecah's brows knitted. She plucked the stone from the top of the cabinet and positioned it above the impression on the cover. Before she had a chance to place it, the stone jumped from her fingers, snapped against the cover and rotated, settling into the impression. A faint, crimson glow encircled the gemstone and winked out.

Reecah touched the gem but it held fast. "Wow," she said, the word long and drawn out. "What's it do?"

"That, my child, is part of your legacy." A spasm clenched Grammy's features.

Reecah wanted to ask what she meant but was put off by Grammy's discomfort.

When the fit eased, Grammy's glistening eyes locked on Reecah's. "Before I go, I need you to promise me one thing."

"Don't say that, Grammy. Please," Reecah whispered.

Grammy slipped a hand free of her grasp and stroked Reecah's wet cheek. "You will always be my precious, little flower bud, just as you are forever Poppa's poppet. Promise me you will…" Grammy choked on the fluid in her lungs but managed to say with a rasp, "Let your spirit soar."

Reecah's Flight

Reecah had no idea what that was supposed to mean but she nodded anyway, unable to speak.

Grammy's eyes smiled of their own accord one last time before the life left them.

Reecah laid her head on Grammy's chest—the light snuffed from her world.

Reecah's Flight

Only Family

Reecah didn't think she would ever get over Grammy's death. The woman had been a cantankerous and brooding old lady, but looking back, Lizzy Draakvriend had done what she thought was needed to protect Reecah from her mother's fate. Grammy had regretted her decision at the end but who was Reecah to gainsay her motives. On her deathbed, Grammy's words had served as the catalyst to reawaken Reecah's childhood dream.

The next day, Reecah buried Grammy beside Poppa at the end of the lane, overlooking the seaside. Returning to the silent cabin, she sat in front of Grammy's loom, unable to figure out the scary machine. She felt like such a failure. Grammy had shown her many times how to work the wooden apparatus but Reecah was never one to concentrate on menial pursuits. Her mind had always been on fanciful notions of adventure.

In the flickering candlelight, she tried to thread the shuttle through the strands of wool Grammy had been working on. Applying the foot pedal, the loom leapt into action and right away it was obvious she hadn't done it right.

She pushed the stool back and looked around the barren hut. Grammy and Poppa's pallet lay under a heap of blankets. The sheets that had kept Grammy warm for as long as Reecah could remember. Her throat tightened. The thought of Grammy lying cold in the ground made her cry again.

She got up and walked to Grammy's pallet, staring at the worn bedding through blurred eyes. She had walked over with the intention of making up the pallet—Grammy would have liked that. Standing there, she couldn't bring herself to do so. The act felt so final.

Shaking with grief, her teary vision caught sight of the diary Grammy had given her. She swallowed the lump in her throat and held the book against her chest. It was the only nice thing she owned besides Poppa's dragon carving.

She stumbled to her own blanket in the back corner and sat dejectedly with the diary in her lap. Grabbing her dragon, she stroked it between its wings like she did every time she felt sad.

With legs crossed, she rocked herself well into the night— long past the last candle sputtering out. Alone with her dragon, she welcomed the darkness.

By the time Reecah woke the next day, the sun blazed overhead. Biting her lower lip to keep her emotions in check; it promised to be one of those rare days Poppa had loved.

She boiled a pot of water and mixed in a bowl of oats. Sitting at the shabby dinner table, she couldn't help feeling that life had abandoned her.

After breakfast, she grabbed her new journal and found Poppa's old inkpot and quill. Prying the brittle cork free, she grimaced. The ink had become rock hard.

She searched the cabin for something else to use, but Grammy had never been one for lettering.

The temperature in the hut rose quickly, the atmosphere corresponding with the chirping and chattering of forest creatures enjoying the glorious weather outside.

Reecah changed out of her dirty clothes and searched out another white tunic—all her clothes basically the same. Grammy had made them.

Throwing the tunic over a thin shift, she laced up the front and pulled on a pair of green breeks. She grabbed her brown, hooded cloak from a wall peg near the door and went out to face the day.

Standing on the porch Poppa had built shortly before his death, she welcomed the sun on her face. It was a wonderful, late spring day. If only she knew what to do with herself.

Grammy's death had sapped her spirit. Running around the mountainside didn't interest her anymore. Unsure of how to proceed on her own, she decided she needed to swallow her misgivings and consult with someone in town. Perhaps she could take the next step in her evolution as a dragon hunter. After all, she wasn't one to work the land like Grammy and Poppa. If she didn't start earning a wage soon, she would starve to death.

Recalling her last foray into town and the confrontation with the Jonas boys, she retrieved Poppa's weapons from the shallow cave behind the hut and strapped them to her back— Poppa's sword belt too loose to hang around her waist

She couldn't remember the last time she'd actually *walked* down the hill into Fishmonger Bay. It was past high noon by the time her black suede boots crunched across the gravel commons and stopped at its centre. Surveying the common area, she contemplated her options.

Several villagers, including the mountain of a man, recognized her and called out. She gave them an obligatory smile and, "Hello," but her mind was elsewhere. She almost laughed out loud when she spotted Jaxon Waverunner exit the warehouse, stare at her for a moment, and quickly disappear back inside.

She glanced at all the buildings surrounding the commons. Who would be the best person other than Jonas to teach her how to wield Poppa's sword?

There was the old blacksmith in his shop behind the mercantile, but she had never really met him before. He was around Grammy's age, so he probably wasn't the best choice.

Reecah's Flight

Her gaze took in the temple. The Father Cloth, perhaps? Clerics were known to be accomplished fighters.

She sighed. That was the price she paid for her seclusion. She had lost touch with everyone in the village after Poppa died. At the time, she had been more than fine with it, but now that she needed something, she was at a loss on who she could trust.

The only people she had dealt with in the last several years were the Jonas family and the witch. She shuddered thinking of the old crone. There was no way.

The warehouse door opened and Jonas Junior appeared at Jaxon's side along with two girls around Reecah's age. The young women looked like Jonas' oldest daughters, but it had been such a long time since Reecah had last seen them. If she was correct, the older girl was Janice and the other was Jennah, the fraternal twin of Janor—the boy carried away by a dragon earlier in the spring.

Junior said something to the sisters. The young women glared at her and rolled their eyes.

Reecah swallowed her discomfort and started toward the temple, not knowing what she'd done to earn the girls' ire.

She stood at the base of the temple's stairs, contemplating whether to bother the Father Cloth and couldn't help glancing at the lavender cabin set back against the cliff face. The small hairs on the back of her neck rose just thinking about its inhabitant.

Out of the corner of her eye, the Jonas children watched her, their arms folded. She would love to smack them silly.

She sighed. What was she even doing here? Nobody liked her. With Grammy gone, the village would probably thank her to continue walking south toward Thunderhead. She caught herself nodding at the notion. Why not? She had nothing to look forward to here but sad memories and loneliness.

Reecah's Flight

Shivers shot up her spine. The stained-glass door of *Grimelda's Clutch* squealed open and Reecah locked eyes with the witch. She gulped, incapable of breaking contact.

"There you are, child. Grimelda is expecting you."

Reecah didn't know what creeped her out more. The fact that the witch had expected her or the way Grimelda referred to herself in the third person.

The witch leaned on her gnarly stick and raised a shaky hand, a withered finger motioning for Reecah to join her. "Grimelda and Reecah have much to discuss now that Lizzy has gone to the faeries."

Reecah's blood chilled. Nobody knew of Grammy's passing. Her mind screamed for her to run away, but her feet started toward the garish building.

Grimelda's crooked grin met her as she held the bottom half of the door open.

Stepping inside, Reecah cringed as the door squealed shut.

The crone swung the upper half shut. Several locking mechanisms clicked with a wave of her hand.

"Don't be alarmed, my child. Grimmy won't hurt you," Grimelda cackled and hobbled past Reecah, disappearing behind the counter.

Grimmy? The similarity to her pet name for Grammy unnerved her. As if feeding off her discomfort, the raven cawed from its usual resting place, imitating Grimelda's disquieting laugh.

Reecah considered the stained-glass door and searched the perimeter of the shop for another way out. Other than the plaid curtain draped over the hole in the wall behind the counter, there didn't appear to be one.

"Come hither, dear child. Join Grimelda in the cellar."

Reecah stared wide-eyed. There was no way she was going beyond that doorway.

Reecah's Flight

The raven emitted a high-pitched caw. "In the cellar! In the cellar!"

Reecah shook her head. This couldn't be happening. She must still be asleep.

"No need to fear Lizzy's sister, child. Grimelda is the only family you have left."

The raven's head bobbed. "Only family! Only family!"

Reecah grabbed onto a display shelf to keep her legs from buckling. She must've heard that wrong. That made Grimelda her great-aunt.

"Aye, dearie. There is much you need to learn now that grandma is gone, eh?" Grimelda disappeared behind the curtain.

Reecah's eyes darted everywhere at once, her throat dry and her tunic soaked with perspiration. She turned to the door, attempting to unlatch the highest lock but it wouldn't budge.

Grimelda's voice reached her from beyond the curtain. "Hee hee, child. You're not versed in magic. Those locks won't move without Grimelda's command."

Reecah spun around. The witch was nowhere in sight. She contemplated the stained-glass door in a panic and unsheathed Poppa's heavy sword. Even after running with it in her hands for countless days on end, swinging the brute of a weapon was an entirely different matter. She had hewn several stumps into chip wood over the last few years, but the blade's weight still gave her difficulty.

"I wouldn't try that if I were you," Grimelda called out.

The raven tilted its head sideways and blinked. "If I were you! If I were you!"

How did the witch know what she contemplated? Her mind made up, Reecah didn't hesitate. Holding the sword with two hands she brought the weapon crashing down from over her shoulder. The last thing she felt as the blade impacted the colourful, glass barrier was the explosion lifting her from her feet and throwing her into a display shelf. The tall stand buckled around her, dropping the shelves and their contents on top of her.

Reecah's Flight

In the Cellar

Reecah screamed as the old crone leaned in close, her breath rank. She remembered trying to escape Grimelda's mystical shop and then a bright light and then…

She found herself lying on her back atop a black marble slab in the middle of a small, candlelit cavern—its vaulted ceiling spiked with rock formations. She tried to push away from the vile woman but Grimelda's stick-like hands pinned her to the stone.

"What are you doing?" Reecah asked, frantically looking around and wondering why her ear lobes hurt. She forced an arm between herself and the witch and touched her right ear, shocked to feel a hard stone embedded there. She pulled her hand back—her fingertips red with blood. She checked her other ear and felt another hard stone.

Her frightened gaze met Grimelda's. "What have you done to me?"

Grimelda's expression made her shiver.

"Relax child. Grimelda has done what Lizzy neglected."

Reecah frowned but didn't want to waste time finding out what the crazy crone meant. She needed to get off the table and escape.

A fount on a matching marble stand stood near her head—perched on the edge of a blood-letting trough surrounding the base of the table.

She swallowed hard. Though not versed in the ways of the occult, Poppa had taught her to read at an early age. She had taken great joy in reading the tomes Poppa kept locked in an old trunk by his and Grammy's pallet. If she wasn't mistaken, she lay upon a sacrificial altar.

Using every bit of strength she had, Reecah bucked her hips and arched her back, driving her shoulder blades and head against the table to escape Grimelda's grasp.

She landed on the floor with bare feet but Grimelda's iron grip maintained control of her wrists.

"Easy child, you're going to ruin everything."

"Get your hands off me, you crazy witch!" Reecah shrieked, jerking her arms free and stepping backward. She bumped into a wooden table covered in crimson cloth. On top of the cloth, sat an array of knives. Some for slicing, some for chopping, one with a serrated edge for sawing, and another with a hooked tip—just like the one Grammy used to skin animals. "Where am I?"

"You're in Grimelda's cellar." Grimelda wiped her blood-stained fingers on her apron.

The witch's cellar? It looked like a cave devoted to demonic rituals. She swallowed a lump of fear and put the knife table between them, her eyes wildly darting about, searching for her boots and Poppa's weapons. She reached up with both hands, rolling the stones in her earlobes between her thumb and forefinger. "What have you put in my ears?"

"I have adorned you with your bloodstones."

"My what?" Her hands were wet and sticky with fresh blood. "Take them out!"

Grimelda shook her head. "That I cannot do. Once the ritual has been performed it would be too dangerous to remove them."

"Ritual? What did you do?"

"Something Lizzy should have had me do years ago if you wish to become a Windwalker."

"You're mad! Leave me alone!" Reecah glanced at the stairs.

Reecah's Flight

"Calm yourself, poppet."

Poppa's endearment snapped Reecah's open-mouthed attention back to the witch.

"Yes, child. Vili's name for you."

"You know that because you're a witch."

"Grimelda has been called many things." Grimelda pursed her thin lips, her tone softening. "The people of Fishmonger Bay labelled me as such. At one time I might have been hurt by the name, but the villagers leave me alone so I live with it."

Reecah noted the witch had started referring to herself in the first person. Her eyes flicked between the woman and various pieces of ornate furniture lining the walls. Pieces that looked as if they belonged in a palace, according to the sketches in Poppa's tomes.

A sudden burst of flapping wings appeared from the curved doorway marking the flight of stone carved stairs climbing into darkness. The raven landed on the near rim of the fount and turned its head sideways, blinking at her.

"Vili spoke fondly of his little poppet whenever he visited."

Reecah's temper rose. "You're a liar."

"You're a liar! You're a liar!"

Grimelda gave the bird a dirty look. "My sister called you her flower bud. You called her Grammy."

The pain was too much. Reecah's eyes misted up. "How do you know all this? Grammy doesn't have a sister."

Grimelda stepped toward her but stopped when Reecah's eyes honed in on the knives before her.

"Lizzy was afraid of what I represent."

"A witch?"

"A witch! A witch!"

"Yes, child, if that helps you understand."

"Understand what? That if I hadn't woken up when I did, you were about to send my spirit to your sick gods?"

"Sick gods! Sick gods!"

Reecah's Flight

Grimelda didn't deny it. Instead she picked up a carving knife and threw it at the raven.

The bird rose in a flurry of feathers and winged its way back up the stairway.

Grimelda shook her head. "Such a pest, that one. I should turn him into a toad."

Reecah's eyes grew wider.

"Witch humour. I can't actually do that."

Reecah wasn't so sure. Everything she had heard about Grimelda from the village children as a youngster attested to the fact that the witch was capable of performing many dastardly tricks.

"Why did you put me on that…that sacrificial altar? Where's my stuff?"

"Your stuff?" Grimelda scratched her head. "Oh, your boots and weapons. I left them in the shop."

Reecah tried to casually step toward the doorway. "Why?"

"Look at me? You may not consider yourself heavy, but it was all I could do to drag you down here without the extra weight."

"Even my boots?"

"Well no, but—"

"But nothing." Reecah took another big step. "What else were you planning on doing to me?" Her eyes went to the knives again.

"You were hurt. I healed you."

Reecah flexed her muscles and surveyed her outstretched arms. "That's strange. I feel alright."

"Of course you do. I healed you after you tried to break my door."

Reecah swallowed. She backed farther away, not believing a word the old crone said.

Grimelda followed with her eyes. "If you insist on leaving, I won't stop you, but…" She let the word hang between them.

Reecah's Flight

Reecah stopped and waited for it.

"You may never know if our family gift has passed down to you."

"What are you talking about?"

"Whether you believe me or not, my child, once I'm gone, you'll be the last in a line of magic that has been in this world for as long as the sun has risen. You're the only one who can prevent our legacy from disappearing from the world."

Reecah adjusted her stance, jutting her hips to one side and leaning her head toward Grimelda. "Huh?"

Grimelda nodded. "It is as I feared. Lizzy never told you, did she?"

Grammy's death had been hard on her. Reecah had been too heartbroken to remember everything Grammy had told her. Grimelda's words triggered the painful memory.

Your great-grandmother possessed the gift.

The implication slammed into her. She hadn't thought of it as anything more than a dying, old lady's rambling.

Grimelda nodded, a smile lifting the corners of her mouth.

It skipped me, but your great-aunt was touched by it. I've been watching for it in you, afraid to see it foster. By keeping you secluded all these years, I have done you a disservice.

Reecah didn't care that her jaw dropped in disbelief. She stood in a witch's cave staring at Grammy's *sister!* Accepting Grimelda's words, she noticed the startling resemblance between the sisters—Grimelda was much older in appearance but there could be no mistake—the witch of Fishmonger Bay was Reecah's only living relative.

The truth left her speechless. Part of her wanted to scream, but deep down, an ingrained desire to know festered. Even so, she teetered on the verge of extricating herself from the witch's cellar. Grimelda's next words held her spellbound.

"You are a dreamer, Reecah Draakvriend. Vili instilled that in you. Lizzy fought against it, but if I'm not mistaken, in the end, she came to understand. Am I right? Did she give you a special item before leaving our world?"

Reecah reached into the secret pocket inside her cloak, half expecting the witch to have stolen it from her, but her fingers wrapped around the smooth binding of her diary. For some reason she felt compelled to pull it out and hold it out for Grimelda to see.

"Turn it over."

Reecah hesitated but did as she was asked. The candlelight reflected off the facets of the crimson gemstone.

Grimelda's awe-filled tone wasn't lost on Reecah. "It worked. I wanted that book ever since the day your great-grandmother died, but for some reason it was given to Lizzy. And the stone! I can hardly believe my eyes. Your grandmother knew the truth all along. Why that little…" Grimelda's voice trailed off.

Tears dampened the wrinkles on her great-aunt's face.

As bizarre as it seemed, Reecah had a compelling desire to comfort the old woman. Hoping she wouldn't regret it, she put her strong arms around the old crone, hugging her head into her bosom. She couldn't imagine how lonely the old woman had been all these years, loathed by the villagers and shunned by her family.

Grimelda wept softly, her skeleton arms returning Reecah's embrace. Separating herself, she stared at the ground. "I'm sorry, my child. Forgive a foolish old maid. I forget my place."

Reecah grasped Grimelda's blue-veined hands. "There's nothing to forgive…great-aunt."

Grimelda looked into Reecah's hazel eyes, a glimmer of hope in her bloodshot stare. Fresh tears rolled down her cheeks as a genuine smile illuminated her haggard face. "You truly are the godsend Vili spoke of."

Reecah's skin flushed with goosebumps. Whether due to Grimelda's words or because of the chill in the cellar and the

Reecah's Flight

cold from the floor entering her body through her bare feet, she didn't know. She released her hands and started for the doorway. "Come on, we need to get you somewhere warm. There's nothing to you."

Grimelda nodded and preceded Reecah up the long, twisting flight of stairs; leaning on her knobby stick to help lift her body.

The steps emptied into a large storeroom burrowed into the mountainside—at its far end hung the plaid curtain.

The welcome heat of the shop drove Reecah's chill away. *Grimelda's Clutch* flickered under the light of several candelabras hanging from the ceiling—through the stained-glass door she realized it was nighttime. Casually surveying the store, the crusty raven had returned to its usual perch. Piled beneath it were her weapons and her boots.

While Grimelda pulled a small table and two short stools around the counter, Reecah retrieved her boots and pulled them on, her eyes following Grimelda's movements. The crone pulled out the octagonal brass bowl covered in runes—the one she had tried to show Reecah years ago—and placed it on the table.

Reecah thought for sure the rickety stand would collapse. "What's it do?"

If Grimelda heard her, and Reecah was sure she had, she never let on. The witch disappeared behind the curtain before returning with what appeared to be the same flask she had used before.

Grimelda emptied the flask into the brass bowl, adjusted its position until she was satisfied, and dipped a yellowed fingernail into the liquid—just enough to break its surface.

A line of ripples surged toward the middle of the bowl, narrowed into the point of a triangle at its centre and disappeared. Grimelda nodded. "It's ready."

"What's it do?" Reecah repeated.

Reecah's Flight

"Sit here, child." Grimelda indicated the stool on the opposite side from where she had dipped her fingernail.

Reecah lowered herself onto the stool, her knees sticking up by her elbows.

Grimelda sat on the other stool, her stooped body making it the proper height. "This, my child, is a magical fount. With it, someone proficient in the gift can do many things."

Reecah had no clue what that meant. "The large runes on the side are directional, are they not? I'm sitting in front of the south rune."

Grimelda nodded. "Yes, dearie. I'm impressed."

Reecah blushed. "Poppa taught me."

"Hmm, he did, did he?" She nodded some more. "Vili was a special man. I'm impressed he taught you runology. It's a dying language. Did he teach you the common language as well?"

"He made me read to him at bedtime when I was three or four. He kept at me until I didn't need his help with the bigger words."

"Excellent. That saves us a lot of time."

"A lot of time? For what?"

"Tsk, tsk. We're getting ahead of ourselves. First, we must discover whether you possess the family legacy. Have you ever experienced a time when you have, um, done something you shouldn't be able to?"

Reecah's brows knit together. She shook her head. "I don't think so. Like what?"

"Oh, I don't know. Like lighting a candle without touching a flame to its wick, or foreseeing something before it actually happens. You know? Stuff like that."

"No. Nothing."

"Hmm."

Her answer appeared to unsettle Grimelda.

Grimelda dipped her pointer fingernail in the bowl and swirled the viscous liquid, deep in thought; her yellowed eyes on Reecah. Without a word, she got to her feet and plucked a couple of strands of Reecah's hair.

Reecah winced, about to protest, but kept quiet.

Grimelda eyed the strands. Picking the longest one, she placed it in the bowl's centre.

Instead of falling limp on the liquid's surface, the hair straightened into a rigid follicle, slowly absorbing into the bowl with a soft hiss—the surface around the hair smoking.

Reecah leaned forward, studying the strange phenomenon.

"Curious," Grimelda muttered. "I've never seen that before."

"Seen what?"

Her features twisted in thought, Grimelda rose and shuffled behind the counter and rummaged in the shelves on the wall. Not finding what she wanted, she slipped through the curtain.

Reecah waited patiently, listening to the sound of jars clinking and objects being relocated. "Can I help?"

"Can I help? Can I help?"

Reecah stared at the raven. It returned her gaze, turning its head from side to side. Without warning it squawked and took flight, banging into the stained-glass door and falling to the ground. It righted itself and flapped at the door, cawing incessantly.

"Raver! If you break a wing, Grimelda will cook you." Grimelda admonished the spastic bird.

Reecah jumped. She hadn't heard the witch approach. Her great-aunt's words did little to calm her nerves.

Grimelda carried a plate-sized object, its obsidian surface refracting the flickering candlelight.

"Is that what I think it is?" Reecah asked, forgetting about the raven.

"Yes, my child. A dragon scale."

"May I touch it?"

Grimelda handed it to her.

Reecah's Flight

She almost dropped it, it was so heavy. "Wow. I've never held a black one.

"I don't imagine you have. They are only found on ancient male dragons, and ancient dragons are becoming rarer as the years pass. The dragon hunt has seen to that."

Reecah tried to hand the scale back.

Grimelda shook her head. "No, that's for you. When I tell you, dip it into the bowl."

Reecah positioned the scale near the bowl's south rim.

"Not until I tell you," Grimelda warned, and sat on her stool. She laid her hands on the northeast and northwest rims of the bowl and threw her head back. A strange noise escaped her throat.

Reecah nearly dropped the scale.

Grimelda's eyes rolled back into her head as she chanted in an unfamiliar language.

It took Reecah a few moments to realize she understood the meaning of Grimelda's words. The witch intoned the runic language—strange to hear it spoken aloud after so many years. Grimelda spoke faster than Reecah could follow. Concentrating hard, she absently registered the raven had stopped fussing and was hopping up the aisle toward them.

Grimelda completed her chant with a dramatic emphasis on the last words, *"Ventus ambil!"*

Grimelda's eyes flicked back, their intensity, frightening.

"Now child! Immerse the scale, but don't let go." Grimelda's wispy hair shook, vehemently directing Reecah to do as she was bidden.

Reecah gaped, afraid of what was to come. As the dragon scale broke the liquid's surface, a peculiar presence invaded her body. She tried to release the scale and distance herself from the rite, but she no longer controlled her movements.

Visions of the ocean flashed past her, hundreds of feet below, leaving her reeling with vertigo. The shoreline north of

Reecah's Flight

the Summoning Stone disappeared as the cliffs wheeled up before her. She scrunched her face in anticipation of slamming into the side of the mountainside, only to feel her momentum change. She stared up at the clouds, a steep mountain façade whooshing by her side.

A mournful cry pierced her brain and she fell from the sky.

Reecah's Flight

Dirty Bird

If not for Grimelda, Reecah would have hit the floor harder than she did.

Accepting Grimelda's hand, she rose shaking, balancing herself against the counter. The shelves tilted back and her equilibrium slowly returned.

The brass bowl lay on the floor beside her, the vertex between the southern rim and the southwest dented—the foreign liquid dissolving into the floorboards in a haze of acrid smoke. The dragon scale lay unaffected amid the spill.

Reecah gazed into the witch's eyes, her mind spinning. "What just happened?"

"Come, child, we need fresh air." Grimelda steered Reecah toward the door. "Raver, to me."

The raven jumped into the air from a shelf near the front of the shop and alit on Grimelda's shoulder.

Approaching the stained-glass door, Grimelda muttered something too fast for Reecah to comprehend and the locks clicked open.

Reecah was surprised at how woozy she felt. She let Grimelda help lower her to the flagstone steps before sitting down beside her.

A cool breeze swept off the ocean, its rolling surface barely visible beneath the new moon.

"Tell me what happened," Grimelda said.

"What happened? What happened?"

Reecah's Flight

"Shoo, you dirty bird or I'll cook you." Grimelda shrugged her shoulder and Raver flew to the outstretched wing of a flying dragon statue at the base of the steps.

"I don't know. It's hard to explain. I remember dipping the dragon scale into the bowl and then…" Reecah shook her head.

"And then?"

"And then…it was as if I was flying. Over the ocean." The vision came back to her. "I flew north of the Summoning Stone. I know the shoreline well. I've been there many times."

"With Viliyam."

Reecah shook her head. "No, by myself."

Grimelda raised her eyebrows. "That's dragon country up there. Dangerous for people."

"Ya, that's what Grammy said. Whenever she found out she gave me the cane." A rueful smile creased her lips at the painful memory. "Anyway, I flew at the mountainside. I thought I was going to hit it but I shot straight into the sky. And then…I don't know. An intense pain filled my head and I fell. The next thing I knew, you were holding me."

Grimelda's face darkened. "Tell me, child, what exactly were you flying?"

"I wasn't flying anything. I flew on my own…at least I think I did."

Grimelda nodded slowly. "Interesting."

"Does it mean I have the gift?"

"I honestly don't know what it means. There's something different about you, but I've no idea what."

"Great." Reecah swallowed. She always knew she was different. She assumed it was because she lived up on the hill. Perhaps the villagers were right to pick on her.

"The good thing, my child, is that you're not normal."

Reecah's Flight

Reecah flashed Grimelda an ungrateful smirk. Shivering in the night air, she stared at the whitecaps rolling into shore, eternally crashing and receding, only to crash again.

Grimelda wrapped a scrawny arm around Reecah's shoulder. "One thing I do know, Reecah Draakvriend. The way your hair sample responded to the scrying liquid was unique. In all my years I've never seen that happen. Nor have I heard anyone experience what you claim."

"So, I'm a freak."

Grimelda tightened her hold, pulling Reecah in close. "Not so much a freak. More like...special."

"Ya, real special. No one likes me. Everybody makes fun of me, and now I'm all alone." Reecah hung her head, fighting the urge to cry.

Grimelda's bony fingers lifted Reecah's chin and looked her in the eyes. "I never want to hear you talk like that again. You're never alone as long as you have me."

"You have me! You have me!"

Through watery eyes, Reecah followed Grimelda's disgusted glare.

Raver bobbed his head up and down—the faint moonlight glinting off his beady eyes.

Grimelda shook her head. "Go on you dirty bird, before I pluck you."

Reecah spurted out a laugh.

Reecah's Flight

Poppa's Deception

Reecah clicked her tongue against the roof of her mouth trying to coax Raver from his perch in the corner of *Grimelda's Clutch*. "Come on. You want breakfast?"

"Stupid bird," Grimelda said sitting behind the counter on a tall stool, slopping oatmeal into her mouth. "He ain't worth the bother." She leaned toward the raven, her voice changing to a higher pitch. "Are you? You're a dirty bird. Momma should stuff you."

Raver turned his head to the side and blinked.

Reecah smiled. "He's so cute. Where'd you get him."

"Cute? Pfft," Grimelda grunted. "A royal pain in the arse, more like. I caught him to use in a spell, but I never got around to performing it."

Reecah stopped chewing, envisioning the witch carving up Raver on the marble altar in the cellar.

Grimelda must have noticed Reecah's appalled glare. "Bah. The ugly bird's lucky I don't dig that spell back up."

Reecah wasn't sure if her aunt was serious or not. "Don't you listen to her, Raver. I think you're a pretty bird."

Raver's head bobbed up and down. "Pretty bird! Pretty bird!"

"Don't encourage him. He'll get a fat head." Grimelda slid off her stool and shuffled around the counter with her stick to stand in front of Reecah. "Now, what to do with you? I'm going to need time to investigate what your episode with the scrying bowl meant."

Reecah's Flight

Reecah glanced at the vessel in question. After waiting for the air to clear in the shop last night, they had cleaned up the mess and retired in the back room where Grimelda kept a cot. Reecah had slept on the cold, stone floor without complaint. She didn't know anything different.

Reecah undid the thong holding the end of her braid, doing her best to gather the loose ends and tighten it up again. "I was just thinking. I came to the village searching for someone."

"Who?"

"I'm not sure. Someone to teach me how to use Poppa's weapons."

Grimelda nodded. "To protect yourself. Not a bad idea."

"Actually, I want to become a hunter."

"A hunter?"

"A dragon hunter. Like Poppa."

Grimelda leaned back. "A dragon hunter? Really?"

Reecah picked up on her aunt's hesitation. "Why? Because I'm a woman?"

Instead of replying, Grimelda retrieved Reecah's weapons.

Reecah went to help her, but Grimelda lifted them with apparent ease. The witch's walking stick was nothing more than a prop. Full of surprises, Grimelda shuffled past and slipped through the curtain.

Reecah followed on her heels.

Grimelda approached a dusty shelf and unceremoniously pitched Viliyam's weapons onto the lower section of four.

"What are you doing?" Reecah stepped between Grimelda and the shelf. "Those are Poppa's."

"You don't need them anymore."

"I don't care whether I need them or not, I'm taking them." She retrieved Poppa's quarterstaff and examined it for damage.

"Suit yourself, child," Grimelda said from the far side of the dimly lit room. "Though I think you'll be hard put carrying them while burdened with these."

63

Reecah's Flight

Reecah peered over Grimelda's shoulder. Her breath caught.

Grimelda's gnarled fingers pulled back an oiled leather cloth, revealing an assortment of stunningly wrought weapons. Three arming swords, a dagger, and an unusual black bow—its matching quiver etched with the same markings as the bow.

"Where'd you get those?"

"Belonged to my mother. Your great-grandma. When she died, she gave Lizzy the book and I got these. We thought she erred in her choices but I'm beginning to think she did so for a reason."

"How so?" Reecah leaned in to take a closer look. "May I?"

Grimelda stepped back. "I believe your great-grandmother knew that Lizzy and I weren't the ones to carry on her legacy, and therefore gave me, the one with an aptitude for magic, her weapons, knowing full well I wouldn't use them. It seems the same held true with Lizzy. She was given a magical journal that was of no use to her."

Reecah processed little of what her great-aunt said, her mind preoccupied with the wondrous weapons before her. She gave the bow a quick look over before grabbing one of the sheathed swords—the one without the fancy, circular guard. She pulled it free of its leather scabbard and admired its perfect balance— much less cumbersome than Poppa's. Though she was taller than the average woman, the length suited her perfectly.

"Now, about Viliyam."

Something in Grimelda's tone made Reecah stiffen. She swallowed and lowered the sword, her hazel eyes searching the crone's.

"Do you know why your grandfather participated in the dragon hunt?"

Reecah shook her head at the strange question. All the men in Fishmonger Bay were expected to do their part safeguarding the community. "Because it was his duty?" she half asked, sensing her great-aunt was about to tell her differently.

Reecah's Flight

"Aye, as you well know he had no choice in the matter. But, do you know why he made certain he was not only the best tracker available, but the *only* tracker to remain alive each season?"

Reecah shook her head.

"To lead the hunt away from the dragons."

"Why would he do that?"

"Viliyam made it his business to preserve the magical beasts as best he could. He went out of his way to lead the hunt astray. To keep them away from the main dragon warrens."

"But…but he often came back battered and bloody. It was his job to locate the nesting holes and urge the babies into the open so that Jonas and the others could dispose of them."

Grimelda offered her a patient smile. "That is what he led everyone to believe. In fact, he purposely found the most roundabout route to the outlying warrens—dragging the hunters over exhausting terrain. Their journeys took much longer than they should have."

Reecah thought of her recent spying adventures and how easy it had been to get ahead of the hunting party. She never stopped to wonder why it took them so long to access parts of the mountains that she could reach in half the time. She just figured she was smarter than them. If what Grimelda said was true, Jonas and the hunters were following the routes Poppa had set out for them years ago. Routes that led them needlessly off track.

"Why would he do that?"

"Because your grandfather was a student of your great-grandmother. That's how he met Lizzy."

Reecah slid the sword into its black leather scabbard and replaced it on the shelf. She'd never met her great-grandmother. "I'm sorry, I'm not following you."

Grimelda grasped her hands. "You come from a line of dragon friends."

Reecah's Flight

"Dragon friends?"

Grimelda nodded. "There aren't many of us left. I don't know of any others like us except for perhaps a family in Cliff Face, far to the north."

"Others like us?"

"Don't you see? Our family is trying to preserve the dragons, lest the high king's men kill them all. The high king is unhappy that mankind is not at the top of the food chain."

"The high king is justified in his thinking. Dragons are dangerous. They killed Poppa, my parents and uncle Davit."

"Oh, they most certainly are dangerous. Deadly, in fact, to those who provoke them." Grimelda's twisted features softened. She released one of Reecah's hands and patted the other. "Your family died defending the dragons."

"That's not what Grammy said."

Grimelda's smile filled with compassion. "Lizzy could never accept their deaths. Had your parents not intervened on the dragons' behalf, a greater travesty would have occurred. Unfortunately, their measures cost them their lives. Your grandmother was never able to bring herself to see beyond that. She believed that in order to protect you, she needed to distance herself from me. She made Viliyam promise never to mention our family's heritage. Poor Lizzy. I cannot fault her. You were all she had left."

Reecah pulled free of Grimelda's grasp and paced around the storage room, pondering her words. She found it hard to digest the news of Poppa's deception, but the more she thought of her time with him, distant memories faded as they may be, the more Grimelda's words made sense. Poppa had revered the dragons like he had all living creatures.

She stopped in front of Grimelda, wanting to ask her more about her best friend—of what else Poppa had kept from her. As much as she understood he acted in deference to Grammy's wishes, Reecah couldn't help but feel betrayed by the one person who had meant the world to her.

Grimelda interrupted her thoughts. "Take those weapons. They're yours."

Reecah swallowed her pain. "They're useless to me."

Grimelda grasped her hands and squeezed. "Think, child. You have been granted a gift. Use it. You have a chance to honour Viliyam's memory."

"And join the dragon hunt? After what you just said?"

"Pick up where Viliyam left off. You're young and strong. Stronger by far than your Poppa ever was. You possess the Windwalker gift."

"Windwalker?"

"Your great-grandmother's family name. One that is not to be mentioned lightly. There are many who would kill you on sight should they discover your true lineage."

Reecah struggled to comprehend Grimelda's meaning. "So, let me get this straight. You want me to join the dragon hunt, but not kill the dragons?"

"Not just join the hunt, lead it."

"But, I'm a woman."

"Exactly!"

Reecah's brows furrowed. "And who's going to train me?"

Grimelda's face lit up in an evil grin. "Why, Jonas, of course."

Reecah's Flight

Parlay with the Enemy

Jonas' eldest daughter, Janice, answered the door. If not for her eternal scowl, Reecah thought the blonde-haired woman would be attractive—she carried her broad frame well, if a little hunched.

The ample busted woman sneered. "What do *you* want?"

Reecah let her cloak open to reveal two circular sword hilts extending from a brown leather belt cinched that was attached to a wide, leather cummerbund for added support. She threw her shoulders back to accentuate her bust and flicked her bangs from her eyes—her thin braid flapping around her waist.

Janice gave her a quick once over and rolled her eyes. "Be gone with you, wench. You think you're so special. Decent folk want nothing to do with tripe like you."

Janice went to close the door but a blonde-haired boy, standing a head taller than either of them, came up behind her.

"Who are you talking to?" Jonas Junior asked with a snarl. His blue eyes took in Reecah. His dour face softened. "Oh!"

Junior cast his sister a dark glare. "Where's your manners? It's no wonder you're still a maiden." Smiling wide, his eyes scanned Reecah from head to foot. "Reecah Draakvriend. Wow...I-I mean, um, what are you doing here?"

Janice scowled and disappeared into the warehouse, muttering, "I'll leave you to the ogling fool."

Reecah smiled for Junior's benefit. "I wish to speak with your father. Is he about?"

68

Reecah's Flight

Junior frowned. "Father? Um, ya, I believe so. What do you want with him?"

"This is the year of the dragon, is it not?"

"Um, ya. What of it?"

"I wish to join the hunt."

Junior's eyes bulged. He seemed on the verge of laughing but kept his emotions in check. "But you are a...a..." He swallowed noticeably, his eyes scanning her again.

"A woman?"

Junior emitted a quick snort. "Yes, of that there is no doubt."

Reecah purposely rested her hands on the sword hilts. "I assure you I'm up to it." She started to draw her great-grandmother's training blades and lifted an eyebrow. "Do you care to find out?"

Junior held up his hands. "Ha-ha! Not really. One moment." He ducked into the warehouse, leaving the door ajar.

Reecah let out a deep breath, thankful Junior hadn't taken her up on her dare. Scanning the village commons to ensure no one watched her, she stepped up to the warehouse doorway and peered in.

She had visited Jonas' warehouse on a few occasions with Poppa, but that was so long ago. She'd forgotten what it looked like inside.

A short hallway led away from the door into a dimly lit interior. She steadied herself on the door jambs and leaned in to see beyond the corridor. So caught up in her inspection, she never heard the gravel crunch behind her.

"Can I help you, Draakvriend?" a deep voice asked.

Reecah jumped. Trying to spin around to see who had snuck up on her, she tripped over the raised threshold and fell to the dirt-lined hallway on her rump. Looking up at the hulking shadow barring the door, she swallowed. "Mister Waverunner. You scared me."

Jonas glared. "A better fate than a robber deserves."

Reecah's Flight

Reecah picked herself up and tried to step over the threshold, but Jonas' bulk prevented her. She struggled to maintain his gaze. "Robber? Me? Oh, no. I was waiting for you, actually."

Jonas crossed his beefy arms. "Really? By sneaking into my building?" He swivelled his head to take in the town around them. "Which, by the way, is still standing."

Reecah swallowed, remembering their last encounter. "I wasn't sneaking int—"

"Wasn't sneaking in?" Jonas boomed. "A strange thing to say when you are standing inside."

"B-but—"

"But nothing. You Draakvriends are nothing but a scourge to our village. I'm willing to forget this…on one condition."

Reecah stepped backward, not appreciating what she read in his suggestive sneer.

Footsteps crunched from around the corner of the building.

"There you are, Father," Junior said, coming into sight. His eyes took in Reecah inside the doorway and the look on his father's face. "I see you found each other."

Jonas turned on his son. "You knew Draakvriend was here and you didn't send her away?"

Junior's smile slid from his face. He stared at the ground. "No Father. She wanted to speak to you about a position in the hunt."

Jonas' eyes narrowed, finding Reecah's.

She couldn't tell if she read anger or confusion. Raising her head with dignity, she straightened her shoulders and forced a smile. "That's right, Mister Waverunner. I wish to take my Poppa's place."

"Your Poppa's place? As a tracker? Hah!" Jonas hocked and spat, the spittle barely missing Junior's boots.

"Please sir, give me a chance. I've been training for years. I know the mountains better than anyone. I'm ready."

Jonas regarded her like a festering boil. He leaned forward.

70

Reecah's Flight

Reecah tried not to flinch as Jonas' yellow-toothed sneer came within a hair's breadth of her face.

"Oh, you are, are you? Have you ever killed anything?"

Reecah hoped she wasn't trembling as hard as she thought. "D-deer and elk. Rabbits and chickens."

"Chickens!"

Jonas roared so loudly, Reecah was sure her hair blew backward. She caught movement in the hallway. Janice walked up behind her, crossing her arms—a smug look on her face.

"We're talking about dragons! Bigger than a hut and breathing fire!"

Reecah struggled to remain positive. "I know, Mister Waverunner. I've seen them before."

Jonas' face darkened. He stepped aside. "Not up close you haven't. Not while breathing fire and carrying off your loved ones! Be gone from here, silly girl. You wouldn't last a day on the hunt."

Reecah struggled to keep her fear of Jonas at bay. Her eyes threatened to tear up. Taking a deep breath, she lifted her chin, careful not to trip over the threshold again. "I saw the dragon carry away your son."

The look Jonas gave her as she passed, chilled her to the bone. She hastened her step, worried he might attack her.

"Hold!"

She stopped obediently, not daring to look back.

The gravel crunched as the brute grasped her shoulder, painfully yanking her around to face him. His shoulders lifted with heavy breaths. "I should strip you bare and flay your sorry hide before all of your peers for speaking such lies."

Her eyes moistened, expecting the worst, and her legs shook, but a dark resolve hardened her features. "Your party was taken unaware high above Dragonfang Pass. Your son climbed a rock face and clung to a dead tree sticking out from the cliff. He prodded a dragonling from its warren at the same time the mother dragon came out of nowhere. She plucked her baby in one foreclaw and your son in the other. His screams still haunt me in the darkest part of the night."

Jonas blinked at her several times. His brows knit together above his softening, purple scowl. "Dragonfang Pass is only accessible to the hardiest of mountaineers. It took us three days to get there." He glanced briefly at Junior and then back again. "Who told you this?"

"Told me? No one. I followed you."

"Don't lie to me, Draakvriend. I'll flog you where you stand."

"What took you and your men three days to reach, I can do in two."

The darkness seeped back into Jonas' face. "Impossible."

"For *your* men, perhaps," Reecah stared him in the eye without blinking. "Not impossible for a Draakvriend familiar with the mountains. I traverse what appears to you and your men as insurmountable obstacles. When your party made it to the Fang, I had been there since daybreak."

Jonas' eyes scrunched together.

Reecah didn't wait for his response. She knew he wouldn't believe her. "I seek someone to train me in the ways of the hunt. I will be a good tracker. Almost as great as Poppa. From what I observed, you're in dire need of a *real* tracker."

"That's my job!" Junior blurted out but looked to the ground when Jonas glared at him.

"How can I prove myself?"

"You can't," Jonas growled, but his brows twisted in thought. He turned his attention south, beyond the town temple. "Are you aware of an old hut near the summit of Peril's Peak?"

"The one at the base of the falls?"

Jonas lifted his brows, clearly taken aback. "Aye, that one. Meet me up there by noon tomorrow. *If* you think you're up to it."

Reecah's Flight

She thought about what he insinuated earlier and shivered. The idea of being alone with Jonas, high in the mountains, set alarm bells ringing in her mind.

"What's the matter, Draakvriend?" Jonas snarled. "Don't think you're up to it?"

"It's not that."

"Are you...scared?"

"Of the climb? No, sir." Reecah didn't know what to say. "Who's going to be up there?"

Comprehension settled on Jonas. He hocked and spat. "Don't flatter yourself. I prefer meat on my conquests."

Reecah fought to control her breathing. Janice stood beside Junior, the siblings enjoying her discomfort. Jonas crossed his arms, a satisfied smirk splitting his bearded face.

If she wanted to join the dragon hunt, Jonas was the man to talk to. If she wished to learn how to wield her weapons effectively, Grimelda claimed Jonas was the man to teach her. Like it or not, unless she made her way to Thunderhead, Jonas Waverunner was her best option. She had been considering leaving Fishmonger Bay but the brief time spent with her great-aunt had changed her mind. Grimelda's words had sparked a curiosity in her about her family. From the subtle innuendoes the crone had imparted, the Draakvriend heritage hid many secrets.

She felt herself nodding before she consciously made up her mind. "Okay. Tomorrow noon."

Reecah started north, toward the trailhead.

Jonas and his children laughed amongst each other.

Reecah's cheeks flamed hot but she wouldn't give them the satisfaction of turning around.

"Draakvriend!" Jonas' voice stopped her before she slipped between the two buildings at the trailhead.

Reecah's Flight

She stiffened. Giving in to her fright, she looked back. The Waverunners stared at her. Not trusting her voice, she waited for Jonas to continue.

Jonas pointed south. "Peril's Peak is that way."

Reecah remained silent.

"Why are you heading north?"

Reecah frowned. What a silly question. "To get some rest."

Jonas and his children exchanged looks.

"The cabin is at least a day's trek from here. With nightfall, I doubt you would reach it until mid-morning if you left now."

Reecah raised her eyebrows. "I know," was all she said.

Slipping between the buildings, she put the Waverunners out of sight.

Reecah's Flight

Peril's Peak

Reecah strolled to the brink of the waterfall overlooking the cabin below Peril's Peak as it tumbled from the heights toward a crag infested drop beyond. The sun had crested the peak a little while ago—beaming warmth into the green valley. Judging by the sun's position, she had plenty of time to spare.

A wisp of smoke escaped the cabin's roof, drifting lazily upon a cool breeze. The aroma of burning wood meant someone had arrived before her.

She located a ledge jutting out on her right and was about to jump down to it but stopped. A squealing hinge disturbed the tranquil setting.

In a small clearing below, Jonas and his sons exited the cabin and made their way to the edge of a steep defile. Several other male figures followed on their heels, not one of them bothering to look up the mountain.

She smiled. They were probably looking for her. Expecting to see her climbing the perilous slopes south of Fishmonger Bay. Without a sound, she leapt to the shelf and clambered down the last stages of the waterfall behind the hut.

Softly padding her way around the thatched-roof hut, she listened to the conversation, recognizing Jonas' voice.

"Anyone see her?"

A huskier man spat off the edge of the cliff. "Pfft. Please. She'll never make it past that first gorge."

Reecah's Flight

Jaxon emulated the husky man beside him and spat. "Uncle Joram's got the right of it. We'll find her crying and lost at its bottom when we return."

Reecah leaned in between the husky man and Jaxon with a mischievous smile, taking in the dizzying view. "Who're you looking for?"

To a man, everyone on the clifftop nearly jumped to their death.

Jonas recovered first, his voice incredulous. "Where'd *you* come from?"

Reecah knew her insolent smile wouldn't win her any favours but she couldn't keep it from her face. She pointed up the falls.

"Over the peak?"

"Not quite, but close."

"But how?" Jaxon asked. "There's no way across to the next peak."

Reecah raised her eyebrows twice in quick succession.

Jonas appeared flabbergasted. "We left shortly after you. How did you get here so fast?"

"I left my hut before dawn."

"This morning?" His face darkened. "Impossible."

Reecah shrugged. "Not if you know the mountains."

She could see her statement unsettled most of the men gathered around. She stepped away from the brink, fearing they might throw her over the edge.

The husky man, Joram Waverunner, spat on the ground at her feet. "I warned you, Jonas. Bringing a woman into the fold is asking for trouble."

Jonas wasn't as large as his older brother but his scathing glare made Joram look away. Without warning, Jonas grabbed Reecah's elbow and unceremoniously impelled her toward the cabin. "Come with me."

Reecah resisted the urge to cry out. She barely kept from tripping as the brute half pushed, half lifted her.

Reecah's Flight

With a final shove, Jonas released her. If not for the cabin wall she would have fallen to the ground. Struggling to keep her pride in the face of such treatment, she was starting to wish she hadn't come. She tried not to look at the dozen male figures studying her like a prize sow.

"Jaxon. Get your sword," Jonas ordered.

Jaxon's face lit up with an evil smirk. He disappeared into the hut and returned carrying a sheathed sword, and a tower shield appearing too big for him to wield. He leaned the shield against the cabin and strapped his sword belt on.

"Girl!"

Jonas' voice snapped Reecah's attention to him.

"Choose your weapons."

Reecah blinked at him twice. He wanted her to fight Jaxon? "Um…" Her gaze flicked to Jaxon and his shield. She opened her brown cloak to reveal two average length scabbards hanging from a drooping sword belt. With practised ease, she unsheathed the shiny blades—her grip against the blades' circular guards.

She didn't know if Jonas nodded to mock her or did so out of a newfound respect. She assumed the former.

Jonas spread his arms wide, motioning the gathering toward the cliff. "Give them room. The gods only know who these two might end up skewering."

Everyone laughed except Reecah and Jaxon. The boy appeared to take offense to his father's slight. She didn't let the man's words affect her. He wouldn't respect her until she had proven herself.

Jonas motioned for Jaxon to start with his back to the cliff. As his son strode up to where he indicated, Jonas leaned toward him and whispered loud enough for everyone to hear. "Alright, boy. Now's your chance to make amends for the last time this wench whooped your sorry arse."

Reecah's Flight

Reecah swallowed. Her eyes flitted from person to person, trying to ascertain whether she had any support in the crowd. From the hard glares she received, she didn't think so.

Red-faced, Jaxon pulled his sword free and grunted, hoisting his tower shield before him.

In response, she threw her cloak back over her shoulders and brandished her swords.

Jonas stepped away. "Fight!"

Reecah had never fought a person before. She hadn't the faintest idea how to hold herself. Trying to recall how the men sparred behind the temple every weekend, she stepped forward with her right foot and awaited Jaxon's advance.

Jaxon clattered his sword off his shield. "Come on, witch. That's who you are, isn't it? A wannabe witch?"

The semi-circle of watchers mumbled amongst themselves, nodding.

Reecah didn't answer, her mind enrapt in nervous anticipation. These were real weapons they were using. Surely, Jonas didn't mean for them to actually maim each other. The men and women behind the temple used wooden weapons.

"I saw you enter the witch's shop the other day. You never came back out." Jaxon taunted. "Come on, put a spell on me."

Reecah adjusted her stance to keep her right-hand sword facing Jaxon's circuitous approach. "Obviously I came back out or I wouldn't be here, would I?"

Her words elicited a few titters from the onlookers. Bolstered by their ambiguous support, she shuffled forward a few steps, preparing to meet Jaxon's approach.

Jaxon's face scrunched up with what Reecah assumed was fury. He thrust his shield toward her, the effort causing him to stumble.

The crowd laughed.

Reecah steadied her stance, waiting on his next move.

Reecah's Flight

Jaxon jumped forward, yelling and pulling his shield aside to swing wildly at her legs.

Reecah sidestepped the lunge but wasn't able to return a swing of her own.

Reecah's Flight

Jaxon recovered his balance and circled. "Whatcha waiting for?"

Reecah swallowed. If she wasn't careful, this would end badly. Judging by Jaxon's attack, he wasn't worried about hurting her. Had she not leapt out of the way, he would have taken her leg off.

Jaxon drove his cumbersome shield at her.

Stumbling on the uneven terrain, she sprung back and whacked the curved shield with both swords—the resulting vibrations jarring her shoulders.

Jaxon took an unbalanced swipe at her face. Fortunately for Reecah, his reach wasn't long enough.

They had barely begun fighting and already her breaths were coming in short spurts—her mouth dry. Her undergarments clung to her skin with sweat. A real swordfight was more taxing than she'd imagined.

Jaxon steadied himself, perspiration beading on his forehead. He flicked wavy bangs from his eyes. "That the best you got, Reeky?"

Reecah saw red. She lifted her sword tips high and battered Jaxon's shield, shrieking with each hit. Jaxon appeared hard put to fend off her flurry but the impacts did nothing more than create a loud clatter.

The onlookers cheered and laughed.

Ceasing her wild barrage, Jaxon moved his shield toward her. She assailed him again, shuffling around to get a clear shot at him cowering behind his defensive barrier.

She feigned one way and stepped the other but Jaxon turned just as quick.

Neither combatant landed a blow and the longer they jockeyed for position, the slower their movements became.

Jonas intervened. "Enough!"

Reecah fought to keep from falling to her knees, exhausted.

Reecah's Flight

She allowed her sword tips to touch the ground, desperately trying to control her ragged breathing. She wanted to swallow but her mouth was too dry.

Jaxon didn't appear any better off. He looked from beneath lowered brows at his father, cowering as Jonas stormed up to him and ripped the shield from his arm. "Get out of my sight! Beaten by a woman!"

"But, Father…" Jaxon pleaded. "I was wearing her down. She never laid a blade on me."

"You're an embarrassment to the Waverunner name." Jonas threw the shield against the hut. It clanged and spun to the ground. "Leave! Now!"

Visibly shaken, Jaxon threw his sword down and tromped around the hut.

Reecah's eyes were as wide as they could get as the brute's attention fell on her.

He pointed a sausage-sized finger, coming at her. "And you!"

She brandished her blades in fear.

Jonas' sneer chilled her to the bone as his thick-bladed scimitar slid free of the thong on his belt.

Reecah barely registered the speed at which Jonas' blade smote her lead sword out wide and stepped inside her reach.

His free hand grasped her other wrist and twisted, the pain so intense she had no choice but to release her sword. He twisted it until she released the second blade and sent her stumbling. Yanking on her slender arm, he pulled her from her feet and slammed her to the ground, dropping a knee across her chest and driving the wind from her.

The pain of Jonas' weight was so severe she feared he had broken her ribs.

"I ought to smash your insolent face." He raised a fist. "You come to me all high and mighty about your ability to join the hunt. Look at you. How do you expect to confront a dragon when you can't even best a weakling runt?"

Reecah's Flight

Reecah trembled in his grasp. Seeing his wavering fist, she closed her eyes tight and turned away, but the mighty blow never fell. Suddenly the weight lifted and Jonas stomped away.

She waited for the hut's door to bang open and slam shut again before she opened her eyes, only to flinch as the rest of the hunt ambled by, each man spitting on her.

"You have no business here."

"Begone, wench."

"Leave before I give you something you've never had before."

"Reeky Draakvriend."

"Disgusting."

"Stupid girl."

Covering her face and trembling, she waited until she thought everyone had followed Jonas into the hut before lowering her shaking arms. She almost screamed.

The husky brute stood over her, glaring with veined eyes and yellowed teeth. "If you ain't gone afore I come back, ye're gonna wish Jonas had killed ya, ya hear what I'm sayin'?" He licked his lips before setting off after the others.

Reecah watched him leave. Squeezing her arms against her aching ribs, she fought to regain control of her breathing.

She got to her feet, tentatively probing her chest for broken bones. Although sore, she didn't believe Jonas had done any lasting damage.

She collected her swords and slid them home as a raucous chorus of laughter arose from the hut. She cringed, her gaze on the door—afraid the husky man would return.

Embarrassed, she limped back the way she had come, her body aching like never before. She skipped across a narrow section of running water and clambered up to the shelf below the main ridge.

If nothing else came of her folly, she had gained a new level of respect for the men and women who practiced behind the temple. Running with weapons strapped to her body and hacking at tree stumps hadn't prepared her for the rigours of a real fight.

She paused to survey the glade, sadness blurring her vision. She had truly believed she was about to begin her journey as a tracker and become just like Poppa. The realization that her dream had ended so abruptly, pained her more than any physical hurt she received from Jonas. She had failed herself, but more importantly, she had failed Poppa's memory.

Fighting the urge to unbuckle her swords and pitch them into the cascading water, she spied the forlorn image of Jaxon sitting by himself on the far edge of the clearing, his legs dangling over the cliff. She hoped he wasn't contemplating what she thought. His father's actions had done little for the boy's confidence. If she didn't despise Jaxon so much, she might have had empathy for the downtrodden young man.

The door's squealing hinge sent her scrambling up the rockfall. Hoisting a long leg over the brink, she hazarded a backward look.

Standing with his hands on his hips, the husky man watched her. His menacing image etched itself in her mind. Sick to her stomach with fear, she traversed the heights of Peril's Peak and made her way home.

It promised to be a long way back.

Reecah's Flight

Inferno

After her encounter with Jonas and his men on Peril's Peak, Reecah was too ashamed to show her face in Fishmonger Bay. The days and weeks following her ill-fated attempt to join the hunt filled her with dread. Nightmares of the husky man catching her alone in her cabin, doing unspeakable things, plagued her restless nights.

She slept with the fine bow Grimelda had given her—the door barricaded with heavy furniture, and the windows covered with Grammy's quilted comforters.

During the day, she set wooden targets in the trees around the outside of the hut to improve her dismal archery skills in case the man showed his face. She spent most of her time hunting for errant arrows.

Weeks passed before she contemplated the swords again, but as she hacked away at a tree stump, she attacked it with renewed determination—swinging and hopping about for hours on end. It was no substitute for the real thing, but she trusted no one. Except great-aunt Grimelda. Unfortunately, the crone wouldn't be much of a sparring partner.

It took her most of the summer before she dared set foot in Fishmonger Bay again. When she did, it was under the cover of darkness.

Sneaking around the backside of buildings, she slipped onto the lavender porch of *Grimelda's Clutch*. She paused behind the nearest dragon statue and scanned her surroundings in the poor light of a new moon. Nothing stirred.

Reecah's Flight

She inhaled deeply and tiptoed to the stained-glass door. Finding it locked, she rapped on the lower section, all the while glancing around, fearing the noise her knock had made.

Grimelda didn't answer fast enough so she rapped a second time, louder than the first. She was about to sneak off into the night and return to her hut, but a flickering light from within, cast the porch in a rainbow of colour through the stained-glass.

The glow approached the door and the magical locking mechanisms withdrew, allowing the door to swing inward.

Grimelda's haggard face appeared scarier in the dim light of her handheld sconce. Wearing a dirty white apron splattered with dark stains, she leaned on her gnarled walking stick, squinting, and Raver perched on her shoulder.

"Gracious, my dear. What took you so long?"

Raver bobbed his head up and down as if he shared Grimelda's worry.

Reecah blinked. *What took her so long?* She searched the darkness of the town centre before pushing past her great-aunt into the mystic shop. "I'm afraid, Auntie Grim."

Grimelda closed the door and waved her hand, triggering the locks. She made a clucking noise with her tongue, placed a hand to the small of Reecah's back and pushed her down the aisle. "Ohhh. Do come in dearie. I've been expecting you."

"Come in dearie! Come in dearie!" Raver mimicked.

Grimelda's words unsettled her, but the raven made her smile. Something she hadn't done in a long time. It felt good to be in the company of another person. Someone who wouldn't pass judgement on her.

"You were expecting me? How did you know I was coming?"

Grimelda cackled and shuffled behind the counter, holding the ratty blanket aside for Reecah to enter. "Auntie knows everything." She placed the sconce on a crude, knee-high table and searched the shelf behind it. "Ah, what do you know? Here it is. I searched for this all day."

"All day! All day!"

"Shoo, you dirty bird." Grimelda shrugged her shoulder and Raver winged to a high shelf near the curving cellar staircase.

Reecah looked over Grimelda's shoulder. The witch held a small vial in her wrinkled hand, a greenish liquid kept inside by a blackened cork.

"What is it, Auntie?"

Grimelda clucked her tongue and held up a crooked finger. "A curious one, eh? You shall see soon enough. Take this and follow me."

Grimelda handed her a grey stick.

"Is this a…?"

"Yes, dearie. Something to write with." Grimelda dropped the vial into an apron pocket and plucked the sconce from the table. Hobbling to the back of the room, she descended the twisting stairwell to the damp cellar below.

Torches burned in racks around the perimeter of the small cavern—the sacrificial altar surrounded by wrought-iron candelabras.

Stepping off the bottom step, it appeared Reecah had interrupted some kind of ritual. The fount at the head of the altar contained a crimson liquid very much resembling…

She swallowed, her gaze falling on the dark stains on Grimelda's apron. Her jubilation at sharing someone else's company forgotten, she approached the fount. "Is…is that what I think it is?"

"Eh, dearie?" Grimelda shuffled off to one side, rummaging through an assortment of stone bowls. Finding the one she sought, she said, "Oh, don't touch that."

Reecah pulled her hand back.

Grimelda hobbled past her with a small ladle. She scooped three precise measures of the crimson liquid into the stone

86

bowl, careful not to spill a drop. Setting the bowl on the altar, she pulled the green vial from her apron pocket and removed the stopper with her teeth. The cork between her lips, she tilted the small bottle and dispensed one, then two, and finally three drops into the bowl.

"Look closely, my dear child, but do not touch."

Reecah bent over, inspecting what she suspected was blood. She shuddered. Where had it all come from? She was about to ask but something pulled on the top of her head, stopping her.

"Ow!"

Grimelda held a few strands of hair between her thumb and forefinger.

"What did you do that for?"

Ignoring her, the crone inspected the hairs and selected three, dropping them one by one into the bowl.

Without hesitation, she reached up and pulled a few of her own grey strands, depositing three of them into the dark liquid one at a time.

Reecah backed away. She had come at a bad time.

The sudden appearance of Raver flapping down the stairwell made her jump. The raven landed on the rim of the fount and stood blinking at Grimelda as if he had been summoned.

Grimelda selected a small knife from beneath the folds of the utensil table on the far side of the altar and leaned her walking stick against the marble slab. "Raver, to me."

Raver squawked and landed on the altar.

In a flurry too fast for Reecah to comprehend, Grimelda's hand closed on the bird and held him against the marble slab—deftly severing the two side toes on his left foot, close to his leg.

Raver screeched and pecked at her hand, drawing blood, but Grimelda didn't let go until she severed a side toe from his right foot; all three toes lying on the altar.

Reecah's Flight

Raver flew erratically into a shelf beside the stairs and dropped to the ground. He fell on one side, making an awful noise. Flapping furiously, he righted himself and disappeared up the steps.

Reecah couldn't believe what had just transpired. The old lady was stark raving mad. She wanted to go after the injured bird but Grimelda's grim face held her. "Auntie Grim, what are you doing?"

"Trust me, child. That hurt me more than it did my little chum."

Reecah's mind reeled. What a nice way to treat your *little chum*. There was no way her aunt's guilt was more painful than Raver losing three toes.

"Before I go, I must ask a boon of you."

Reecah's brow furrowed, unable to take her eyes off the toes and offending knife still clutched in Grimelda's hand. Where did the crazy witch think she was going?

"Are you familiar with Dragonfang Pass?"

Reecah had travelled as far as the Fang, a towering rock formation at the head of the pass, but had never ventured far into the dragon-infested valley itself. She wasn't sure she wished to entertain Grimelda's question—the image of the knife severing Raver's toes wouldn't leave her.

"North of here, deep within the pass, is an old temple. Built centuries ago by the first Windwalkers." Grimelda put the knife on the utensil table, grabbed her stick, and hobbled to confront Reecah. "Do you hear me, child?"

The intensity in the witch's bloodshot gaze made Reecah's breath catch. She nodded out of fear.

"Good, because this is important. When I'm gone, you'll be the only one left on this side of the Great Kingdom capable of saving the dragons."

Reecah's Flight

"Saving the dragons?" Reecah was incredulous. "I can't swing a sword to save myself. How do you expect me to face a dragon? I wouldn't survive its first breath."

Grimelda held up a hand. "Shhh, child. Listen. You must *save* the dragons, not fight them."

"Then why did you give me great-grandmother's weapons?"

"To protect you from everyone else."

"I don't understand."

Grimelda gave her a patient smile. "I wish I could train you in the ways of the Windwalker, but my time is at hand."

Reecah gaped. Where was her aunt going?

"Ah, ah," Grimelda wagged a crooked finger. "I'm out of time. You must go to the Dragon Temple." She raised an eyebrow. "Aye, guarded by a beast old enough to have seen the mountains formed. Locate the earth's schism to claim your heritage. Remove the Dragon's Eye from the Watcher and bring it back here."

Dragon's Eye? Watcher? Schism? "What are you talking about? Locate a temple protected by a dragon?"

Grimelda's expression told her that the witch knew of her fear. "What I ask is *very* important. Can you do that for an old lady, child?"

What could she say? Deny her great-aunt's dying wish? The relevance of that sobering thought hammered itself home. "You're not dying, Auntie Grim. Look at you. You are, um…" She didn't know how to express her alarm.

Grimelda grabbed her wrists. "Shh, shh, shh. It's time you left. You mustn't witness the transfiguration spell."

Reecah mouthed the word 'transfiguration' in horror. She had no idea what it meant but it sounded prophetic. "You'll wait until I return, won't you? Promise me you'll be here when I return."

The compassion in Grimelda's smile confirmed her fear.

Reecah's Flight

"Auntie Grim, I can't go on without you. You're all I have." Her watery gaze darted around the cellar. "I know. Come with me. We'll find this Dragon's Eye together. We can—"

"Reecah Windwalker!"

Grimelda spoke with such conviction Reecah wasn't convinced the feeble, old woman had said it at all. A quick scan confirmed there was no one else in the flickering cavern.

"Promise Grimelda that no matter what happens tonight, you will return with the Dragon's Eye."

Reecah swallowed. Conscious of the tears falling from her cheeks, she nodded. "I promise."

"Heed these words well, for they're the only thing standing between you and a long, lonely death." Grimelda's features twisted into a hideous effigy of her wrinkled self—her voice taking on a manly timbre. "There'll come a time in the not too distant future that you'll be required to accept your heritage if you want to survive. Pray, child, you are wise enough to open your heart. Let the truth guide you."

Reecah swallowed, the crone's crazed words lost on her. All she wanted to do was pull away.

Grimelda released her. "Now run. Get away from here. Whatever you do, don't look back. Not now. Not ever. You hear Grimelda?"

Reecah didn't think she could talk past the lump in her throat. She nodded, unsure what to do to save her great-aunt.

Grimelda's face transformed into a frightening mask. Her voice dropped lower than a woman's ought to. "Leave me!"

Reecah took the stone steps two at a time. Bolting across the shop, the magical locking mechanisms released and the door opened on its own. She stepped onto the porch, not bothering to close the door.

Guilt at leaving the old woman to face death by herself weighed heavily on her. Whatever insane ritual Grimelda had planned, she should be there to help. She turned in time to

90

witness the door slam shut with such force it blew her loose strands of hair around and fluttered her cloak. She grabbed the handle but already the locks were clicking into place.

The large bells above the temple next door rent the silent night. A clamour arose as parishioners descended the steep, wooden staircase fronting the village's place of worship, their attention directed her way.

Pounding the stained-glass door with the sides of her fists, she had no time to spare for them. "Auntie Grim! Auntie Grim! Open the door! Open it up! Don't leave me!" Conscious of the commotion she was making, she didn't care. Let them think what they wanted. No one liked her anyway.

The villagers' curiosity brought them to gather in front of *Grimelda's Clutch*, watching her.

Realizing she wasn't getting back into the shop, panic set in. She turned her wild eyes on the crowd. "Someone, help me. Auntie Grim is dying. I need to save her. Please!"

The Father Cloth appeared on the top step of the temple as a spectrum of light splashed through the windows and front door of *Grimelda's Clutch*.

Reecah, and those gathered around the mystical hut, covered their eyes to shield them from the intense glare.

"Witchcraft!" someone shouted as the crowd backed away.

"Jaxon!" the Father Cloth called out. "Fetch your father!"

Reecah's eyes went wide. A dark figure darted away from the crowd, his blonde locks bobbing behind him as he made his way across the commons toward the large warehouse on the shoreline. She shook her head and dropped into a crouch, holding clenched hands in front of her mouth, muttering, "No, no, no. Not Jonas. Please not Jonas."

Another series of bright flashes emanated from the interior of Grimelda's Clutch, lighting up the night.

Reecah's Flight

The crowd "oohed and aahed" at the spectacle. People stared at Reecah quaking against the door, but no one bothered to comfort her.

Crunching gravel announced Jonas carrying a large warhammer, with Joram and Jaxon in tow. They ran up to the porch and bent over, covering their heads as a third series of multicoloured flashes illuminated the mystic shop and a deep rumble shook the ground.

As soon as the light died away, Jonas shouted, "Move her away from there!"

Jaxon met Reecah's scared eyes and held out a hand to assist her. "You need to get away from the door."

Reecah shook her head. A new fear replaced her distress, dreading what the brute Jonas planned to do to Auntie Grim once he got through the door.

She pulled her great-grandmother's dagger from her belt and held it to Jaxon's face. "Get away from me!"

Jaxon's eyes crossed as the blade hovered over his nose. He stumbled backward and fell off the porch.

Reecah stood, threatening to chase him, but Joram thundered onto the porch, swatted aside the hand holding the dagger, and slammed her into the glass door.

The husky man's hand enveloped hers and squeezed hard, breaking her thumb.

Crying out in pain, she was vaguely aware of her dagger clattering to the porch at her feet. Before she could fully appreciate what was happening, Joram spun her through the air and chucked her off the porch to land in a heap in front of the dragon statue.

Jonas hefted his warhammer and smote the stained-glass door. Shock twisted his face as he flew backward through the air, propelled by the repulsion spell warding the door, and landed heavily in front of a scattering line of villagers. His wayward warhammer smashed the face of an unfortunate spectator.

Tears streaming off her face, Reecah hugged the statue as if drawing a sense of security from the inanimate object.

Jonas gained his feet and brushed himself off. His angry glare silenced anyone thinking his flight was comical. "Burn it down!" he commanded. "Being me torches!"

Reecah stared at him. She shook her head quickly, unable to speak past her rising fear.

Men scattered to various buildings and returned bearing torches and sconces.

Jonas snatched the first one to arrive and walked up to the porch overhang. "Vex this town no longer, witch!"

Leaning back, he tossed the torch high in the air, the flaming brand spinning lazy circles before landing near the roof's peak. Oil from the wrapped cloth spread the flames around the torch as it rolled along the wooden shingles.

Reecah couldn't believe what was happening. She staggered backward from the corner of the porch, seeing the damage perpetrated by the villagers as torch after flaming torch whirled onto the roof.

Watching on in helpless horror, the villagers set brands against the lavender walls, fanning the flames until they caught.

It wasn't long before the fiery wooden shingles fell into the interior and flames ripped through the shop, catching the various accelerants Auntie Grim kept on cluttered shelves. Small explosions rocked the night, turning *Grimelda's Clutch* into a raging inferno.

Reecah covered her face with her hands, stumbling away from the nightmare. She butted up against the side of the temple and slid to a sitting position, trembling uncontrollably. By the time the walls crumbled into the heart of the conflagration she was so numb it barely registered. The only person left to her in all the world was gone.

Reecah's Flight

It had become apparent to the villagers that they needed to get the fire under control lest it spread to the temple and buildings beyond.

Reecah stared vacantly as a bucket brigade formed across the commons to the shoreline, their actions not registering through her grief-laden fog.

As the buildings in Fishmonger Bay became visible in the first light of morning, Reecah tried to pull herself out of her emotionally draining stupor—her back still pressed against the temple wall. Nothing remained of *Grimelda's Clutch* but blackened dragon statues poking through the charred remains.

The villagers had returned to their homes during the night, abandoning her to her sorrow. She didn't think they were even aware of her against the temple. If they were, they hadn't bothered to show her any compassion.

Bereft of feeling, she staggered to the skeletal remains of the porch awning fallen upon the numerous statues fronting the ruins. She swallowed hard. The stained-glass door had fallen outward, surprisingly still intact. She stepped over a charred timber and knelt in the embers, barely aware of the heat emanating from the ruins.

She ran fingers through the soot covering the multi-coloured glass door—tears dripping onto the ground as her shoulders shook. She lifted the charred remains of the dragon shingle that had hung in front of the door—the word, *Grimelda's,* barely legible through the black soot coating it.

A glint of metal caught her eye. She reached out and tried to grab at it only to realize there was something horribly wrong with her thumb. She didn't care. Let it hurt. She used her other hand and discovered her discarded dagger.

Attempting to walk amongst the destruction, the heat radiating from the centre of the ruins drove her back. She walked around the building's exterior to where it abutted the cliff, hoping to access the stairs to the cellar. Examining the gaping hole from afar, the rumbling heard during the night had been the storage room's stone ceiling collapsing, burying the cellar beneath tons of rock.

She stared at where the stairwell had been, not knowing what to do. There was nothing left for her in Fishmonger Bay, but she had nowhere else to go. With hunched shoulders and a bowed head, she dragged her feet away from *Grimelda's Clutch*.

Rounding the rear corner of the temple, she stopped. A muted 'caw' sounded behind her. She shook it off as a distant memory until it sounded again.

Goosebumps dimpled her skin.

She scanned the ruins but saw no sign of the bird. "Raver?"

Nothing moved.

She was about to turn away when a flutter of black wings lifted the maimed bird from beneath a bush against the base of the cliff. It tried to fly toward her but it was obvious, even from where she stood, that its feathers had been singed. It landed on its crippled feet and fell to its side.

"Raver?" Reecah ran to the bird and gently scooped him off the ground. Her tears flowed anew. Somehow, Raver had escaped the inferno. Judging by his poor condition, he wasn't long for the world.

Cradling him to her breast, she stumbled out of Fishmonger Bay and ascended the north hill, vowing never to set foot in the demented place again.

Reecah's Flight

First Encounter

The intervening years between Grimelda's death and the next dragon season passed Reecah in a blur. She had devoted the first few months after the inferno caring for Raver, hoping to ease him toward his eventual death, but the resilient bird had surprised her. Not only did he grow new feathers to replace most of the ones damaged in the fire, but he learned to stabilize himself on thin branches with his remaining toes. The raven struggled to walk across flat surfaces, falling to his side more often than not, but his antics proved to be the magical elixir that kept Reecah's mind from sinking into the depths of despair.

Late in the summer of her eighteenth year, she got back into running the trails and exploring the heights with Raver as a constant companion. Though her promise to Grimelda remained in the back of her mind, they never made it as far as Dragonfang Pass—her healing thumb had precluded any extensive climbing.

A couple of times over the next few years she entertained searching out the temple, but with Auntie Grim dead, it didn't make sense to put herself in harm's way. Her archery skills had improved somewhat, but without someone to spar with, the extent of her sword skills came from building up her arm, shoulder and back muscles by mercilessly hacking at downed trees. She was no match for a dragon, let alone an entire colony of them.

Reecah's Flight

Recovering from the melancholy of Grimelda's horrific death, she found joy exploring the mountains with Raver—deeper than she had ever been. On more than one occasion, he led her back home after she had gotten hopelessly lost. If she had to guess, she would say he'd been in the mountains before.

Celebrating what she believed to be the date of her twenty-first birthday in the drafty cabin on the hill, Reecah took solace in the fact that she had kept her pledge to remain clear of the village at the bottom of the hill. Whenever she ventured south, she did so via the route she had taken to the hut below Peril's Peak. Many were the times she stayed for a night or two in the dragon hunt training cabin, relying on Raver to inform her of anyone ascending from the village.

The dragon hunt would likely commence within a fortnight if the weather held. The days were becoming increasingly warmer and that meant the mating season would be in full swing—much sooner than in past years.

She planned to search out the new warrens on this side of the Fang. Those were the nesting grounds the villagers would concentrate on. According to Auntie Grim, Jonas and his band weren't foolish enough to venture too far into Dragonfang Pass.

Eleven days after her birthday feast of seeds and berries with her feathered friend, she awoke to an unusually warm cabin—the morning sun cutting through the grimy windows, heating the interior.

She stretched on her pallet—Grammy and Poppa's old bed—and scanned the hut. Raver was absent. During the warmer weather she left the hut's east-facing window ajar.

Reecah's Flight

Protected from the winds blowing off the ocean, the window provided Raver a means to escape into the wilds whenever he liked.

She stood up and looked at her simple, threadbare shift—stained and smelling of sweat. It was high time she washed it, but given the fact she had few remaining clothes to her name, she decided today wouldn't be that day.

Stepping through the cabin door, she embraced the glorious day—a slight morning chill raising goosebumps on her bare legs and arms. It promised to be one of Poppa's 'rare days'—a day not to be wasted on menial tasks. Rather, a perfect day to scout out the routes the hunt would follow on their way to the Fang.

She emitted a shrill whistle to alert Raver she was up and about and ducked back inside to get dressed.

By midmorning, with a healthy sweat dampening her brow, Reecah tossed her great-grandmother's black quarterstaff above her and pulled herself up to a high ledge. The vantage point overlooked the path Jonas' men would take any day now. Studying the soft ground earlier in the day, she knew they hadn't passed this way yet.

She sat on the ledge with her boots dangling above the trail and caught her breath, smiling and content with her solitary life. On the days she craved another person's company, she recalled the night of Grimelda's fire and any use she had for human companionship dashed itself against the wall of her grief.

Raver sat high atop a pine, the tree jutting out from the top of a boulder north of her position. As far away as he seemed, she knew he saw her clearly. She didn't bother whistling. Instead, she dug inside a leather pouch lashed to her sword belt and held a palm out.

Sure enough, the distant bird ducked his head and launched into the air, covering the distance in a long graceful swoop to land on one of the leather vambraces she wore on her forearms. She steadied him on her arm until he gained the purchase required to keep from slipping.

His beak and little tongue tickled her palm. Watching him eat, she appreciated how he had become the gift her soul had so desperately needed.

She set off along the ridgeline paralleling the path below, searching for key locations. Whenever the trail narrowed to a pinch point between the ridge and a deadly drop, she set to work dislodging boulders and pitching fallen brush over the edge, congesting the route Jonas' men would travel.

Her efforts would only prove as temporary setbacks to the hunt but she didn't care. Anything she did to impede their progress might give the dragonlings a chance to escape their fate.

Caught up in congesting the hunt's path, it wasn't until Raver cried overhead that she realized the sun had dropped toward the ocean; the waves unseen beyond the heavy forested slopes. Dragonfang Pass still lay another solid day's journey north of her present position.

Without the sun's direct rays, cooler air settled across the heights. Not prepared to weather nightfall on the mountain face, it was time to head home.

Scanning the sky, she couldn't locate Raver. She emitted a shrill whistle and started home. If she hurried, she would be past the more dangerous section before darkness encroached.

On the days the torrential spring rains didn't prevent her from going out, Reecah spent the next week and a half venturing deeper into the northern heights, continually adding to her previous trail blockages at strategic points, ones that would leave the hunt no option but to waste time clearing them away.

Reecah's Flight

Three weeks after the spring solstice, the day the dragonlings were expected to hatch, Raver landed on a small bush close to where she worked at uncovering a decent-sized boulder and cawed at her hysterically.

"What is it?" she asked, laughing as the bird lost his grip on the twig he sat on and flapped furiously to adjust himself. "You see something?"

"See something! See something!"

The raven never ceased to amaze her. In her estimation, Raver was smarter than the entire population of Fishmonger Bay put together.

She stretched her sore back, wiping her hands on her filthy green leggings, and stared back the way they had come. At first, she couldn't see or hear anything other than the wind blowing in the treetops and the distant sound of running water. A bird calling out from far away and the buzzing of bees hovering over new blossoms were the only other indication of life on the mountainside, but she trusted Raver.

Ducking behind the bush Raver sat on and waiting, it was quite a while before the sound of a twig snapping in the distance caught her attention.

Raver jumped into the air and flew to the top of a nearby tree, cawing twice.

Nobody would pay attention to a raven making noise, but to Reecah, it was his signal that whoever was coming was close.

Crouched on a ridge immediately above the path, she didn't dare move. The path below wasn't visible. Hopefully, whoever travelled the heights wouldn't see her either.

It wasn't long before voices rose above the breeze. Boots crunched on rocks and the chinking and creaking of leather and metal bespoke of armed men approaching. The hunt!

Her eyes widened. Of course. Today was the day the dragonlings were supposed to begin hatching. According to

Reecah's Flight

what Poppa used to tell her, once hatched, the mothers abandoned the nests and foraged for food.

"Not another one," an angry voice snarled.

"Damn!" That was Jonas' voice. Reecah would recognize it anywhere. "Get that shit cleared out."

The sound of branches being hacked and rocks tumbling off the narrow ledge on the far side of the path to the brush below, echoed through the woods.

Reecah enjoyed their plight but her fear of discovery kept her cowering behind the bush.

Raver cawed several times.

An arrow zipped through the branches he perched on, sending him winging away. Reecah restrained from crying out.

"Damned bird. It's like he's following us," a higher-pitched male voice growled.

"Don't be stupid. How can you tell one raven from another? The woods are infested with the blasted vermin," Jonas said. "Put that thing away before you take out someone's eye and concentrate on where we're going. We've never encountered this many road blocks before. Someone's purposely impeding us. Are you sure you know where we are?"

"Yes, Father. This is the trail we always take."

"If you've led us astray, Jaxon, your days as a tracker will be short-lived."

"Yes, Father."

Reecah breathed a huge sigh of relief when the troop moved on. Jonas was smarter than she gave him credit for. She would have to be careful.

Waiting a while longer for the hunt to pass beyond the next ridge, she stretched her back, grinning. It wouldn't be long before they encountered the next hazard.

Reecah's Flight

Not wanting to risk being caught, Reecah returned to her hut. It was time to prepare herself to venture all the way to Dragonfang Pass.

The hunt would experience half a dozen more road-blocks before their path cleared sometime tomorrow. If she left early in the morning, she was confident of reaching the Fang before Jonas and his men.

Arriving home long before midnight, she lay in the darkness, recalling Poppa's teaching. It never meant much to her all those years ago, but as she thought about it now, she marvelled at the miracle of a dragon's birth.

Poppa claimed dragons mated once every three years on the spring solstice. She loved the coincidence—her birthday. The female would burrow a hole into a cliff face and squeeze herself into it to lay a clutch of eggs. Poppa called the nesting holes, warrens.

Three short weeks later, the first egg would hatch and the mother would pull herself free of the warren, leaving the dragonling to feed upon the unhatched eggs until she had sated her own hunger.

Poppa claimed this was when the dragonlings were the most vulnerable—thus the timing of the hunt. Tomorrow would prove interesting, provided she remained unseen. She needed to figure out a way to divert the hunt from their task until the baby dragons were ready to leave their nests or their mothers returned. Poppa claimed that could take anywhere from a day to two weeks depending on the dragon.

She thought about everything she should pack, making a point of locating the special journal Grammy had given her. It might be a long time before she returned home.

In the middle of the afternoon, Raver's cry alerted Reecah to the hunt. From his height, that could mean Jonas' men were far ahead or had stopped around one of the crags along the way. At least she knew to be wary. Jogging along the high ridge above the trail, she slowed her pace to keep her gear from rattling.

She hadn't travelled this far north often. Over the years the mountainside changed with new growth, fires, avalanches and landslides. She suspected the hunt wouldn't reach the Fang before morning. The monumental rock spur would be visible long before then.

Raver folded his wings and dropped headfirst out of the sky, alighting with practised ease on her outstretched forearm. She steadied him until he gained purchase, and took a moment to drink from Poppa's old waterskin.

She wasn't used to carrying her rucksack loaded with sleeping blankets and camping utensils, on top of all of her weapons. Breathing heavily, she was thankful she chose to only bring her fighting sword, dagger and quarterstaff. The double training swords and bow would have been cumbersome climbing and scaling down the steep embankments she traversed at regular intervals.

"Where are they, Raver? Close?"

Raver tilted his head to the side.

"Far away?"

Raver nodded emphatically and took to the air.

"Circle them!" she called after his diminishing form.

It took Raver a while before he altered his flight and began gliding in great arcs over a stand of pines barely visible in the distance. The mountainside jutted out with what appeared to be, from where she stood, an impassable crag.

She nodded to herself. She knew exactly where they were. She'd have to be careful. There was only one way around the crag, and that meant descending to the trail.

Reaching the edge of the ominous spur, she dropped to a knee and listened. Nothing. Nor did she know where Raver had flown off to. Probably still tracking their quarry on the crag's far side.

She waited a while longer, just to be sure, and picked a spot to scale down from the ridge.

Jumping the last several feet, she dropped into a crouch, cringing at the sound she made. She'd have to be more cautious if she planned on remaining hidden. Though she hadn't seen him, she knew Joram likely accompanied the hunt. A shudder ran through her.

Scanning the skies above and to the west, she instinctively ducked against the rock face as a small, brown dragon swooped to the forest far below, its flight erratic. They were hatching!

She remained still, enjoying the spectacle. The first baby dragon of the year. Most likely on its maiden flight. That meant...

She searched the surrounding area and spotted it, skimming the distant treetops—the mother dragon—its massive wingspan riding the air currents with little effort. Had she not seen the baby, she would never have noticed its mother—her scales blended in with the terrain.

Reecah experienced a euphoric terror. Her journey was getting real. From this point onward, the dragon hunt was the least of her concerns.

Waiting until she no longer saw the mother dragon over the treeline and the baby but a speck in the partly cloudy sky, she looked away. When she looked back, she had lost sight of the baby as well.

Searching her immediate surroundings, a bad feeling tingled her skin. She hadn't seen Raver for a while. The bird would be a perfect snack for a passing dragon.

A pebble skipped off the wall of rock directly behind her. She froze. Hazarding a look skyward, her blood ran cold. Perched on the trunk of a dead tree, extended high above the path, a baby dragon looked down on her.

Reecah's Flight

Her breath caught in her throat. She'd never been this close to a dragon before. It was a magnificent creature—at least as large as she was. Stunning emerald eyes stared at her from beneath prominent brows. Ivory horns twisted back from where she imagined its ears would be. Its leathery, green wings wrapped around its scaly hide. Swallowing her discomfort, she regretted her decision to leave her bow behind.

As insignificant as the lurking dragon seemed compared to the mother dragon she'd seen moments before, she didn't relish fighting it with a sword. And yet, she didn't get the sense that it meant her harm. It just stared down at her, unblinking.

She swallowed and searched the sky. Where was its mother?

Raver cawed close by and her heart sank. Forgetting about her own safety she yelled, "Raver! Away!"

The black raven either hadn't heard or he ignored her. He flew around the outcrop and landed on her vambrace. She ducked her arm under her cloak, fearing the dragon would fall on them to get at Raver. Lifting her quarterstaff over her head, she waved it back and forth. "Shoo, dragon! Begone!"

The baby dragon tilted its head sideways, much like Raver liked to do, and opened its mouth, revealing rows of jagged teeth. It fluttered its wings before extending them wide and leaping from the trunk, winging in a tight circle and disappearing beyond the ridgeline.

Legs and hands trembling uncontrollably, Reecah found it hard to remain standing. The Fang was a good day's trek away and already she wanted to go home. She hadn't been this shaken witnessing Janor being taken by a full-grown dragon three years ago.

Raver latched onto her tunic and clawed his way to an opening under her chin. She tried to hold him inside but he wiggled free and took to the air.

"Raver, no!" She reached up and missed as he followed the dragon over the ridge. She emitted her shrill whistle, not caring about the hunt. "Raver, to me!" It was no use. Raver wasn't coming back. It wasn't like him not to return when called.

Furious at the stubborn bird, she stormed around the remainder of the rock spur and searched the skies up the slope. Neither the dragon nor Raver were in sight. Fearing the worst, she pictured the dragon snacking on her friend.

The hunt was nowhere to be seen. Forgetting her earlier misgivings, she scaled the far side of the crag, searching for Raver.

She shook her head and talked to herself as she broke into a slow jog. "What a stupid bird. Auntie Grim was right. She should've cooked you!"

She felt her eyes welling up, which infuriated her further. She didn't know what she'd do if she lost him. Raver was her rock.

The sun appeared to rest on the treetops far below when Reecah slowed her pursuit of the hunt—the smell of burning wood reaching her. The crackling of a fire and the hunters' voices disturbed the slopes.

She crouched low and crept along the ridge, careful where she placed her feet. Any sound now might prove fatal, but she couldn't resist getting closer to the encampment. The hunters had likely stopped for the night, taking advantage of the last vestiges of light to set up camp before the sun dropped into the ocean—the steely waves visible beyond the treetops.

Her heavy heart lifted when Raver cawed from somewhere below the path and fluttered to a shaky landing on a sapling's branch beside her.

Relieved he was safe, she watched him struggle to hang onto the branch with his mangled feet. "There you are, you crazy bird. I ought to fletch my arrows with you. Don't ever do that again or I'll feed you to the dragon myself."

Raver bobbed his head as if he understood.

Reecah's Flight

She laughed out loud. Mortified, she slapped her hand over her mouth and hazarded a look below but saw no one.

The dragon hunt sheltered at the base of a tall cliff—one she would either have to descend to the pathway to circumvent or climb over. She didn't relish giving them an opportunity to catch her. That left ascending the crag. It had proven a tough climb the last time she had been through here, so she decided it best to get it over with tonight.

By the time she scaled down the far side, stars sparkled overhead. The noise of the hunter's camp lay behind her, the smell of their fire downwind, almost unnoticeable. She located a flat patch of grass amongst a jumble of rockfall and spread a small blanket out.

Sharing a meagre supper with Raver, she lay down and covered herself with the thin blanket to ward off the chill. Her pack under her head, she stared at the stars through breaks in the clouds, ever fascinated by the sky. Oh, what a joy it would be to soar the winds and experience the land from above.

Raver hopped about the rocks, stumbling more often than not and flapping his wings to keep upright.

The bird melted her heart. He had survived a brutal amputation and a raging inferno. His will to survive and make the most out of what life had given him, humbled her. Many *people* would have wallowed in their misery had their lives taken such a dire turn, but not Raver.

She glanced skyward again, following the silhouette of the towering crag beside her and gasped. Framed in the full moon a baby dragon perched at the top of the crag staring down.

It was tough to tell with the moon at its back, but she was sure it was the same dragon that had spied on her earlier.

Curiously, even though it was dark, she wasn't as frightened as she had been during their first encounter. If the dragon wanted to harm her, it could have done so long before now.

Reecah's Flight

She wasn't sure it was aware of her or Raver, but something told her that was why it sat there.

Poppa had often spoken about a dragon's intelligence. She wondered how he knew stuff like that. As a young child she had accepted everything he told her. Now, as a rational thinking adult, she couldn't see any reason to think differently.

"Look at you lurking up there," she said softly. "Are you following me?"

"Following me! Following me!"

Raver's emphatic mimic of her voice jarred her. "Shh, you silly bird!"

"Silly bird! Silly bird!"

She cringed. Listening to the wind, she feared the hunt might have heard them. No one seemed to have noticed but it took a while for her nerves to settle down.

Having Raver around when stealth was required had its drawbacks. He was great at tracking things from considerable distances but being discreet was another matter. It wasn't until Raver hopped over and settled under the blanket that she felt she could stop worrying about the hunt.

Staring at the baby dragon, she wondered what it was thinking. Was it waiting for her to fall asleep? Just the thought unnerved her. As enthralled with the wondrous creature as she was, she began wishing the beast would fly away.

As the night wore on, it became increasingly hard to keep her eyes open. On one of the occasions her eyes closed, she drifted off. Opening them again with a start, the dragon was gone.

Reecah's Flight

Dragon Slayers

Raver nibbled at Reecah's ear lobe, his little tongue flicking in and out. She awoke laughing until she remembered where she was. Dawn broke over The Spine, the snowy peaks refracting the early morning sunlight, though it would be a long time before the sun rose high enough to crest the mountains.

Making sure Raver had cleared her blanket, she rolled onto her side, reflecting on yesterday's strange encounter. Glancing up, she wasn't prepared for the sight of the green dragon peering down at her.

She shivered at the relevance that it could've attacked her while she slept. Afraid to move, she hoped it would fly away now that she was awake.

Pulling the covers tightly around her to ward off the cold, her hand came to rest on the journal inside her cloak's inner pocket. Despite her rising anxiety, a peculiar thought crossed her mind. It was as good a time as any to begin her dragon journal. If the dragon remained still.

She retrieved the stick of lead Grimelda had given her, oddly fearing her movements might cause the dragon to fly away. That made her chuckle. She had just wished it would fly away and now she wanted it to stay so she could write down her observations.

She opened the leather-bound book, proud of the embossed gold lettering: *Reecah's Diary.* Besides Poppa's wooden dragon, the journal was surely her most prized possession—dearer than her great-grandmother's fine weapons.

Reecah's Flight

Propped on an elbow, she deliberated how to begin. She wanted the first entry to be as special as her grandparents. "Hmmm?"

The dragonling fluttered its wings and settled again. That gave her an idea. 'Dragons: Day One.' She placed the lead stick to the parchment and tried to write, but it didn't leave a mark.

She examined the tip. It appeared okay. She tried again. Nothing.

Perhaps it needed sharpening. She located a flat rock near her pack and rubbed the stick against it, leaving grey lines on the rough surface.

She returned to write in the journal but nothing happened.

She closed the book and rubbed the stick against the cover, leaving a faint grey line. "What the...?" Shocked she had marred the cover, she scribbled her name on the flat rock. Other than being messy due to the rock's even surface, her name was clearly legible.

Opening the book again she scribbled in circles. The paper creased but her efforts did nothing to mark the page. She slammed the book shut. What good was a journal if she couldn't write in it?

She turned the diary over, trying to solve the riddle of the journal. As the back cover came to face the lurking dragon, the gemstone glinted. That seemed odd. Searching the area for the source of light causing the refraction, she couldn't find one.

A low growl escaped the baby dragon.

In the distance, Raver squawked out of control.

She sat up, looking around. Something was wrong.

Raver flew closer with each caw, an odd pulsating swoosh following his approach—the significance dawning on her a moment before he streaked across the sky—a winged leviathan rose into view, giving chase.

She jumped to her feet. "Raver, to me!"

Reecah's Flight

The mangled bird tucked his wings in and dove, followed closely by a green dragon many times the size of the one perched above.

Everything happened in rapid succession. Reecah held up her hands in defense as Raver slammed into her vambrace, bounced off her arm, and rolled on the ground, screeching and flapping. Ducking, she expected to be raked by the dragon's claws—the screaming vision of Janor went through her mind.

Her hair and cloak blew around in the wind created by the adult dragon's great wings as it hovered in the air between her and the dragonling—its attack seemingly thwarted by the pulse of light emanating from the journal's gemstone.

"Windwalker?"

Her great-grandmother's maiden name resonated in her mind. Wondering what made her think of that name, she heard, *"Only a Windwalker may command the Communication Stone."*

The words hadn't been spoken aloud. Not knowing where they came from, she shook her head. She'd never heard of a 'communication stone.'

The mother dragon bent its long neck to regard its offspring. *"Come my child. Dragon Killers are at hand. We must be away."*

Reecah thought she was going mad.

The mother dragon nudged her baby off the rock with her giant snout, and they quickly became small in the sky, winging northward.

Reecah followed their flight until they disappeared in the mountain shadows. She swallowed at the ludicrous notion forming in her mind. The idea of a talking dragon!

She hadn't eaten much, nor drank enough water over the past couple of days. Perhaps the anxiety of being watched by the dragonling and then the one she believed to be its mother had made her delusional.

Raver jumped into the air, flying over the trail below.

Reecah's Flight

"There it is again!" A deep voice sounded as if it was right beside her.

"Probably stirred up by the dragons," Jonas' voice answered. "Did you see how well that dragonling flew?"

"That's a bad omen. They're hatching early. I told you we should've set out last week."

"Ya? Well it's too late to worry about it now, so drop it!" Jonas' angry voice passed directly below where Reecah lay flat against the ledge.

A bowstring twanged and Raver squawked, winging higher in the air—the missile missing its mark by the length of a raven's feather.

"See its toes? It's the same bird as yesterday," Jaxon's high-pitched voice sounded beyond Reecah's position. "It's following us."

A bowstring released from where Jaxon's voice originated.

Raver squawked his displeasure, but the arrow fell short.

"Save your arrows for the dragons, you fool. It'll take a hell of a shot to hit the blasted varmint in the air," the deeper voice scolded.

Reecah shuddered. She couldn't be sure, but she imagined the voice belonged to Joram.

Several other voices passed beneath her location, following Jaxon up the trail.

As the voices faded beyond the next bend, Reecah breathed a sigh of relief. She waited a while longer before feeling safe enough to stand. Shaking out her blanket, she stowed her gear and climbed higher into the mountains, her direct course cutting out hours of needless switchbacks and arduous ascents the hunt would take as they approached the Fang.

Reecah's Flight

Before high noon, the notorious curved monolith marking the southwestern end of Dragonfang Pass appeared in the distance.

She had wandered far from the route the hunt travelled and had no way of knowing their present position, but unless they had broken into a fast march, she was confident she'd passed them long ago.

Raver rode on her shoulder until she grew tired of his scratchy claws digging through her cloak, tunic and shift. She coaxed him onto a forearm and walked with him like that as she approached a precarious descent to the ridgeline paralleling the trail.

The sun descended above the whitecaps of the Niad Ocean, the expansive waterbody visible from Reecah's perch on the Fang a few leagues away. Had she been afraid of heights she never would've been able to cling to the small ledge a third of the way up the towering pillar of pale stone.

From a distance, the Fang had looked every bit its namesake—as if carved by the hands of a giant. Up close, it was nothing more than an odd-shaped, naturally occurring rock formation.

She had no idea where Raver had taken off to. The last time she had seen him, he was circling the Fang's pinnacle. She gazed up at the dizzying height, wishing she possessed the ability to fly. There wasn't a place in the world that wouldn't be accessible to her. Well, perhaps not the depths of the ocean. She had no use for the frigid waters. Tales of serpents and other unspeakable terrors from the deep had kept her feet firmly planted on the ground for her first twenty-one years.

Movement along the trail the hunt followed interrupted her thoughts. Pulling her cloak tightly around her, she crouched low, feeling exposed. If someone knew where to look, they might pick her out, especially if she moved. Hunkering beneath her brown cloak, she blended into the multi-coloured textures of the towering rock, its sides riddled with scrabbly trees and lichen.

Her biggest fear, however, was catching the attention of a passing dragon. Clinging to the rock face, she had nowhere to go. It had taken her a good while to scale to the ledge—it would take even longer to descend again.

Jaxon and an older man strode several paces ahead of the rest of the hunt. Jaxon carried a quarterstaff in one hand and a bow slung over his opposite shoulder. His companion carried a long, barbed pike.

Bile rose in her throat upon seeing the hulking form of Joram waddling beside Jonas at the head of the trailing pack. Both men had battle-axes strapped to their backs, the large, double-bladed heads protruding above their shoulders.

Reecah counted nine more men comprising the hunt. She recalled Poppa's words to Grammy one night at the dinner table. *"Jonas likes carrying thirteen men in the hunt. A witch's quorum, he calls it."*

She had no idea why that conversation had stuck in her mind. Perhaps the witch reference or the odd word, 'quorum'—one she'd never heard until that day.

The hunt passed below her position. Three of the men carried nothing but bows and long swords, one of them sporting blonde hair and a long nose—Jonas Junior. They were obviously the dragon slayers, along with Jonas and Joram.

The six stout men bringing up the rear had great tower shields strapped to their backs. Poppa called them the firebreakers.

Reecah remembered the firebreakers three years ago. The large, friendly man she fondly recalled from the village, towered above the rest. She had wondered how overweight men like him trekked all this way burdened by thick shields and the heavy, leather armour they wore to protect them from the worst of the dragon fire. Despite their size, they must be in incredible shape.

Watching the last of the firebreakers pass beyond her field of vision, Reecah searched the sky before getting to her feet and edging her way around the backside of the massive rock formation. It took her a while to position herself to peer into Dragonfang Pass and the trail winding far below.

Jaxon came into view first, pointing to a cliff on the first hill lining the pass—the embankment separated from the backside of the Fang by a wide gap. The other tracker stepped beside him and started climbing.

Reaching a small ledge, the second tracker pulled a coil of rope from his shoulders and tied it to the base of a pine tree growing out from the ledge.

Jaxon tested its strength and stepped aside to allow the three firebreakers access.

Reecah held her breath as the heavily burdened men took to the rope. She thought for sure they would tire and fall, but before long, they joined the tracker on the ledge and waited for Junior and the two slayers Reecah didn't recognize.

When all seven men were on the small ledge, the older tracker, with the help of the firebreakers lifting him on top of one of their shields, reached up to grasp the bottom edge of a fissure in the rock. Pulling himself up, he studied the fissure for a while before the firebreakers lowered him back to the ledge.

The tracker gave a thumbs up to the men on the ground and pulled the barbed pike strapped to his back over a shoulder. With the firebreaker's assistance, he climbed until his chest was at the height of the hole. Taking a moment to search the skies, he inserted the pike into the hole.

Reecah's Flight

A muted squeal pierced the quiet. The tracker jabbed and pulled on the pole, his actions threatening to topple him from the upturned shield to a certain death.

The rest of the hunt urged him on with unbridled excitement.

The strain on the tracker's arms was evident even from Reecah's position as he struggled to hang onto his pike.

He bore down and the squealing grew in volume—a blue, dragonling's wing appeared at the edge of the hole, snagged on the barbed weapon.

The firebreakers lowered the tracker to the ledge as he gave the dragon one last yank, pulling it free of the warren. It fell past the men on the ledge, crying out in panic and trying to flap its wings but the embedded pike prevented it from going anywhere.

Reecah cringed at the squishing thud of the poor beast impacting the trail below. It emitted pained squeaks and backed away from Jonas and Joram, but it was obvious even from where she watched that the dragonling was in no shape to elude them.

Two battle-axes churned in unison, each massive blade striking the defenseless baby with killing force. A quick yelp followed by a decisive silence settled over the entrance to Dragonfang Pass.

A great cry rose up from the members of the hunt, everybody patting each other on the back.

Joram and Jonas grabbed an ivory horn and lifted the dragon's corpse into the air between them—the animal easily as large as Jonas. The brothers grinned, soaking up the adulations of their peers.

Jonas nodded to Joram and they let the carcass drop to the trail. Pulling daggers from their belts, they set to work cutting the ivory horns from the baby's head, then stood with their gory trophies held high.

The men cheered again.

Reecah's Flight

Reecah slid down to her backside, afraid she might be sick.
The body of the dragon lay in an expanding pool of blood,
its lifeless blue eyes catching the last of the dying sunlight.

Reecah's Flight

The Love it Never Knew

Dragonfang Pass was deathly quiet as darkness crept across the mountains. The dragon hunt had disappeared up the trail into the pass, out of sight of the Fang.

It took everything Reecah had to summon the strength required to scale down from her perch. She had witnessed the hunt three years ago but, for some reason, the dragonling's violent demise affected her more this time.

She sat at the base of the Fang, oblivious to the cold air wafting from the heights. Shadows lengthened into night before a distant caw echoed off the surrounding cliffs. Raver crash-landed on the ground beside her, rolling into her hip. Normally she would have laughed. Not tonight.

She helped right the mangled bird and placed him in her lap. He blinked up at her as she gently stroked his back—the silence of the mountains deafening. Everything she had done to stall the hunt had been for nothing. A dragonling had been killed and butchered no sooner than the hunt had entered the pass and all she had done was watch it happen.

"What are we doing here?" she asked Raver, and immediately felt even guiltier. Dragon Pass was nowhere to bring her little friend.

A tear dropped on the bird's head. He shook it off and clawed his way between her cloak and tunic, ostensibly to get out of the cold. The bird was smarter than her.

She sighed and unslung her rucksack, digging out the thin blanket and draping it over them.

118

Reecah's Flight

Gazing at the clear sky and the infinite stars, she caught sight of something big flying toward the pass, its great wings flapping slowly as it soared overhead.

Reecah grabbed onto Raver who painfully nipped at her hand. She pulled him from her cloak and set him on the ground, her attention on the dragon.

The moonlight reflected off the dragon's blue scales. She gasped. The mother!

Jumping to her feet, she clambered up the steep slope abutting the backside of the Fang.

The dragon stretched its wings out wide and back-flapped until its talons grasped the ledge below its warren. Extending its head into the hole, it quickly pulled out again—a mighty roar echoing off the heights.

It searched the area. Looking down, another roar, fiercer than the first, made the hair on Reecah's neck stand on end.

Unfurling its wings, the dragon dropped to the path below, its head dipping to inspect its baby's lifeless body.

Reecah dropped to her hands and knees in fright.

A great gout of flames escaped the enraged dragon's mouth, its head twisting one way and then another. She feared what might happen if it spotted her.

The mother dragon extinguished its flames and dropped prone to the ground, her head lying across her dead baby. Emitting the saddest mewl Reecah had ever heard, the dragon's sorrow broke her heart.

Raver's call as he winged away in the early light of the new day woke Reecah from a disturbed sleep. Her friend rose high overhead and disappeared up the pass.

Reecah shivered beneath her thin blanket, her mind weary from the emotion of the previous night. She half expected to see the mother dragon still draped over her baby, but the dragon had departed sometime during the night—the blood stain on the path and a scorched cliff face, the only sign either dragon had been there at all.

Her efforts to stop the hunt had been for nothing. Disheartened, she had decided last night to head home come morning. She had fooled herself into thinking she could make a difference. She was relieved Poppa wasn't here to see what a failure she had turned out to be.

Those sentiments had filled her *before* the mother dragon arrived to discover its slain baby. *Before* she witnessed the mother dragon's heartrending grief.

Fueled by a new conviction, she was done with hampering the dragon hunt. It was time to put a stop to it altogether. But first, she had a promise to keep.

Though she reluctantly commiserated with the villagers and the reasons behind the hunt, she couldn't justify the brutality of the hunt itself. Everyone knew dragons were predators who didn't discriminate what they killed for food. That being said, they generally stayed clear of Fishmonger Bay—probably more from fear of being killed themselves. Unfortunately, they were known to feed on travellers wandering the wilds.

Dragons were meat eaters. People were meat eaters. Reecah struggled to see the difference. Wasn't that the way of the world? She would fight a dragon in self-defence, or to protect anyone with her, without a second thought—just like she would defend against a bear or a troll. What angered her was the hunt purposely slaughtered helpless dragonlings to prevent them from reaching adulthood. In her mind, that would be like the dragons eating the villagers' babies for no other reason than to keep them from growing up.

Jonas and his men weren't protecting the village, they were committing brazen acts of mass murder. The organized obliteration of a species.

Reecah's Flight

Reecah wasn't clear on what her family's heritage had to do with her, but according to Auntie Grim, her distant relatives were somehow connected with the dragon community. It was high time she put aside her self-doubt and followed her calling. Ever since she was a young girl, she'd been fascinated with the idea of soaring through the skies. Where better to chase that dream than amongst those capable of flight?

It was time to stop dreaming and start acting. She smiled. If she thought too hard on what she was about to do, she'd likely talk herself out of it.

Stowing her gear, she grabbed her quarterstaff, ensured her sword was properly seated in its scabbard, and set forth on a journey she wasn't sure she would survive. It was time to locate the Dragon Temple and lay claim to her ancestry.

Raver rode the wind currents over the divide separating the southern mountains from their counterparts in the north—his diamond-shaped tail sticking out behind him like a flattened arrowhead.

Dragonfang Pass curved and twisted eastward, the opposing sides never coming together nor spreading too far apart—as if cloven by a gargantuan harrow, its operator staggering left and right as they went.

Reecah made her way to the trail the hunt followed, the terrain easier to navigate. She didn't want to test her luck finding another path as she had never scouted the pass before. She didn't know what she would do if she caught up to Jonas' men but she envisioned a violent outcome.

She cursed herself over and over for leaving her bow at home. She needed to stop the hunt without engaging them one-on-one. A task that seemed impossible without the ranged weapon.

Reecah's Flight

Raver's sporadic calls from farther down the canyon informed her he'd located Jonas' men, but the bird was nowhere to be seen. The hunt was still far ahead.

On her left, it was a long way down to the valley floor. The cliffs on the far side appeared impassable. She wished Auntie Grim had been more specific about the location of the Dragon Temple. For all she knew, it could be hidden in any one of the many mountain crags—perhaps only accessible through a warren. Her previous bluster waned. It would be a miracle if she ever found it.

As the morning wore on, she began doubting herself about her role in stopping the hunt. She would be wise to avoid a confrontation she couldn't win.

Rounding a bend, she came across a sight that made her sad. It was nothing more than a trampled section of brush and blood stains, but looking up she spied the hole the dragonling had been pulled from. The absence of the victim meant another mother had discovered her slain baby.

She crouched low, searching the sky—a cold feeling flushing her body. It would be just her luck for the mother dragon to be hanging around. Her fear got the better of her. She ran up the trail, putting the gory scene behind her.

Rounding a sharp bend to the right, she stopped and stared. Lying across her path lay the body of a deep purple dragon, smaller than the one slaughtered last night—barely half her size.

She approached the dragonling, its mutilated forehead nothing but a blur through her welling tears. Her inner senses screamed at her to run. The mother might return while she stood out in the open.

Raver cawed from a great distance. She studied the valley, searching the skies for danger.

A feeble whimper at her feet made her jump with fright. The baby was alive!

Reecah's Flight

It lay unmoving on the ground, blood seeping from the ragged gashes where its horns had been ripped from its head. More blood pooled on the ground from two deep cuts on either side of its neck. The evident blood loss was staggering, and yet, the baby dragon's side rose and fell with shallow breaths.

Reecah dropped to her knees, stroking its nose. "You poor thing. Look what they've done to you."

The baby's lavender eyes flicked open, exquisite pain reflected in them, beseeching her for help.

"I don't know what to do," she cried, her hands trembling. It would be humane to put it out of its misery, but she couldn't bring herself to do it. All she could do was be there to comfort it as it died and hope for her own sake that its mother didn't happen by.

The dragonling's leathery skin and soft scales were cold to her touch. She shrugged out of her rucksack and draped her blanket over the dragon to give it a bit of warmth. Lying down beside the dying creature, she draped her arm over it, careful not to touch its grievous wounds.

Dragon blood soaked into her blanket, but she didn't care. She refused to let the baby die cold and alone.

Time stood still. The dragon wheezed, its breath interrupted by raspy gurgling as it slowly drowned in its own blood.

It shuddered and moaned, trying to lift its head to see her. When their eyes met, she was positive its great mouth curled up in a tiny smile. She hugged it closer.

"You poor, little thing. You never got a chance to experience life." She couldn't say anymore, her words choked by emotion.

"Well look who it is."

The male voice made her heart leap.

Jonas Junior stepped out from behind a rockfall with Jaxon at his side. "You were right for a change, Jaxon. Someone *is* following us."

Reecah's Flight

"Reeky Reecah!" Jaxon said with a smirk. "I never thought I'd see you out here." His gaze took in the dragon beneath the blanket. "What are you doing?"

Reecah grabbed her quarterstaff from the ground behind her and rose to her feet, contemplating whether to draw her sword. She wasn't afraid of Jaxon, but Junior's size gave her pause. He had grown bigger than his father.

Junior scanned her from head to foot, a strange look in his eyes. He scowled at Jaxon. "That's no way to speak to a woman."

Jaxon laughed, slapping his quarterstaff against a tree trunk. "Reeky ain't no woman. She's nothing but a slimy brat who's about to get a what for."

Junior grabbed Jaxon by the bicep, yanking him off stride. "Back off!"

Jaxon shrugged out of Junior's grip with a contemptuous glare. "Father said to deal with our follower. We can't let her be just because you're sweet on her. That's Reeky for goodness sake. You're disgusting, brother."

Junior glowered at Jaxon but directed his words at Reecah, his voice strangely higher pitched. "What are you doing way out here, Miss Draakvriend? Dragonfang Pass ain't no place for a lady."

Reecah bristled. "I'm no lady."

"You can say that again," Jaxon snorted but his brother's dark look kept him from saying more.

"My apologies, Miss Draakvriend," Junior said with a mollifying tone. "Please excuse my brother. He can be a real boor. We're just surprised to see you this far away from your home. You need to be careful out here. We believe someone is following us. Have you seen anyone?"

Jaxon cast Junior an odd look.

The baby dragon at her feet coughed up a wad of blood.

Reecah's Flight

Reecah crouched to stroke its nose. "Shh, shh, shh." She glared at the brothers. "Look at this poor thing. Look what you've done. You should be ashamed."

Junior's face creased with confusion, but it was Jaxon who spoke.

"Ashamed? Of what? Killing a monster? You really are a crazy witch. We're risking our lives to save the village."

Reecah straightened and strode toward the brothers, her hand pointing at the baby dragon. "Saving the village from what? A baby that can't defend itself? Is that how you justify butchering an innocent life? Look how it suffers."

Jaxon's brows lifted. "It's still alive?"

He unsheathed his sword but Reecah stepped in front of him.

"Get out of my way or I'll slap you down," Jaxon snarled.

Reecah threw her quarterstaff to the ground and pulled her own sword free. "Over my dead body."

A wicked grin twisted Jaxon's complexion. "Even better."

"Enough!" Junior unsheathed his sword, swatting Jaxon's sword tip to the ground.

Jaxon glared, his face purple. "I'm telling Father."

"Fine. Go tell him."

Jaxon didn't move.

Junior grabbed him by the shoulder and pulled him away from Reecah, shoving him up the trail. "Go! I'll deal with you later."

Reecah thought the brothers were about to engage in a sword fight but Jaxon broke Junior's stare and stomped around the rockfall out of sight.

Reecah tried to steady her breathing. She walked back to the baby dragon, her eyes never leaving Jonas Junior. "Look what you've done."

Junior looked abashed. He took a couple of steps toward her. "Let me kill it."

Reecah's Flight

Reecah raised her sword. "How about I kill you, instead?"

Junior stopped, holding up his free hand. "Whoa, Miss Reecah. I ain't meaning you no harm." He slid his sword into its sheath. "Why don't you come with me. We can protect you."

"From what? Helpless babies?" Reecah was so angry she spat on the ground, the act shocking her almost as much as the look on Junior's face.

"I, um…no, but…there are adult dragons flying around. If they get wind of you, you're finished."

Still clutching her sword, Reecah crossed her arms below her chest. "I'll take my chances."

"But, Miss Reecah, there's someone else out here. Following us and blocking our path."

Reecah shook her head. "You're as stupid as your father."

Junior frowned.

"Who do you think is following you?"

It took Junior a moment for realization set in.

"You?"

Reecah raised her eyebrows. She nodded at the dying dragonling, fervour returning to her voice. "Judging by your trail of *murder*, I've obviously failed at stopping the hunt."

"Stopping the hunt? What would possess you to do that?"

Reecah was done with talking. The baby dragon didn't have much longer. "Leave me alone."

Junior appeared to be struggling with what he should do.

Reecah pointed her sword at him. "Are you deaf? Get out of here, you butcher, before you share the dragon's fate."

Junior's gaze flicked from her to the dragonling and back again. He swallowed and without another word, followed his brother around the rockfall.

As soon as she lost sight of Junior, Reecah's composure left her. Her hands shook so badly she found herself incapable of sheathing her sword without sticking herself or severing her fingers.

She threw the blade to the ground and dropped beside the purple dragon. Her whole body trembled as she looked into its vacant eyes. It had died alone while she argued with the Waverunner brothers. She wanted to scream. Letting her tears flow, she stroked the baby's face, giving it the love it never knew.

Reecah's Flight

Incensed

Jonas Waverunner cupped his sore knuckles in his other hand, glaring at his boy sprawled beside the campfire.

Jaxon stood off to the side with his arms crossed.

Jonas Junior rose up on an elbow, cupping his chin. "Geez, why'd you go and do that for?"

Jonas spat on the ground, just missing Junior's knee. "Next time you decide to get sweet on that Draakvriend troublemaker, I'll show you what I *really* think. You got that?"

Junior knew better than to say what he was really thinking. He pulled his hand away from his mouth. He was bleeding.

Jonas kicked him in the thigh. "I can't hear you, boy!"

Junior nodded, unable to keep the anger from his voice. "Yes, Father. I got it."

Junior feared his father would kick him again but Jonas grunted and stormed around the campfire, past the stares of the rest of the men who pretended to be busy eating their evening meal.

Junior flashed his brother a dirty look. This was his doing.

Jaxon raised his eyebrows. He spat on the ground, emulating their father, and joined their peers around the fire.

Junior stared after him. Jaxon was exactly like their father in every way except size. He couldn't wait to get him alone. His brother would pay for his loose lips.

Getting to his feet, Junior brushed the worst of the dirt from his clothes and found a spot on the far side of the campfire from Jaxon. Without meeting anyone's gaze, he grabbed a bowl

128

from a stack beside the fire and spooned his share of gurgling gruel from an iron pot suspended above the flames. The thick paste stung his split lip.

He kept his own counsel as conversation resumed around the fire. The men spoke glowingly of the day's exploits. One dragon last night and five more today.

He bristled when Grog, the beefiest firebreaker and largest man on the hunt, said, "Jaxon, today's success is a tribute to your exceptional tracking skills. I don't recall a more successful first day."

Junior watched Jaxon's reaction from beneath a lowered brow. His brother's arrogant smile irritated him.

The second tracker, Portus, lifted his grey-haired head from his supper, scowling, but remained quiet. Portus had taken over as lead tracker of the hunt when Viliyam Draakvriend had reportedly slipped off a high cliff while extricating a baby dragon. Many of those who had been on that hunt fifteen years ago, secretly claimed Viliyam died trying to set the dragon free. Thinking back, Junior couldn't refute those claims.

Junior had been ten years old back then—delighted to partake in his first hunt. Ignoring his mother's heated protests, his father had insisted on bringing Junior along as a spectator, stating that if his boy were to take over the hunt one day, he needed to learn it from an early age.

"Yep. Six dragons in less than a day's span." Jaxon puffed his chest. "Two green, a blue, a brown, an orange that had already flown at least once, and…" He glanced at Junior. "Despite the intervention of our local hill witch, a rare purple."

His brother's words grated in his skull, but Junior refused to rise to the bait. Jaxon needed to be knocked down a notch or two.

"I hope whoever follows us has his way with Draakvriend," a gaunt man with greasy black hair draped over half his face said, his voice nothing more than a snake's rattle. "I'd have at her, if you take my meaning."

The men seated around the fire imitated his chilling laugh.

They humoured the man, not because they thought he was funny, but because they were afraid to get on Viper's wrong side. Even his father seemed wary of the man clad from head to foot in black leather. There was no doubting Viper's proficiency with his wide-bladed scimitar.

Junior hadn't bothered mentioning that Reecah was the one following them. He shuddered to think what these scoundrels would do if they caught her.

"What's the matter, JJ? Does your brother speak the truth?" Viper nudged the gruff firebreaker sitting beside him, motioning to Junior with a subtle jut of his pointy chin.

Junior met the snake's icy glare.

A cynical sneer lifted the corner of Viper's thin lips. "I've said for years you're too soft to be a Waverunner. I'm thinking Jonas got it wrong naming you Junior." Viper's tone dared Junior to respond.

Junior held his gaze, the tension around the campfire palpable. He was almost twice Viper's size but he broke eye contact first.

Viper hocked and spat into the flames. "Just as I thought."

Junior took a couple of heavy breaths. He tossed his unfinished bowl to the ground. Ignoring the laughter around the campfire, he stormed down the path—back toward where he knew Reecah would be coming.

Reecah's Flight

Lurker!

Reecah awoke cold and hungry in the wee hours of the morning. She had tracked the hunt into the darkness but the uneven terrain precluded her making up any more ground.

It took her a long time to fall asleep in the hollow between a thick pine and a cliff wall. She couldn't get the purple dragonling out of her head. What bothered her most was her inability to exact retribution for the travesty. She begrudged the fact she hadn't spent the years since Grammy died finding someone to train her on the proper use of her weapons. Since she hadn't, they were barely more than sentimental ornaments hanging from her belt.

Even so, wearing them made her *feel* dangerous. In still water reflections she *looked* like someone to be reckoned with, kitted out in great-grandmother's spectacular gear. Unfortunately, perception wouldn't help her confront the people whose actions haunted her.

The image of Jonas Junior's surprise when he discovered she was responsible for sabotaging their route jumped into her mind. She thought it strange he hadn't reacted worse than he had—like his father would have—but the damage was done. Once Junior reported her to his father, Jonas would run her out of town. Or worse.

Everything about Jonas gave her the chills. Although she had never ventured anywhere else in the kingdom, she couldn't imagine anyone nastier than the dragon hunt leader. And his brother! Just the thought of Joram made her skin crawl.

Reecah's Flight

Tucked beneath her cloak, Raver emitted a soft coo, pushing away her dark thoughts. Shivering in the pale darkness, she didn't think she would ever be warm again.

Her chills brought her full circle to the purple dragonling—remembering how cold the dying baby had felt to her touch. She had spent a good part of the previous day covering its body with stones, hoping to keep mountain scavengers from desecrating its corpse any further, all the while afraid its mother would catch her in the act. She left her blanket wrapped around it—the massive amount of blood the cloth had soaked up rendered the blanket useless to her.

The moon drifted into a gap in the leaden clouds, illuminating the mountainside. A coyote called out, the feral animal sounding leagues away but she wasn't naïve to the way the mountains distorted sounds and distances. For all she knew, the coyote might be on a ledge above her.

Her gaze followed her thoughts, gasping at the sight staring down at her. The green baby dragon—its emerald eyes glinting in the moonlight.

After her initial shock, she found herself staring at the creature in wonder—a twinge of fear tingling the periphery of her consciousness. She'd been so preoccupied with chasing the hunt and stumbling across the grizzly killing grounds left in their wake that she had forgotten her encounter yesterday morning. She almost laughed. She had come close to being eaten by a full-grown dragon—how could anyone forget something like that?

Her eyes grew wide. The journal!

She reached into her cloak and withdrew the leather-bound book, its gold lettering sparkling in the moonlight.

Raver struggled to free himself from her cloak. He nipped her side, the pinch of his beak felt through her tunic.

Reecah's Flight

"Ow!" She dropped the book and scooted sideways, trying to distance herself but Raver was caught in the folds and nipped her again.

"You little bugger!" she screeched and stood up, opening her cloak.

Raver dropped to the ground and emerged from under the cloak's hem. He poked his beak at her. "Little bugger! Little bugger!"

She wanted to kick him, but her concern that she may have hurt him when he fell, kept her foot at bay. She crouched to check, but he took to the air, flying onto one of the prickly pine boughs.

Glaring at her impetuous friend, she scolded, "Auntie Grim was right. You're a dirty bird."

He bobbed his head up and down. "Dirty bird! Dirty bird!"

The baby dragon adjusted its wings, drawing her attention.

Even with the distance separating them, she was positive it smiled at her. She stepped away from the pine tree to get a better look and stumbled over her journal.

Shaking her head at her clumsiness she bent down to snatch up the book but stopped and stared. The journal lay open with its first page showing. Written in what appeared to be black ink were bold runes. She read their message.

Windwalker?
Only a Windwalker may command the Communication Stone.
Come my child. Dragon Killers are at hand.
We must be away.

She frowned as it dawned on her. Those were the same words that had resounded inside her head when the mother dragon hovered over her yesterday.

"But how?" she mouthed, stunned.

She glanced at the baby. Holding the journal up, she almost dropped it again. The gemstone flickered.

Reecah's Flight

Looking from the gemstone to the dragon and back, her mind flooded with a vision of a little girl and a grey-haired man standing on the crest of a steep hill overlooking the Niad Ocean. A clear image of Poppa flashed through her mind as if he stood right there in front of her.

Poppa put her down and reached inside his tunic to pull out a walnut sized, crimson gemstone she had never seen before. He crouched down to her level.

"Wow." Reecah accepted it in her small palm. "For me?"

Poppa smiled. "That was your mother's. I need you to take good care of it for me until I come back. Can you do that?"

Reecah nodded.

"Promise me you won't tell anyone else about it."

"Not even Grammy?"

Poppa's response surprised her. "Especially not Grammy."

Reecah turned the multi-faceted stone over in her hands, running a finger along its one flat side. "What's it do?"

Poppa swallowed, his eyes on the verge of tears. "There's no time to explain it to you now. When the time comes, it'll all become clear, okay?"

As the vision faded, comprehension shocked her to the core. The red gemstone was the communication stone the mother dragon spoke of.

She spurted out a wet laugh, conscious of the tears flowing down her cheeks. If she was right, the gemstone allowed her to converse with dragons! At least one of them anyway.

She smiled at the baby dragon, giddy with newfound knowledge. "Hey you, lurking up there, can you hear me?"

The baby dragon didn't respond as such but it blinked twice.

"You *can* hear me. I knew it." Reecah raised her voice. "Speak to me. Say something."

The baby blinked several more times.

Reecah frowned. She was missing something. The gemstone glowed softly. Its light fluttered and became constant again.

She gazed at the dragon. "Did you just nod your head at me?"

Reecah's Flight

The gemstone flickered again.

"No!" she said in awe as the relevance of what she was witnessing struck home.

Inside the journal, inscribed in bold runes below the three original lines were the words;

Yes.

I did. You just can't hear me yet.

Yes.

Goosebumps rippled across her skin. She nearly dropped the journal as she staggered against the cliff for support.

Stepping into the open, it took a moment to find her voice. "My name is Reecah. I'm glad to meet you."

She dropped her gaze to the journal. Nothing happened at first but when the gemstone shimmered, runes printed across the page.

Mother said your name is Windwalker.

Reecah struggled to read the text through watery eyes, overwhelmed by the fact that she was actually communicating with a dragon. She nodded at the text. "Yes, yes. Windwalker. That was my great-grandmother's last name.

Last name? I don't understand.

Giddy, Reecah laughed. "My first name is Reecah. My last name is Draakvriend, given to me by my grandfather and…" She paused. She'd never thought about it before. She hadn't inherited her father's last name.

The gemstone's light wavered.

You have more than one name?

Dragons only have one.

Reecah swallowed, trying to come to terms with why her last name wasn't her father's. "Um, yes. So, what's your name?"

A long rune that Reecah had never seen before printed across the page, comprising an entire line.

"I'm sorry, I can't read it."

Mother said people can't pronounce our names.

Reecah's Flight

Reecah stared at her new friend. "What should I call you then? You need a name. One that I *can* pronounce."

An important thought took root. "Are you a boy or a girl? You know, male or female?"

At once the gemstone flashed.

Male.

"Male, hmm?" Chin in hand, she pondered, "What shall I call my friendly lurker."

Raver scrabbled out on the limb. "Lurker! Lurker!"

Reecah stared at the raven. "Lurker. That's it! You're a genius, Raver."

Raver bobbed his head up and down. "Genius Raver! Genius Raver!"

The baby dragon turned his head sideways, watching Raver.

Reecah pointed an admonishing finger. "We need to set some ground rules if you and I are to be friends. Rule number one: friends don't eat each other *or* each other's friends. You understand me? Raver here," she indicated the raven, "is Reecah's friend."

"Reecah's friend! Reecah's friend!"

Mother says dragons and people are enemies.

Lurker extended his head to glance up and down the valley.

I'm supposed to stay away from people.

I should go.

"Please don't," Reecah pleaded. "I would never hurt you."

Several dragons were killed yesterday.

"That saddens me as well."

They were killed by the people you were with.

Mother said to stay away from you.

That took Reecah by surprise. "No, please. I don't have anything to do with them."

I watched you from afar.

You spoke with two of them.

Since you didn't kill them, you must be with them.

136

Reecah's Flight

"I assure you, we're anything but friends. Just because I didn't kill them doesn't mean I like them."

If they are not friends, they are enemies.

She didn't know what to say to that. "I guess you could say they are kind of like enemies. I certainly don't like them."

Why didn't you kill them?

Reecah spit out a nervous laugh. "*They* would've killed *me*. I'm not strong enough to fight them. Just because we're not friends doesn't mean I should kill them."

Reecah waited for the next line of runes but they never came. She felt the euphoria of bonding with the dragon slipping away.

Without warning, Lurker bent his rear legs and sprung into the air, his wings wide, cutting the air with graceful beats as he flew toward the far side of the valley and headed east.

Moving to the edge of the trail, conscious of the steep drop to the treetops below, she watched until the light of the moon no longer glinted off his scaly hide.

Reecah's Flight

Dance with Death

Jonas Junior walked beneath the muted light of the full moon shining through a thin layer of clouds; attempting to come to terms with his feelings. He had tried so hard to fit in with the hunt—to be the man his father desperately wanted him to be, but the harder he tried, the more he made a mess of everything.

The moon emerged from behind the clouds, illuminating far-off rock faces and stretching the deep shadows cast by crags and tors lining both sides of Dragonfang Pass.

He had been a disappointment in his father's eyes for quite some time. At first, it had gutted him, leaving him hollow—unworthy of bearing the Waverunner name. One day that guilt had changed. He wasn't sure when, but some time last year he began to rise out from beneath his father's shadow to assert himself as his own man.

At least that's what he believed. The truth was a different matter. Whenever his father was near, Junior conformed to the Waverunner philosophy of dominance at any cost—never display weakness or compassion.

In his father's estimation, that was how Waverunners conducted themselves. Lead by demanding respect. Gain obedience by invoking fear.

He ducked behind a boulder as a dark shape flew by on its way eastward—the silhouette of a small dragon—its green scales glinting in the moonlight.

Reecah's Flight

He had seen that one a few times since rounding the Fang. It was like it stalked the hunt.

He sighed and slid his back down the boulder until he sat on the ground. His leather jerkin and hooded black cloak barely kept the cold at bay, but he didn't care. A cold nose and trembling lips were better company than the members of the hunt.

As much as he enjoyed the thrill and excitement of finding and wrestling baby dragons, he always found it sad when they cried out in terror as blades cut them down and despoiled their carcasses. It was a grizzly affair. The slayers cared little if the babies were dead or not before cutting those damned horns free.

He bit his lips and shook his head. What good were the horns to anyone? Useless trophies that sat in cradle holders or were placed on mantle tops. Ever since his first hunt at the age of ten, he'd detested seeing the severed horns in someone's house. Being a Waverunner, he couldn't escape the sight. His father and uncle owned the largest collection in the village.

His eyes were closing when a dark form crossed the face of the moon. He sat up, instantly alert. A dragon! One too large to be a baby, glided on the wind, its head craned toward the ridge where he sat.

Green scales refracted the moonlight as the creature adjusted its flight, closing the distance between itself and the trailside ridge he sat on.

The dragon emitted a loud shriek, setting his nerves on end.

Stiff with fear, he found he couldn't move. The dragon flew toward him, close enough to hear the wind in its leathery wings as it banked, screeching loudly and crunching into the mountainside not far up the path. The hunt camp!

Junior scrambled to his feet and rounded the boulder as shouts rose into the night. The members of the dragon hunt were under attack.

Reecah's Flight

Junior's heart almost stopped. A second dragon materialized from the valley below, its dark purple hide so close he could've hit it with a rock. Through the trees, a spout of flames escaped its mouth as it joined the green dragon on the trail.

Finding it harder to breathe than his short sprint merited, he slowed on the periphery of the campsite to reconnoitre the scene. In the surreal lighting of a scattered campfire, moonlight, and dragon fire, Junior located two banks of three tower shields—the rest of the hunt cowering behind the defensive lines.

Grog's bulk was easily identifiable. Behind him and the two other firebreakers in his wall crouched Viper, Joram, Jaxon and Jonas senior—the green dragon stomping toward them on thick legs of muscle and sinew.

The second firebreaker wall was trying to coax the purple dragon to the ground—the dragon hovered before them, its nostrils emitting spurts of fire. The members of the hunt were taught at an early age never to engage a dragon in flight. Without the aid of a ballista, it was nearly impossible to take down an adult dragon.

It was the job of the slayers and the tracker to coax the dragon to the ground by taunting it, without ever fully exposing themselves. The firebreakers were their safety barrier—their thick shields constantly moving to position themselves between the slayers and the fire breathing beast.

The veteran tracker, Portus, stood up and shouted at the purple dragon. He darted out from behind the firebreak to cast a stone before darting around the back of the wall and repeating the action on the other side.

Portus did this to provoke the dragon into dousing him with flames. Dragons were prone to draw their heads back in preparation to spew their deadly swath of flames, leaving them vulnerable to anyone not within their fire's path.

Reecah's Flight

The purple dragon blasted the area Portus had just vacated, following his progress behind the shield wall. The firebreak spread the fiery wrath high and wide.

The slayers behind Grog's shield wall stood straight and released arrows and a crossbow bolt into the purple dragon's mouth. If the volley proved effective, the dragon would cease spitting fire and land.

The combined forces of two shield walls were utilized to take one dragon down. Jonas' men battled two.

Afraid to draw the green dragon's attention his way, Junior fretted. He couldn't just leave his family and fellow huntsmen to deal with the two enraged monstrosities that were forcing them back toward the steep slope behind them. Once the shield wall's movements became hampered by the hillside, the dragons would surely tear through them.

Grog caught his eye.

Junior held his hands up, shrugging his shoulders, silently asking the experienced veteran what he should do.

Grog shook his head at him and returned his concentration to keeping the wall together. "Left twice, right three times, back once."

The men holding the shields, and those cowering behind, moved in unison—their course pulling the landed green dragon one way and then another, buying them time.

The purple dragon's head coiled back and thrust forward, spewing a volley of flames.

Jonas roared, "Now!"

Grog's shield wall stopped its manoeuvre while Jonas, Joram and Viper dispatched three missiles into the purple dragon's gaping maw.

The purple dragon cut its fire short, recoiling under the painful barrage.

"Move!" Jonas ordered, ducking low.

Reecah's Flight

"Four right, one back, two left, three right!" Grog gave the direction and the shield wall staggered away from the green dragon.

Sweat dampened Junior's undergarments. He was well versed in the dance with death. He had taken part in them several times throughout the years. It was something one never got used to.

The wall's job was to keep the dragon off-balance. Antagonizing it enough to rush at them at the right moment. That was the pivotal point when dealing with grounded dragons. If the slayers weren't prepared, or the wall not fast enough to turn the dragon at the right moment, their formation would fall apart and the dragon would be in their midst.

Junior grimaced. The purple dragon refused to land. Opening its mouth to screech at the shield wall and the veteran tracker who goaded it, two arrows were clearly lodged in the roof of its mouth.

It flapped its mighty wings, the wind stirring ground debris around in swirls. Flames roiled at the back of its mouth. Its teeth came together and its head recoiled. Emitting a great roar, it threw its head forward, dousing the far shield wall with fire.

"Now!"

Grog's wall stopped. Two more arrows and Viper's crossbow bolt found their mark.

"Move!"

"Two right, one back, four left, one forward, three right!"

Grog's wall danced with the green death.

The purple dragon turned its wrath away from the shield wall provoking it and concentrated on the exposed flank of Grog's wall as the firewall went through its assigned steps.

Portus ran out between the shield walls, trying to divert its attention, but it ignored him.

Recoiling its head, the purple dragon screeched, the sound so terrible Junior's teeth ached. It landed, shaking the ground, but instead of going after the veteran tracker it closed its mouth and pulled back.

"Grog, right face!" Jaxon's high-pitched voice rose above the chaos. Grog and his shield brothers turned to absorb the torrent of flames.

Junior gaped. By turning to face the purple dragon, Jonas' group were now exposed to the green dragon.

The green dragon charged. Just before it snapped at Grog's left side, Grog spun his shield to intercept it, the action allowing the purple dragon's flames to set his right side ablaze along with the firebreaker crouched beside him.

Wrestling to free his shield from the green dragon's mouth, Grog tried to grab onto his shield mate as the middle firebreaker dropped his own shield and stumbled into the open, his leather armour fully ablaze.

Screaming, twisting and turning, the firebreaker dropped to his knees and fell on his face—the disgusting smell of burnt flesh filled the glade.

Junior hoped the man was dead before the purple dragon snatched his flaming body in its mouth and lifted him into the air.

The man cried out in agony, his bones snapping like dry twigs. The purple dragon shook its head back and forth until pieces of the man scattered about the clearing.

Jonas roared, leading Joram around the far side of the shield wall to engage the green dragon—all semblance of order gone from Grog's wall.

The dragon's emerald eyes caught Jonas' movement and craned its head to intervene, the action throwing Grog's bulk to the ground, ripping the shield from him.

Junior withdrew his sword and forced his incapacitating fear aside. His father and uncle were about to suffer the same fate as the firebreaker. He had to do something.

Reecah's Flight

Dashing across the clearing, he leaped over Grog rolling on the ground, and vaulted off the remaining firebreaker's hunched back. Swinging his sword arm out wide, he aimed its point at the dragon's eye and drove it home. The breath left him as his body smashed against the side of the dragon's head. Falling away, he lost his grip on his sword.

The green dragon reared high on its back legs, flailing its wings out wide. Its head thrashed back and forth, screeching in anguish and billowing flames soared into the night sky.

Jonas, Joram, Viper and Jaxon hacked at the dragon's exposed underside with wild abandon, spilling the creature's entrails to the ground.

The purple dragon screeched, running at Joram and his men but the second shield wall charged forward, the slayers expertly sliding their blades up and under its protective scales.

The purple dragon turned on them, spewing a tremendous blast of dragon fire. The flames hit two of the slayers and Portus head-on, killing them instantly.

Viper's scimitar slashed at its stomach, followed closely by Joram and Jonas' lethal axe swings. The purple dragon fell to its chin, dead.

Dazed, Junior tried to get up, but he slipped in the gore at his feet. Landing on his side, his gaze caught the agonized expression of Grog—the right side of the man's face burnt beyond recognition.

Reecah's Flight

Those Left Behind

Frightening sounds echoed throughout the valley. Angry roars accompanied by thunderous screeches of agony. A great battle was being fought somewhere up the trail from where Reecah and Raver huddled behind the pine.

She had just settled between the tree and the cliff to pass the night away when the terrible noises started up. Trembling, she hoped that whatever was fighting wouldn't turn its attention her way. She debated running as fast as she could in the other direction, but she wasn't familiar with this part of the mountains. It would be foolish to navigate it in the dark.

Raver made soft noises beneath her cloak, his body shivering in her lap. She pulled her arms from the cloak's sleeves to comfort her frightened friend and stroke his head as the commotion echoed down the pass.

A terrifying shriek made her hunker down further—followed by an eerie silence—the complete lack of noise more frightening than the uproar before it. She feared whatever had been fighting was now coming after her. If the attacker had been a dragon, like she believed, she was sure it had found the dragon hunt. Their trail would lead the creature straight back to her.

She sat shaking against the wall, her eyes darting everywhere at once, barely blinking. The remainder of the sleepless night dragged on. As the valley lightened with the new dawn, Reecah wasn't sure what to do. Afraid to venture further into the pass, she was equally reluctant to return home—she might never get

Reecah's Flight

a chance to speak with a dragon again. She sighed. After the way her conversation had ended with Lurker last night, the opportunity may have already gone.

Her stomach growled. Her eyes were dry and her head ached from the lack of sleep. The emotional highs and the devastating lows she had experienced over the last couple of days had mentally exhausted her.

Checking her rucksack, her lack of food made the decision for her. She was ill-equipped to be frolicking deeper into the heart of dragon territory.

Pulling her cloak away from her chest she looked at Raver. "What was I thinking, feather brain? Who am I fooling? It's none of my business what the hunt does."

Raver blinked at her.

"It's time we headed home."

She undid the thongs lashing her cloak together and lifted Raver free. The raven took to wing and disappeared around the pine.

She gathered her waterskin and shrugged into her pack, ready to step out from behind the tree but a voice up the trail stopped her.

"There it is again! Look, the raven!" The high-pitched voice could belong to none other than Jaxon Waverunner.

Reecah took a chance and leaned out. Sure enough, Jonas' youngest son marched down the trail toward her location with several others close behind. To a man, they appeared bedraggled.

She slunk behind the tree, fearing the boughs weren't thick enough to hide her. Pulling her cloak tight, she made herself as small as possible and peeked through an opening in her hood.

As Jaxon strolled in front of her, she resisted the urge to rush out and push him over the edge. Had his friends not been with him, she might have.

Reecah's Flight

Including the halfwit, Reecah counted eight men—the last four struggling to carry a makeshift litter.

Joram and Jonas strutted by, their sour faces tracking Raver's flight. Jonas stopped right in front of the tree, searching the sky and the surrounding mountainside.

Not daring to breathe, Reecah fought to keep her body from trembling. Because she had foolishly told Junior, the hunt would know that she was the one responsible for their hardships. If they found her, she would be the one sent flying over the edge.

Jonas seemed to look right at her, but he turned away and pointed at what she could only imagine was Raver in the distance. "Jaxon's right. That raven's following us. Five coppers to whoever brings it down. Perchance I'll even put a good word in for you with Janice or Jennah, eh?"

The thought of the boorish man offering his daughters as a reward to someone just because they killed a bird repulsed her. What kind of father did that?

The litter bearers caught up and stopped to wait on Jonas and Joram, unable to pass them on the narrow trail. The strain of their burden clearly evident in the bulging veins on their red faces, but no one dared to complain.

The litter consisted of four long, ivory horns lashed together—pointed on the front end, and thick and encrusted with blood and gore on the back end; the horns much too long for the body on the litter.

Reecah frowned. Where had they acquired such ghastly poles? She tried to see who lay under the blanket but couldn't see his face. She assumed it was Junior until she looked farther down the trail and saw him talking with the greasy-haired man who reminded her of a weasel.

Jonas regarded the sweating men for a moment and grunted. "Let's be on then, we've rested long enough. The sooner we get Grog off the mountain, the sooner we can form a new party and get back."

The litter bearers rolled their eyes as Joram and Jonas started up the trail. Without a word, they stretched their necks and stomped after the leaders.

Coming up behind the litter, Junior's eyes were on the crossbow the greasy-haired man held. "Viper, you think you can outshoot a bow?"

"Pfft, please. This thing is more accurate and powerful than any bow I've ever seen."

"What about the high king's longbows?"

Viper narrowed his eyes. "Don't rightly know. They certainly pack a wallop. Fine if you're stationary, I guess, but if you're chasing men through the bush, I would think they'd be unwieldy."

They stopped in front of the pine tree. Junior pointed east up the valley. "Think you can hit that bird?"

Reecah sucked in her breath.

"Don't be daft. He's halfway to the other side." Viper cast Junior a disgusted glare and followed the litter west.

"You go ahead. I'll stay back and make sure the bird doesn't come back," Junior called after the man but received no response.

The eldest Waverunner boy stared out over the valley, long after the noise of the rest of the hunt receded past the next ridge. His voice sent shivers down her spine.

"You can come out now."

Reecah almost choked. She cast a furtive glance up and down the trail. No one else was visible.

Junior peered through the boughs. "Come on, Draakvriend, I know you're back there. Heck, I can smell you."

Putting aside her misgivings, she stood with the help of her quarterstaff. She unsheathed her sword and slipped out from behind the pine tree. "I'm not afraid to use this."

Reecah's Flight

Junior smiled at the sword tip pointed at him. "I don't doubt it." He held up empty hands. "I'm not meaning to hurt you."

Reecah searched the immediate area before stepping onto the path.

"If I meant you harm, don't you think I would've told the others you were there?"

She searched him from head to foot. "How'd you know?"

"Your friend gave you away."

She frowned.

"The raven. He's yours, is he not?"

She swallowed, refusing to comment.

"He's the bird from Grimelda's Clutch." Junior's words were a statement, not a question.

Saying nothing, Reecah backed down the trail.

"Look, I'm not going to hurt you. I wanted to warn you. My uncle suspects the raven belonged to the witch. Through your association, he has tied the bird to you. It's just a matter of time before they put it all together and realize you're the one behind the delays along the route. When that happens, you'll be in serious trouble."

Reecah cast a glance behind her, fully expecting to see the other three men from the hunt sneaking up behind her.

"If you're looking for the rest of the hunt, they're dead."

"Huh?"

"We were attacked by dragons last night."

Reecah gaped, lowering her sword. That explained the commotion. "And?"

Junior shrugged. "And what? We defended ourselves. We killed them."

"What colour?"

"Huh?"

"What colour were the dragons?"

Junior stepped toward her. "What's it matter? They're dead."

149

Reecah's Flight

Reecah raised her sword again, her eyes narrowing. "What colour?"

"Easy with that thing." Junior back stepped. "Purple and green, why?"

"No!" Reecah slid her sword into its sheath and sprinted up the trail.

"Reecah, wait! It's too dangerous."

His words didn't register. The vision of the ivory poles making up the litter's frame flashed through her mind. All she could think of was Lurker's mother as she bolted up the trail, deeper into Dragonfang Pass.

She glanced over her shoulder, expecting to see Junior giving chase, but he just stood there, staring at her, bewilderment written on his face.

It didn't take her long to stumble across the gory scene. Two full-sized dragons lay dead across a wide clearing—blood and gore splattered around their midsections and heads. She stumbled to a stop in front of the green dragon, her mind numb.

The dragons were massive. Judging by the size of their mouths, either one of them would have been able to swallow a man whole.

Between the dragon corpses, the remains of a large campfire lay smeared across the ground, but the burn marks close to the purple dragon were definitely not caused by a campfire.

She dropped to her knees in shock, staring at the green dragon's head. It lay on its side, its visible, lifeless, emerald eye open and infested with flies.

Her body convulsed but she hadn't enough food in her stomach to bring it up.

A sad mewling noise made her jerk her head up and look around. It came from the purple dragon.

Reecah stood and fingered her sword hilt, not sure what to do. If the dragon was still alive, she was in trouble.

Reecah's Flight

The massive body didn't move. Its butchered head as lifeless as the green dragon.

The sad noise came again.

Pulling her sword free, Reecah walked around the purple dragon's head, giving it a wide berth. On the far side of the clearing, she caught sight of a man-sized, purple dragonling nuzzling its head beneath the dead dragon's foreleg. It looked identical to the baby dragon she had covered with her blanket.

Afraid she was making a deadly mistake, she approached the baby dragon—the poor creature trying to rouse its mother. It was either oblivious or uncaring of her presence.

Tears blurred Reecah's vision but another noise, one much more ominous, had her staring around the clearing searching for the cause.

Lurker appeared between a gap in the trees, his wings beating slowly as he hovered at the brink of the precipice looking in. His eyes took in the purple dragon and then the green before locking on Reecah. He never broke eye contact as he landed beside the green dragon's tail.

Reecah walked between the fallen dragons, but Lurker's angry glare stopped her. A look so intense it was like he was trying to talk to her.

The journal!

She withdrew the book and opened it to the second page.

You did this!

Her heart caught in her throat. She shook her head. "No! I would never do this. It was the men we spoke of yesterday."

Your friends!

"They're not my friends. They're bad men."

Why didn't you kill them?

My mother would still be alive!

"Oh, Lurker, I'm so sorry. I had no idea they would do this."

Look what you've done!

Reecah's Flight

Reecah gasped. "B-but, it wasn't me. I didn't do it. Lurker, you're my friend. I would never do this. I tried to stop them."

Lurker charged up to her so fast she couldn't have gotten out of the way if she wanted to. He stopped, his long snout level with her face.

She waited for the fire that never came. Searching the dragon's face, the sight of tears escaping his beautiful eyes was like a dagger to her heart. Holding the journal up in a shaking hand, his words drove the dagger home and twisted.

I'm not your friend.

Leave here and never come back.

The next time I see you, I will kill you.

She lowered her eyes. The journal slipped from her hands. It fell to the ground on its cover, its pages rustling in the breeze. With her head hung low, she started for home.

Reecah's Flight

The Hill Witch

"**Viper** tells me you spoke with the hill witch again," Jonas growled, his meaty fists lifting Junior off the trail and pinning him against a tree beside the drop. "Is that true?"

Junior caught Viper's sneer out of the corner of his eye.

Viper scoffed, "Don't be thinking I'd forget your weakness just because you slew a dragon. Lucky for her, I didn't catch on until it was too late."

Junior frowned at the weasel-faced snake. "What're you talking about?"

Viper spat on the ground. "Please. One minute you're distracting me with questions about my crossbow, and the next you're volunteering to wait on the raven. When it dawned on me what you were up to, I went back and saw you speaking with the witch just before she took off up the valley."

"Why does everyone insist she's a witch?"

Jonas jammed his fists under Junior's chin and said with a tooth-clenched snarl, "Think, bonehead. She's related to the witch we burned in town."

"Grimelda?" Junior asked. "No way!"

Jonas grunted, his angry sneer boring into Junior for a tense moment before he released him. "If you'll take your mind off your crotch, you'll recall Reecah's grandmother was Grimelda's sister. In my book, that makes the hill witch Grimelda's great-niece. You thinking on populating the village with ill-begotten spawn?"

Junior looked at the ground. "No, Father."

Reecah's Flight

Stretching his neck and rubbing at it where his father had threatened to crush his windpipe, Junior struggled to keep from running from his father's wrath. He knew that if he did, his punishment would be more severe when he returned home.

Trying to appear contrite, he kept his eyes diverted and thought about the night the witch's shop had burned to the ground. Reecah had pled with his father and uncle to leave the witch alone. Now that he thought about it, he recalled the rumours of the Draakvriends. He'd never made much of it, but if his father was right...

He shook off the thought, thankful the rest of the hunt had continued down the path, including Joram and his brother. He couldn't bear Jaxon watching their father pummel him. His brother received too much joy from it.

Jonas started to walk away but came back and went face to face with him. "What am I going to do with you?"

Junior mustn't have answered quick enough because his father slammed his palms into his chest. He stumbled toward the brink. Using his hands to grab at the brush on the ground, he prevented himself from pitching over the edge.

If Jonas was concerned at how close he had come to killing him, he never let on. Stepping close, he seemed on the verge of giving him one final shove.

If not for Viper's intervention, Junior was fairly certain his father would have.

"Jonas! Enough! Deal with him when we get off the mountain. If we're attacked again, we'll need every man."

Junior gave the snake a sideways look. So that was it. Viper wasn't concerned with his welfare, he was ensuring his own sorry hide had enough protection in case a dragon attacked.

Even with Viper between them, Junior feared his father wouldn't be put off, but eventually, Jonas stormed off.

Reecah's Flight

Viper cast Junior an angry glare. "Don't be thinking we're done with your wench, neither. Fishmonger Bay ain't no place to be harbouring witches anymore."

Junior stared at the greasy-haired man striding after his father. The last thing he wanted to do was go with them but what choice did he have? He couldn't remain on the mountainside. Surely not within the pass.

He thought of Reecah who had gone the other way. He shook his head. Perhaps she was a witch.

Heaving a sigh, he straightened his clothing, adjusted his gear, and started along the trail—making sure he walked slower than his father.

Reecah's Flight

No Going Home

Reecah's feet hurt, her stomach ached, her head pained her, and her heart was broken. Descending the mountain heights, she looked forward to secluding herself within her lonely hut on top of the hill. Despite her misery, she experienced a faint warmth deep inside as the familiar terrain passed beneath her boots. There was nothing quite like the peacefulness and sense of security offered by the weathered boards of Grammy and Poppa's cabin.

Raver squawked somewhere in the trees behind her but she wasn't worried about him. They were far enough away from Dragonfang Pass. With the exception of dragons and people, ravens didn't have many predators. Reecah pitied any hawk or owl deciding to tangle with her black feathered friend.

Four days had passed since witnessing the gory scene with Lurker's mother and the purple dragon. The image still made her sick to her stomach. Lurker's accusations and his open threat to kill her had left her numb.

Despite Lurker's harsh words, she lamented dropping her diary. The journal and the magical gemstone were special gifts from Grammy and Poppa. She fought to quell the tears blurring her vision, something that happened more often these days. The journal was lost to her.

To console herself, she focused on the fact that she had been granted a once in a lifetime opportunity to speak with a dragon. She didn't know of anyone else ever doing that.

Reecah's Flight

She sniffled and forced a smile, wishing for the countless time she had a friend in the village. A friend anywhere. One that she could sit down with and share her amazing experience with. She had never been a braggart but the event was too exciting to keep to herself. She scuffed the toe of her boot on the grassy hillside. Who would believe her anyway?

She had made a point of following the route the hunt would take, not wanting to overtake Jonas and his thugs. Watching the faint trail at her feet, her breath caught in her throat. If not for the heavy rains last night, she would have missed the boot prints in a quickly drying mud puddle. She had recently departed the main trail. Nobody else took this side route off the mountain except her. It led to only one place. Home.

She ducked beneath the height of the spring undergrowth lining the hilltop above the clearing around the hut and listened. Nothing.

She studied the tracks. Four sets. Judging by their size, at least three of them were men's.

Raver fluttered into view, silently winging his way to the cabin. Her mind eased. She had grown used to his habits. If he'd seen anything untoward from the sky, he would've called out, folded his wings in, and dropped to her like a rock.

Fingering her sword hilt, she quietly padded the rest of the way down the hill behind her home, stopping at the edge of the small clearing. It wouldn't hurt to be careful.

Raver was nowhere in sight. Nor was anyone else. She scanned the ground. Faint tracks much bigger than her own led from the trail toward the hut.

An excited cawing caught her attention. It grew in volume until Raver appeared from around the front of the hut and flew straight at her. She caught him on a vambrace and held him steady. "What is it? Is somebody in the hut?"

Raver bobbed his head up and down. "In the hut! In the hut!"

Reecah's Flight

She ducked low, feeling exposed. If someone had bothered to look through the back window, they would know she was there.

Afraid to move, she studied the area, ready to bolt up the hill, but nothing moved. Nor did she detect any sound coming from her cabin.

Swatting at a gnat buzzing around her head, she decided to risk a closer inspection. If someone *had* seen her it wouldn't make a difference how she approached, so she stood and threw Raver into the air. "Be my eyes."

The raven cawed twice and flew to the hut's peak. As frightened as she was, she couldn't help smiling when he slipped on the roof and tumbled to his side. She envisioned him rolling off the roof in a flurry of frantic feathers, but he righted himself.

Stifling a nervous laugh, she hurried to the back wall of the hut and crept over to the window. She held her breath, rolled her head to the side and peeked through the window.

It was difficult to see the dark interior but right away she knew something was wrong. On the opposite side of the cabin, the front door stood ajar.

She pulled back, debating whether to make a run for it or charge into the hut with her sword drawn.

A wind swayed the treetops and the door banged in the wind. The noise had her doubting herself. Perhaps she hadn't closed it properly. That still didn't explain the boot prints.

Risking a better look, she cupped her hands against the window. Her mouth dropped. The contents had been tossed.

Without worrying about the ramifications, she raced around the hut and burst through the door, her sword held in front of her, but no one was inside.

Sliding her sword into its scabbard, she walked amongst the jumble of upset furniture and broken adornments. The sheets were torn off her pallet and the drawers of Grammy's old dresser lay upended on the floor.

She jumped as Raver flew into the hovel and crash-landed on the countertop beneath the back window.

The sight of Grammy's loom smashed beyond repair left her reeling. Covering her stricken face with trembling hands, she stumbled to the old weaving machine and set the old stool back on its feet so she could sit before her legs gave out.

"Who would do something like this?" she said out loud, but she already knew the answer.

A cold chill gripped her. Everything she'd ever known lay strewn around the interior of the hut. Her gaze drifted to the corner where she used to sleep on a blanket. Her wooden dragon lay in splinters against the wall.

The stool tipped from underneath her as she dropped to her knees and stretched a shaking hand toward her most special possession. She couldn't bring herself to actually go to it. She was crying so hard she found it difficult to breathe. She didn't care. They had taken everything from her.

Raver squawked excitedly just before the sound of booted footsteps approached the hut and stomped across the porch—stopping in the doorway.

"Reecah?"

Junior's voice called to her but she didn't bother meeting his gaze—her hurt too profound. If the son of Jonas wished to run her through with his sword, let him. She had nothing left.

She had no strength to flinch as his footsteps approached and stopped directly behind her.

"I'm so sorry."

A tentative hand dropped on her shoulder but she shrugged it off.

"I had nothing to do with this. I can't believe they did this to you."

Reecah's Flight

The presence of Jonas' son did little to soothe her grief. With swollen eyes, she regarded him, not caring how she must look—face streaming with tears and her nose running.

Junior glanced around the hut, shock and sadness on his face. When their eyes met, he appeared on the verge of tears himself.

"I apologize for the actions of my family, but I'm sure nothing I say will ease your pain. If it's any consolation, I'm ashamed to be a Waverunner."

Reecah swallowed but didn't think she could find her voice. She shook her head and cried even harder.

Junior knelt and put an arm around her shoulder.

She tried to shrug him off but his strong grip held on, pulling her into his embrace. She wanted to resist but the hurt was too intense. Lacking the strength to break free, she resigned herself to his arms and cried into his shoulder.

She wasn't used to being held, not since Grammy had left her. She couldn't recall a time anyone other than her grandparents and great-aunt had bothered to show her affection. It felt strange being in Junior's arms, and yet, she found it oddly comforting. Had he not been a Waverunner, she might have returned the hug.

To his credit, Junior held her patiently until she finally sniffled loudly and separated herself, wiping her face on the inside of her cloak.

Junior rose, watching her, his lips pursed to speak but he remained quiet.

Her voice came as a harsh whisper. "What are you doing here? Shouldn't you be killing babies?"

He wrung his hands together. "I came to warn you. You can't stay here."

If her heart hadn't been so heavy, she would've laughed at the absurdity of his statement. "You're too late."

"No, Reecah, listen."

Reecah's Flight

He stepped forward trying to grasp her by the hands, but she stepped out of reach.

"Members of the hunt did this on their way to the village. They were hoping to find you here. They'll be back."

"I don't care anymore. What more can they do to me?" Even as she said it, visions of all the ways Jonas and his men might make her life worse went through her mind. She shuddered.

"You don't understand. My father has convinced the rest of the village that you're a witch."

Reecah scowled. "I've been called worse."

Junior's cheeks reddened. "Ya, well, that was before." He lifted his face, his vibrant green eyes pleading as he blurted out, "They mean to burn you."

Reecah blinked. "Burn me?"

Junior nodded. "You need to get out of here." He went to the door and looked out. "I don't know how long you've got, but if I know my father, they'll be back soon. If they catch you…"

Reecah's mind raced. They wanted to burn her? For what? Blocking the route into the mountains? "But why. What did I do to deserve that? Roll a few boulders in their way?"

Junior turned in the open doorway. "It's not what you did. It's who you were born to."

"My parents didn't do anything wrong."

Junior nodded as she spoke. "It's not your parents they're worried about, though according to father, they weren't welcome in the village either."

"Then who…"

Raver jumped into the air.

Junior ducked sideways as the raven flew outside.

Almost at once, Raver squawked in a cadence Reecah knew well. Her little friend had spotted someone.

Reecah took a quick look around the hut. There wasn't anything salvageable. She went to her old sleeping spot in the corner and picked up a broken dragon wing—her tears starting again. She let it fall through her fingers and sniffed loudly. Everything gone.

Taking a steadying breath, she crossed the hut and reached beneath the pallet. "Thank goodness," she said as she unclipped the black bow from its hidden cradle. She pulled back the heavy dresser and revealed a hidden panel in the wall. Prying it open, she produced a black leather quiver etched with the same two white 'X's' marked on the bow. The training swords were propped up in the tight space, but there was nothing she could do about them.

Replacing the panel, she kicked its bottom to jam it back into place. She spun, scanning the devastated interior. "Where's my quarterstaff?"

Junior searched through the mess and stopped near the broken loom. "Here!" He held it out for her. "Now go. I'll try to stall them."

He tore from the hut and ran down the path.

She wondered why he had helped her. He had been one of the worse boys while they were growing up. Being the eldest, he had encouraged the others.

Raver squawked nearby.

She didn't have time to worry about Junior. Passing through the door, she paused to take a last look, not sure she'd ever see Grammy and Poppa's cabin again.

She willed her tears away. She had no time for them if she wished to live to fight another day. Gritting her teeth, she lamented not having much when it came to worldly possessions, nor did she have anyone to fall back on, but one thing life had taught her while growing up on the hill overlooking Fishmonger Bay, was to be a survivor. If the villagers thought they were going to take her easily, they were in for a big surprise.

Reecah's Flight

She spied her rucksack and ducked back in to retrieve it before slipping through the door and running up the faint trail into the mountains.

She thought briefly about returning to Dragonfang Pass. Grimelda's dying words nagged at her. *When I'm gone, you will be the only one on this side of the Great Kingdom capable of saving the dragons…Locate the Dragon's Eye embedded in the Watcher and bring it back here… Promise Grimelda.'*

As much as she wished to honour her pledge, she dared not expose herself to the dragon community. Not after her encounter with Lurker. He claimed she was as much to blame for the death of the dragons as the hunt.

The sound of distant boots stomping up the main trail spurred her into motion.

Raver flew overhead, following her south into the heights toward Peril's Peak.

Reecah's Flight

Ambushed

Peril's Peak towered over the dragon hunt cabin, it's grey summit devoid of snow. Despite its elevation, the mountain height was pleasantly warm in the late summer heat as Reecah went through her morning ritual with her swords—swinging them around and practicing her footwork. She was no match for a formally trained swordsman—or anyone with experience really, but at least her strength continued to grow.

With nothing but time on her hands and her dependence on her ability to hunt food, her accuracy with the bow had improved considerably. She had become proficient with stationary targets and now enjoyed jogging around a small course she had set up to shoot while on the move. It had taken the loss of many arrows over the cliffside, but as the spring months blended into summer, she found herself able to hit her intended target more often than not. If only Jonas and the hunt could see her now. She doubted even the greasy snake, Viper, could best her.

Leaning her weapons against the cabin she climbed the tiered waterfall tumbling behind the hunt camp, removed her boots, and dangled her feet in the cold water cascading from the heights. She smiled at the irony of her recent journey. She had fled her home to escape the villagers, especially the members of the dragon hunt, only to hole up in their training cabin. When the men returned here in the fall, they were in for a shock. She planned on leaving a blatant message about her time spent in her summer abode.

164

Reecah's Flight

Using the writing stick Auntie Grim had given her, she wrote a brief account of her time spent at the cabin, itemizing her training regimen on the large, central table.

She laughed out loud. She doubted the dullards were capable of reading.

For the time being, the villagers would be busy fishing and farming the lower heights with little time to spare for formal training. She recalled Poppa leaving for a few weeks around the autumn solstice to train with the hunt, and then again in the early spring.

Smiling at the turn of events, the small hairs on the back of her neck stood on end.

Raver squawked excitedly from somewhere far away.

She couldn't locate him at first, but when he appeared from beneath the ledge of the cliff fronting the cabin, she knew her time at the hunt camp had come to an end. Someone ascended the heights from the village far below. It was time to move on.

Struggling to pull her boots over her wet feet, she scrambled down the ledge and ran to the cliff's edge. At first, she couldn't see anyone, but movement to her left made her drop to her knees. Jaxon Waverunner led a group of men in matching surcoats up the trail.

She thought about slipping away to Thunderhead, but the men were already on this side of the junction she needed to access the southern route.

A voice echoed off the cliff face at her feet. Jaxon ran up the last steep slope leading to the plateau, pointing straight at her. Well armed men followed on his heels, their chinking armour and clanking weapons clearly audible.

Reecah darted to the cabin, gathered what scant food stock she had, and ran back outside to collect her weapons. She briefly entertained the idea of using her bow to stop the men's advance, but she didn't have the heart to actually kill a person.

Reecah's Flight

"Raver, home," Reecah called and climbed the waterfall, confident she could easily outpace her pursuit. With no other way open to her she headed home—the eastern face of Peril's Peak too sheer to circle around.

Jaxon's group came hard after her for the first part of her trek but she put considerable distance between them by the time the afternoon sun dropped over the ocean.

Descending the heights toward her cabin, the aroma of a cookfire forewarned her long before she got within sight of her hut. Careful not to alert whoever it was, she crept through the underbrush until she came within sight of the cabin.

Scores of men and women sat around numerous campfires around her yard. Several of the interlopers wore long robes but most of them were outfitted in coloured uniforms matching those that had been travelling with Jaxon, except one. Jonas Junior. The lying scoundrel had led an army of men to apprehend her.

Ever since the day he had held her, she had thought of little else. She dared to hope that he was somehow different than the rest of Jonas' clan. That Junior actually possessed a shred of decency and even cared for her. Never having entertained feelings for anyone other than Poppa, Grammy and Grimelda, something about Junior made her heart flutter. Seeing him amongst an armed camp on her doorstep affected her more than she thought possible.

That troubled her. She had no real reason to believe that Junior liked her, but a profound sense of betrayal fueled a deep resentment. She'd been a foolish girl to entertain notions regarding the blonde-haired man.

She wiped at her eyes to keep them from brimming over and wondered why the villagers had felt the need to employ armed soldiers to bring her in. She might know the lay of the land better than most but she was barely capable of defending herself. They were taking this 'witch' thing far more seriously than they ought to. She didn't possess a magic bone in her body.

Raver cried out overhead, gliding on the wind over the hut.

She cringed. The fool bird was going to give away her location.

Imitating a cardinal's chirrup, she called raver to her—realizing too late what a mistake that would be.

Junior stepped away from the largest campfire, following Raver's flight across the yard toward where she crouched in a thorny thicket.

Reecah entertained pulling her bow from her shoulder and ending the traitorous man. His broad chest made him an easy target.

"Junior!" A gruff voice sounded from over by the hut. Jonas appeared on the edge of the porch, an angry scowl twisting his face. "Where are you…?"

"There!" Junior pointed up the slope at the copse Reecah hid amongst.

The sound of leather and metal erupted across the clearing as the camp rose to their feet and checked their weapons.

Raver crashed into her outstretched arms. "No Raver. Away again." She threw him into the air.

He'd no sooner cleared the thicket than an arrow whistled overhead.

Reecah's heart lurched but Raver escaped unharmed. She stared through the underbrush. Junior had another arrow nocked but he held back. All he had to do was aim at the bush Raver had emerged from. He couldn't miss her.

Grabbing a fist-sized rock she tossed it to her left. The rock struck a tree and rolled down an embankment into the backyard.

Reecah's Flight

Hearing the thump, Reecah sprinted up the trail to her right as cries of, "There she is!" rang out all over the camp.

"Don't let her get away!" Jonas boomed.

Fearing at any moment to be taken down by one of Junior's arrows, Reecah never looked back, but the shot never came.

Running for her life, she felt more confident eluding the new pursuit than she did those she had encountered below Peril's Peak. This was her terrain. She knew the mountainside like it was her backyard—from the hidden climbs and caves to the deepest crevices and everything in between.

If not for the number of people Jonas had employed to catch her, she might have considered finding such a cave and lying low—the mountainside was expansive. It would be next to impossible to find her if she decided to hide, but the appearance of the uniformed troops unsettled her. She couldn't remain hidden forever.

The uniformed troops struck her as professional warriors. In her mind, her best defense was to put as much ground between them and herself and hope they would eventually tire of the chase.

As she ran, a slow rage simmered in the back of her mind. Junior's betrayal bothered her to distraction. She wasn't used to this level of anger. How dare he show her compassion and then shoot an arrow at Raver the next time they met?

Two days of steady jogging and fast walking saw Reecah and Raver enter the great valley beyond the Fang. From the noises Raver had made while they ventured up the coast, she was sure they were still being followed. By the time they rounded the Fang, however, Raver had lost sight of them.

Pausing to catch her breath in the shadow of the monolith, a slight smile spread across her glistening face. She'd outdistanced the special troops brought in to catch her. Unless

Reecah's Flight

they'd learned to fly, she was confident it would be a long time before Jonas' men ever got another whiff of her.

Satisfying as that thought might be, she couldn't escape the fact of where she was headed. The way north was precluded by an impassable landfall. The only route available to her lay east, up Dragonfang Pass. She searched the sky, thankful the only flying creature in sight was no bigger than a raven.

The last vestiges of daylight had left the valley of the dragons by the time Reecah entered the wide clearing where the hunt had slain Lurker's mother and the purple dragon all those months ago. She hadn't been sure it was the same clearing at first—the dragon bodies were gone and the signs of battle had been all but washed away with time.

It was tough to see in the dark but upon closer inspection, she could still see the faded scorch marks of dragon fire and the remnants of the scattered campfire.

Raver landed on a high tree limb jutting over the valley and watched her gather scattered wood from the hunt's campfire.

Using a flint stone to light a small fire, Reecah spread a thin blanket on the ground and called Raver to her. Together, they huddled beneath her brown cloak and listened to the night sounds as sleep overcame her. It had been a grueling stretch of days.

Reecah screeched, trying to throw off the weight that had suddenly fallen on her as she slept. Raver squawked, freeing himself from her cloak and winging away.

"There's the raven! I told you it was hers!" A high-pitched, male voice declared on the other side of the scratchy burlap sack thrown over her.

A raspy voice belonging to whoever pinned her shoulders answered, "Ya, ya, big deal. Help me hold her down! Where's the rope?"

Reecah's Flight

She kicked and punched, twisting and turning. "Let me go!"

"Easy, Reeky, or I'll gut you right here and be done with you."

A sharp point poked through the burlap and scraped her shoulder below her chin.

She screamed. "Jaxon! You creep. Let me go or else."

A strong hand reached beneath the shroud, feeling its way down her arm to her wrist and reefed her arm backward. If Jaxon's weight hadn't lifted from her, her arm would've surely broken as they flipped her on her side.

She kicked out, not hitting anything, but as soon as her legs were extended, someone wrapped their arms around her calves, pulled her boots off, and bound her ankles with rope.

Another hand pried at her other arm, wresting it free from beneath her, and wrenched it behind her back, rolling her onto her stomach.

Raver called out continuously from the treetop.

The more she strained, the more the thin ropes binding her wrists and ankles dug into her skin.

The pointed toe of a filthy black boot dug under her cheek and lifted her head off the ground. The shroud was ripped free and she found herself looking into the sickly, yellowed eyes of the weasel-faced, Viper.

He gave her a crooked-toothed grin and a slight nod, raising a single eyebrow. "Aye, missy. You're in a heap of trouble now."

The sight of Viper sapped the fight from her.

Jaxon strode up beside Viper, holding the burlap shroud over a forearm, a beaming grin splitting his impudent face. "And you thought you could outrun us. Maybe the fat ones like my uncle and father, but not me and Viper."

His words grated at her, filling her with revulsion. She wondered what she had ever done to Jaxon to deserve this type of treatment—other than giving him a deserved bloody nose on more than one occasion.

"You almost gave us the slip back there but you never counted on being tracked by someone skilled like me." Jaxon thumbed his chest.

Glancing from one man to the other, it was apparent they were quite happy with themselves. She was beginning to think the arrival of Jonas and the uniformed soldiers wouldn't be a bad thing. She might be able to talk sense into whoever the uniformed men were. Lying in the dirt at the feet of Jaxon and the snake was the last place she wanted to be.

"Now's your chance," Jaxon turned his attention on Viper, "to shut that damned bird up."

Viper grinned and pulled his crossbow over his shoulders. He reached into his bulging cloak and withdrew a small-tipped bolt.

Reecah rolled onto her side. "Raver, away!"

Raver took to the air, cawing incessantly into the darkness.

A blinding pain erupted in her stomach at the end of Jaxon's boot. "Silence, witch!"

"Stupid woman," Viper grunted and lowered his crossbow. "Don't you worry. I'll get the varmint yet."

Leaning his crossbow against a rock, Viper applied a heel to Reecah's shoulder, rolling her onto her back. He stooped over her waist and slid her sword from its sheath, nodding his head. "What have we here?"

Viper handed the thin handled sword to Jaxon.

"Wow, this is nicer than your sword." Jaxon tested the weight before handing it back to Viper.

Viper glared at him but didn't object. Placing the tip of Reecah's blade against her cheek, he asked, "Where does a worthless wench like you come by weapons like this?"

Reecah jerked her head sideways but didn't respond.

Viper followed her with the sword. "Steal them?"

Reecah's Flight

The campfire at her back prevented her from wriggling any farther. She glared at him, refusing to answer.

Viper placed the sword tip under her nose. "Have you ever tasted steel before?"

Her eyes crossed. She shook her head ever so slightly, sweat casting a flickering sheen on her face in the close proximity to the flames.

"Come on Viper. Joram won't be happy if you damage his prize," Jaxon said placing a hand on Viper's forearm.

Viper cast him a dirty look. "His prize? We caught her. She's rightfully ours."

Jaxon threw his hands up and stepped away. "Whatever you say, but don't expect me to lie for you when he gets here."

The sword in Viper's hand left Reecah's face and sliced up at Jaxon.

Jaxon jumped back. "Really? Have you lost your mind?"

Viper followed Jaxon away from the campfire, the sword still threatening. "Ain't no reason anyone needs to know we found her, is there?"

Jaxon appeared uncertain whether he should unsheathe his own sword and engage the greasy-haired snake or acquiesce. "Come on, Viper, what're you doing? That's Reeky. Nobody wants anything to do with her."

Viper tried to spit on the ground but it got caught on his lower lip and dribbled down his chin. He wiped it with a black cuff. "Pull your head out of your arse, boy. You need to forget your past and appreciate what lies before you."

Reecah didn't care for the sound of that. Nor did she like the way the confrontation was going. Jaxon would either back down, or Viper would kill him. Either way, it would end up the same for her.

She searched her surroundings—the edges of the clearing lost in shadow. Her bow lay on the ground along with her quiver and quarterstaff. They were useless with her hands tied behind her back.

Ducking her chin to her chest, she searched her belt. Her dagger! She squirmed and contorted, painfully reaching with her bound hands, trying to drag the sword belt along the ground to twist the dagger sheath to the side.

The dagger's handle touched the tip of her middle finger but she couldn't manoeuvre it any closer. With a painful stretch she grunted and slid the dagger free.

Raver sounded somewhere over the mountain nearby.

Viper and Jaxon looked skyward for a moment before casting their gaze her way. Their personal grievances temporarily forgotten, they walked toward her.

She tried using her bare heels to push away from them, but it was no use. She had nowhere to go.

"What are you up to, Reeky?" Jaxon asked and pointed his sword at her waist. "What's that in your hands?"

Viper caught sight of the dagger and dropped a knee on her chest, driving the wind from her lungs. She twisted one way and then another, almost throwing him, but quickly tired.

The vile man painfully twisted the dagger from her grasp. She thought for sure he would cut her with it as he held it for a moment between her eyes, but he rose to his feet.

"See, I told you. Nothing but trouble," Jaxon said. "Aren't you, Reeky?"

She nodded, a slow smile forming on her dirt-smudged face.

Both men frowned. Realizing she wasn't smiling at them, they spun around and were met by two angry dragons. One green, the other purple.

Lurker's mouth opened wide, a great roar splitting the night.

Viper's lightning fast reflexes lifted Reecah's sword in defense but Lurker was quicker.

Reecah's Flight

Reecah looked away as Lurker turned his head sideways and clamped his mouth on Viper's head. She cringed as Lurker's dagger-length fangs crunched into the man's skull.

Viper's scream made her skin crawl, as muffled as it was with his face firmly entrenched in Lurker's mouth. A moment later, the weasel-faced man was silenced forever—his throat ripped out with a vicious swipe of Lurker's front claws.

Jaxon stumbled away from the purple dragon.

Reecah rolled sideways, lifting her bound legs to trip him.

He tumbled into the campfire and scrambled to his knees—flames licking at his cloak. Without looking back, he ran screaming into the night, his arms flailing around to throw his burning cloak to the ground.

Reecah expected the dragons to go after him, but with slow, measured steps, they came for her.

Reecah's Flight

Circle of Trust

Reecah resisted the urge to scream but she couldn't stop herself from moving backward as fast as possible, sliding on one shoulder and then the other to keep from hurting her arms. She couldn't get the last words Lurker had spoken to her from her head:

I'm not your friend.
Leave here and never come back.
The next time I see you, I will kill you.

Lurker, noticeably bigger than the last time she had seen him, turned his head one way and then the other, matching her progress across the clearing.

The purple dragon, smaller than Lurker by a head, remained beside the campfire.

Raver called out from somewhere above. She stopped and glanced at the yawning abyss at her back.

Time stood still as Lurker towered over her, an emerald eye studying her from one side of his large head. Without warning he wrapped his mouth around the bottom of her legs.

Too scared to move, she expected to lose her feet but the pain never came. Lurker tugged at the rope binding her ankles, working it between his pointed teeth.

She frowned. "Are you freeing me?"

Lurker paused. He sniffed loudly through his nostrils and resumed gnashing his teeth back and forth.

Without the journal, she wouldn't be able to converse with him, but she knew he understood. "Thank you for saving me."

Reecah's Flight

Lurker's administrations pulled her back from the edge of the drop-off. At one point her backside lifted off the ground only to be dropped again as the binding loosened.

Raver fluttered to a lower branch and bobbed his head as if approving of Lurker's actions.

The rope shredded and her feet separated. She rolled herself until she could get to her knees and rose to her feet.

Lurker flung his head to the side, casting the rope to the aside.

Reecah considered her wrists. She didn't trust Lurker to sever the smaller binding without taking her hands with it.

She caught sight of her dagger beside Viper's mutilated body and went to retrieve it. Kicking the dagger away from the disgusting sight, she bent at the knees. She reached blindly behind her, struggling to keep from falling until she clasped the dagger's handle.

Carefully spinning the handle toward Lurker, she waggled it. "Here, take this. Can you hold it in your mouth so I can saw the rope apart?"

"Of course I can."

Reecah dropped the dagger and jumped forward, spinning to face him. "Did you just speak to me?"

Lurker's mouth never moved, but a voice sounded in her head, *"I don't see any other dragon around here but my purple friend over there and she doesn't say much."*

Reecah glanced around the dark clearing. The purple dragon hadn't moved. Other than Raver watching on with interest, there was only herself and Lurker in the clearing. "But how?"

"I sense magic in the rocks attached to your ears."

"Ahh." Reecah touched her earrings, a look of wonder on her face. "That's why Auntie Grim did this to me. How come I couldn't hear you before?"

"Because I hadn't allowed you into my circle of trust."

"Circle of trust?"

176

Reecah's Flight

"According to my mother…" He trailed off.

Reecah respected his silence, the pain of his mother's loss displayed in his eyes.

"According to my mother, dragons and people are different. Besides the obvious, we are inherently intelligent beings…" He must've noticed Reecah frowning at him. *"Yes, yes, so are people, but dragons are born from magic. Our growth is incredible in our early days. I hatched from an egg that was perhaps twice the size of your head. After eating the other eggs in the nest, I grew half my size again overnight."*

Reecah blinked at him, his words barely registering as she tried not to forget all the questions bumping around inside her head. He hadn't answered her question, but she couldn't help asking, "How old are you?"

As soon as the words left her mouth, she realized it was a silly question.

Lurker blinked, craning his neck to see the three-quarter moon in the western sky. *"Judging by the moon cycle, I am five."*

"Five years?"

A strange noise escaped his throat.

If Reecah wasn't mistaken, she had just heard a dragon laugh.

"Five months," Lurker said and lowered his mouth to the ground, grasping the dagger by the handle.

"That's what I thought. How, then, do you know so much? You speak as though you are many years older."

"I'm a dragon," he said as if that explained everything.

Reecah nodded, accepting his answer. Positioning her wrists over the dagger's edge, it didn't take long for the keen edge to sever the cord. Shaking the thin rope free, she massaged her chafed wrists and relieved Lurker of the dagger, all while trying to stifle a deep yawn.

"You're tired. Go lie by your fire. Nothing good will come of it if you don't sleep."

"But there are so many things I want to ask you."

Reecah's Flight

"There'll be plenty of time in the days to come. You'll need to be rested if you wish to keep ahead of those chasing you."

"You know of them?" Her heart pounded faster, fearing Lurker thought her responsible.

"We've been watching them since they entered our valley."

Reecah wondered who *we* were. Lurker and his purple friend? A sudden wave of guilt gripped her. She felt responsible for bringing the armed men and women into the dragons' territory. They were after her. She hung her head, unable to look Lurker in the eye. "I'm sorry they're here."

"I believe you."

She looked up in wonder. The guilt she'd been harbouring since Lurker's mother was killed lifted from her. She dared to smile.

"Now sleep. My friend and I will watch over you."

Relieved of the crushing burden she walked halfway to the fire and stopped. "One more thing."

Lurker inclined his head.

She swallowed, debating whether it was wise to broach the subject, but she had to know. "The last time we met, you told me to leave and never come back. That you would kill me if I did."

"Turn around."

She fretted, uncertain that was the best course of action in light of the conversation, but did as she was told. She emitted a short scream—the purple dragon stood right behind her. It lowered its chest to the ground and bowed its head. Clutched within the four claws of its right forepaw, was her journal.

"Take it."

Reecah accepted the journal.

"She is the reason."

Reecah faced Lurker. "I don't understand."

"The last time you entered the pass, you came across a dragon identical to my silent friend. She came from the same clutch. The one you comforted

178

Reecah's Flight

was pulled from their nest right after he was born and slaughtered on the ground. The evil men made a point of smashing the remaining eggs but they missed one." Lurker nodded toward the purple dragon. *"She hatched shortly afterward and witnessed the compassion you showed her dying brother."*

Reecah observed an excessive amount of moisture in the purple dragon's amethyst eyes.

"After I sent you away, she told me what you had done. It has taken me until now to reconcile my error. I see how your people treat you. I apologize. I believe you are as mother thought. A Windwalker. A dragon friend."

Something startled Reecah awake as the early morning light lifted the darkness from the pass. She had suddenly become cold and yet, the ground beside her felt unusually warm. As did the outside of her cloak, even though the fire appeared to have gone out long ago. Shivering, she needed to get up—her feet were like ice and her bladder was about to burst.

Raver made an unhappy chirp inside her cloak—the musty raven snuggled between her chest and chin.

She stroked the back of his head. "Come on, silly bird, I need to get up."

Raver pecked at her hand.

"Hey!" Reecah pushed him away and received a face full of flapping feathers. She sat up, watching him land on a nearby branch. "If you're not careful I'll feed you to the dragons."

"Too bony."

Reecah's nerves jumped. She wasn't used to the foreign presence in her head. Glancing toward the drop-off, Lurker stood where she had left him last night. Scanning the clearing, the purple dragon was gone. "Where's your friend?"

"She just left. I think she has taken a liking to you."

Reecah's Flight

Reecah located her boots sitting neatly beside each other and pulled them on. "Where'd she go?"

"Didn't say. You woke up as soon as she left you."

"Left *me*?"

"She slept next to you to keep you warm."

Reecah's eyes widened.

"It appears I'm not your only dragon friend."

A happiness filled her unlike anything she had ever experienced—a large smile dimpled her cheeks. Shaking the debris from her blanket, she folded it and placed it in her rucksack, before locating a nearby boulder. "I'll be right back."

Returning to the clearing, she fetched Viper's crossbow from the rock it leaned against. Just touching the weapon revulsed her. She carried it to the brink, leaned back, and hurled it away. The offensive weapon spun out of sight.

"I hope no one was down there."

"The men won't be down there. And even if they are…" She shrugged.

Lurker shook his head. *"I didn't mean people."*

Reecah cringed. "Oh. I never thought."

"Mother said people are often guilty of that."

She couldn't argue the point. Pulling a strip of dried meat from her pack, she tore a small piece off for Raver, but before she offered it to the raven, she considered Lurker. Glancing at the meagre portion she said, "Um, do you want some?"

Lurker tilted his head, regarding the scrap. His gaze took in the crimson stain on the ground behind her. *"I ate while you were sleeping."*

An eerie sensation crept up her spine. She swallowed her apprehension. Viper was gone. "Y-you mean…?"

Lurker nodded. *"Very greasy."*

Reecah spurted out a nervous laugh. "I wouldn't be surprised if he gives you indigestion."

Lurker burped. *"Too late."*

Reecah's Flight

She smiled. Never in her wildest dreams had she envisioned having a conversation like this with a dragon, and yet, here she was. It didn't seem real.

"You should continue into the valley while I scout the people following you. They were a full day behind when I left them to investigate the noise your friend was making."

"My friend?"

Lurker glanced at Raver pruning himself, a scruffy wing held high as he pecked at the feathers underneath.

"Oh!"

"For a little guy, he makes a lot of noise."

"Tell me about it."

"If not for him we wouldn't have known of your trouble."

She smiled, considering her best friend. "Ya, he's a real gem."

"I'll find you later."

"Wait! What do I do if I come across a dragon?"

"Pray they don't like greasy meat."

Reecah's Flight

Swoop

Travelling through the forested slopes of Dragonfang Pass, the midday sun streamed long rays through the forest canopy. Reecah questioned what she was actually doing there. Yes, she was being hunted by Jonas and the people in uniform. Why they wanted her so badly, she couldn't fathom. Just because they claimed she was a witch didn't justify the lengths they were going through to catch her.

She debated her options. With her climbing skills, she was far enough into the pass that eluding them wouldn't prove too difficult. Someone like Jaxon might give her trouble, but once she got beyond them it would be a simple matter of slipping across Peril's Peak and making her way to Thunderhead.

The idea resonated with her. Other than the mountain slopes around Fishmonger Bay, she'd never been anywhere. Perhaps it was time to see the world. She had loved studying Poppa's old maps and listening to him go on about wondrous cities like Madrigail Bay or the duke's city of Carillon where a magnificent castle was being built. Poppa said the castle had been under construction for hundreds of years. He claimed it would someday surpass the high king's palace at Sea Keep—wherever that was.

The ridgeline she followed bent sharply around a massive spur of bare rock. Rounding its base, the trees fell away, revealing a stunning vista. A lush green valley, interspersed with waterfalls tumbling from inaccessible heights, stretched away to the eastern horizon. The lofty crags on the far side paralleled the one she stood on—the valley seemingly an endless furrow, carved out of the living rock during the world's creation by a harrow wielded by the gods.

As stunning as the view was, it paled in comparison to what filled the air. Dozens of dragons both near and far soared upon the wind, lazily curling one way or another, their horned heads searching the steep slopes.

So absorbed in their fantastical beauty, she never saw the dragon drop out of the sky above her. With nary a sound, it touched down behind her—the wind its wings produced as it caught its descent fluttered her cloak.

She jumped, screaming, and held her hand over her heart. "You scared the life from me."

Lurker tilted his head as if contemplating her remark. *"You seem alive to me."*

Frowning at first, she broke into a smile. "It's a figure of speech."

Lurker tilted his head the other way.

"It's an expression. I didn't mean it literally."

"Literally?"

"Yes. I didn't mean you killed me, I just meant…" Flustered she threw her hands in the air. "It doesn't matter. You scared me. Let's leave it at that."

Lurker nodded once, apparently accepting her explanation.

He had grown a head taller since their first meeting in the spring. Reecah found herself having to look up to meet his gaze. "Any news on the others?"

His face became serious.

"What is it? Are they close?"

"They are still a long way off. I left them where we slept last night."

That was alarming. She glanced back but the western end of the valley was hidden from view by the rock spur. Jonas' men were half a day away. If she wasn't careful, someone like Jaxon might catch her unawares.

Reecah's Flight

"I'm surprised the dragon community allows a force like that into the valley."

"We don't like it, but they are properly armed. To go against them will bring much death to my kind. Our numbers are dwindling. We dare not lose any more dragons."

Walking at a faster pace, she said, "I must keep moving."

Lurker followed her around an outcropping of fallen boulders into a thicker patch of forest. *"I had better remain with you if you plan on going this way."*

"Why? Isn't it a good idea?" Reecah asked, but she already knew the answer.

"The colony is stirring. They're aware of those following you."

Reecah considered his words but a movement in a wide clearing to her right caught her attention.

The forest parted at the base of a steep hollow in the mountainside. Approaching the concaved rockface, she froze.

High above, a brown dragon swooped from a ledge, its nose coming dangerously close to hitting a tree that protruded from the cliffside. It adjusted its wings to swoop up and over the tree before diving toward the clearing.

184

Reecah's Flight

Reecah pulled back, bumping into Lurker. She clung to his scaly shoulder to keep from stepping on his toes and offered him the innocent smile she used to undermine Poppa. "Oh. I'm so sorry. I stumbled."

"No need to apologize Reecah. I will always support you."

She took a chance and rubbed his neck. "Aww, thank you. I'll always support you too."

Lurker's smile left her giddy. Even now, she couldn't believe it. Her hand on Lurker's scaly hide, they observed the brown dragon, no bigger than Lurker, ride the currents swirling around the unusual hollow in the mountainside.

"Pretty, isn't she?"

Reecah glanced at her dragon friend but his attention was on the brown dragon. "Very. That's a female dragon then?"

Lurker regarded her with a funny expression. *"Is it not obvious?"*

Reecah studied the brown dragon. Other than her colour, and two extra horns sprouting from each cheek, and two smaller horns near the end of her snout, nothing differentiated her from Lurker. "Um, yes. Of course."

Lurker stared at skeptically but she kept her attention on the female dragon.

Landing on what appeared to be nothing but the side of the cliff, the brown dragon's claws dug into the rock face. She remained there for a moment before dropping earthward. Spreading her wings wide, she caught an updraft and swooped up and over the treetops behind them, before soaring back into sight and finding another place to land.

"What's she doing?"

"Nothing really. She does this all the time. Just enjoying how she can ride the wind, I guess."

Enraptured, Reecah gazed in wonder, imagining how amazing it would be to do just that. "What's her name?"

"You wouldn't be able to pronounce it."

Reecah's Flight

"Oh, right. You said people can't pronounce dragon names."

"People have short memories."

"Ha-ha. Selective, more like."

"Selective?"

"Never mind."

"People are hard to understand."

"You're telling me," Reecah said. Staring at Lurker's puzzled expression she laughed. "Ya, I know. You just did."

She stood at the edge of the clearing with her dragon friend, observing the brown dragon play in the wind and couldn't help feeling envious.

She was about to say as much but noticed the peculiar way Lurker watched the female dragon; a subtle smile on his lips, and longing in his eyes.

"Do you know her?"

"I know of her. I've never actually met her. She comes here everyday."

"Why don't you introduce yourself?"

Lurker's scaly face scrunched up. *"Oh no. I couldn't do that."*

"Why not?"

Lurker didn't respond. Instead, he hung his head and started back into the forest.

"Where are you going?"

"We should get moving before the people catch up."

Reecah smiled. The thought of meeting the female dragon intimidated him. "Wait a minute."

Lurker stopped.

"You're sweet on her, aren't you?"

"Sweet on her?"

"You know? You like her. You have feelings for her." She wasn't positive but it appeared like Lurker's green face flushed. "Come on. Introduce yourself."

"It's okay. We should go."

Reecah contemplated the bashful dragon and nodded to herself. Stepping into the middle of the clearing, she looked up.

Reecah's Flight

It took a moment to locate the brown dragon perched on a broken tree trunk near the top of the cliff. Putting her fingers to her lips, she whistled.

"What are you doing? Do you want to get eaten?"

She swallowed. She hadn't thought of that. "You'll just have to protect me."

She couldn't be sure, but it seemed like the brown dragon watched her. To make sure, she jumped up and down waving her arms. "Swoop down here! There's someone who wants to meet you!"

"Reecah!" Lurker backstepped farther into the woods.

She glanced at him with a mischievous smile. "Aw, come on. Don't be shy. Look, I think she's coming."

The brown dragon dropped off the trunk without flapping her wings—plummeting headlong. An ear-piercing shriek echoed off the mountain face.

"Reecah!"

The brown dragon dropped like a stone, adjusting her wings to fly straight at Reecah.

By the time Reecah realized her folly, it was too late. Throwing her hands over her head she fell to her knees and crouched low.

Lurker rushed from the trees, stepping over her and sheltering her with his body.

The brown dragon adjusted its wings at the last moment to land heavily beside them. Her eyes on Reecah, she shrieked again.

Lurker shrieked back.

Reecah feared they were going to fight right on top of her.

Lurker sounded in her head, *"She wants to eat you. Says you look tasty."*

Reecah crawled farther beneath his body, unsure whether to take that as a compliment or not.

A lengthy silence ensued.

Reecah's Flight

Reecah hazarded a glance from between Lurker's forelegs. "What's happening?"

"*It's okay. You can come out. I explained to her who you are.*"

She hesitated. "And that is?"

"*A Windwalker.*"

"Heh. I don't know what that really means myself. Are you sure she won't attack?"

"*Pretty sure.*"

Reecah started crawling out but stopped. "That's not reassuring."

"*I promise I won't eat you,*" a female voice sounded in her head. "Lurker?"

"*That wasn't me. That was...*" Lurker said a word that sounded like a jumble of mumbled grunts.

"How can she talk to me? I thought you were the only one."

"*I have allowed you into my circle of trust. Temporarily,*" the brown dragon answered.

Reecah attempted to steady her breathing. She was now capable of talking to two dragons! Crawling out from beneath Lurker, she kept him between them. She forced a nervous smile. "Hi, my name is, Reecah Draakvriend. Pleased to meet you."

The brown dragon took her gaze off Reecah. "*I thought you said she was a Windwalker?*"

"*She is descended from the Windwalkers. For some reason she goes by another name,*" Lurker responded.

"*Perhaps she's ashamed of being a Windwalker. How well do you know this human? Grimclaw claims the king's men are coming this way. How do you know she isn't with them?*"

The king's men? Reecah unconsciously fingered her sword hilt, ensuring the blade sat properly within its sheath. So that's who the people in uniform were. Why would king's troops be after her? According to Poppa, the royal palace was weeks away by foot.

Reecah's Flight

An awkward silence ensued. Judging by their changing facial expressions, the dragons were communicating privately.

Lurker's voice startled her. Mentioning the brown dragon's name, he said, *"...is satisfied on my word that you are not a threat. You may relax."*

"I hope her trust lasts." Reecah cringed as soon as she spoke. The brown dragon could hear her as well.

Reecah lowered her eyes, embarrassed. "My apologies..." She searched for a way to address the female dragon. "I cannot say your name. Do you go by a different one?"

The brown dragon glanced at Lurker.

The dragons' conversation sounded in Reecah's mind. *"I told you. People are different. They go by many names."*

"That sounds confusing."

"She refers to me as Lurker."

"Lurker?" The brown dragon smiled and turned her attention on Reecah. *"I like that. It suits you."* She winked at Reecah.

The astonishing gesture allowed Reecah to relax—she sensed they had just shared an intimate secret.

"What would you name me?"

The brown dragon's question threw Reecah. She was afraid to call the female dragon anything in case it offended her and broke their tentative bond.

\The brown dragon leaned in closer, waiting for an answer.

Reecah gulped. If the dragons spoke in her head, did that mean they were able to read her mind? She would have to speak to Lurker about that. Glancing at him, it didn't appear as though her thoughts had registered.

She had named Lurker because of his habit of perching above her and lurking when he had first started following her. Thinking about the brown dragon's penchant to dive through the air and glide back up again, she said, "If it's alright with you, I shall call you Swoop."

Reecah's Flight

Exposed

Lurker flew off halfway through the afternoon to scout the progress of the king's men and hadn't returned by the time the sun dropped behind the western spur of the great valley.

Pulling her cloak tight to ward off the evening chill, Reecah watched Raver flit from one nearby tree to another, keeping pace at his leisure. With the increased dragon activity, she feared for his safety, but Lurker's earlier comment about Raver being a poor food source provided her with a little consolation.

Unable to see sufficiently in the encroaching twilight, she stopped at the bottom of a small waterfall. The cascade fell from unseen heights, through the leafy forest canopy, into a large pool. The pool overflowed and tumbled across her path—a babbling brook meandering lazily down the forested slope.

Checking her rucksack, she sighed and let it fall to the ground. She was out of food. She filled her waterskin and drank her fill of fresh mountain water, hoping to ease her cramping stomach.

Watching the eddies at the base of the falls, she couldn't recall the last time she'd bathed. She followed the stream a short way through the darkening forest to where it dropped over a precipice to the valley below. Standing on the edge of the forest, she scanned the dark skies for nearby dragons. Shrieks echoed throughout the valley but none of the calls sounded close, so she returned to the waterfall and risked a quick wash.

Reecah's Flight

Getting a small fire burning, she removed her boots, cloak and breeks, and waded into the pool up to her knees; pleasantly surprised at how warm the water felt compared to the air.

Raver landed on her cloak and watched her remove the rest of her clothing. Rubbing her clothes together to wash away the worst of the accumulated grime and sweat, she wrung them out and tossed them on a flat rock at the water's edge. Undoing her tight braid, she shook out her long hair, enjoying how good it felt to scratch her scalp.

A sudden premonition of someone watching caused her to submerge herself up to her neck and examine the darkening shadows in the flickering firelight.

The only one visible to her was Raver, watching her and blinking. That provided her with a momentary sense of relief until he abruptly turned to stare off into the forest as if something had caught his attention.

She swallowed. Surely if someone was nearby, Raver would have known of their presence before now. She followed his eyes to the deeper forest shadows. *Something* had diverted Raver's attention.

"Lurker?" she whispered.

Other than distant dragon song and crickets, she heard nothing except the incessant cascading water.

After a while, she released her apprehension in a long slow breath and dunked her head beneath the water to scrub at her hair. Breaking the surface, she shook the water from her eyes. If her heart hadn't caught in her throat, she would have screamed.

Jonas Junior stood at the water's edge, his unbuckled sword belt in hand.

Raver squawked from the boughs of a tree, his warning too late.

Junior dropped his sword belt and hopped around on one foot, struggling to remove a boot. "Are you okay?"

Reecah's Flight

Reecah glanced at her clothes. They might as well be on the far side of the valley. Sinking lower in the water, she asked, "What're you doing here?"

Junior stopped pulling his boot off, his cheeks red. "I, um, came to find you. I thought you were drowning." His stare intensified. "What happened to your shoulder?"

"My shoulder?" She tucked her chin against her collar bone and looked at the scabbed over abrasion Jaxon's knife had left. "Oh that. A present from your brother."

Junior nodded, not appearing surprised by her answer.

She didn't know what else to say. All of her possessions lay beside the campfire. Looking behind her for an escape route, the thought of running naked through Dragonfang Pass didn't strike her as a good idea, but what choice did she have?

"You need to get out of there." Junior glanced around the flickering clearing. "Jaxon will be here shortly with a bunch of others. If he finds you…" He lowered his eyes to the ground, not meeting hers. "…especially like this, you'll be in serious trouble."

"Were you spying on me?" she asked, an edge to her voice. It seemed like a moot question considering the danger she was in, but she couldn't help herself—her cheeks flamed red. She felt violated.

"Huh?"

"How long have you been watching me?"

"Watching you?" he squeaked, the lie plainly apparent. He laughed nervously. "I just got here."

"Liar! Liar!"

They both looked at Raver, the flames glinting off his shiny feathers.

"Well," Junior started but seemed to struggle with what he wanted to say. "I, um, didn't want to intrude, but when you went under—"

Reecah's Flight

"You *were* spying on me!" Reecah moved to stand up and have a go at the insolent man but stopped herself in time.

"Okay, okay, sorry. I didn't see anything. Well, not really." He wouldn't meet her gaze. "Look, I just wanted to warn you."

"You led the king's men to my hut and tried to kill Raver."

Junior frowned. "Raver?"

"My bird. You shot an arrow at him."

Junior nodded. "Ah. The other day? I had no choice. They were watching me."

Reecah didn't believe him. "Watching you?"

"My father. My uncle. My brother. They're waiting for me to expose myself. Father keeps me on a short leash. They suspect I tipped you off in the spring. Father's looking for an excuse to disown me."

Reecah didn't know what he was talking about. Nor did she care. Junior was a Waverunner, and like Raver so aptly said, Waverunner's were liars.

She cast a worried glance into the forest. "Where are the others? If you're on such a short leash, how come you're here on your own?"

"I pointed the trackers up that crag." He pointed to where the waterfall fell through the trees. "I slipped away and followed you here."

"How did you know where I was without the trackers?"

A smile brightened his chiselled features, his vibrant green eyes finding hers. "Father doesn't know it, but I can track better than any of them. I found the routes you used to outdistance us back home."

That threw her. Not knowing how to respond, she continued glaring her displeasure.

"I learned from the best at an early age."

She couldn't help herself. "Oh yeah, and who would that be?"

"Viliyam Draakvriend."

Reecah's Flight

Reecah made a conscious effort to keep her jaw from dropping. "You're a liar."

"Liar! Liar!"

Junior cast an irritated glance at Raver. "Whether you believe me or not, it's the truth."

She didn't know if she should be appalled or angry that Poppa had taught one of the Waverunners anything. She was sure Poppa hadn't held Jonas in high esteem and Grammy had detested him.

"Come on." He glanced at her clothes. "Get dressed. You need to get away from here. Jaxon isn't as stupid as he looks. He'll soon realize I sent him the wrong way."

If Junior thought she was about to just step out of the water stark naked, he was gravely mistaken. Her narrowed eyes darted between him and her clothes.

Junior lowered his gaze, looking at her from beneath lowered brows. "I, um, I'll go stand over there." He pointed at a large boulder on the edge of the brook. "Just make it quick."

"My clothes are soaking wet!"

Junior shrugged. "I don't know what to tell you. I'd offer you my cloak but the others will wonder what I did with it."

"Put my cloak on the rock and leave me." Reecah indicated the same stone her clothes lay on.

He did as she asked and disappeared behind the boulder.

Not trusting him for a moment, she crawled through the water to the shoreline and stretched an arm out to grasp her cloak.

It was impossible to tell whether he peeked around the boulder. "You better not be looking!"

His muffled reply mollified her. "I'm not. Just hurry."

She jumped to her feet and lifted her cloak in front of her. Looking around, shivering, she wondered, *now what?* Her clothes were soaked. If she pulled her cloak on, it would be also.

Reecah's Flight

She sidestepped to stand with her back to the fire and her eyes on the boulder, appreciating the warmth.

"Are you decent?"

"Stay where you are!" she snapped, humiliated.

"What's taking so long? Jaxon will be along anytime now."

She sighed. Struggling to keep her cloak from exposing her to prying eyes, she rummaged through her rucksack and dried herself with her blanket as best she could.

With the deftest of movements, she slipped into her cloak and tied it tight. Stepping on her blanket she dried her feet and sat down to pull on her boots.

Getting to her feet she gathered her wet clothes and jammed them into her rucksack along with her blanket—the bag nearly bursting at its seams. She grabbed her sword belt attached to its wide cummerbund and buckled them around her midsection. Throwing her bow and quiver over opposite shoulders, and sliding her vambraces over her forearms, she retrieved her quarterstaff and faced the boulder.

"Okay, you can come out, but don't get too close, or else." She swallowed. Or else what? She felt silly standing there looking the way she did. The cold night air blew against her bare shins between the hem of her cloak and the top of her calf-high boots. Her wet hair hung in tangles down her back, soaking her cloak anyway. The amused look on Junior's face as he gave her a once over did little to appease her self esteem.

"I think it's best if you come with me," Junior started to say but stopped when Reecah hastily strung her bow and pulled an arrow from her quiver.

He put his hands up. "Whoa, girl. It's just an idea. You can't keep running. If I can catch you, you can bloody well bet it's only a matter of time before the *real* trackers do."

Reecah didn't respond. There was no way she was about to go off with Junior. For all she knew, he could be trying to trick her like he had on more than one occasion.

Reecah's Flight

"What're you doing way out here?" He gestured at the forest with open hands. "Even without my father after you, parading around Dragonfang Pass is hardly a sane thing to do."

"I can take care of myself."

He gave her another once over. "I can see that. I found you in the dark, unarmed and without any—"

"Ya, ya. You got lucky. It won't happen again."

"You never answered my question. What're you doing out here? And don't say running from my father. I know you better than that. You're more skilled in the mountains than all of Jaxon's tracker friends put together. You could easily get by them and escape this cursed place if you wanted to."

She lowered the bow. "For one thing, I don't find this place cursed. For another, it's none of your business."

Junior blinked at her. "Then you're as crazy as Father says. The dragons are agitated. Unless you travel in a pack, you won't survive long on your own. Come on, I'll help you get past Father. From there you can go off to Thunderhead or wherever you wish."

Reecah tilted her head. "Why would I trust you? Not only are you a Waverunner, you look exactly like your father."

Junior's voice gained an edge, a hurt look transforming his features. "I'm nothing like my father."

She was shocked at his reaction. If she wasn't so worried about what he really had planned for her, she might have apologized.

"Look. I can't help what you think about me. Was I an ass to you when we were growing up? Yes. Believe it or not, if I could take back all the stupid things I said and did to you back then, I would. Heck, I would take back everything I said and did to everyone. Don't think you're special."

He sighed, staring with concern to the west—toward the place where Jaxon would be coming. "Like it or not, you're

Reecah's Flight

going to have to trust me. Tell me where you're going and I'll do what I can to direct my father in the opposite direction."

"Tell them I went home."

"Reecah, they're not stupid. Jaxon will find your tracks. Besides, they aren't leaving the pass anytime soon. The king's men are here to eradicate the dragon colony. The farther away from here you are, the better."

A cold chill passed through Reecah. "Eradicate the dragons? I thought they were here to—"

"What? Kill you?" Junior laughed. "You think highly of yourself, Draakvriend. They're here to put an end to the dragons once and for all. More troops have landed in Fishmonger Bay and are on their way to join us. Elite forces, according to Father."

Reecah swallowed her horror. Lurker and Swoop were in grave danger. She needed to warn them. Thinking it was odd they hadn't returned to her, she felt like she'd been punched in the stomach. Maybe they were already dead.

"H-have they killed any more dragons?"

Junior muttered, "How would I know? I've been too busy trying to find you. As far as I know, we have nothing to do with the king's men other than showing them how to access the pass. We travel with them to keep safe while we search for you."

Her mind reeled. She had to do something. "How well do you know the valley?"

Junior seemed taken aback. "I-I don't, really. Less than you, I would imagine."

That wasn't the answer she wanted. "Have you heard of the Dragon Temple?"

Junior frowned, nodding. "Aye. Many times. It's rumoured to be protected by a legendary black dragon. Why?"

"No reason. Do you know where it is?"

"Why don't you ask your dragon friend?"

Reecah's Flight

She studied his face. She wasn't happy Junior knew about her relationship with Lurker. "Okay. Well, like you said, I've got to get going."

"Let me come with you. You'll be in grave danger from both sides once the king's men engage the dragons. What's so important that you want to risk your life?"

Her hands tightened on her bow and arrow. She couldn't decide whether to trust Junior or not. He was a Waverunner, after all, but other than Lurker, she had nobody to confide in. Junior had been the only person since Auntie Grim's death who had shown her any kindness, and yet...

"I need to find something. In the temple. Please, if you know where it is, I need to know."

Junior shook his head. "I already told you I don't. This is the farthest I've ever been down the valley. If it were up to me, I'd be high-tailing it home. Let me help you."

She desperately wanted to trust him, but given his family history, that would be foolish. Gritting her teeth, angry at herself for divulging her intentions, she restrained from verbally lashing out at him. "I'm better off on my own."

Adjusting her equipment, her mind returned to the fact that she wore a cloak and nothing else. She pointed the arrow at him, searching for a way to cross the brook without getting wet. "Don't you dare follow me or I'll put this between your eyes."

Junior glowered but made no attempt to stop her.

She skipped across several rocks in the stream and landed on the far bank, not quite believing she had threatened Junior with his life. It had been her voice talking, but it certainly felt like someone else had said it.

"Raver, to me!"

Raver squawked and flew unerringly to her, landing on her raised arm.

Reecah's Flight

She half ran, half walked sideways, ensuring Junior didn't follow.

The man's profile flickered in the dying light of her abandoned campfire. He called after her, "If I had wanted to shoot your bird, I wouldn't have missed."

She frowned. What was that supposed to mean? When she had put enough distance between them, she concentrated on the ground in front of her, careful not to trip over the underbrush or go falling off an unseen cliff in the darkness.

\

Reecah's Flight

The Drop-off

Swoop found Reecah wandering aimlessly across an open expanse of mountainside halfway through the night.

Stumbling across a wide glade, her mind not fully on the task at hand, she couldn't push Junior from her thoughts. What was the eldest Waverunner boy up to? He had betrayed her twice already, and yet, there was something strangely comforting about his presence. She shook her head, her cheeks reddening as she imagined what Junior might have seen at the base of the waterfall. Just thinking about it raised her dander.

Hearing Swoop's approach, Reecah dove into the tall grass and Raver flew away.

"Fear not, Reecah. It's me." Swoop's voice sounded in her head.

"Swoop. Thank the gods, you're okay. Where's Lurker?"

"He comes. I just let him know where you are. He was worried about you. He said you scared the life from him, whatever that means. He seems alive to me."

Despite how tired, hungry and cold she was, Reecah couldn't keep from laughing out loud.

Swoop's dark form detached itself from the cloud cover as she spread her wings, catching the wind and easing herself gracefully to the field. She craned her neck to the west. *"Here he comes now."*

Reecah couldn't see what Swoop was looking at, but Lurker's voice sounded in her mind, *"There you are. I feared you were taken by the king's men or worse."*

Reecah's Flight

Lurker appeared over the edge of the forest, back flapping as he landed in front of her—his emerald eyes catching the little light filtering through the clouds and glowing in the darkness. He sniffed at her. *"Are you alright?"*

"I'm okay. I was beginning to worry the hunters had…" Shivering uncontrollably, she couldn't finish her thought. "Anyway, I see they didn't."

"What happened to you? Your hair's a mess and your clothing is different."

"It's a long story. Apart from freezing to death and feeling a little hungry, I'm okay. Just tired."

The concern on Lurker's face was obvious. *"You're freezing to death?"*

"My clothes are wet but I'm afraid to stop and make a fire in case the men catch me." She went on to describe her encounter with Junior at the waterfall. Both dragons listened closely.

Swoop padded over when she finished. *"You needn't worry about being caught tonight. They're a good way back. Lurker and I will watch over you."* She turned her horned head Lurker's way. *"People are fragile things. Lie down and keep her warm."*

Lurker didn't question Swoop. He dropped low and lay on his side—his bottom wing stretched out on the grass like a large blanket.

"Remove your wet clothing and lie close," Swoop instructed as if it was a natural thing to do.

"Most of my clothes are in here." She shrugged out of her rucksack. "I'll keep my cloak on."

Swoop examined her. *"The back of your cloak is wet. Take it off and throw it onto a pile with the rest of your clothes. I will see to them."*

Reecah wasn't convinced stripping naked was a good idea. Unconsciously searching the clearing and the wall of trees for peeping eyes, she admonished herself. Of course, there was no one around. Even so, she was bashful about baring herself in front of the dragons, which, as she thought about it, was silly.

Reecah's Flight

Taking into consideration their scaled bodies, leathery wings and ivory horns, they couldn't be any more different from her. To them, she was just another animal.

She sighed. If she didn't get warm soon, she would be in trouble. Unbuckling her sword belt and undoing the ties on her cloak, she took another look around before slipping free of the wet garment and looking questioningly at Lurker's outstretched wing.

"It's okay, Reecah. You won't hurt me. Get on."

"Wait. Where's Raver?"

Swoop cast a glance around the clearing. *"Over there in a tree. He'll be okay."*

Reecah tried to identify which tree Swoop looked at but couldn't see much in the darkness. The cold night left goosebumps all over her body. Swallowing her misgivings, she timidly crawled onto the underside of Lurker's wing, surprised at how soft the leathery surface felt on her skin.

"Get close to my body," Lurker said, curling his wing around her and holding her against him.

As bizarre as the scenario struck her, she snuggled into Lurker's warm embrace. A huge smile creased her face as her worries seeped away. Lying vulnerable in a dragon's embrace, she felt more content than she had in her entire life, with the exception of that magical day she and Poppa had sat on the hill discussing how high she could fly.

Swoop's voice sounded as if from a dream. *"Reecah, dear. Wake up."*

"Leave her. She had a rough night," Lurker purred, squeezing his wing tighter around Reecah.

"Humans are coming. We must be gone from here."

Lurker sighed. *"Alright. Give me a moment. She's so soft."*

Swoop rolled her eyes.

Reecah's Flight

Reecah snuggled in, never wanting the magical experience to end. If she were to die right then in the dragon's embrace, she would die happy.

"You'll be sorry if they catch her."

"Did you bring her clothes back?"

Reecah's eyes popped open. She wasn't sure whether they knew she could hear them or not. What had they done with her clothes?

"Of course. Dry as brimstone."

"I'm surprised they did it at all."

"They weren't happy about it, but after I explained who we think she is, Grimclaw insisted on doing it himself."

Reecah felt Lurker shudder.

"You actually spoke with him?"

Swoop laughed. *"Grimclaw? You're kidding, right? I waited outside the temple gate."*

"Temple gate?" Reecah asked, putting her hands against the edge of Lurker's wing and popping her head into the bright sunlight.

"You're awake. Good." Lurker adjusted his wing to help her stand on the ground and glanced at Swoop. *"Did you bring her food?"*

Swoop hung her head. *"I don't know what humans eat."*

"No worries. I'll be back." Lurker spread his wings, jumped into the air, and disappeared west, beyond the treeline.

Reecah wrapped her arms around herself, looking for her clothes. The air temperature had risen considerably since last night but after enjoying Lurker's warmth, the morning breeze was fresh on her exposed skin.

\"Here, I had someone dry your clothes while you slept." Swoop stepped sideways revealing her garments.

Conscious of her nakedness, Reecah scanned the area as she pulled her breeks on. "How did you dry them so well? They aren't damp at all."

Reecah's Flight

"Fire."

"Fire." She inspected them for damage, but found none. "I didn't think you were old enough to spout fire."

"An adult did it for me."

"The one called Grimclaw?"

Swoop's head perked up. *"You know him?"*

Lacing up her tunic she laughed. "No, silly. I heard you talking about him. Is Lurker afraid of Grimclaw?"

Swoop nodded. *"Everyone's afraid of Grimclaw. At least the smart ones."*

"Why's that?"

"Why's that? Grimclaw is the ancient wyrm of the Draakclaw Clan," Swoop answered as if that explanation was all that was required.

Buckling her wide cummerbund, with attached sword belt beneath her breasts, Reecah frowned. "What makes old Grimclaw so scary? Is he mean?"

Swoop looked around like she feared another dragon might be listening. *"Grimclaw is our leader. He protects the ancestral tomb."*

"Is that the same place as the Dragon Temple?"

Swoop's eyes narrowed. *"Why?"*

Reecah stopped dressing, sensing she had hit a nerve. She couldn't very well tell Swoop she was thinking of stealing the Dragon's Eye from their sacred tomb. "Um, no reason. Just curious."

Swoop's brow furrowed but thankfully didn't pursue the matter.

Pulling on her boots, Reecah grabbed her sword belt and pretended to be busy concentrating on getting the buckle adjusted properly. She was relieved when Lurker's voice entered her mind.

"Reecah, good news. I brought you something to eat."

Swoop must have heard him as well. They both searched the western sky.

Reecah's Flight

Raver had no sooner squawked from the tip of a lofty pine when Lurker appeared over the treeline, gently flapping his wings. Something small dangled from each of his front feet.

He landed with barely a sound on his rear legs and held his front feet forward, a toothy grin directed at Reecah. *"You shall hunger no longer."*

Reecah stepped forward to inspect what he had brought and stepped back in disgust. "They're still alive! That's gross. I don't eat rats."

Swoop regarded the catch, licking her lips.

Lurker looked puzzled. *"I don't understand. I thought humans were meat eaters."*

Reecah turned up her nose. "We are, but we don't eat vermin."

Swoop's voice sounded demure. *"I'll have one if she doesn't want it."*

Lurker looked between the two, not seeming sure how to proceed.

Reecah smiled for his benefit and used her eyes to direct him to give one to Swoop.

Lurker threw the largest one at Swoop who snatched it out of the air with her mouth and crunched into it—the rat emitting a loud squeak.

"Mmm. Thank you."

Lurker smiled shyly, the second rat biting at his claws. *"You want this one too?"*

"Sure." Swoop swallowed the first one, bones and all, before catching the second, flailing rat.

Reecah wrinkled her nose, cringing at the sound of crunching bones.

Lurker's happy gaze remained on Swoop until Reecah asked, "Did you happen to see the men while you were off chasing rats?"

Reecah's Flight

"Huh?" Lurker refocused on her. *"Oh, yes. They were at the waterfall you spoke of last night."*

"I'd better get moving."

"What about food?"

Shrugging into her quiver and bow, Reecah said, "Can't do much about it right now. Hopefully I'll catch something as I go."

"I'll fetch you something more befitting a human. I know just where to find one. Swoop, take Reecah to the drop-off. It's time we introduced her to the colony. I'll find you." Lurker didn't wait for a response. He took two quick steps and launched himself into the air.

Watching Lurker wing up the mountain and disappear over a distant ridge, Reecah couldn't keep her knees from shaking. She wasn't ready to meet a colony of dragons.

Using her quarterstaff as a walking stick, Reecah grimaced at the way Swoop clomped along behind her. With the female dragon crashing about, she would be lucky to get within a league of something to shoot with her bow. She hoped Lurker wouldn't be too long. She was starving.

Not far into their trek, Swoop said, *"Follow me."* And led Reecah to the edge of the steep bluff separating the mountainside from the valley below. *"I'll meet you at the bottom."*

Reecah studied the edge of the drop-off. "How am I supposed to get down there?"

"There aren't many ways on this end of the pass for non-fliers to access the valley floor. If you look closely, you'll see the way down. At least that's what Father says."

"Your father?"

"Yes. He told me a moon cycle ago about humans visiting Dragon Home."

"Dragon Home?"

"Our colony. It lies close to here, across the valley."

Reecah's Flight

Reecah raised her eyebrows but said no more. Studying the landfall at her feet, she couldn't see anywhere to even begin descending the sheer drop. Kneeling to inspect the edge, she shook her head. "You sure this is the right spot?"

Swoop prepared to take to the sky. *"Pretty sure."* She jumped into the air and spread her wings, gliding into the valley far below. Her distant voice reached Reecah. *"According to Father, Marinah and Davit Windwalker often came this way."*

If she hadn't been kneeling already, Reecah was certain she would've fallen over the brink. Marinah and Davit? Her mother and uncle? They weren't Windwalkers. They were Draakvriends. Swoop's father must have been mistaken.

A heated exchange Grammy once had with Poppa came to mind. One she had replayed many times in her head after Poppa's death.

She couldn't recall where her grandparents were standing but she could still hear Grammy saying, *"We agreed not to fill her head with this dragon nonsense."*

"I know, but—"

"But nothing! You want Reecah to end up like her mother, father and uncle?"

"No, but—"

"Dammit, Viliyam! She's all we have left of Marinah."

Staring at Swoop's receding form, another conversation bombarded her. One she had with Grimelda three years ago, while arguing about the dangers of dragons.

She remembered it like it had happened yesterday. Her own words sounded in her mind, *"The high king is justified in his thinking. Dragons are dangerous. They killed my parents and uncle Davit."*

"Oh, they most certainly are dangerous. Deadly, in fact, to those who provoke them." Grimelda's twisted features softened. She released one of Reecah's hands and patted the other. *"Your parents and uncle died defending the dragons."*

Reecah's Flight

"That's not what Grammy said."

Grimelda's smile filled with compassion. "Lizzy never accepted their deaths. Had your parents not intervened on the dragons' behalf, a greater

Reecah's Flight

travesty would have occurred. Unfortunately, their measures cost them their lives."

Sitting on the edge of the drop-off, gazing across the valley, Reecah had trouble focusing on the present. There was no way the two names were a coincidence—*especially* combined with the Windwalker surname. Unless her mother and uncle were named after distant relatives. She wished Grimelda hadn't left her. There were so many questions she needed answered. If only she had thought of asking them when she had the chance.

Raver landed beside her, startling her back to the present. Looking into the valley, Swoop was nowhere to be seen.

"Great. Leave me up here by myself while you fly down there," she said to the wind.

"Fly down there! Fly down there!" Raver bobbed his head and flew after Swoop.

"No, Raver! Wait! I didn't mean you."

The raven disappeared beyond the face of the cliff.

Smiling at the irascible bird's departure, she spotted an irregularity along the edge and went to inspect it. From a distance, the crevice hadn't appeared out of the ordinary, but on closer inspection, it looked as if it might provide a way down.

Easing herself into the cool shadow of the fissure, she hoped the subtle pathway continued beyond a sharp bend below. The cleft ended on a narrow ledge curving across the face of the cliff at a precarious angle. From there, the route didn't appear fully intact. Looking up to see how far she had come, she almost lost her balance. Leaning against the rock to catch her breath, she tried not to think about how far the fall would have been.

Edging her way down the ledge, she caught sight of Raver soaring over the forest, a tiny black speck amongst a leafy, green ocean.

Reecah's Flight

Twice she slid on loose scree after jumping a precarious section of the ledge. By the time she clambered to the bottom and jumped onto a mound of spongy moss, she could barely stand. Dropping to her backside, she hung her head between her knees.

Weak from hunger and the physical toll of the descent, she ignored Raver squawking overhead, but jumped as a larger presence dropped in front of her. Swallowing her fright, she blinked twice at Swoop's smiling face.

"Fear not. Lurker is on his way with proper food. Can you hear it squealing?"

Squealing? Reecah couldn't hear anything but birdsong from the thick forest spreading out from the base of the cliff. And then she heard it. A panicked cry. Raspy.

"There he is."

Reecah followed Swoop's gaze up the drop-off.

Lurker soared into view, flying erratically. Struggling to remain aloft, a man-sized creature dangled from his claws.

Reecah gaped. Surely, he wasn't holding what she thought.

Swoop let out a high-pitched shriek, catching Lurker's attention.

Lurker craned his neck and returned the call, his excited voice startling Reecah, *"Get ready to kill it!"*

Reecah feared he had captured someone from the hunt. "What is it?"

Neither dragon answered.

Lurker dropped from the sky like a falling boulder, his wings beating rapidly in an attempt to slow his descent. Just before hitting the ground, he opened his claws, releasing a six-foot, black-haired troll—the enraged beast clearly unhappy.

Reecah's Flight

Swarm

Traumatized by the ordeal, Reecah never thought about drawing her sword or stringing her bow.

The troll's yellow eyes glared at her and Swoop, its shoulders and chest matted with dark blood oozing out of puncture wounds caused by Lurker's claws.

Keeping its eyes on Swoop, the troll backed away and roared.

Swoop returned a roar so loud, Reecah had to cover her ears.

The troll squeaked its fright, skirted around them, and jumped at the cliff, its claws scratching for purchase as it scaled the granite wall.

Looking from Lurker to Swoop and back again, Reecah was flabbergasted. "A troll? Really?"

"It's getting away!" Lurker called out, altering his flight to intercept the climbing monster. He stretched out his back legs to pluck the troll from the rock—the creature already a third of the way up the cliff.

"Let it go. I'm not eating that."

The troll roared and hissed, baring yellowed fangs. It swatted at Lurker's feet and slipped, but caught itself.

"Lurker, no!"

Lurker played with the troll for a few more wing beats before tiring of the sport and landing. *"I don't blame you. They're almost as greasy as people."*

"Ew. That's disgusting."

"You don't eat them either? I thought people killed trolls."

"We do, but we don't eat them. That's gross."

211

Reecah's Flight

Lurker pulled his head back and blinked. *"What do you do with them?"*

Reecah returned his bewildered look. "Nothing. Burn them if they get near the village."

Lurker glanced at Swoop. *"Seems like a waste to me."*

"Me too."

Lurker shook his head. *"People are picky. What do you eat?"*

Reecah didn't appreciate talking about food when her stomach pained her so. She shrugged. "I don't know. Fish. Small animals like rabbits and certain birds." She followed the dragons' gaze to Raver. "Not that kind! More like chickens and turkeys."

Lurker nodded. *"Leave it to me. Go with Swoop to the river and I'll meet you there."*

Sitting on an old log on the banks of the wide river cutting through the centre of the valley, Reecah tended to the wild hen Lurker had scavenged for her as it cooked over a small fire.

Swoop and Lurker waded in the middle of the river, submerged up to their necks.

"Aren't you afraid they'll eat her?" Swoop asked.

"They wouldn't do that, would they? She's with us." He swung his head in Reecah's direction. *"Do you really think they would?"*

"I wouldn't count on them welcoming her. Not with the king's men hunting us."

"I thought Grimclaw liked Windwalkers."

Swoop laughed and splashed toward the far bank, water flowing from her scales like a small waterfall. *"Grimclaw doesn't even like himself."*

"Do you think we should tell her?"

"I'd hate to scare her, but I guess I'd want to know if someone was going to eat me."

Reecah's Flight

Reecah stood up with her hands on her hips, glaring. "I can hear you!"

"Oops." Lurker hung his head, his chin dipping into the river. *"Don't worry. We won't let that happen. Will we, Swoop?"*

Reecah couldn't tell from the distance separating them, but by the way Swoop lifted her head on the far bank, Reecah was sure the brown dragon had rolled her eyes.

Shaking her head, Reecah studied the pile of feathers on the ground, thinking they would make good fletches. Not liking the thought of dirtying her satchel any more than it was, she dismissed the idea and sat back on the log to await her meal.

Pulling her boots on, Reecah stood on the far bank and examined the jagged heights rising over the treetops. Several large dragons flew from one ledge to another or drifted down the valley. With more than a little trepidation, she ran after Lurker as he bustled onto the forested slope at the base of the north rim. Judging by his burst of speed, Reecah speculated about his sudden urgency. Had the king's men entered the valley?

Swoop had flown ahead, stating that she wanted to make sure everything was ready for Reecah's arrival at Dragon Home.

Reecah suspected the female dragon was really trying to ensure there weren't other dragons hanging around where they were headed. Overhearing Lurker and Swoop's conversation in the river had done little to reassure her the colony would be receptive to her arrival. If Lurker hadn't remained with her, she might have followed the troll up the ridge and fled back home.

The thought of returning home made her sad. Unless she decided to flee to Thunderhead or beyond, she may as well remain with Lurker. She had nothing to lose. She smiled wryly. Other than her life.

Reecah's Flight

"What's so funny?"

Lurker's voice startled her. She didn't think she'd ever get used to someone else's voice sounding in her mind. She gave him her best 'vexed' look. "I wish there was some way to warn me."

Lurker frowned.

"I'm sorry," she said, appreciating everything he had done for her so far. Showering her with kindness in the wake of her people's nefarious actions. "It's just hard to get used to your voice in my head."

"I will stop, if that pleases you."

Reecah stopped walking. "No! Please don't. It's my issue. I shouldn't have said anything. I would be devastated if you stopped talking to me."

Lurker continued on without a word.

She caught up to him and kept pace. Forcing herself to cheer up she said, "So, let's talk about Swoop."

"Swoop? What about her?"

"Have you made any ground with her?"

Lurker's forehead furrowed. *"Made ground with her?"*

"Ya, you know. Made a move?"

Lurker stopped, his frown deepening. *"What are you talking about?"*

"Have you told her how you feel about her?" Reecah raised her eyebrows and licked her lips. "Huh?"

Lurker's eye grew wide.

Reecah thought he blushed but couldn't be sure. "Yes. That's exactly what I'm talking about."

Lurker hung his head and looked away. *"Gosh, no. I couldn't do that. What if she doesn't like me?"*

"Think, silly. Why is she hanging around us if she doesn't like you? You said she preferred to spend her days at that waterfall. If that's the case, why is she here?"

"She's a nice dragon, I guess."

Reecah's Flight

"She certainly seems nice. Nice enough to make *ground* with." Reecah winked.

He tilted his head. *"Do you have something in your eye?"*

"Huh? No." She laughed. "Do you need me to put in a word for you?"

He looked away again, his answer softly registering in her mind, *"Gosh, no. I would be too embarrassed."*

Reecah considered that and decided she might be pushing the matter too far, too fast. She thought about how she would feel if she were in Lurker's position and let it drop.

"I can't wait to see your home. Is it far?"

"It is if you're not a flier. We're almost directly below the southern reaches but to get there you will be forced to climb a long way. I wish I could carry you."

Reecah stumbled and almost fell into the underbrush. She swallowed and gazed into Lurker's eyes. "Do you really think you could?"

Lurker gave her a bemused grin as she extricated herself from a bramble of blackberries. *"I would be afraid to drop you. Someday maybe. I'm not strong enough yet. At least not without hurting you."*

"No, I guess not," she said dreamily, imagining what it would be like to soar through the sky, suspended from a dragon's claws. She pictured the troll wiggling in his grasp, and swallowed. Then again, perhaps it wasn't such a great idea…unless. A faint thought formed in the back of her mind on how to make that work without causing her serious injury. Perhaps some kind of harness she could hang in.

She nodded, plucking blackberries from a vine. Gathering a handful, she held out her palm. "You want some?"

Lurker glanced at her and pushed his snout into her stomach, nudging her aside.

"Hey!"

Reecah's Flight

Ignoring her, he clamped his mouth over a large patch of berries and ripped a section of vine free. He grinned as his sharp teeth gnashed back and forth, consuming everything.

Amused at her friend's antics, she picked as many as she dared carry in her rucksack, sucking the juice from her fingers. Their previous conversation came back to her. She glanced at the towering cliffs. "Is there an easy way up there?"

"There's an animal trail not far from here that will take you to the lower colony. From there you can access the rest of Dragon Home from within. As far as easy, I'm sure it won't give someone like you much difficulty."

It made her happy to know Lurker thought highly of her skills. She had worked hard to become proficient in the mountains. Up until that moment, she had wondered why she spent so much time on the meaningless endeavour. It was invigorating to realize her hard work had actually been for a reason.

"Is that where Swoop went? To make sure no one watches me climb?"

Lurker stopped chewing. *"She is gone to…to make sure you are welcome."*

That didn't sound promising. "What if I'm not?" She recalled Lurker playing with the troll clinging to the cliff. "I'd rather not get halfway up and find out I'm not welcome."

Lurker started walking again. *"If Grimclaw says you're okay, you have nothing to worry about."*

Reecah watched him strut into the shadows beyond two tree trunks, unconvinced he believed what he said. She was still getting used to dragonspeak, a term she made up, but even hearing the voices in her head, they contained certain nuances and inflections. If she were to interpret Lurker's last statement, she would say he was being elusive.

From back the way she had come, a blood-curdling scream pierced the relative silence of the valley floor. The mournful

216

sound went on for what seemed a long time before abruptly ending.

Not knowing what else to do, she bounded after Lurker toward a colony of people-eating dragons.

Finding the place to start her climb hadn't been an issue, but as she rose above the treeline, Reecah found it increasingly difficult to choose the best route. Twice she stopped, clinging to the rock with fingertips and tiny toe holds, searching for the best way to go. Unless her mother and uncle had been spiders, she didn't think they would have taken the route she chose.

At one point, though she didn't dare search the skies to see him, Lurker asked, *"Are you sure you're going the right way?"*

Clinging to the rock face, fearing her next move would be her last, she bit back a sarcastic reply. It was obvious she had chosen the wrong path at some point. To make matters worse, Lurker and Raver continuously glided past her with ease, not bothering to flap unless absolutely necessary while they checked on her progress. Her stamina was wearing thin as they drifted by together.

"Are you going to be much longer?"

"Much longer! Much longer!"

She cast them a dark look, refusing to honour them with a response. Gritting her teeth, she dragged herself along, fully cognizant of the danger she was in.

The sun had drifted into the western sky, toward the Niad Ocean many leagues down the valley, by the time Reecah was able to relax enough to catch her breath. All along the higher elevations, dragons of varying colour and size came and went, but if they saw her clinging to the cliff, they never paid her any attention. The higher she climbed, the more noticeable the dragons' movement became—the upper reaches of the north rim abuzz with frenetic dragonsong.

Reecah's Flight

Sitting on a steep incline, in a horizontal crack along the wall, Reecah screeched as Lurker dropped out of the sky, his claws grating on the rock beside her feet. Reecah jumped again as Swoop crunched gracelessly on her other side.

Before she could ask them what they were doing, Lurker spread out a wing, the cold leather slapping her in the face.

"What are you doing?"

"*Shh.*" The voice was Swoop's. *"If they see you, we're all in trouble."*

Deep roars and high-pitched shrieks echoed up and down the valley accompanied by the commotion of hundreds of wings flapping, the noise thundering off the cliff face.

At the risk of slipping from her precarious resting spot, Reecah grasped the top of Lurker's wing and peered at the spectacle. A swarm of dragons—the term she thought best summed up what she witnessed—winged their way across the valley toward the south rim.

"What's going on?"

Lurker relaxed the pressure on his wing and Reecah almost pitched over the edge. His wing went rigid again, preventing her from falling. *"Stay back. Something's happening."*

Reecah shot him a frustrated look. "I can see that."

"Shh!" Swoop appeared to be concentrating on something Reecah couldn't hear. The dragon's face went from bewilderment to awe and finally twisted with concern. "They're attacking the king's men! We need to get Reecah out of here before they return!"

Reecah looked from one dragon to the other. There was no way she was scaling back down the cliff.

Reecah's Flight

Dragon Home

Swoop peered over the edge, looking down at Reecah clinging spread eagle to the cliff below. *"Hurry up, Reecah."*

Raver perched beside the brown dragon, also staring at her. "Hurry up! Hurry up!"

Reecah barely heard her raven over the tumult taking place across the valley.

Every now and then she sensed in her mind Swoop or Lurker flinching—how this was possible, she had no idea. It was as if she was attuned to their fear.

Lurker hovered below her position, ostensibly to catch her if she slipped. The selfless act wasn't lost on her but she wasn't keen on it. She feared she would take him to his death were that to happen.

Looking up, the last bit of energy left her. She was a couple of arm lengths away from the safety of the ledge but she may as well have been on the far side of the valley. There were no imperfections in the rock anywhere around her—the uncompromising granite sloping slightly outward from where she clung for her life offered her no further handholds.

Seeing the treetops far below, there was no way she would be able to scale back down without falling. She was stuck. If the dragons weren't with her, she would've screamed her frustration. Instead, she said as calmly as her trepidation allowed, "It's no use. I'm done. I can't go any higher."

Lurker sounded alarmed. *"You need to go back down, then."*

Reecah's Flight

She forced a fake smile, shaking her head. "I can't see where to put my feet."

"What can I do?"

Biting back her anger for getting herself into such a predicament in the first place, she sighed. "I don't know. Nothing." She grimaced, the futility in her situation came through in her voice like a whine. "I can't go up, and I can't go…hey!"

Lurker's snout butted into her backside, lifting her feet off their tenuous footholds. *"Swoop, grab her!"*

Swoop dropped to her scaly chest, one foreleg dangling over the precipice.

Reecah's equilibrium pitched forward and then backward on the edge of Lurker's face. With his assistance, the weight had been taken from her arms, but she had nowhere to go. Swoop's foreleg was too short. Maintaining her grip on the wall wasn't easy with Lurker shifting below her, his body undulating with each beat of his wings.

A gust of wind blew him to the side. *"Now Swoop, I'm losing her!"*

With the bulk of her weight on Lurker's snout and him blowing around, Reecah's fingers pulled free of the cliff face. She flailed her arms out wide, feeling him fall away.

She screamed.

A brown leather wing whapped her in the side. *"Grab on!"*

She clasped Swoop's bony wingtip with one hand and attempted to latch on with her second but lacked the strength to pull her weight up. Her aching fingers slipped from Swoop's wing.

"Hang on!" Swoop's frantic voice thundered in her head.

A throaty growl sounded beneath her. Lurker rammed her against the rock face, the painful manoeuvre providing her enough height to latch onto Swoop's wing with both hands.

Reecah's Flight

Before she knew what had happened, she sprawled on the ledge above—a noisy raven cawing in her ear.

"Hang on! Hang on!"

Reecah sat up and caught her breath, staring at Raver. The raven was gifted with imitating others' voices, but as far as she knew, the only time he talked was after someone else had spoken first. No one had spoken that last phrase out loud.

Lurker flapped up to the alcove and landed on the lip. He stretched his neck and nuzzled Reecah's cheek with the side of his rough face. *I thought we were going to lose you.*

Reecah wrapped an arm around his head and hugged him close. "I thought so too, but thanks to you and Swoop, I made it."

"We need to get her out of here before they return. I can hear snatches of my father's conversation. It's not going well. If they return to find her here, we won't be able to protect her." Swoop's attention lay across the valley.

Lurker pulled out of Reecah's embrace, but he didn't respond to Swoop—he considered the deep recess at the rear of the alcove.

Reecah peered into the shadows, startled by a pair of amethyst eyes staring back at her. "Is that the dragon from the campsite?"

Lurker nodded. *"Yes, it is."*

"Am I in trouble?"

"Not sure." Lurker waddled to the purple dragon. Considering each other, they were obviously conversing without including Reecah.

Swoop's head perked up and whipped around. Scrambling to Lurker's side, her sudden movement caused Raver to fly to a small ledge near the roof of the alcove.

As one, the dragons turned their attention on Reecah, but it was Lurker's voice she heard.

221

Reecah's Flight

"Our silent friend says we must hurry if we wish to get you out of Dragon Home."

Swoop's voice jumped in. *"What about the elders? I'm sure not all the adults are fighting."*

There was a long pause as Lurker and Swoop listened to the purple dragon, nodding several times.

Lurker's voice informed Reecah, *"She claims to know a secret way through Dragon Home only big enough for dragonlings."*

"What's her name?"

Lurker turned to the purple dragon who shook her head. *"She was never given a name. Shortly after discovering her brother's body, her mother was killed in the clearing with my mother. She doesn't know who her father is."*

Sadness filled Reecah. It was as if fate had brought her together with the purple dragon. Hearing of the dragon's heart-wrenching story, Reecah understood her silence.

Walking up to the purple dragon, she declared, "Then we shall call her, Silence."

"Silence! Silence!"

Lurker and Swoop regarded the raven with a frown but Silence nodded her head, a faint smile curling the corners of her mouth.

Lurker's eyes widened. *"I've never seen her react to anything before. Reecah, I believe you have made her happy for the first time in her life."*

Afraid of what her actions might provoke, Reecah patted Silence's snout between her nostrils and eyes. Silence didn't pull away, so Reecah stroked the ridges below her eyes.

"Would you look at that," Swoop said in wonder. *"She's never let anyone get close to her before."*

"She did once. A few nights ago, actually. She kept Reecah warm."

Reecah raised a cuff to her eyes to wipe away tears of happiness. She wrapped her arms around Silence's head, ignoring the rows of dagger-like teeth lining her muzzle.

Reecah's Flight

Pulling Silence in tight, she whispered, "We're your family, now. Don't you ever forget that."

Poppa's words came to her. "We'll always be here for you." She placed a palm against Silence's chest. "No matter what happens, as long as you feel us here, we'll always be together."

Wetness dampened the side of Reecah's head. She pulled away. A dragon tear had fallen into her loose hair. She didn't bother to wipe it away.

Swoop stepped to the edge of the lowest tier of Dragon Home and stared out. She returned just as quickly. *"I hate to spoil the moment, but we need to go—now!"*

Without a word, Silence led them into a rounded passageway large enough to accommodate an adult dragon—the lightless tunnel curving northward into the mountain.

It wasn't long before Reecah had to keep a hand on Lurker's shoulder to navigate the dark without hitting the unforgiving walls. Occasionally, Raver's wings rustled behind them; the old raven maintaining its own pace.

Reecah sensed tunnels branching off by the difference in the sound of their footsteps and a change in air temperature. They never encountered another dragon until Lurker's words startled her—their sudden inclusion in her thoughts exacerbated by the darkness.

"We're approaching the lower level common area. Silence has gone ahead. She says there were several older dragons and a bunch of dragonlings there earlier."

Lurker stopped walking as a faint light seeped into the tunnel ahead. A soft snort from behind told Reecah that Swoop was still with them.

Though the passageway was cool, sweat dampened Reecah's underclothes. Shivering in silence, she wished she could listen in on the colony's dragonspeak to learn what was going on.

A shadow filled the far end of the corridor, but didn't come any closer.

Reecah's Flight

"Silence says there are four adults in the common area and several dragonlings."

Swoop stepped back and forth. *"Now what?"*

"Silence will distract the adults. If Reecah keeps hidden beside me, I'll stick to the back wall. We'll be out the far side before they know we're there." Lurker started forward. *"Stay close."*

The outside light shone brightly at the end of the tunnel, leaving Reecah half blind. An expansive cavern opened up, its southern face exposed to the sky. The area was dominated by a pool of water at its centre—fed by a waterfall cascading down the rear wall of the cavern. The overflow from the pool plunged to the forest below.

Two white dragons, a black dragon and a grey dragon sitting beside the pool craned their horned heads, watching Silence saunter to the edge of the drop before she turned to face them.

Reecah whispered in Lurker's ear. "Am I right in guessing that the white dragons are older females, the black one an older male and…what?"

"Shh!" Lurker warned. *"Yes. The grey dragon is a male in the process of turning black. Now be quiet. Just because they're old, doesn't mean they're deaf. They probably have eyes in the back of their head too."*

Despite her nervousness, Reecah smiled. She knew all about old people. Grammy *always* knew what she was up to, *especially* when she thought she was being her sneakiest.

She peeked beneath Lurker's chin. Between the four adult dragons, five dragonlings splashed about in the water—two blues, an orange, a yellow and a brown—flicking water with their wings and spouting at each other.

"Ready?"

Reecah patted Lurker's shoulder. They started into the common area, clinging to the back wall as it curved away from the pool.

224

Reecah's Flight

Two of the dragonlings were instantly aware of Lurker and Swoop's presence. They stopped splashing—their heads following Lurker as he walked across the back wall.

"We're being watched," came Swoop's voice.

"Just keep moving."

The rhythmic splash of the waterfall grew in volume, its splattering runnels sprinkling Reecah's skin. A movement on the far side of the cascade drew her attention. A red dragonling stepped away from the far side of the waterfall.

Lurker's focus was on the adult dragons.

Reecah patted his shoulder and said in the quietest, yet firmest voice she could muster, "Um, Lurker."

Lurker didn't respond. Whether because of the waterfall's noise or his attention on the adults, Reecah didn't know. She nearly slipped on the wet floor as she pulled down on his neck and spoke into his ear slits. "Lurker! Dragon. Straight ahead!"

The dragonling in the waterfall watched their approach with more interest than Reecah liked—its ruby eyes spotting her sneaking along beside Lurker.

Swoop recognized the danger and rushed past to distract the red dragonling. The remainder of the dragonlings in the water stopped splashing, their eyes following Swoop.

Finally noticing the dilemma in front of them, Lurker said, *"Oh, great. A red dragon."*

Reecah made a note to ask him about that later, but for now, she tried to make herself as small as possible.

The red dragon's eyes locked on her. It opened its mouth wide, emitting a high-pitched screech.

"Time to run!" Lurker picked up his pace, splashing through the base of the falls.

"Run! Run!" Raver flapped high overhead.

Unable to hang on, Reecah ran beside Lurker surprised at how fast he moved. She stumbled in the stream, her feet

Reecah's Flight

slipping out from underneath her. Grabbing onto Lurker's passing wing, she righted herself.

Alerted by the red dragonling, the adult beasts emitted a community roar that shook the cavern.

Swoop pushed the red dragon against the wall but it forced itself past her and lunged at Reecah.

Clutching Lurker's wingtip, Reecah swung her feet into the air, her backside eluding the red dragon's snapping mouth by a hair's breadth. Her momentum carried her onto the far shore. Hitting the ground running, she fled toward the darkness of the far exit tunnel cut into the back corner.

Silence ran toward them—the four adult dragons uncoiling to give chase. Cutting Reecah off, Silence pointed her snout into a thin crevice Reecah hadn't seen, her amethyst eyes pleading for Reecah to hurry. *"In there, quick."*

Reecah frowned at the dark cleft but Raver never slowed his flight into the gap.

Lurker nudged her after the raven, following closely behind Swoop—the space barely wide enough for the dragonlings.

Silence backed into the crevice behind them, stopping to bar the red dragonling from giving chase.

Running down the narrow passage, Reecah slowed and called over her shoulder, "Thank you, Silence. Remember, we're with you always!"

The angered roars of the adult dragons reverberated through the escape tunnel; their raucous displeasure accompanied by the gnashing of teeth.

Silence had engaged the red dragonling.

Reecah's Flight

Dragon Fall

Flames scoured the ridgeline as far as Jonas Junior could see.

Following Jaxon's lead, Jonas's group and the high king's men had pursued Reecah's flight to a narrow cleft along the brink of the drop-off and lost track of her.

One of Jonas' men entered the cleft to inspect what lay below. Encumbered by his heavy equipment he got caught up on something. In an effort to free himself, he slipped. An eerie cry escaped his mouth as he fell to his death.

Undeterred, Jaxon was adamant Reecah had descended the drop-off at this point. The surly commander ordered his men to hammer spikes into the rock and secure ropes to lower their heavier equipment to the valley floor.

They were joined by a larger group of reinforcements who had lugged disassembled ballistae and their accompanying missiles. It took a while to construct a proper harness to house the precious ballistae. Before they had a chance to secure the parts and lower them, a thunderous din echoed off the heights. A wave of dragons flew toward them from across the valley, sending them scurrying back to a line of tumbled mountain debris to make a stand.

The faces of Jonas' dragon hunters paled at the sheer number of flying leviathans, but the king's men never faltered. Shield walls formed an outer perimeter with practiced precision, protecting a line of archers with longbows and heavy shafted arrows.

Reecah's Flight

More shield walls went up around a black-bearded hulk of a man—the commander of the royal forces. Twelve robed figures, bearing staffs adorned with twinkling baubles and fiery-gemmed trinkets, intoned a litany of spells.

"Cover the ballistae!" the commander roared.

Jonas and his men retreated to the centre of the structured formation, his dragon hunt firebreakers adding their defensive bulk to the crews hastily assembling four daunting machines capable of hurling tree trunk-sized missiles.

The first line of dragons dropped on their position, hitting them hard; a solid wave of fire scorching anything not sheltered beneath heavy iron or protected by rock. Several unlucky victims engulfed in dragon fire rose screaming from behind the defensive lines and dropped to the ground, writhing in agony.

The wizards filled the air with ice spells and cast balls of lightning at a wall of dragons so thick they couldn't miss.

Longbows thrummed into the pack—the power behind the heavy arrows enough to penetrate all but the toughest of dragon scales.

Hundreds of king's men hit the dragon wave hard—their combined efforts bringing down a solitary dragon that had taken an arrow in its azure eye.

The injured dragon hit the mountainside hard near the outer line, churning up earth and plant life as it ground to a halt. Still alive, it struggled to right itself. Several men emerged from behind the closest shield wall, cut it to shreds with heavy axes, and scrambled back to safety.

Junior cowered beside the mutilated bulk of Grog who had insisted on accompanying Jonas and his fellow dragon hunters. One look at the massive man confirmed that he should still be lying in a bed recovering from the burns he'd received in the spring, but Grog wasn't an ordinary man. He was tougher than a boiled owl and had the tenacity of an angry hornet when provoked.

Grog was one of the few men Junior admired. The bear of a man had always struck him as a mild-mannered, bashful gentleman when not in Jonas' employ.

Just being beside the disfigured firebreaker provided Junior an odd sense of calm in the face of an all-out dragon attack.

The ferocity of the assault fell away as the last dragon soared overhead. Junior risked leaning out from beneath the line of shields to observe the dragon formation turn in two arcs, one south and the other north. They were preparing to hit them from opposite directions.

"Get yourself down here, laddie, else you'll be frying. I ain't to be the one to tell your old man you got yourself burned like old Grog." Grog wrapped his free hand around Junior's forearm and yanked him down like he was a little child.

"He'd probably thank the dragon," Junior muttered, but he appreciated Grog's concern.

Grog frowned at him, half of his face hideously scarred. "What's that, boy?"

Junior shook his head. "Nothing."

Grog tipped his thick tower shield to one side. The dragons rounded on their position from the east and the west. "This isn't going to go well."

Rising so all could hear, Grog shouted, "Lock shields overhead! Squeeze tight! Flanking units form walls! Nothing gets through to the punchers!"

Junior was pushed toward where the crews of the 'punchers' had the ballistae almost together. If they could keep the siege engines from harm for one more attack, he believed they would be operable for the next wave.

The wizards formed a square around the launchers, powering their staffs in anticipation. Squires stirred mixed small

Reecah's Flight

cauldrons of acid and poison for the surrounding archers to dip their iron-tipped arrows into.

Junior searched beneath the canopy of metal for his family. Jonas and Joram barked orders at the Fishmonger Bay dragon slayers from the far end of Grog's shield formation. The familiar faces of the village trackers huddled behind the heaviest of the shields, their expertise of little use now that the dragons were engaged. There was no sign of Jaxon.

Junior extended his neck to search the burnt corpses within view, but a violent yank from Grog almost tanked his arm from his socket.

"You got a death wish, boy?" Grog's words were lost to the thunderous roar of raging dragon fire—beast after terrifying beast laid down a wall of flames.

Agonized screams rose above the din. Several gaps appeared in the ranks of the defenders—the shield bearers consumed in fire.

Bowstrings thrummed. The dull 'thwap' of deadly arrows piercing scales sounded from every direction.

Explosive concussions rattled the shield lines as volatile wizard spells tore into the dragon ranks.

Through it all, the flying nightmares kept coming—spewing fiery death on anyone not holding their shields just right.

Long after the second wave soared away to gather for a third attack, the cries of the dying mixed with the mournful screeching of several downed dragons. Two of the massive creatures had fallen amongst the shield walls, crushing men and women alike.

The flailing beasts were made quick work of by an army of slayers who faced them without hesitation.

Grog parted his shield with the rest of the firebreakers to assess their situation. "Close the gaps! Toss the dead!"

The surviving defenders pulled and carried their dead comrades to the outside perimeter and tightened their ranks around the wizards and ballistae crews. If they were to survive, they needed to keep a tight formation until the punchers were ready to unleash their deadly bolts.

"They'll come at us from the north and south! Turn and lock!" Grog ordered.

Junior had to admit that Grog knew what he was doing. The mass of dragons, no less impressive with the loss of several of their number, banked in formation and commenced a third attack. Judging by the attrition rate of the king's men, the dragons would soon have the upper hand.

Junior stretched to the tip of his toes but couldn't find his brother. In the back of his mind, he dreaded what would happen if the dragon army decided to land and rush their position. Ballistae or not, they'd be overrun in moments.

Ratcheting cranks turned the winches of the ballistae, disturbing the bizarre calm that had settled over the battlefield between attack waves. Wooden missiles hewn from small trees were loaded into the beds of the cumbersome machines and drawn back as the ropes attached to the throwing arms tightened their hold, charging the gigantic, crossbow-like weapons with incredible tension.

Junior's eyes bulged. Two of the pointed projectiles seemed like they were levelled in his direction. He ducked before Grog had to yell at him.

The nerve-rattling crackle of dragon fire erupted along the northern flank, followed closely by the roar of the beasts attacking from the south. Junior bent low, covering his head with his hands, hoping that insignificant feat would protect him should Grog falter.

Arrows whapped dragon scales, and wizard spells concussed the field. Shield edges clattered against each other as the fiery roar closed on Junior's position.

The commander's gruff voice rose above the din. "Loose!"

Reecah's Flight

Four distinct whooshes came from where the ballistae sat. No sooner had the mighty weapons released than the noise of the attack took on a new sound—the ballistae bolts finding their marks, skewering full-sized dragons and dropping them out of the sky.

Calls to action accompanied the dragon fall as the third wave passed beyond the defensive lines. Axe blades rang out—slayers performing the grizzly task of slaughtering the fallen beasts.

"Reload!"

The winches creaked again.

Not waiting for the firebreakers to lower their shields, Junior crawled away from Grog toward the ballistae and beyond, searching for Jaxon. Passing the last puncher, Junior questioned why he even cared. Since becoming Jonas' head tracker, Jaxon had stopped being afraid of Junior's superior strength. His younger brother had been elevated in the eyes of the dragon hunt while he, himself, had suffered nothing but humiliation. All because of Reecah! He gritted his teeth. His brother was right. The woman was nothing but trouble.

A sudden vision of the way Jaxon had described Viper's death made Junior stop and shudder. What an awful way to go.

"Watch where you're going!" a broad-shouldered man, half Junior's height, grumbled.

Junior had crawled across the handle of the stumpy man's battle-axe. He swallowed. "Sorry, sir. It won't happen again."

The short man put his unproportionally huge face against Junior's, his breath reeking of ale. "You bet your britches it won't, or you'll be getting me axe in your pretty boy face. Hear me?"

Junior gulped. The man was half his size but equally as wide. The bulging gut beneath his black beard bespoke of a slovenly individual but the diameter of his corded forearms testified he wasn't to be trifled with. Junior nodded. Without a word, he crawled away.

A gruff voice barked an order and the shield rows around Junior adjusted their stance to face the east—their well-drilled precision thundering off the mountain slope. He stared in awe at the sight but couldn't help gagging at the greasy pall left by the burned corpses as they were hastily dragged between the ranks to the front line—the grotesque husks deposited beyond the firebreakers.

In the distance, the dragon wave circled to begin its next pass.

"Lock!"

The command sounded behind Junior. Ducking beneath the iron ceiling clicking into place, he caught sight of Jaxon's blonde head. His brother huddled on the southern end of the front line with a score of king's men. Outfitted in black surcoats they stood out from their peers. Junior remembered them arriving with the reinforcements. The shield bearers' tight formation prevented him from crawling farther until the next wave passed.

Junior shivered as ear-piercing shrieks rattled the metal field covering the dragon hunt. Longbows released and the ground shook several times shortly afterward.

Thunderous gouts of fire erupted across the defenders—flames licking between small breaks in the protective cover. Holding the massive shields aloft, strong arms trembled under the force of the flame waves.

The punchers released their dragon killing missiles moments before the shield cover adjusted their angle to repel the fiery assault hitting them from the west. Junior cringed. The greatest casualties to the king's men happened during the transition. Cowering on hands and knees, he was certain the hair on his head had shrivelled under the infernal blasts.

Reecah's Flight

The earth shook three times in rapid succession—the ballistae had taken down three more flying beasts.

The attack was over quicker than before—the heinous din of the receding dragons replaced by the cries of their recent victims. Dragon fire was a horrible way to die. It clung to its victim like molten metal—rapidly incinerating its target.

The firebreakers stood and parted their shields, allowing the slayers to jump forth and deal with the creatures squirming and snapping on the charred ground.

Junior was shocked by the number of mangled dragons littering the field. Half of the beasts still aloft flew erratically, bristling with arrows or missing scales where wizard blasts had damaged their hides. Despite his earlier belief that the dragons would soon gain the upper hand, the king's men were winning the day.

The line of dragons flying east turned and winged their way over the valley. Junior held his breath and looked behind him—the remainder of the dragons followed suit.

A victory shout rose from the king's men.

Junior flinched at the sound of gauntlets, axes and hammers ringing off tower shields in celebration.

Movement on the eastern flank drew Junior's attention. Jaxon and the small host of black-armoured knights broke across the battlefield, ignoring the fallen dragons and following the ridgeline deeper into Dragonfang Pass.

Grabbing a firebreaker by the shoulder, Junior pointed. "Who are they?"

The grizzled man squinted. "You don't want to be messing with them. Those are J'kaar's elite troops."

Junior furrowed his brow. "J'kaar?"

"The high king, you twit." The firebreaker shook his head and stomped away.

"Right, High King J'kaar," Junior said abashed but the man never looked back.

Reecah's Flight

He remembered hearing about J'kaar's elite troops. More a band of assassins than chivalrous knights if rumours held any sway. "What is Jax doing with them?"

A stocky man, no taller than his chest, walked by and turned with a sneer. The man's thick hands clenched the handle of a well-used battle-axe. "What did ye say?"

Junior's face paled. He hadn't realized he had spoken out loud. "Ah, nothing mister. Just talking to myself."

The dwarf's thick brows came together. "Humph," was all he said before continuing on his way.

Junior exhaled the breath he had been holding. Curious as to where Jaxon was leading the infamous troop, he started after them.

Reecah's Flight

Grimclaw

Swoop led Reecah and Lurker through a twisting passageway—the dragonlings struggling to squeeze through several narrow sections but they never quite got stuck. Tell-tale claw scrapes informed them that someone came after them. Reecah hoped it was Silence.

Her hand upon Lurker's shoulder to guide her in the wider sections, Reecah wondered about his reaction at the falls. "Why don't you like red dragons?"

"Red dragons?" Lurker asked, his voice accompanied by Swoop's nervous laugh. *"Stupid know-it-alls. They think they're superior."*

"Why's that?"

"You tell me."

Apparently, a sore subject. Reecah let it go.

They travelled through the darkness for a long time. Swoop led, Reecah hung onto Lurker while Raver had settled upon his neck. On a few occasions, Reecah stumbled on the ground as it steadily slanted upward, or was bashed by an encroaching wall. Ignoring her mishaps, she feared the tunnel might be closing in on itself, but Lurker and Swoop never faltered. Every now and then, light at the end of a side passage informed her that their path paralleled the mountain face.

"Do you know where we're going, Swoop?"

"Kind of. Silence said to follow the tunnel to the end. It's supposed to empty out on the ancestral tomb level."

236

Reecah's Flight

Reecah's stumble had nothing to do with the tunnel floor. "Ancestral tomb? You mean the Dragon Temple?"

Although they never spoke a word, nor could she see them in the dark confines, Reecah knew both dragons were puzzled by her comment. She frowned. It was like she was inside their head.

"Dragon temple? You mentioned that name before. What is this place you speak of?" Lurker responded, an air of hesitancy in his words.

She wasn't sure she should continue. Something about the name made her dragon friends uneasy. But she had to know. She might never get this close again. "Your ancestral tombs. They wouldn't by chance be guarded by an…um…old beast, would they?"

She felt Lurker miss a step but it was Swoop who responded with a nervous laugh. *"I guess you could call him that, but I wouldn't suggest saying it to his face."*

"Call who that? What are you talking about?"

"Lurker, tell her who guards the tombs."

Lurker shuddered beneath Reecah's palm.

Swoop answered for him. *"Grimclaw watches over the tombs. And yes, he's the oldest dragon in the five kingdoms."*

Lurker stopped walking. *"Can we not talk about him, please? Let's just get out of here."*

A low growl sounded from behind.

Reecah's hands went to her sword hilt but Lurker's voice stayed her.

"You made it. Are you okay?"

"I'll live." Silence's voice came in low.

"You're hurt."

"Not as bad as Scarletclaws, but we better keep moving. She won't stay down long."

"Scarletclaws?" Reecah asked, sensing rather than witnessing Silence's nod.

Reecah's Flight

"I used your technique for naming us. She's a red dragon, so…"

Reecah smiled. Patting Lurker, she urged him forward. "Let's go, then. Take me to this ancestral tomb of yours."

Again, the shudder, but Lurker started forward. *"Only death awaits anyone foolish enough to go there."*

Silence growled her displeasure. *"The ancestral tombs are sacred. Humans aren't permitted."*

The hostility in Silence's voice threw Reecah.

Swoop interrupted. *"How much farther, Silence?"*

"Two more levels up."

"Do you know how the assault went?"

Silence didn't respond at first. When she did, her voice barely registered. *"Not well. Many dragons were killed."*

"They're back?" Swoop asked.

"What's left of them. They're preparing for an assault on Dragon Home." She went silent for a while, leaving everyone to their thoughts. When she spoke again, Reecah shivered.

"We need to be careful. If they find Reecah, they'll kill her."

Reecah had no idea how long they travelled the winding passageway but Lurker tensed beneath her palm long before she sensed the tunnel lightening ahead.

Swoop stopped. *"Let me go first. If they're looking for us, I'm sure they know where the tunnel ends. It doesn't take long to get here through the air."*

Reecah swallowed her discomfort. She hadn't thought about that. She checked her sword.

The vision of Viper's last moments made her shiver. A seasoned fighter, he had faced a baby dragon and it hadn't ended well. What good was her sword against a full-grown, fire-breathing dragon? They would use her blade to pick their teeth when they were done with her.

"How many exits does this tunnel have?"

Reecah's Flight

Silence answered, *"Many, but I suspect if they were going to watch one in particular, it will be this one."*

"That's not good."

Swoop's angular silhouette filled the exit, sunlight spilling across her horned face. She turned her head in all directions. *"Looks clear."*

Lurker started forward. *"Remain here until we check the area. Silence, stay with her."*

Reecah took a few steps toward the light and stopped. Removing her hand from Lurker's back, she let him go ahead on his own. Silence stepped up beside her but said nothing.

Outside the exit, Swoop unfurled her wings and sprang out of sight.

Clearing the tunnel, Raver leapt from Lurker's neck and followed Swoop. Lurker turned a slow circle, scanning the area. He took two quick steps, fluttered his wings and took flight. In moments, he was lost to view.

Distant screeches sounded from outside—how far away, Reecah had no way of telling.

A larger shadow darkened the exit, one much bigger than Lurker or Swoop would throw. An adult had touched down.

Silence's words made her jump.

"Run!"

Reecah swung her head to question the purple dragon but Silence pushed her forward. If she didn't move her feet toward the dragon waiting outside, Silence would trample her.

Hadn't Silence noticed the dragon's shadow? Reecah wanted to voice her concern but a rapid clawing noise from deeper within the tunnel had her running toward daylight.

Swoop appeared out of nowhere, dropping out of the sky— barely missing the ground before disappearing from view. A shriek grated Reecah's nerves, followed by the flap of huge wings. The shadow chased after Swoop.

Reecah's Flight

"Go as fast as you can. Don't stop until you come across the vine-covered wall. Be careful you don't miss it. We'll find you when we can."

"What? Where am I going?" Reecah tried to keep the panic from her voice.

"The ancestral tombs. Whatever you do, do not disturb Grimclaw. He doesn't hear well, but if he sees you, well…"

Silence didn't have to elaborate. Reecah gave her a quick pat on the side of the face. "Take care of yourself. Don't get hurt because of me."

Silence nudged her with her snout. *"Go, before it's too late."*

Reecah thought she saw the dark outline of Scarletclaws charging up the tunnel. Without looking back, she sprinted into the sunshine. She expected to be eaten but the way was clear. Lurker and Swoop had led the dragon away.

The sun sank into the western end of the valley, taking with it the staggering heat of the afternoon. Although cool in the tunnel confines, running across the forested slopes of the valley's north rim proved exhausting. It had been a long day.

Reecah slowed her pace, worried she had missed the entrance to the dragon tombs. Silence had mentioned a vine-covered wall, but she had no idea what that meant. Was it like a hedgerow? Was the wall a natural formation? Out here, she couldn't imagine it being anything else. Was it sitting against the side of the slopes rising on her left, or did it form a protective barrier against anyone foolish enough to slip off the ridge? She couldn't understand why anyone would've built a wall way out here in the first place.

She stopped against a cabin-sized boulder that appeared to have fallen from the heights recently. Leaning her quarterstaff against the rock, she shrugged off her rucksack and dug out her waterskin.

Reecah's Flight

Drinking sparingly, she realized she'd soon need to find a water source. She grimaced. The last one she had passed was the waterfall in the lower tier of Dragon Home. That probably wasn't the best place to return to.

Combing her long hair with her fingers, she gathered three equal clumps and spun it into a tight braid, securing its tip with a leather thong.

She slipped free of her bow and quiver with the intention of relieving herself. Worrying at the knot in the thong securing the top of her breeks, she ducked low. A shadow sliced the sunlight radiating through the trees.

A screech echoed off the mountainside. Grabbing her quarterstaff, she searched the forest behind her, expecting to find the red dragon coming after her.

Nothing moved.

Her need to relieve herself forgotten, she stepped around the boulder with long, quiet strides, careful not to tread on anything that might make a noise.

A large branch snapped from the direction of Dragon Home. She crouched against the rock, wishing she hadn't left her bow on its far side.

Two more branches snapped in rapid succession, coming her way.

Trying hard to control her breathing, she reproached herself. Sounds travelled far in the forest—their direction often misleading. For all she knew, someone might be descending the slopes far north of her position. With great care, she stepped around the backside of the rock, her eyes darting everywhere. Where was Raver?

Leathery wings snapped twice overhead. A grey dragon circled a gap in the treetops. Hovering on the winds, it craned its neck, searching the forest floor.

Reecah's Flight

Reecah didn't dare breathe. She couldn't tell one dragon from another with the exception of Lurker, Swoop and Silence, but it looked like the grey dragon from the waterfall cavern.

Clinging to the boulder, her hazel eyes followed the drifting leviathan until it passed beyond the gap. She didn't fool herself. It was still up there, waiting. Watching.

Another branch snapped, closer—definitely from the direction of Dragon Home.

"Silence?" she dared whisper. Receiving no response, she glanced at the gap in the treetops. The grey dragon remained out of sight but she heard the flap of its wings.

Several branches snapped in rapid succession. Through the trees, a flash of crimson caught her eye. Scarletclaws!

Forgetting her gear, Reecah jumped free of the boulder and sprinted through the undergrowth, afraid to look back and see the red dragon on her heels.

The sound of pursuit died away, replaced by one of combat. High-pitched shrieks and a guttural roar filled the forest behind her.

Her sword whapped against her right leg, threatening to trip her—its tip catching her boot as she high-stepped fallen trees and moss-covered rocks.

Raver's call pierced the forest. Searching the air, she stumbled and stopped. The motley raven flew up behind her and settled on a vambrace she held out. Steadying him with her free hand, she leaned on her quarterstaff to catch her breath—the forest eerily silent.

The absence of sound wasn't necessarily a good sign. Growing up on the mountains had attuned Reecah to the nuances of nature. A quiet countryside usually meant a predator prowled nearby. Though, given the noise she had made running with abandon, she may have been the reason.

Self-assured in the mountains, she was out of her element in Dragonfang Pass. Disconcerted at being lost in the realm of the dragons distorted her ability to think rationally. Tendrils of panic trickled through her.

"Vine covered wall! Vine covered wall!"

Raver's voice startled her. Where had he heard that? The raven's ability to master human speech always amazed her, but she was beginning to think his intelligence went beyond that. Up until a little while ago she hadn't imagined him capable of uttering a coherent thought on his own.

Frowning, she inspected him closer. No one had spoken those words out loud. Silence had mind-spoken them. How did…?

Reecah wondered whether Raver was attuned to dragonspeak? "Can you hear Lurker?"

Raver tilted his head and blinked as if processing her question. He bobbed his head. "Hear Lurker! Hear Lurker!"

Reecah was dumbfounded. Surely Raver hadn't understood. It had to be a coincidence. He had repeated her words, not answered the question. Or had he?

She swallowed the implications. Searching the still forest, she put it off as absurd. And yet, she was about to ask him another question when he launched from her forearm.

She followed his flight high overhead, circling nearby trees. Emitting a shrill caw, he winged his way toward the steep slope of the mountain climbing beyond the treeline.

Without warning, his flight ended in midair. He stopped flapping and turned to look at her from a distance, somehow hovering above the forest floor without the use of his wings.

Reecah squinted. Camouflaged against the backdrop of the forest, Raver stood upon a high wall covered in ivy. The dragon tombs! She'd found it—or rather, Raver had. If not for his intervention, she would've run right by it. Even knowing the wall was there, it blended in so well with the forest that if she took her eyes off it and came back to where the wall stood, she had difficulty picking it out again. Raver's presence enabled her mind to process the fact that a wall bisected the trees a short distance away.

Nearing Raver's location, the wall distinguished itself from the landscape. A magical illusion had kept it hidden from view. Parting the vines with her hands, the leaves around her quivered like they were ruffling in a breeze. In the deathly still atmosphere of the forest, the sensation was unnerving. A feathery tingle ran up her spine as solid stone met her probing inspection of the wall.

Three times her height, the wall ran through the trees in both directions, blending into the foliage and disappearing. Beyond the barrier, the mountain rose out of sight.

Wondering how to get past the wall, she considered climbing the vines. A glance sideways revealed a rectangular doorway.

Her skin crawled. Either the entrance had materialized when she wasn't looking or she had lost her mind. The doorway hadn't been there moments before.

She observed the serenity of the forest. Nothing moved. As peaceful as it seemed, the small hairs lifted on the back of her neck. There wasn't anything remotely natural about this place.

Against her better judgement, she poked her head through the doorway. To her left, toward Dragon Home, the wall receded into oblivion, but on her right, another moss-covered stone wall bisected this one, rising straight up to lose itself in the trees.

She almost balked and fled back into the forest. The towering second wall should have been visible outside the perimeter wall.

Trying hard to still her nerves, she examined a red stone path at her feet leading beneath an arched entranceway through the second wall—the tunnel-like passage thicker than the outer wall was high.

A broken gate of lashed tree trunks lay buried beneath fungus and moss on the far side of the path while its counterpart hung neglected from the near edge of the short tunnel.

Raver startled her, squawking his impatience and flying through the archway.

Inhaling a deep breath to calm her building excitement, she searched the skies. Silence had said they would meet her. She hoped they would get here soon.

Marvelling at the manmade walls, she experienced the euphoria of accomplishment. If she was right about the ancestral tombs, they were what Grimelda referred to as the Dragon Temple.

She steeled herself and followed Raver, marvelling at how the arched tunnel appeared to be chiselled from the mountain itself.

Passing beyond the tunnel, she nearly swooned. The path veered left toward a dark cleft into the mountain, its frontage carved in the likeness of an immense dragon's head. The path she trod passed between curved fangs taller than a large man and disappeared into the mouth of the beast. Breathless, she stopped to appreciate the grandeur. This had to be the Dragon Temple.

An odd scraping noise arose from the courtyard where the ivy-covered wall stood. Turning to listen, her courage left her.

Silence's words ran through her mind. *Whatever you do, do not disturb Grimclaw. He doesn't hear well, but if he sees you, well…"*

Swallowing her fear, she placed her hand on the hilt of her sword. If the ancient one was aware of her presence, there was little she could do about it now.

Turning back to the dragon head carved from the side of the mountain she wondered where Raver was. It took her a moment to realize he perched atop a dragon fang at the entrance, his mangled feet finding purchase on the stone.

Remembering that fateful day she had lost Grimelda, filled her with dark memories. The look on her great-aunt's face just

Reecah's Flight

before dismissing her with an unearthly voice had scared Reecah more than she cared to admit.

Reecah's Flight

The sound poor Raver made when Grimelda severed his toes haunted her dreams to this day. And the blood in the fount...she shivered.

Grimelda had been adamant that Reecah retrieve something she referred to as the 'Dragon's Eye,' and return it to her. Forlornly studying the dragon's head carved out of the mountainside, Reecah wondered what could be gained by recovering the Dragon's Eye now. Auntie Grim was gone.

Staring at Raver, one thing Grimelda had said the night of the inferno echoed deep within her. *"Promise Grimelda that no matter what happens here tonight, you will return with the Dragon's Eye."*

Reecah squinted at nothing in particular, going over the words...*no matter what happens here tonight...no matter what happens...no matter what!*

Of course! Grimelda had foreseen her death. She had come right out and said it. Then what would posses her to demand Reecah bring her the Dragon's Eye if she were dead? Unless...

She shook her head. It made no sense. Perhaps, her aunt hadn't expected her shop to burn to the ground, but the more she thought about it, the less convinced she became. Auntie Grim had an uncanny way of prophesizing the future. The old crone had mentioned on more than one occasion that she had been expecting Reecah. She thought it had been an old woman's mutterings, but now she wasn't so sure.

Raver squawked a warning and took to the sky.

The suddenness of his distress filled Reecah with dread.

A shadow blotted the light, and the earth shook under the weight of the biggest dragon Reecah had ever seen—its hooked claws crunching into the path between her and the mountain entrance.

Blacker than a moonless night, the dragon filled the courtyard, its massive head an arm's length away. Sulphurous smoke wafted from nostrils larger than her head. Had she been able to catch her breath, Reecah would have screamed.

Reecah's Flight

Cantankerous Curmudgeon

"You don't look worth my while. How did you get in here?" a deep, gravelly voice sounded in her head. *"I'd be better served disemboweling you and letting the raven have your innards."*

On the verge of blacking out due to fright, Reecah struggled to regain her breathing.

"It has been some time since I've dined on human meat. You're nothing but gristle if truth be told."

A quick breath snuck past the back of her mouth, followed by another. Gulping in great gasps of air, Reecah didn't care that her knees knocked together. It was a relief she hadn't wet herself.

"You act like you've never seen a dragon before."

Reecah nodded in small, quick jerks, her gaze averted by the dragon's twitching tail thumping against the face of the mountain entrance.

"A shame I must eat something as pretty as you."

Reecah's breath caught again. She held trembling hands before her. "Please, I mean you no harm."

"You mean me no harm? Ha!" The dragon's incredulous voice thundered in her head. *"What could a pitiful human do to one such as I? Surely you don't think I fear a pathetic creature like you. If I feel generous, I might permit you the opportunity to run. I do miss such sport in my advanced years."*

"Please Mr. Grimclaw—"

"How do you know my human name?"

Reecah's Flight

Reecah swallowed but before she could respond, Grimclaw bellowed, *"Speak, before I end you!"*

Flames licked at the edges of his nostrils. Even if Reecah had the courage to attempt an escape, she didn't think her legs would move.

"S-s-swoop t-told me."

Grimclaw's tail smashed the ground beside him. *"Swoop! Who is this Swoop? Lead me to him and I'll end him, too. Arrogant humans!"*

"H-he's, I-I mean, she's not human. She's a dragon."

Grimclaw's head pulled back. *"A dragon? Impossible. Never heard of her. You're trying to deceive me. For that, you shall burn."* He pulled his head back farther, opening his fanged maw. Flames roiled at the back of his throat.

Reecah lifted a knee and covered her head with her hands. "Swoop *is* a dragon. She led me here. You dried my clothes!" Her voice rose to a squeak as Grimclaw thrust his head forward—flames spewing through rows of jagged teeth.

Reecah shrieked but the stream of instant death crackled overhead. Grimclaw's aborted attack shrivelled the loose hairs on top of her head.

Opening her eyes, she recoiled in fright. Grimclaw's eye, the yellow orb almost as tall as she, wasn't more than a finger's length from her face—his great head tilted just so.

"You're the one the dragonling claims is a Windwalker?"

She stepped back. "M-my name is Reecah Draakvriend. M-my...wait!"

"Not a Windwalker?" Grimclaw turned his head and opened his mouth wide.

Reecah screamed, anticipating a horrific death. "My great-grandmother was a Windwalker!"

Grimclaw paused, the points of his teeth poised on either side of her head.

Reecah's Flight

His breath was enough to make her retch. The sight of his dark purple tongue caused her to shudder. It felt like an eternity before Grimclaw's mouth withdrew.

Grimclaw's nostrils twitched. His tongue licked his black lips. *"And just who is this great-grandmother of yours?"*

Reecah's stomach dropped. She couldn't recall ever hearing her great-grandmother's name. People had simply referred to her as great-grandmother.

"I-I don't remember."

Grimclaw's eyes narrowed.

Reecah held her hands out, shaking her head. "No. Wait. It's true. I just, um, I mean I've never…" She started to panic and then it hit her. The stories Poppa had read to her were about a young woman—her great-grandmother's history! Until this moment she thought they were make-believe. "Katti! Her name was Katti Windwalker!"

"Was?"

"She died years ago. Around the same time as my mother."

Sorrow replaced the anger in Grimclaw's eyes. The great dragon lowered his head. *"Most unfortunate. It would explain why she never comes by anymore."* He cast her a sad glance. *"That also explains how you got this far into the temple grounds without dying."*

She had no idea what he meant, but felt it best to let him keep talking.

"Who are Marinah and Davit Windwalker to you?"

Reecah swallowed. How did Grimclaw know about them? Swoop's earlier comment came back to her, *…Marinah and Davit Windwalker often came this way.* The revelation stunned her. Had her mother spoken with Grimclaw?

"My mother and uncle went by those names, but they were Draakvriends just like me."

A deep growl escaped Grimclaw. Reecah feared she had upset him again, but instead of becoming angry, the black dragon nodded. *"Ahhh. It's making sense to me now. I seem to recall Katti mentioning something to that effect many years ago."*

"I'm not sure what you're talking about."

Grimclaw leaned his head close. *"You don't seem to know much. Perhaps you aren't who you say you are, hmm?"* Puffs of smoke escaped his nostrils.

Reecah waved her hands to disperse the caustic emission. "Katti was my great-grandmother. I never knew her last name until auntie Grimelda mentioned it to me."

Grimclaw withdrew his head, furrowing his scaly brow. *"Grimelda Windwalker?"*

"I only knew her as…" Reecah imitated his puzzled expression. What was Grimelda's last name? Come to think of it, she never knew Grammy's maiden name either. Of course, if they were both descended from Katti…

Reecah's face lit up. "Yes. Yes! Auntie Grim was a Windwalker, just like her sister, Lizzy."

"Pfft! Not that one. She's a disgrace to the Windwalker line."

Despite her deep-rooted fear, his words fueled her quick temper. "Who? Lizzy?"

"Please! Don't mention her name around me. If not for her, things may have been different for many of us. Including your mother. I should have eaten her when I had the chance. I know where she lives."

A door hidden deep within Reecah's mind squealed open, releasing her pent-up sorrow. She fought back tears but couldn't keep the bitterness from her voice. "She died three years ago."

"That is good news."

Before she had the sense to stop herself, Reecah pulled her sword free and brandished it at Grimclaw's chin. She had no idea why he didn't like Grammy, but she refused to let him badmouth her grandmother. "You take that back!"

Grimclaw eased his head into the air. A guttural rumble shook the courtyard.

Reecah's Flight

It took Reecah a moment to realize he was laughing. She wanted to impale the impertinent beast but doubted her blade would even scratch one of his scales. Helpless, she fought the urge to scream her frustration.

"What do you plan to do with that? Scratch my itchy back?"

"I demand you take back what you said about Lizzy Draakvriend, or else."

Grimclaw laughed harder. *"Or else what? You're nothing but a harmless tick."*

"Ya? Well you're nothing but a..." She searched for a term to express how vehemently she despised his attitude. Unable to think of a term that would cut as deeply as she felt, she blurted out the first thing that came to mind, "a cantankerous curmudgeon!"

"Cantankerous curmudgeon?" Grimclaw thundered, his amber eyes narrowing to slits.

Reecah swallowed, holding her sword before her as she slowly stepped backward. It probably wasn't the best idea to argue with a mythical leviathan older than time remembered, and able to breathe fire.

Grimclaw stepped after her, his footfalls shaking the ground.

Reecah considered turning and running but she bumped against a peculiar, rough surface. Grimclaw's spiked tail, thicker than she was tall, blocked her progress.

Grimclaw's head thrust toward her.

She dropped her quarterstaff and held her sword in shaking hands, but he stopped out of reach.

"You have your mother's pluck, I'll give you that. Marinah never suffered anyone she didn't agree with. Perhaps there is hope for us after all."

Reecah's sword tip wavered. "How do you know my mother?"

Grimclaw blinked several times. *"How old are you? You don't appear old enough to be Marinah's child."*

252

Reecah's Flight

Reecah lifted her chin in defiance. "Twenty-one."

His nod barely noticeable, Grimclaw said, *"So you never really knew your mother, then, did you?"*

"How do you know that?"

"She came to me not long after you were born, brimming with excitement. Boasting she had secured the Windwalker lineage. She insisted on championing our cause with the rulers of the land to put an end to the dragon hunt."

"My mother spoke with you?" Reecah asked with a squeak.

"No one told you about Marinah and Davit? That explains a lot."

"They told me dragons killed them."

Grimclaw stiffened. Anger burned within his eyes. *"That sounds like Lizzy talking!"*

Reecah wanted to lash out at his accusation, but her rebuttal caught in her throat. He was right. Grammy had always resented the dragons. Distant memories—convoluted conversations she had with Poppa—coalesced in the forefront of her mind. It was as if Poppa and Grammy had been on opposite ends of the dragon debate.

Her recollections of the time when Poppa was alive were reduced to nothing more than a collage of happy emotions. Other than a few instances that remained rooted in the back of her mind, like the last day she had ever seen him, she couldn't remember her Poppa clearly anymore.

A tear dripped off her cheek. Looking up, she shook her head. "Nobody told me anything. I guess I was too young."

"Too young for the truth?" Grimclaw's voice boomed. Flames crackled from his nostrils. He shook his massive head, his voice dropping to a compassionate whisper. *"That is truly unfortunate. According to your mother, you were destined for great things. She and Davit were trying to lay the foundation for a new era when J'kaar intervened."*

"The high king?"

Reecah's Flight

"J'kaar Dragonscourge is the bane of my kin. Because of his intervention two decades ago, your uncle and your parents were lost to us. The high king is responsible for their deaths."

Gaping, Reecah couldn't believe what she heard. Why would the high king want to harm her family? Grimclaw's hostile voice grated at her as she tried to come to terms with his revelation.

"Do you see now why dragonkind cannot tolerate humans? We're fighting for our very existence. Apparently J'kaar isn't content with his lot in life."

Reecah stared hard at the angry dragon.

"In the grand scheme of life, dragonkind sit atop the food chain. J'kaar, in all of his royal arrogance, aims to change that." A deep bitterness crept into his voice. *"By virtue of his attack this morning, he has declared war on us. Twenty three dragons lost their lives today. Twice that number are injured and may not recover. The king's men are crossing the valley floor to continue the fight. What do you have to say to that?"*

Reecah was speechless. What could she say? She hung her head. Too despondent to care anymore, she allowed her sword tip to fall to the ground.

Her whole life had been a sham. Everyone had lied to her or bullied her into believing mankind's storied association with the majestic creatures was one of antagonistic survival, not one of harmonious rapport.

Torn between Grammy's views and what she remembered of Poppa, she had wanted to become a member of the dragon hunt. If for no other reason than to avenge her parent's death, and maybe someday, fit in with the rest of her people. If what Grimclaw said was true, the high king had killed her parents.

She swallowed, unwilling to release the ingrained hatred and fear society had instilled in her. "How can I believe you? Of course you see things the way you do. You're a dragon."

Trying to judge Grimclaw's silence, she grew concerned she had upset him again.

Reecah's Flight

Raver cawed, breaking the ominous silence.

Her thoughts drifted to the boulder in the forest and her abandoned gear. She could sure use a drink of water. And what of Scarletclaws? Had it tracked her to the temple? She craned her neck to peer beyond the tunnel gateway.

Grimclaw's voice made her jump.

"You are in possession of something that should prove to you the folly of your high king."

She glared at him—his head lifting high, sniffing at something.

Without looking at her, he said, *"I thought it lost with your mother, but I've sensed its presence ever since you approached the Dragon Temple."*

Reecah's mouth dropped open hearing Grimclaw validate the ancestral tombs were indeed the Dragon Temple.

"I'm the guardian of the ancestral tombs. The hallowed halls behind me can only be entered by a true Windwalker. The entrance guardian will crush anyone unworthy. You come seeking what many have died for, am I correct?"

Reecah reeled, her gaze drawn to the dragon head entrance. How did Grimclaw know of her intention? She feared his reaction if he discovered she meant to steal what she sought. Grimelda's raspy voice echoed in her mind, *"Locate the Dragon's Eye embedded in the Watcher and bring it back here."*

The Watcher. Reecah gasped. Surely Grimelda hadn't sent her to take out Grimclaw's eye.

"Am I correct?"

She jumped. "I-I don't know what you're talking about?"

"Show me the other eye!"

"Other eye. What are you—?"

Grimclaw struck so fast she didn't know it until she lay flat on her back, staring at a chilling set of curved teeth—her sword discarded beside her. She fought to regain the breath knocked out of her as a result of him driving his closed mouth into her.

Reecah's Flight

"It's in your clothing! I can sense it."

The pain eased as her lungs filled. Running her hands over her cloak in a panic, she grasped the leather-wrapped journal and pulled it free—the walnut-sized stone radiating a blinding white light. She almost flung the book away. The ruby stone had become a light blue crystal.

Grimclaw withdrew, his voice filled with awe. *"You* are *a Windwalker. By all that is good in the world, Dragon Home has been blessed."*

Reecah got her elbows beneath her and watched in shock as the mammoth beast prostrated itself before her.

"Reecah Windwalker. I pledge to you my life. May it be forfeited so you may live. Forgive my transgression for I truly believed your line had vanished from the world. From this day forth, you shall know the protection of the Draakclaw Clan. Through you, may we yet live on."

Reecah's Flight

Dark Heir

Jaxon's blonde locks were visible ahead of the file of black-cloaked knights—the chinking of their black-plated armour echoing off the heights.

Junior stopped to wipe the sweat from his brow. Chasing them for the better part of the afternoon, he had no idea how the knights maintained the grueling pace dressed as they were. Identical kite shields, strapped overtop baldrics bearing long-handled swords, exacerbated the weight they carried.

Searching the skies, Junior feared they would be spotted by one of the many dragons patrolling the valley.

He crouched behind a clump of pines on the edge of the drop-off. The greatest concentration of dragons was barely visible on the north rim, to the west. If his suspicions were correct, they guarded the main colony of Dragon Home. There were other dragon colonies throughout the realm, but according to his father, Dragon Home was only rivalled by the Draakvuur colony in the eastern wilds of the Great Kingdom.

It didn't make sense to Junior why Jaxon led the elite guard this deep into Dragonfang Pass. Surely, they knew they were well beyond their intended target. If High King J'kaar wished to make serious inroads on his campaign to rid the realm of dragons, Dragon Home was where they should concentrate their efforts.

A cool breeze filtered through Junior's thick hair providing him a welcome respite from the heat. He forced his gaze from the distant dragons to where he had last seen his brother's group. They were gone!

He expected them to sneak up behind him and scanned the immediate area. A troop of two dozen men couldn't simply vanish. They either went to ground or had slipped into an unseen cave in the side of the mountain.

Checking the steep hillside for movement, Junior stepped free of his concealment and light-footed through the trampled heather left in their wake. The path meandered along the brink of the escarpment to where Junior had last seen them, and disappeared.

A clatter of metal on rock sounded from the direction of the drop-off. A path ran along the cliff face not far below the lip, sloping steeply out of sight back the way they had come. Jaxon had located a second way down the escarpment. One that wouldn't leave them exposed to the dragons patrolling in the west.

Taking a deep breath, Junior dropped to his rump and eased himself over the lip. His sword belt caught on the ground, threatening to pitch him outward. Dropping to the ledge in a crouch, he thanked the gods he hadn't lost his balance entirely. It was a long way to the valley floor.

Once on the trail, he caught sight of the line of knights over halfway down the steep incline. If he didn't hurry, he feared he would lose them in the forest at the base of the drop-off.

Although wide enough to descend comfortably, the loose scree coating the trail made it treacherous. At one point, Junior fell so hard he dislodged a large stone. It careened down the trail, skipped off a rock and careened over the edge—plummeting to the trees far below.

He held his breath, expecting the elite guard to turn and see him. Being Jaxon's brother didn't mean anything, especially where his brother was concerned. Jaxon would rather see him fall off the ledge than help him. His father and uncle likely wouldn't be put out either if he suffered that fate.

The knights searched the area where the rock had fallen. Fortunately, they never cast their gaze up the slope.

He lay on the path until the last man disappeared into the forest. Studying the expansive valley, he muttered, "What am I doing?" And started down the trail.

There was no sense going back. Jonas would demand to know where he'd gone. If his father found out he was spying on his brother, Jonas might toss him off the cliff himself.

He was greeted by warmer temperatures as he descended to the valley floor. He mused he must've lost weight by the time the trees provided him with a welcome reprieve from the afternoon sun.

Although he couldn't see Jaxon's troop, the occasional voice or snap of a twig let him know he wasn't far behind. Traversing the dark shadows of the thick woods, he didn't envy spending the night alone down here. Despite his fear of being discovered by those he chased, he picked up his pace.

Junior shivered as he donned the last of his clothing. The river had been refreshing, but dripping on the far bank in his wet shift left him riddled with gooseflesh. Overhead, the sky had darkened, threatening the valley with an oncoming storm.

The cliff leading up to the north rim appeared in glimpses through breaks in the trees. He didn't have to be a tracker to follow the knights' path—their boots left ample impressions in the soft ground.

Approaching the far side of the valley, he ignored the hunger gnawing at him. Unable to stop thinking about Reecah Draakvriend, he didn't think the ache in his stomach was purely food deprivation. Thoughts of the hill witch angered him. Why was he so fixated on her? Why had he been for years? Ever since that day she came looking to join the dragon hunt.

Thinking on it, that had been around the time his relationship with his father had begun to turn sour. It made no sense why Jonas resented Reecah. Sure, she had busted Jaxon in the nose a few times. In fact, he recalled being the recipient of her fists, himself. The pretty lass knew how to punch. Looking back now, he was ashamed of how he and the other kids had treated her. They had all deserved every bloody nose they received throughout the years.

Reecah hadn't been the only one to take exception to their rudeness, but for some reason, she had come to the attention of their father's wrath. Junior assumed the hatred derived from his father's previous dealings with Reecah's family.

He vaguely recalled Reecah's parents, Marinah and Kruid, arguing profusely with Jonas on more than one occasion outside the village temple. Junior hadn't been any older than five, but the confrontations stuck out as some of his earliest childhood memories. Other than a time years later when Viliyam Draakvriend threatened to disrupt the dragon hunt, Junior had never seen his father as upset. That disagreement had cost Viliyam his life.

He swallowed, fearing Reecah's reaction if she ever discovered the truth. The thought saddened him more than he believed it should have. Sighing, his lips turned up—a warm feeling pushing his melancholy away. The vision of Reecah at the water hole was ingrained in his mind. A most perfect vision he wouldn't soon forget.

Entranced in his thoughts of Reecah, Junior failed to see the two men standing behind the trees on opposite sides of the knights' trail. Before he could raise his hands to defend himself, a gauntleted fist crushed his nose against his face.

Reecah's Flight

Incoherent voices filtered through Junior's addled thoughts. Words slowly came together to make sense, strung together in disjointed sentences, but he couldn't identify the speaker.

"Leave the guardian to us. Once you get us to the temple, you're free to do what you will. Do you seriously think she's made it this far?"

A familiar voice answered. "I find it hard to believe, but according to my brother, she befriended a dragonling and is searching for the same thing you are."

Pain struck Junior's face, first on one cheek, and then the other—slapping his head violently back and forth. It took him a moment to realize why his upper-arms hurt so bad. Two of the elite guards held him upright—his legs dragging behind him.

"Leave him," a black-plated knight, his armour inlaid with golden piping, ordered. The man approached from the direction of a crackling fire, a smug-faced Jaxon at his side. Shrewd eyes on either side of an angular nose observed Junior from above a well-kept, black goatee.

The painful grip released and Junior fell to his stomach. Blood dripped to the forest floor, running freely from his broken nose.

"That's your brother?" the newcomer asked.

Jaxon hocked and spat, the spittle smacking the dirt near Junior's head. "Ain't no brother of mine. A waste of skin if you ask me, Prince J'kwaad."

The prince! Junior's arms shook as he tried to lift himself off the ground to offer the prince his subservience.

The dark heir to the throne lifted Junior's head to one side with a sickening crack of his boot.

Junior was unconscious before his body hit the ground.

Reecah's Flight

Dragon Temple

Grimclaw's amber eyes never blinked as the hill-sized dragon genuflected before the doorstep of the Dragon Temple.

Reecah couldn't stop her hands from shaking or her legs from trembling. A giddy wave of vertigo had her on the verge of swooning in the lengthening, twilight shadows.

She wasn't sure how long she stood rooted to the spot, staring in disbelief. Prostrated at her feet, Grimclaw remained silent, as if awaiting her command.

The declaration of Dragon Home's elder resounded in her mind as if she basked in an unbelievable dream. Her ragged emotions had run the gambit from the fear of being eaten by a beast many times her size, to having an ancient dragon swear allegiance to her. *Her*, of all people. A pitiful wretch despised by her people for the misfortune of her ancestry. She quaked at the revelation that she had earned the fealty of an entire dragon clan. Nothing in life had prepared her for this.

Shadows lengthened into darkness as brooding clouds coalesced overhead. In a daze, Reecah took the time to gather her weapons and her senses. Daring to stroke the ancient wyrm's snout, she smiled as Grimclaw closed his eyes in contented supplication. She moved around his great head, rubbing her knuckles raw on his rough skin.

A high-pitched squeak of surprise escaped Reecah as Grimclaw jumped to his feet, fiercely sniffing at the air.

262

Reecah's Flight

His eyes narrowed. *"Into the temple. Someone approaches from the valley."*

Reecah blinked, scanning the darkened tunnel leading to the ivy wall.

Grimclaw roared, *"In the temple! Now!"*

Snapping out of her shock, she withdrew her sword.

"What're you waiting for? I have only just found you, Windwalker. I refuse to lose you like I did, Marinah."

She couldn't imagine a safer place in all the world. Who in their right mind would be foolish enough to confront a magical beast as old as time?

Despite her mounting fear that Grimclaw believed he wasn't strong enough to protect her, she was consoled by his insistence on referring to her as a Windwalker. If her ancestors had been involved with the dragons in years gone by, she was okay with being considered a part of that history.

Summoning what little courage she had left, she squared her shoulders, puffed her chest out and held her chin high. "We face them together."

"I have no time for your silliness. You're nothing but a hindrance. Until you realize your legacy, you're vulnerable. Into the temple. Now!"

His acrimonious words drained her resolve. Hanging her head like a berated puppy, she jogged around Grimclaw's bulk, careful not to get swatted by his agitated tail.

A tumble of ancient volcanic spillover, pitted and glass-like, fronted the cliff face. Three large steps carved from the lava, their surface smooth and shiny in the moonlight, rose to meet a vaulted marble bridge in the shape of a dragon's tongue. The pathway bisected towering fangs that curved up taller than she was—almost connecting with those hanging down from above.

Reecah paused at the back of the marble dragon's mouth to look back.

Reecah's Flight

Grimclaw's large eyes blinked once, the action unable to quench their underlying sadness.

It broke her heart. It was as if the ancient wyrm had foreseen this day.

He nodded once, his voice soft in her mind. *"Go, Windwalker. I'm honoured to have finally met you."*

Crouching low, Grimclaw unfurled his expansive wings and took to the night sky, his black scales blending into the darkness and out of sight faster than Reecah wished. She had a sinking premonition she would never see him again.

Thinking she should cross back over the tongue bridge to search the grounds for something suitable to make a torch, Raver cawed from inside the temple—the black raven invisible in the dark interior—his fluttering wings informing her he flew toward her.

Holding an arm out, she scooped him out of the air, hanging onto to him until his mangled feet found purchase on her leather forearm cover.

"Hey!"

Raver pecked at her cloak, trying to pull the opening aside.

From within her cloak, the gemstone embedded in her journal had sparked to life. Its light jumped free of her cloak and radiated into the temple.

Holding the book outstretched before her, she leaned across the threshold and jerked back in fright as a piercing light flared overhead, followed closely by another and then another in quick succession—each one radiating the same light as that of the journal.

Raver squawked and flew into the tunnel.

Gemstones much bigger than the one in her diary blinked on, one after another into the distance, as if tracking Raver's progress. The artificial light illuminated a wide corridor of masterfully carved rock, its walls, floor, and ceiling intricately carved with a continuous scene of dragons, mountains, ocean, and people.

She couldn't prevent her lower jaw from dropping. Ambling along the tunnel, her head swivelled in every direction, unable to take in the entirety of intricately depicted scenes.

A lifelike depiction of a dragon flying over a valley that resembled Dragonfang Pass drew her imagination. She ran her fingertips along it. Carved from the living stone, a woman sat astride the dragon; long hair flowing behind her.

Goosebumps riddled her skin. She had envisioned this scene her whole life. Had dreamt it time and again in so many different ways. She recalled the giddy feeling of weightlessness she experienced in her dreams—the wind blowing through her hair and the world slipping by far below as she clung to the neck of a dragon.

If the scene surrounding her bore any truth to the past, people had once lived in harmony with the majestic beasts and soared the skies.

If not for Raver squawking a warning at the last moment, Reecah would have tumbled over the brink at the end of the tunnel. The passage terminated at a cavernous, cone-like chute rising to dizzying heights before opening up to display the stars in the night sky. Dark clouds roiled across the gap, their edges illuminated by the unseen moon.

She swallowed. The Dragon Temple had been carved into the heart of a volcano. An unusual sense of vertigo dropped her to her knees. Mustering her nerve, she crept to the brink and peered down. The cleft fell away into impenetrable blackness.

A narrow ledge branched off the end of the entrance tunnel, circling the interior of the crater in both directions. Numerous passages ran off the inner circle at random intervals—the side tunnels glowing in the same light as that of her journal.

Reecah's Flight

Backing away from the defile, Reecah brushed volcanic dust from her clothes. She glanced back the way she had come, wanting desperately to return to the courtyard and search for Grimclaw.

She sighed. He had made it abundantly clear he didn't want her out there. Not knowing where to begin looking for him now that he'd flown off, she was loath to wander the forest at night.

Her mind returned to her near-encounter with Scarletclaws in the woods. If the red dragon was running around the forest, that meant Silence had been...

She swallowed. She should have never left the purple dragon.

A shiver gripped her. One that had nothing to do with the chill in the temple. Where were Lurker and Swoop? They were supposed to join her on the temple grounds.

Withdrawing her sword, she sprinted up the entrance tunnel. Whether Grimclaw liked it or not, she wasn't prepared to allow another dragon to suffer because of her. If she couldn't stand by them, she didn't deserve their fealty.

Halfway to the exit, the tunnel shook under her feet. Losing her footing, she went down hard in a puff of dust. Inhaling a lungful of airborne silt, she struggled to her feet, coughing. She leaned against the wall, scanning the passage through watery eyes, searching for the cause of the tremor. Her knees and elbows felt like they were on fire. Without having to look at them, she knew they were badly scraped.

A fearsome roar thundered outside. The inside of the marble dragon head flickered in an orangey-red glow—the sound of flames crackled; stronger than any fire she'd ever witnessed—including the one that had gutted *Grimelda's Clutch*. Dragon fire!

Ignoring her skin abrasions, she winced at the pain in her lungs as she bounded up the corridor—despairing, not for the first time about leaving her bow and arrows behind.

Reecah's Flight

The closer she got to the exit, the louder the noises of a battle raging outside filled the tunnel. The din alone made it sound like two great armies were clashing on the temple's doorstep.

Reducing her pace, a sense of self-preservation warned her of an impending death if she ventured into the marble dragon head.

Spoken tales of her parents—the only memories she had—whirled through her mind. Grammy's stern voice despising the dragons for stealing her children, thundered its alarm. Reecah envisioned Grammy with a raised finger, berating her for casting her lot with the feral beasts. Her pace slowed to a walk.

The many faces of villagers she hardly knew mocked her. Who gave an orphaned girl the right to oppose the edict of the high king? Shame on her.

Raver cawed up ahead, his silky feathers refracting another bout of roaring flames.

The raven reminded her of Auntie Grim. The eclectic crone's mannerisms and bizarre rituals had reinforced the villagers' belief that dragons and magic were devices wielded by dark forces—the epitome of all that was wrong with the world. How dare she gainsay the mandate of the high king?

Distant memories of Poppa stepped forward, brushing those thoughts aside. Not disagreeing with the villagers' sentiments—more like assuring her it was okay to come to her own conclusions. To trust in herself and not waste her time worrying about what others thought. It was her life. If she believed she could fly, however impossible people said that would be, Poppa's philosophy was to never dismiss her dreams. It was up to her to make them happen.

Goosebumps riddled her skin. She cast her gaze at the wall—at the picture of the woman flying the dragon. Humans didn't possess the ability to fly, but that didn't mean flight was impossible.

Reecah's Flight

The tunnel shook. Dust filtered down from the thick edges of carved rock, diffusing the light from the gemstones and blurring her view of the exit. A shriek of agony reverberated down the tunnel. Grimclaw's torment called to her.

Springing into action, she ran faster than ever before. The ancient wyrm was in trouble and it was up to her to save him. Proficient with a sword or not, they would face the aggressors together or die in the attempt. She no longer feared for her life. If she didn't do what she could to help Grimclaw, she would die inside anyway.

A ball of ice exploded against the back of the marble dragon's throat. The revelation of the magical bolt struck her. Grimclaw faced more than blades and arrows. He was dueling with a wizard.

Pressing her soft-soled boots against the dusty marble floor, she slid, trying to avoid the aftermath of the strike. She held her forearms in front of her face, shrieking as the leather vambraces absorbed cold from the dissipating wizard's bolt.

Arresting her slide against a marble tooth, she hung onto the curved pillar for support and cast a stunned gaze at the scene unfolding outside.

Flames engulfed the courtyard, their erratic path running beyond the thick wall to the ivy parapet. How the dozens of black-plated knights stood amongst the burning fires without shriveling, Reecah couldn't comprehend, and yet, there they were, facing an enraged dragon.

Grimclaw's hide bled from several locations—thick blood oozing from beneath damaged scales. His head swung back and forth trying to keep the black knights at bay but they kept coming—fearlessly venturing forth the moment his attention fell on the next man.

"Reecah!" A familiar voice rose above the din.

Searching the grounds, she located the one responsible.

Reecah's Flight

"Reecah?" Grimclaw's head craned back to find her, desperation written in his pained eyes. *"Run, Windwalker, run!"*

She ducked as Grimclaw's massive tail swung at the marble dragon head, violently impacting the entranceway.

Stumbling backward to avoid being hit, she held up her arms. A thunderous crack rocked the exit. Chunks of marble collapsed to the entry bridge—the ensuing avalanche of broken rock sealed off the tunnel from the outside world.

Running through the dark forest, it wasn't hard for Junior to discover where Jaxon had led the prince and his elite guard. Concussions rent the mountainside ahead, the area flickering from the glow of many fires.

To the west, distant dragon cries and the occasional grumble of something large colliding with the ground could only mean the original army of king's men had engaged Dragon Home.

An ear-piercing shriek split the night air, full of intense pain.

Materializing out of the dark wood ahead, Junior ran for the smoldering breach in an ivy-covered wall—the area beyond awash in fire.

Running through the gap, a moss-covered wall rose into the trees to his right, the granite barrier penetrated by an arched tunnel. From where he stood, he witnessed a battle taking place beyond the second wall.

Gritting his teeth, wondering what possessed him to run toward certain death, he passed through the tunnel and stopped. His jaw dropped.

Lightning flashed, illuminating what the unchecked banks of fire didn't. A ring of black knights confronted an enormous dragon—the midnight black leviathan spewing swaths of deadly fire. His knees felt weak.

Leaning against the tunnel wall, his attention was diverted by an errant ice bolt issued from the hands of the prince. The crackling sphere, no bigger than his fist, missed the dragon's swinging head and flew into the open maw of what appeared to be a marble statue of a massive dragon head.

The ice-ball exploded against the back of the marble dragon's throat, freezing the wall and disintegrating into a thousand frozen shards.

Junior gaped at the unexpected sight appearing in the ice-ball's wake. Reecah stared out at the scene, a sword in one hand and a quarterstaff in the other.

Junior pulled his sword from over his back. "Reecah!"

The dragon turned his attention on her.

Unable to do anything but watch, Junior winced as the dragon's tail smashed the marble entranceway. The last thing he saw of Reecah was her throwing her hands up in a futile attempt to hold back the ensuing avalanche.

Reecah's Flight

Blind Truth

Marble crashed to the ground in front of Reecah, accompanied by granite boulders and dirt—the grating noise, one she would not soon forget. When the dust cleared, the rockfall muted the raging battle outside to a distant rumble.

Pushing and kicking at the rubble, she clambered to the tunnel's ceiling and pushed with everything she had but the rockfall was too heavy for her to move.

She half climbed, half slid down the pile until she sat with her back to it. Throwing her weapons to the ground, she buried her face in her hands and cried, infuriated at her inability to help Grimclaw.

Her chest falls came in great, angered heaves. She had spent her life ignoring those intent on abusing her physically and emotionally—playing cruel tricks on her when she was young and slandering her family as she grew older. She had learned to turn her cheek on the people who professed their superiority. She had endured a lifetime of avoiding people who went out of their way to voice their opinions on the pitiful Draakvriend family secluded on the hill.

She abhorred the bitterness darkening her soul. Poppa and Grammy had raised her better than that, but she had had enough. Everyone she had come into contact with acted the opposite of what she was taught to be the proper way to behave. Perhaps they were right. Perhaps *she* was the odd one. Gritting her teeth, she wiped her face on a vambrace, smearing the smooth leather with tears and snot.

Reecah's Flight

She jumped to her feet and pushed and pulled at the rubble, as if the passage of time had made a difference to its composition. Kicking out in despair, she grimaced and hopped around. There was a good chance she'd broken her big toe. The self-inflicted pain enraged her further.

Grimclaw's muffled cry reached her through the barrier. Its tone of finality got her moving. She had to find another way out of the temple. Empowered by the ancient dragon's plight, she sheathed her sword, grabbed her quarterstaff and sprinted away from the danger, swiftly arriving at the end of the tunnel.

Storm clouds drifted beyond the unreachable gap high overhead, their swirling mass flickering with lightning that flashed eerily off the crater's walls. Visible in the glow of the surrounding side tunnels, a heavy rain fell into the heart of the volcano.

Raver called out from somewhere to her right. Turning in that direction, she pulled her journal free and used the shining stone to search for the bird. Perhaps Grimelda's pet knew more than Reecah gave him credit for.

She came across a tunnel branching off into the mountain, but Raver called again, farther along.

"Where are you?" she shouted, her voice echoing and fading into the depths. "To me!"

"To me! To me!"

She panned her journal around, but the stygian pitch of the crater swallowed its light. The notion of Raver actually communicating with her rather than just repeating her words made her wonder at his response. Could it be true?

"Raver, to me!" Her voice echoed.

"To me! To me!" Raver answered.

It wasn't like the raven to disobey her command. He usually returned as soon as she called him.

The next tunnel was a fair hike around the interior of the crater. If she didn't find an exit soon, she feared Grimclaw would be long dead before she made it back to him. The gods only knew where another exit would take her.

Her footfalls barely made a sound along the inside ledge as she thought about Jonas Junior. A numbing cold seized her heart. Embarrassed at being caught bathing below the waterfall, she had foolishly told him of her destination. The traitorous cretin had led the king's men right to her. If Grimclaw died as a result, she vowed to kill the bastard with her bare hands.

Screaming at how everything had worked out, her high-pitched wail echoed into the depths, mocking her.

Raver's call prevented her from sinking into a pit of self-loathing. The bird stood on the threshold of a tunnel she hadn't noticed in the dark crater. On closer inspection, with the aid of the journal's light, a small landing led to the top of a steep stairwell spiralling into the earth.

"What is it, Raver?"

The raven blinked.

The foreboding passageway didn't look promising. She needed to find a fast way out of the temple—not descend into the bowels of a volcano. "Is the exit down there?"

Raver bobbed his head. "Down there! Down there!" He skittered to the top step and took flight, his black form swallowed by the impenetrable darkness. No gemstones illuminated this tunnel.

Unperturbed, she chased after the bird. Her journal would show her the way.

Setting foot on the top step, her gemstone blinked out. A tooth-rattling scrape of heavy stone rumbled behind her, shaking her to the core.

If not for the tightness of the stairwell she might have fallen down the gaping shaft. Bracing her hands against the stone wall, she felt behind her. In the absolute darkness, her touch confirmed that a slab of rock had sealed her inside the tunnel.

Reecah's Flight

She leaned against the barricade, wanting nothing more than to drop to the ground in despair, but Grimclaw's plight kept her moving. Stashing the journal inside her cloak, she descended into the ground, patting the unseen wall curving in on itself, hoping the rock wasn't about to drop away and send her tumbling into oblivion.

If not for Raver's occasional caw, each one sounding farther into the ground than the last, she might have faltered. The irony struck her. Had she been anywhere else, she would have applauded Raver's fortitude. It wasn't the first time the silly bird had proven itself braver than her.

The stairwell seemed to go on forever in her heightened state of fright, but she eventually reached the bottom step—almost pitching forward when her next footfall landed on stone level with her last.

Her quarterstaff rattled off the edge of the wall and flailed out beside her—the clatter echoing hollowly ahead. Just as she feared, the wall had fallen away. From what she could ascertain, she stood on the edge of a subterranean cavern.

Probing the floor ahead with her staff, she was puzzled. There didn't appear to be any ground in front of her. It was as if...

A 'snick' from the staircase behind, accompanied by an ominous rumbling of rock grating together, jarred her senses. Using her quarterstaff, she probed where she believed the steps to be but was met by solid rock. The stairs had disappeared!

Lowering herself to her hands and knees, she felt for the edges of the cold stone beneath her, her eyes growing wider with each subsequent touch. If what her investigation told her was true, she knelt on a small ledge, barely large enough to accommodate her—a stone wall at her back and nothing else around her. A quick search with her staff confirmed that if there was a ceiling within the shaft, it wasn't within reach.

Reecah's Flight

"To me! To me!" Raver's voice echoed from somewhere ahead.

"Raver, where are you?" Oh, what she'd give to be able to fly. To not fear stepping off a ledge and falling to her death. Examining the small area around her by touch, she carefully sat on her rump and cradled her quarterstaff in her lap. If she had only hung onto that rucksack, she could've used her flint to set something on fire and give her light.

She grimaced. The only thing she had to burn was her journal. Pulling it out of her inner pocket, she turned it blindly in her hands, feeling the faceted surface of the gemstone. She attempted to will it to life but nothing happened.

Pondering the gemstone's significance did little to ease her worry. The magical bauble somehow linked her to the dragons—spurred to life in Lurker's presence. Her brain came to a full stop. What if the power in the stone was tied to Lurker's life?

She shook her head, unwilling to travel down that path.

Whatever the reason, something had quenched the gem's vitality. Perhaps her distance from the dragons and the thick slabs of rock that trapped her beneath the ground.

Putting the journal away, fluttering wings grabbed her attention. In futility, she searched the dark for her little friend, marvelling at his ability to see anything, until he thumped against the wall and fell to the ledge beside her.

"Raver!" She searched with her hands, afraid he had dropped into whatever abyss lay below. Her fingers brushed his feathers, instilling her with a new fear. He wasn't moving.

Wrapping shaking hands around his body, careful to fold his wings against his side as best she could in the darkness, she hugged him to her chest. Tears welled up, thinking he was dead, but his chest rose and fell beneath her fingers in quick succession.

Reecah's Flight

Spurting out a laugh, she hugged him closer, rubbing his neck. "Silly bird. You've gone and knocked yourself out."

She dreaded the thought of Grimelda looking down from wherever dead witches went if she had been responsible for leading the crone's pet to his death. Raver had been Grimelda's only friend for years.

The night of the inferno jumped into her head. Some friend Grimelda had been. Who in their right mind hacked the toes off a friend? Or anyone, for that matter.

Stroking his feathers, she considered his age. She was twelve the first time she visited her aunt and Raver was present. That made him at least ten.

Her thoughts settled on Grimelda. It was hard to imagine being related to such a strange woman. And yet, there was something compelling about the brief snippets of information the witch had shared. Grimelda had made Reecah's great-grandmother sound like someone extraordinary. Magical, if Reecah had interpreted the gist of Grimelda's mutterings correctly.

The bizarre words of their final conversation consumed her. *"Heed these words well, for they're the only thing standing between you and a long, lonely death. There'll come a time in the not too distant future that you'll be required to accept your heritage if you want to survive. Pray, child, you are wise enough to open your heart. Let the truth guide you."*

She hadn't given Grimelda's ramblings much thought at the time. She'd been too preoccupied by her aunt's assertion of her impending doom. *"…a long, lonely death…accept your heritage if you want to survive…let the truth guide you."*

What had the old crone been getting at? Surely, Grimelda couldn't have foreseen her being trapped in such a…

Reecah's eyes widened. "No," she said out loud—Auntie Grim's instructions forming on her lips. "Locate the earth's schism to reclaim your heritage. Is this the schism?"

If she only had the faintest of light to see by.

Reecah's Flight

"Think Reecah! Think Reecah!" Raver's throaty voice disturbed the stillness of the cavern.

She almost dropped him in fright. Instead, she hugged him to the side of her face. "Crazy bird. You scared the life out of me."

Realization set in. Raver had proven again his penchant to speak his mind. Holding him out at arm's length to look at him in a new light, she laughed through her tears at the foolishness of her actions. She couldn't see the nose on her face.

Raver pecked at her hands.

"Ow, you dirty bird." Without thinking, she threw him into the air.

"Dirty bird! Dirty bird!" Raver cried, his wings flapping noisily away from the ledge.

Reecah worried he would fly into something and knock himself out again. Following his flight with her ears, he wasn't aloft for long before his erratic, tell-tale landing could be heard somewhere across the defile. Schism, she corrected herself.

Carefully dropping to her stomach, she stretched her quarterstaff over the abyss to investigate the darkness, hoping to find the far edge of the gap. Her staff found nothing.

Letting her arm hang down in surrender, Auntie Grim's words bombarded her. *"...accept your heritage if you want to survive...let the truth guide you."*

She gritted her teeth. What did it mean? She rubbed at the side of her head in frustration. Why hadn't the crazy old woman said what she meant instead of speaking in riddles? If she truly was Grimelda's great-niece, one would think...

Grimelda's great-niece! A Draakvriend by virtue of Poppa, but through her mother and Grammy, she had descended from a Windwalker.

Grimclaw had said as much. So what?

"Save the dragons! Save the dragons!" Raver's words startled her.

Reecah's Flight

Reecah's fingers brushed her earrings—the bloodstones embedded in her earlobes without her consent. She recoiled from the brink as Grimelda's bloodshot visage loomed in her mind, as real as if she were right there in front of her. *"When I'm gone, you'll be the only one left on this side of the Great Kingdom capable of saving the dragons."*

She swallowed. Her heritage. Like her mother, who Grimclaw claimed to have allied with, it was time for Reecah to latch onto her destiny and take up the dragons' cause. She saw it now. Thinking back, she'd always known it. She distinctly remembered when her family's legacy had made itself known to her—sitting with Poppa and pointing at a butterfly. She just hadn't known it at the time.

Why else would Grimclaw, a fearsome, fire breathing beast, prostrate himself at her feet? He sensed the truth in her even if she had not. She wasn't merely descended from the Windwalkers, she *was* a Windwalker!

Raver squawked, his wings beating furiously.

Across the schism, a faint glow pierced the darkness, growing in intensity until it's light shone so brightly, Reecah couldn't bear to look at it.

Shading her eyes with a forearm, Reecah gaped at the sight revealing itself. She stood on the flange of an immense sculpture carved into the side of a shaft that fell out of sight—similar to the volcanic crater but much smaller in diameter.

Careful not to step off the edge of what appeared on closer inspection to be a larger than life-sized journal under her feet, she gaped at the scope of the female caricature carved out of the wall behind her. Draped in robes, the beautiful woman bore a staff in one hand and held aloft the stone beneath Reecah's feet with her other. Some ancient sculptor had chiselled the woman's hair from the veins of marble shooting through the dark granite of the schism. The grandeur of the scene encircling the chamber left her breathless.

278

Reecah's Flight

The anguished bodies of fallen men, women and dragons lined the walls encircling the abyss amongst massive, stone tree trunks climbing high overhead—the trees' limbs branched out to form the cavern's ceiling. A myriad of gemstones sparked to life within their entangled limbs like tiny faeries dancing around the petrified canopy—their light illuminating the fantastical chamber in an ethereal glow.

Rising from the darkness on the far side of the schism, a great stone dragon, bigger than Grimclaw, spread massive wings around the chamber's perimeter, their detailed folds encircling the fallen men, women, dragons and trees.

Everything about the magical environment enthralled Reecah beyond comprehension, but the dragon itself mesmerized her.

Carved out of a plume of fossilized lava, the dragon's head leaned into the middle of the shaft, its enormous mouth parted to reveal a small cavern of its own, lined by a row of curved fangs twice Reecah's height. Above its gaping maw, the dragon stared directly at her—one eye blackened while the other sparkled with the light of a small gemstone set in its centre like a tiny pupil.

She had found the Watcher and the Dragon's Eye! The stone her great-aunt made her promise to return to her. It would be a shame to deface such a beautiful sculpture. And to what end? Grimelda was long dead.

Realizing she was holding her breath, Reecah exhaled and inhaled in rapid succession as she searched for a way to cross to the dragon. Unless she learned to fly, she was condemned to remain stranded upon the stone journal.

Raver squawked from his perch on the limb of a stone tree towering over the abyss. "Reecah's diary! Reecah's diary!"

Her journal? Why would Raver say that? Withdrawing the book from her cloak filled her with relief—its gemstone shining brightly. Tears blurred her vision. If it had any connection to Lurker, it meant her friend was still alive.

She turned the blinding glare of the book away from her face. As its beam broke that of its twin in the Watcher, the cavern trembled. Countless years of dust sifted down the walls, diffusing the light.

The journal beneath her feet shook so hard she dropped to her stomach and pushed herself backward, thinking to hold herself against the rock face. Alarmingly, she wasn't able to touch the wall. The journal platform rattled its way toward the Watcher, extending from the wall like a flat bridge.

Raver called out a belated warning, but it was too late. It was all she could do to hang onto her quarterstaff with one hand and her journal with the other; trying to keep herself from vibrating off the side of the bridge.

Daring to glance up at the approaching dragon head, she winced, expecting the bridge to crash into the beautiful carving, but the tremors stopped abruptly, pitching her onto her face. The bridge stopped a hair's breadth from the dragon's bottom jaw.

It took her a moment to calm her breathing and steady her shaking hands. Rising unsteadily to her feet, afraid the bridge might collapse beneath her movement, she gazed around the cavern. The new vantage point filled her with a fresh sense of wonder at the detailed work that had gone into the lava dragon's lair.

Looking down did little to bolster her courage. She stood in the centre of a seemingly bottomless cavern upon a tenuous platform. There was no use going back, nor could she see a way forward beyond the dragon.

She spotted a black hole at the back of the dragon's mouth, emulating its throat. The outside of the dragon's neck plummeted straight down, out of sight. There was no way she was entertaining that route.

Reecah's Flight

Not knowing what to do, Grimelda's plea to retrieve the Dragon's Eye nagged at her. She had made it this far. It was time to see her promise through.

Taking measure of the height of the dragon's upper jaw, she wished again for her rucksack and the small coil of rope at its bottom. Leaving her quarterstaff on the bridge, she took a deep breath, wiped her clammy palms on her breeks, and latched onto a longer fang shooting up from a corner of the dragon's lower jaw. Her years of climbing the mountain heights allowed her to shimmy up with ease—quickly reaching the corresponding upper jaw fang.

She transferred her grip over the slight gap between the teeth and steadied herself for the second part of the climb. The upper fang required more concentration and all the strength she had as it curved outward, disappearing beneath the statue's upper lip.

Clinging to the top of the upper fang, she was forced to release her tenuous grip and reach out to grasp the top of the lip. Her aching thighs strained to remain wrapped around the upper end of the tooth.

She berated herself for looking down. Hanging suspended over the gaping abyss, any mistake now would be her last. She dragged her attention away from certain death and readjusted her grip. Taking a few quick breaths, she pulled her torso over the curved dragon lip—her feet swinging wildly in the air until she got a heel up and over the edge. Digging her foot on top of the dragon's snout, she dragged her trailing leg to safety and lay on her stomach, panting hard. How she was going to get down again was another matter altogether.

Raver dropped from the ceiling headfirst like a black stone, spreading his wings at the last possible moment and righting himself. With little grace, he alit between the dragon's raised eyes. Steadying himself, he studied Reecah.

Reecah's Flight

Reecah pointed a finger, raising her eyebrows. "One of these days you're going to misjudge the drop and become a feathery splat. Don't expect me to scrape up your sorry hide."

He bobbed his head. "Sorry hide! Sorry hide!"

She shook her head, unable to keep the smile from her face. "I must admit. You did good. You found the Watcher. In your roundabout way, showed me how to cross the schism."

"Schism! Schism!"

The mirth left her as she regarded the dragon's eyes. Beautifully carved from the lava and polished smooth, one eye had a tiny indent in its centre matching that of the journal's gemstone.

Her focus fell on the other—too bright to look at directly. Turning her head to one side, she squinted and joined Raver between the raised eye sockets.

Judging by the intense beam of light, the gemstone would likely be too hot to touch. She huffed. Her gloves were in her rucksack. If she survived the day and made it back to the forest, she swore to stitch the rucksack to her cloak so as to never be parted from it again.

She unsheathed a dagger and contemplated the eye from above. "How am I supposed to get it out without dropping it?"

"Get it out! Get it out!"

Raver jumped into the air. Wings flapping rapidly, he hovered beside the Dragon's Eye, his black feathers white in the intense glow. Reaching out with his hooked beak he plucked at the stone.

Reecah cringed, certain he would burn himself, but he didn't make a fuss. After several unsuccessful attempts, she called him off. "It's okay. You showed me its not hot. Let me try."

Raver dropped away and flew around to the back of the dragon.

Reecah's Flight

Lying on top of the eye socket, Reecah hung down and tentatively touched a finger to the stone. Feeling nothing, she pressed her finger against it. It was surprisingly cool.

She placed the tip of her dagger at the edge of the eye and hesitated, thinking again what a shame it was to spoil such a glorious sculpture. She almost pulled herself back up, but the thought of having to come down here again made up her mind. With Grimelda dead, there seemed little point, but she had promised. Reecah prided herself—her word was her bond.

Carefully inserting the dagger's tip behind the upper edge of the eye, she twisted the blade. Without any resistance, the gemstone slid free and fell into her upturned palm. She stared at it, puzzled. Raver had tugged and pulled at it with more vigour than she had.

As soon as the Dragon's Eye lost contact with the dragon, it winked out and a deep rumble thundered throughout the cavern.

Standing upright, Reecah searched for the cause of the disturbance.

The slab blocking the stairwell at the far end of the bridge had slid into the wall, exposing the stone steps.

Reecah nodded. By removing the eye, she had sprung the means to her escape. Now if she could only get back down to the bridge before it retracted.

She approached the end of the dragon's snout and looked down. A straight jump would likely cause her to turn an ankle at the very least. If she wasn't careful, she might not be able to prevent herself from falling over the side of the narrow causeway.

She dropped to her knees and prepared to hang down as far as possible before letting go, but stopped. The clinking of metal-shod feet descending the stairwell echoed throughout the cavern.

Reecah's Flight

Her lower lip trembled and her heart sank. For anyone to enter the Dragon Temple, they would have to get by Grimclaw. The only way to do that would be if they had killed the ancient guardian.

A torch's flickering glow illuminated the bottom of the stairwell. Confirming her worst fear, two black-clad knights clattered onto the causeway.

Momentarily distracted by the splendour of the cavern, their attention fell on Reecah.

"There she is!" One of the knights pointed. "Quick. Tell J'kwaad we found her and the dragon altar."

The other knight disappeared up the stairwell leaving Reecah facing a man at least six and a half feet tall.

He strode to the centre of the causeway and stopped, pulling a crossbow from over his shoulder. Watching from behind the upturned visor of his pointed helm, his attention never left Reecah.

Reecah searched the cavern for another way out. She was trapped.

The knight bent over his crossbow, reached down with both hands and pulled the string into the open nut, securing it into place. Levelling the stock, he dropped a quarrel into place and took aim. "The prince will reward me for your head, you nettlesome witch."

Reecah's Flight

Reecah's Flight

Something had caused the knight to miss his shot. Whether it was Raver suddenly taking flight or the puff of smoke that escaped the stone dragon's throat, Reecah didn't care. She had bigger things to worry about. The dragon's head had moved beneath her feet.

Cursing his rotten luck, the knight stooped over his crossbow and pulled the string back into firing position. Notching another bolt, he stepped closer and took aim.

Reecah contemplated running off the front of the dragon to jump onto the knight, but she couldn't see that ending well. Even if he missed his shot, falling four times her height onto an armour-plated man didn't seem like a sane thing to do.

She swallowed her nerve. What choice did she have?

Taking a deep breath, she leaned into a crouch and sprung forward. One step, two steps…

The dragon's head shook violently, throwing her to its surface as a wave of flames shot out from between its teeth, the blast taking the knight full in the face.

Reecah's momentum carried her to the edge of the dragon's upper lip. If not for the handholds provided by its smoking nostrils, she would have fallen into the fire's path.

Unable to keep her legs from sliding over the front edge she screamed, folding her legs at the knees. The heat of the roaring fire threatened to burn through her breeks and melt her boots.

Hanging by her fingers, her wild eyes were drawn to the knight. A horrifying noise escaped his helmet as he cooked inside his metal sarcophagus. His anguish lasted long enough for him to drop to his knees and tumble off the bridge, wailing like a banshee and plummeting out of sight. She was certain she was going to wake up in a cold sweat for many nights to come remembering his agonized cry.

The blast of flames petered out moments before Reecah's strength gave out. Straightening her shaking arms, she lowered her body across the glowing hot fangs and fell to the stone journal with a yelp. Landing hard, she fell to her rump. She winced, lifting her tunic away from her waist and seeing her pale skin bright red where her body had come into contact with the fangs.

As soon as she landed, the bridge retracted into the wall from which it extended. Reecah jumped to her feet, not waiting to see if the stairwell would remain accessible once the journal settled back into place against the arm of the female wall carving.

"Raver, to me!" She picked up her quarterstaff and ran without looking back.

Raver flew by her head as she ducked inside the stairwell and disappeared up the spiralling shaft.

Taking two steps at a time, her thighs burned by the time she reached the landing. The sight of the soft glowing tunnels on the far side of the volcanic crater lifted her spirits—the upper stone slab no longer barred her way.

Before she entered the crater, she heard men shouting.

"There's the bird! Shoot it down!"

Reecah burst onto the circular ledge and gasped. A small group of knights ran at her from the mouth of a tunnel farther around the crater. Behind them, a man with Waverunner blonde hair pointed. "There she is!"

All around the perimeter of the crater, knights stopped their progress and turned to see Jaxon's group chase after her.

"To me! To me!" Raver called.

Reecah's Flight

Several crossbow bolts zipped through the air, missing Raver by the narrowest of margins as he dropped headfirst out of the air and disappeared into the second tunnel on her left—the exit tunnel. If the knights were in the crater, that meant the avalanche blocking the courtyard entrance had been cleared.

Her legs carried her faster than her heavily armoured pursuit—all but Jaxon, who had separated himself from the pack.

Slowing just enough to slam into the far wall of the exit tunnel, she looked back, surprised. Jaxon had gained on her.

She sprinted toward the rockfall at the end of the tunnel. If she was wrong about her theory, she would be trapped. Her heart caught in her throat. The fallen rock didn't appear to have been touched at all, but Raver tucked in his wings at the last possible moment and disappeared into the blackness beyond.

Lightning flashed, illuminating a fair-sized breach at the top of the blockage. Her spirits lifted. All she had to do was reach the far end of the tunnel and she would be free.

Approaching the debris, Jaxon's high-pitched voice reached her from halfway down the tunnel. "Reeky! Don't make this harder than it has to be. It's just a matter of time now."

Reecah swallowed her mounting fear. Scrambling up the side of the rockfall she glanced back before slipping through the gap and into the pouring rain.

Gaining her feet on top of the pile, she raised shaking hands to her face. Even knowing Grimclaw must have been killed in order for the knights to enter the temple, nothing could have prepared her for the sight sprawled across the courtyard— Grimclaw's glistening corpse illuminated by lightning. A magical creature, alive for as long as time could remember, slaughtered while protecting her. An amber eye stared back at her, pale and lifeless.

"No. No. No, no, no, no." Reecah dropped to her knees— her legs too weak to bear her weight.

Reecah's Flight

"Got you!" Jaxon exclaimed triumphantly. Extending his arms through the breach atop the debris pile, he latched onto Reecah's ankles and pulled.

Reecah looked back in horror. Devastated by Grimclaw's demise, she had forgotten about Jaxon. Forgotten about the brat who had vexed her for as long as she could remember. Forgotten about the man who had ridiculed her family. The detestable human being who, with his brother, had led the black knights to the temple and killed Grimclaw.

Rage replaced her fear. She no longer cared what happened to her, but she did care what happened to Jaxon. A sadistic smirk twisted her face—one noticed by the blonde-haired man hanging onto her.

He sneered. "What're you going to do now, huh?"

Reecah's answer came at the end of her quarterstaff as it cracked Jaxon between the eyes.

He released one of her ankles to staunch the blood pouring down his face. Examining his hand, blood washed onto the marble in the rain. He growled and wrenched her other boot toward him. "You little witch! You'll pay for that!"

Reecah twisted in his grip and slid toward him as he hoisted himself through the gap.

Kicking out with everything she had, she caught him square in the face with the bottom of her boot.

Jaxon's head snapped back with a yelp, his body tumbling backward and impacting the tunnel floor with a thud.

Reecah experienced a burning desire to re-enter the tunnel and stomp on his face. Her adrenaline demanded she smash his insolent sneer into a gory pulp, but the sight of Grimclaw's body sucked the fight from her.

She slipped down the outside of the rockfall and stumbled to Grimclaw's rain-soaked head.

On his side, Grimclaw's jaw was still higher than her. She slopped through a puddle to stand before the top of his face.

Reecah's Flight

With a trembling hand she stroked the space between his lifeless eyes.

Speaking through heaving sobs, she whispered, "I'm so sorry. This is all my fault. I should never have come. Please forgive me, you beautiful soul. You deserved better than this."

The horrid damage the knights had inflicted on the timeless creature twisted her gut. Her gaze fell on the temple entrance, hoping Jaxon, or anyone, would appear so that she could avenge Grimclaw's death.

Something deep inside warned her that her wish would soon be realized if she didn't leave soon. It wouldn't be long before the black knights emerged from the gap and seized her. She swallowed. If that happened, Grimclaw would have died for nothing.

A building resolve crept from the depths of her soul. If it was the last thing she did with her life, she vowed to avenge the needless slaughter perpetrated by the high king's men on the dragons.

The rain had stopped and the clouds parted. Moonbeams lit up the mist rising off the ground as she leaned in to kiss Grimclaw's face. "Good-bye, my brave friend. I will not let your death be in vain. I, Reecah Windwalker, pledge to you, oh noble beast, that I won't rest until the plight of the dragons is remedied or I die in the attempt. I promise I will not go down quietly."

Stepping away from Grimclaw, her delicate fingertips trailing on his rough skin for as long as possible, she located the tunnel leading to the ivy-covered wall. Steeling herself not to look back, she strode boldly away from the dead guardian.

Jonas Junior separated himself from the shadows of the courtyard tunnel, his face looking more beat up than it had a short while ago. "Reecah!"

Reecah's eyes narrowed. Soaked to the skin, she wiped the tears from her face to see Junior clearly. Her sword slid from its sheath. "You traitorous bastard!" She extended the blade behind her. "Look what you've done! You've stolen the beauty from the world!"

Junior's sword appeared in his hand, his head shaking.

She didn't give him time to respond. Running through the muck, she ran headlong to engage the man twice her size.

"Reecah, no!" he cried out and grunted.

His eyes went wide and his sword fell to the ground. Dropping to his knees, he said through clenched teeth. "Run, Reecah, run."

Reecah frowned at the strange behaviour. What kind of foolery was this?

Junior's eyes rolled into his head and he fell face first into the mud, his hands not breaking his fall—an arrow buried in his back.

Before Reecah realized the inference of the arrow, dozens of men in king's livery stormed through the courtyard tunnel and fanned out, crossbows and longbows brought to bear.

Reecah spun one way and then the other searching for an escape route. Not that it mattered. The archers would cut her down before she took a second step.

A clamour arose from the temple entrance as the first of many black knights emerged.

Raver called from atop the thick wall. "To me! To me!"

On the brink of her death, Reecah laughed half-heartedly at the silly bird. If only she *could* fly. Perhaps when her spirit left her body, she would finally get to experience the rapturous joy of spreading her wings and soaring through the air. She dropped her arms, welcoming death.

"Up there!" someone shouted.

Reecah smiled. Perhaps she and Raver would meet Grimclaw together.

"And there!"

"There's another one!"

Reecah's Flight

"And another!"

Reecah snapped out of her stupor. What were the knights looking at?

Dropping out of the sky came a brown dragonling, plunging headlong at the line of king's men, raking two with her claws before swooping back into the air.

"Swoop!" Reecah cried, afraid for her friend but ecstatic to see her.

A green dragon dropped to the ground between Junior's prone body and the scrambling king's men.

Lurker roared louder than Reecah would have thought possible as he ran at the nearest man. An arrow bounced off his scales. Another one impaled his wing.

Reecah stared in horror. The archers had stopped their retreat and were pulling their strings taut. "Lurker, no!"

If Lurker heard her, he didn't respond. One man lay at his feet, his arm mangled beyond repair while two more backed away from the enraged dragon.

From out of the gloom, the red dragon Silence had named Scarletclaws crashed into the line of archers and crossbowmen. She never bothered catching her fall—just kept driving through the knights until her momentum dropped her into a heap beside Lurker.

Together, the two dragons chased after the knights who had broken rank and were running for their lives.

Behind Reecah, three black knights emerged from the temple, cursing the lesser knights for not maintaining their formation.

Reecah turned to intercept them, but a purple blur dropped behind the black knights.

Silence's fanged mouth closed on the nearest man's helmet, crushing the metal helm into his screaming head. She twisted her neck with such fury that the man's body whipped into the air at an unnatural angle from his trapped head.

Reecah's Flight

The remaining black knights charged at Reecah, but Swoop fell out of the sky, smashing into them.

Reecah didn't know where to look. More black knights streamed out of the Dragon Temple and reinforcements were pouring through the courtyard tunnel, shoring up the lines and blocking any chance she had of escape.

Lurker and Scarletclaws were surrounded, each of them bristling with more than one missile protruding from their scales.

Silence backed away from several black knights, doing her best to keep them from getting at Swoop as the brown dragon finished off the two knights she had fallen upon.

Reecah despaired. The dragonlings still had a chance to escape but they wouldn't leave without her. "Lurker! Leave me. Fly. Get away before they kill you!"

Swoop swung her bloody-toothed grin Reecah's way. *"Grimclaw gave his life for you, Windwalker. What kind of friends would we be if we left you?"*

"But you can fly. I can't. There's no other way out. Go, before its too late," Reecah pleaded. "I release you of Grimclaw's vow. Now, please, I beg you."

Wracking sobs shook her to the core. They weren't listening.

"Reecah, to me!" Lurker's voice filled her head.

Blinking away tears, Reecah stabbed at a black knight sneaking around the backside of Swoop, her sword tip diving between the man's shoulder armour and helm. She pulled her sword free, shaking at what she had just done, staring in horror at the blood dripping off the sword's tip

The knight's axe fell to the ground, his hands clutching at his throat as he fell with a clang at Swoop's feet.

"Reecah, get on!" Lurker broke away from the fight and ran to her. He dropped to his chest beside her. *"Come on, it's the only way."*

Reecah's Flight

Out of the corner of her eye, she noticed a longbowman steadying himself to shoot Lurker in the head.

The archer drew his string, set his sight and cried out— his errant missile slamming into Grimclaw's uncaring hide as Raver clawed at the archer's face with his mangled feet.

Shaking uncontrollably, a numb detachment washing through her, Reecah turned her wrath on the archer, incensed he had further desecrated Grimclaw's corpse. Before the archer could rid himself of Raver, Reecah ran him through.

Lurker chased after her. *"We're out of time. Get on!"*

Reecah cried out, half-crazed with battle-lust. "I have to avenge Grimclaw's death!"

"I do too, Reecah, trust me, but if we don't leave now, we won't survive the day. We need to retreat to a safe place and regroup if we're to have any chance of fighting another day. Come on. Get on." He lowered his chest to the ground.

Reecah frowned, realizing what he was suggesting. "You want me to ride on your back?"

"How else are we going to get you out of here?"

"I'm too heavy."

"We don't have a choice," Lurker pleaded. *"Besides, I carried a troll, remember."*

How could she forget the troll dangling from Lurker's back claws? She shuddered. "That was different. You can't fly with me on your back."

"Climb on my shoulders and hug my neck. Hurry! We're out of time."

She followed his gaze to the temple entrance. The black knight with the gilded piping pulled himself from the gap. The wizard!

Sheathing her sword, she wrapped her arms around Lurker's scaly neck and swung her inside leg over his shoulder. She couldn't believe she was doing this.

"Hang on tight!" Lurker straightened to his full height and stretched his wings experimentally, wincing.

293

Reecah's Flight

"What's wrong?"

"Remove the arrow from my wing."

Reecah laid back and grasped the offending shaft with both hands. "Ready?"

Not waiting for a response, she ripped the arrow free and threw it to the ground.

Lurker roared, almost bucking her off.

"Now, Lurker!" Reecah shouted, her eyes meeting the wizard's across the courtyard.

"Swoop, Silence, Scarletclaws, away!" Lurker ordered. He took two quick steps and launched himself into the air. His great wings flapped quickly but Reecah's added weight over his shoulders threw off his coordination.

Reecah screamed as Lurker nose-dived over the defensive line set up by the regular king's men.

An ice-ball exploded against the moss-covered wall where Lurker's trajectory would have taken him had he been able to remain in the air

Lurker's front feet hit the ground hard, jarring Reecah from his shoulders. Clinging to his neck, her feet hit the ground beside him.

Lurker ran into the high arched tunnel. *"Hang on!"*

She kept pace with his frenzied flight, her feet touching the ground sporadically. Newcomers emerging through the breach in the ivy-covered wall scrambled to get out of the way of the charging dragon. All except one.

The biggest man in Fishmonger Bay stepped out in front of them, a large tower shield strapped to his back and a mighty battle-axe held overhead.

Covering a grotesquely scarred face, his unkempt, pepper-grey beard lifted off his chest as he swung his weapon behind him to deliver the killing stroke.

Reecah released her grip on Lurker's neck and tumbled on the ground. "Nooooo!"

Reecah's Flight

Grog's gaze fell on Reecah for the briefest of moments.

Unable to react fast enough to save her friend, all she could do was watch Grog step into his attack. She held an arm out before her, closing her eyes and looking away as the battle-axe chunked into the ground.

A collective gasp sounded from the scattered knights and villagers of the dragon hunt.

Reecah lowered her arm and surveyed the damage, stunned by what she saw.

Grog stood before Lurker, his meaty hands held up as if they were enough of a barrier to keep the dragon from ripping his head off. "Do with me as you like, my scaly friend. I'm done with killing majestic beasties!"

Lurker roared, the sound lifting the small hairs on Reecah's neck.

Everyone stepped back, except Grog who simply lowered his tree trunk arms, awaiting his fate.

Reecah fondly recalled the gentle giant from her youth. One of the few men who had never been anything but kind to her.

"Lurker, no!"

On the verge of clamping his jaws over Grog's head, Lurker stopped—his emerald eyes beseeching an explanation.

"There's no time to explain. Just don't."

The wizard entered the tunnel behind them.

"We need to fly!" Reecah ran alongside Lurker as he stepped around Grog and began moving.

Clearing the tunnel, Reecah bounded high into the air and landed heavily on Lurker's shoulder. The sudden weight nearly toppled him but he kept his feet. Without warning, he sprang into the air as a volley of arrows zipped past where his next step would have taken him.

The ivy-covered wall came up fast. Reecah ducked her head and closed her eyes tight but the collision never happened. Unsure she wanted to open her eyes, she felt the rhythmic up and down lurch of Lurker's body as his wings pushed air beneath them, rising and falling in cadence.

Wind whipped at her tight braid and tore at her cloak. Fearing she might lose her journal and the Dragon's Eye stashed in her inner pocket, she dared to open her eyes. Locating the journal with her elbow, she squeezed it against her body, afraid to remove her hands from Lurker's neck.

With the greatest of willpower, she let her gaze drop to the moonlit ground glistening far below. She gasped to catch her breath, and tightened her hold on Lurker's neck. The chaotic scene in the Dragon Temple courtyard dropped away as lofty treetops became smaller with each flap of his wings. Far to her left, the river sliced through the valley, glinting as it wound its way toward the ocean unseen beyond a bend in the pass.

Far to the side, Silence soared on the prevailing winds. It took her a moment to locate Swoop, much higher still, the brown dragon silhouetted in the moon. Of Scarletclaws, there was no sign.

The smoking ruins of Dragon Home slid by to the north before she was able to calm her breathing. Her eyes watered in the wind, but she didn't care. She was flying!

Reecah Draakvriend, the awkward girl who lived on the hill and spoke of silly dreams, sat astride a real live dragon and flew through the air. If only her doubters could see her now.

Amid the heavy pall of grief, a strange calm settled over her and the leagues passed by in silent exhilaration. If not for the approaching coast and the edge of the mountain range falling away to the south, she would never have located the pin-sized monolith of the Fang.

They were over the Niad Ocean before anyone gathered enough composure to speak.

It was Lurker's voice she heard first, his tone subdued, *"Where now, Reecah?"*

Reecah's Flight

Reecah struggled to prevent her emotions from getting the better of her. She couldn't allow herself weakness while fighting to remain on a dragon's back high over the world, but it was tough. Lurker's entire colony had been destroyed. Other than Swoop and Silence, Reecah wasn't sure any of the dragons had survived.

It soon became apparent that Lurker was tiring. They needed to land, and fast.

Searching the night sky, the newly snow-capped summit of Peril's Peak shone brightly in the moonlight.

She didn't dare loosen her grip upon his neck to point. "Head to that snow-covered peak. At the base of the upper waterfalls lies a cabin. We should be safe there."

Lurker never responded. He adjusted his wings and flew toward the suggested destination.

She didn't mind the silence. She was enjoying the view.

A long-ago memory tingled her skin. If only Poppa could see her now, he would be so proud. His little poppet was flying as high as a dragon.

Reecah's Flight

A New Beginning

Reecah focused on the flames leaping into the darkness, her mind a million leagues away from the hunt camp at the base of Peril's Peak summit. Reminiscing on days gone by and how different life might have been if not for the unjust prejudices between mankind and dragonkind.

After landing through the night, she had tended the wounded dragons. Silence had taken the worst damage, but given enough rest, Reecah was confident the purple dragon would recover.

The day was spent lazing around the field below the tumbling waterfalls. At one point, Swoop flew off and returned a short while later with a small deer in her claws.

Blinking several times, her mind returning to the present, Reecah grunted at the irony of those sitting outside the dragon hunt cabin. Three dragons and the woman the hunt leader had rejected.

She lifted her head and studied the beautiful faces of Silence, Swoop and Lurker. How could anyone wish them harm? Her anger began to rise so she forced herself to think of something else.

Withdrawing her journal, she checked for the countless time that the Dragon's Eye remained stashed at the bottom of her deep pocket. It did. What good it was going to be to her, other than an endless worry, she had no idea. A part of her considered throwing it over the edge of the ridge fronting the fire pit, but she couldn't bring herself to do it. She couldn't

Reecah's Flight

bring herself to part with the subject of Auntie Grim's dying wish.

She swallowed, fighting back the tears that seemed to be her constant companion lately. If she wished to confront the high king and convince him of how wrong the dragon hunt was, she needed to toughen up. How did she expect the reigning monarch of the Great Kingdom to listen to the whiny ramblings of a snot-nosed girl?

She sighed and bowed her head. So much death and misery weighed down on her and her friends. It would be a long time before she thought she would genuinely smile again.

Turning the journal around in her hands, she absently flipped through the pages. "What the…?"

Lurker lifted his head from his own contemplation.

She hadn't realized she'd spoken out loud. Studying the back pages of the journal she considered the bold runes printed there. "I don't remember these words being here."

Lurker didn't respond.

Silence and Swoop moved closer to her to see what she was talking about.

A few of the words were unfamiliar, but it didn't take long to realize she was staring at a spell of some kind. Flipping to the last page, she pointed. "Look! It's signed: Grimclaw."

"I wonder what it means?" Swoop asked.

Lurker and Silence shook their heads.

"Beats me. It looks like something only a wizard would understand."

With that revelation, the clearing fell silent. The fire crackled and popped, its heat driving away the high mountain chill.

Fighting to keep her melancholy at bay, she forced a smile for Lurker's benefit and reached up to stroke his beautiful face. "You miss her, don't you?"

Lurker frowned.

"Your mother."

Reecah's Flight

Lurker's sad expression was answer enough.

Reecah didn't care about the tears flowing down her cheeks. They all needed to heal mentally if they were to move on. She leaned into Lurker, nuzzling her wet face against his shoulder. "I miss my mother too. I never knew her, but I still feel so empty knowing she's gone." She fell quiet.

Lurker tilted his head to rub against the top of hers.

"What about your father? You never talk about him."

Lurker shuddered.

Leaning away, she gazed into his magnificent eyes, the emerald colour aglow in the leaping flames. 'What is it?"

Lurker hung his head. *"Grimclaw was my father."*

A cold wave of comprehension washed through Reecah. She stared hard at her mourning friend, seething at what the king's men had done to him. Swallowing her unease, she stirred the embers with a stick, sending a flurry of sparks into the air.

Letting her ire simmer in the back of her mind, she stared him in the eye. "I'm going to find the high king and demand he put an end to this atrocity. You should come with me. Together we can show the people of the Great Kingdom you aren't their enemy."

A single tear rolled off Lurker's cheek. *"You mean that?"*

She gave him a scathing look for doubting her. "I pledge to you," her gaze included Swoop and Silence, "to all of you, that I will not rest until I convince the king of his folly."

"They'll kill you for speaking such blasphemy."

Reecah's spine tingled, a mischievous grin dimpling her cheeks. "Not if I have three dragons at my back."

The End...

...is but the means to a new beginning

I hope you enjoyed Reecah's Flight.

Your opinion is important and means a lot to me.

Please consider leaving a review on Amazon and Goodreads. Reviews are vital to an author's livelihood.

If you prefer, you can send me your thoughts at: richardhstephens1@gmail.com

Reecah's Gift

Reecah's journey continues in book two in the Legends of the Lurker Series.

Enjoy the first chapter.

Reecah's Gift

End of Silence

𝕬 fortnight had passed since that horrific day in Dragonfang Pass—a day that had witnessed the annihilation of the Draakclaw Colony from Dragon Home. All except for the three dragons waiting for her to pull herself together and get on with her life.

Every passing day since Grimclaw's death filled Reecah with crushing guilt over her role in the beautiful creature's demise. She should never have left him, no matter how vehemently he insisted she save herself. Grimelda said her role was to save the dragons—not run away and allow the annihilation of the colony.

Confounding her melancholy were the faces of the two knights she had killed in the courtyard of the Dragon Temple. Visions of their blood dripping from her sword woke her in a cold sweat, night after sleepless night.

In contrast to her unease, her companion, Raver, casually pruned his feathers—his shiny raven's head pecking away at whatever irritated him. She envied him his simple pleasures—

Reecah's Gift

admiring the way he had moved on after such a traumatic event.

Dust motes shimmered in sunbeams shining through the solitary window in the cabin below Peril's Peak, despite the grime coating its thick glass.

Had she planned on remaining at the dragon hunt camp, she would have turned her attention to tidying up the slovenly interior. If not for her fear of the owners returning to lay claim to their property, Reecah fancied she might have been content to start a new life high atop the world.

Lying on a crude pallet with her hands behind her head, she grimaced. If only life were that simple.

A clamour outside the cabin's lone door made her sit up. The dragons were scuffling about, impatiently waiting for her to pull herself together and decide on their next course of action.

Something about the sunshine flooding the hut melted away her languishing despair. It looked to be a glorious day. Perhaps that was the omen she had been waiting for. A reminder of her pledge—not only to Grimelda, but to dragonkind as well.

They had outstayed their welcome. The king's men had seen them escape the battle at the Dragon Temple. They would no doubt be searching the area. It wouldn't do to tarry under their noses.

Reecah shuddered. If the burning intensity on the face of the wizard she had seen at the Dragon Temple was any indication of his determination, her scaly friends were in peril anywhere near Fishmonger Bay.

It was time to put aside her guilt. A dragon war had been set into motion. Facing certain death at the Dragon Temple, she had vowed to avenge Grimclaw's death. To remain mired in self-recrimination was a grave misjustice to the noble wyrm's sacrifice. It was time to make good on her promise.

She stretched her neck one way and then the other, raising her arms overhead and taking a last deep breath of peaceful

Reecah's Gift

solitude. Pulling on her black suede boots, she jumped to her feet to gather her gear.

Silence had risked her life returning to the forest between the Dragon Temple and Dragon Home to retrieve her discarded equipment. Thankful, Reecah slipped her quiver over her shoulder and secured her unstrung bow to her rucksack before shrugging it on.

Pausing at the door, her gaze fell on the large table at the centre of the hut. A smirk tightened her lips at the irony. Wait until Jonas and his lackeys discovered who had sheltered at their dragon hunt camp. Reecah Draakvriend. She tilted her head, smiling a little deeper as she corrected herself. Reecah Windwalker, the hill witch, had sheltered here—along with three dragons. If only she could stick around to see the look on their faces.

The door opened with a squeal, drawing the attention of her new friends, Lurker, Swoop, and Silence—green, brown and purple dragonlings, respectively. Judging by their sheepish looks, they were up to something.

Allowing Raver to fly through the open door she let it slam back into its frame. The raven made his way to the tiered waterfall cascading from the snow-capped peak behind the hut.

Drawing her brown cloak around her, slipping on its hood, she raised her eyebrows, staring at the green dragon. "Well, are you going to tell me, or do I have to figure it out myself?"

Lurker lowered his head, his emerald eyes alight with mischief. He glanced at his cohorts.

Reecah almost vomited when the dragons parted to reveal the remains of more than one shredded troll's carcass. She turned away from the mound of hairy gore. "Do you have to eat those here? That's disgusting."

"Sorry, Reecah. We didn't think you'd be up and about," Lurker said—his voice sounding in her head. He motioned for Swoop and Silence to get rid of it.

Reecah's Gift

It was a fair assumption. She had become less and less social as the days went by. She waved a hand. "Ugh. Leave it. It's time for us to leave."

The dragons considered the carcasses, obviously not done with them yet. While Lurker and Silence ambled over to Reecah, Swoop snapped up a last chunk of troll flesh; noisily chewing it.

Reecah winced at the sound of bones snapping. The brown dragon swallowed, offering her a bloody-toothed grin. It was going to be an adjustment getting used to the habits of her new companions.

Lurker accompanied Reecah to the edge of the cliff fronting the field around the cabin; following her gaze over the rugged terrain to where the land abutted the glimmering ocean many leagues away. *"Where're you going?"*

The question threw Reecah. "Are you not coming with me?"

Silence and Swoop joined them—all three dragons avoiding her hazel eyes.

"What? I thought we agreed? We need to convince the high king that his mandate to eradicate dragonkind is not an acceptable solution to settling our differences." She paused, staring at each of them individually. They refused to meet her gaze.

She grasped Lurker by the chin, forcing him to look at her. "You can't be serious. I need you."

A sadness came through in his voice. *"I'm sorry, Reecah. We've struggled with this. Dragon Home is our colony. We can't abandon it in its darkest hour."*

"But...but..." Reecah searched the faces of the others. They nodded, confirming Lurker's words. "There's nothing there for you but death. Dragon Home is destroyed. Everyone is dead."

"We don't know that."

Reecah's Gift

"Silence went back and scouted the area." She turned to implore the purple dragon. "You said no one was left alive."

Silence bowed her head.

Reecah returned her attention to Lurker. "If you go back, you risk being killed yourself…"

She spun to face the drop-off. "Damn it!"

She promised herself not to cry anymore. She must be strong if she wanted to face the high king. Wiping her cheeks, she turned back to her friends. "It would kill me if something happened to you."

"We feel the same way about you, pretty Reecah. Nevertheless, we cannot leave our home. Besides, our presence will likely hinder you than help. You won't make it anywhere near the castle with us at your side."

"Then I'm going back to Dragon Home with you."

Lurker glanced at his dragonkind, shaking his head. *"That we cannot allow. You're the last Windwalker. Grimclaw pledged Draakclaw Colony's allegiance to you. We forbid your return to the killing zone."*

Reecah didn't want to vent her frustration on her companions but she had no one else. Sounding off at Raver wouldn't be nearly the same.

Lifting her chin, she straightened her shoulders and tried to cast them a stern look. "If you're supposed to obey me, then I command that you take me with you."

As soon as she said it, she hated herself. Who was she to order *anyone*, let alone three dragons who had lost everything? She, of all people, knew what that was like.

"I'm sorry. That was wrong of me. I won't order you to do anything you don't want. Please forgive me."

"You're a Windwalker. Of course we'll do as you command," Swoop said, looking at the other two, who nodded. *"But we respectfully ask you not to come. If Grimclaw's death is to mean anything, you must go to your king and plead our case before there aren't any dragons left in the world."*

Reecah's Gift

The dragon faces blurred before her. Her tears flowed freely but she didn't care. Let them exhaust themselves so that she could move on. Unable to speak past the lump in her throat, she kept her eyes on the ground at her feet.

A soft breeze wafted up the mountainside, ruffling her cloak and blowing her brown hair in front of her face. A hawk's call echoed off the peak.

Lurker nuzzled his face against her stomach, almost sending her stumbling over the brink. *"Remember what you said to Silence in Dragon Home?"*

Reecah shook her head. She couldn't think beyond the moment.

"We'll always be here for you. No matter what happens." Lurker nuzzled his snout beneath her left breast. *"As long as you feel us here, we'll always be together."*

His words gave her goosebumps. He'd remembered. Those were words spoken by Poppa a lifetime ago. Instead of pacifying her, it made her cry harder.

Shoulders shaking, she smiled and laughed through her tears, half spitting as she spoke. "Oh, great. Now look what you've done. Come here."

She wrapped her arms around Lurker's head and held him close. Eyeing Silence and Swoop on either side, she motioned for them to lean closer. Arms stretched wide, she included them in the embrace.

"I pledge to you with my last breath. Today marks the end of silence. From this day forth, the Great Kingdom shall know we will no longer suffer the people's prejudice."

She sniffled loudly and squeezed their heads together. "I will never forget you."

She kissed Lurker's cheek and laid her head against the top of his nose. "Especially you, my dear friend. Thank you for allowing me into your circle of trust."

Reecah's Gift

"Circle of trust! Circle of trust!" Raver landed on top of one of Lurker's horns, surprisingly gripping it the first time with his mangled toes.

Reecah looked up at the crazy bird and laughed, her heart warming despite the fact it had just broken.

. . .

Books by Richard H. Stephens

The Royal Tournament

The Royal Tournament has at long last come to the village of Millsford. For Javen Milford, a local farm boy, the news couldn't be better. Finally, Javen can perform his chores on the homestead and partake in the biggest military games in the Kingdom, hoping beyond hope that just maybe, he might catch the eye of the king. Javen enters the kingdom's flagship tournament only to discover that in order to win, one must be prepared to die.

Of Trolls and Evil Things

The (standalone) prequel to the Soul Forge Saga series!

Travel down an ever-darkening path where two orphans battle to survive upon a perilous mountainside, evading the predators and prowlers preying upon its slopes, and within its catacombs. When the dangers they face force them from their mountain home, they end up in the cutthroat streets of Cliff Face plying their hands as beggars to survive.

Soul Forge - The Epic Fantasy Trilogy

Soul Forge
Book 1

Loyalty, betrayal, fantastic creatures, breathtaking vistas and one man's need to rescue his darkened soul come together in this amazing epic fantasy.

Accompanied by a band of eclectic characters, Silurian Mintaka embarks upon a journey seeking revenge on the those responsible for the murder of his family. Those closest to him fear his decisions will end up killing them all, and the fate of the kingdom hangs in the balance.

Wizard of the North
Book 2

The Royal House of Zephyr is in shambles. A beast is unleashed, and the only hope the kingdom has to survive the imminent firestorm, lies in the hands of an eclectic band of giants, a rogue vigilante, an old man, an orange furred creature and a pair of female pranksters.

A catastrophic spell reunites two lost souls, setting them on an epic journey of discovery to discover the source of an ancient magic.

Into the Madness
Book 3

The epic conclusion of the Soul Forge Saga.

A carefully hidden truth is revealed. The key to the kingdom's salvation if the Wizard of the North and her unstable companion can unlock its secret and survive an encounter with a wyrm bent on destroying the world.

Far to the south, a motley group of assassins set out to end the land's suffering. Waylaid by an eccentric necromancer, and suffering a tragic loss that threatens to ruin their poorly laid plan, they stagger toward a fate no one ever envisioned. An obsidian nightmare is summoned and Zephyr will never be the same.

Legends of the Lurker Series

Reecah's Gift – Book 2

Braving the perils of a cutthroat city, Reecah discovers that as bad as life may have seemed, nothing had prepared her for what her future has in store.

Surviving hardships no one should ever have to endure, she finds herself face-to-face with those seeking her demise.

Without the intervention of an eclectic warrior, and the assistance of her dragon friends, Reecah might never realize the gift so many died to protect.

Coming December 2019—Legends of the Lurker Series
Reecah's Legacy – Book 3

About Richard H. Stephens

Born in Simcoe, Ontario, in 1965, Richard began writing circa 1974; a bored child looking for something to while away the long, summertime days. His penchant for reading The Hardy Boys led to an inspiration one sweltering summer afternoon when he and his best friend thought, 'We could write one of those.' And so, he did.

As his reading horizons broadened, so did his writing. Star Wars inspired him to write a 600-page novel about outer space that caught the attention of a special teacher who encouraged him to keep writing.

A trip to a local bookstore saw the proprietor introduce him to Stephen R. Donaldson and Terry Brooks. His writing life was forever changed.

At 17, Richard left high school to join the working world to support his first son. For the next twenty-two years he worked as a shipper at a local bakery. At the age of 36, he went back to high school to complete his education. After graduating with honours at the age of thirty-nine, he became a member of the local Police Service, and worked for 12 years in the provincial court system.

In early 2017, Richard retired from the Police Service to pursue his love of writing full-time. With the help and support of his wife Caroline and their five children, he finally realized his boyhood dream.